The item should be returned or renewed by the last date stamped below.

Dylid dychwelyd neu adnewyddu'r eitem erbyn y dyddiad olaf sydd wedi'i stampio isod

To renew visit / Adnewyddwch ar
www.newport.gov.uk/libraries

DOCTOR WHO

DOCTOR WHO AND THE KRIKKIT MEN

JAMES GOSS

BOOKS

1 3 5 7 9 10 8 6 4 2

BBC Books, an imprint of Ebury Publishing
20 Vauxhall Bridge Road,
London SW1V 2SA

BBC Books is part of the Penguin Random House group of companies
whose addresses can be found at global.penguinrandomhouse.com

Penguin
Random House
UK

Copyright © Completely Unexpected Productions Limited 2018
This novelisation copyright © James Goss 2018

Completely Unexpected Productions and James Goss have asserted their right
to be identified as the author of this Work in accordance with
the Copyright, Designs and Patents Act 1988

Doctor Who is a BBC Wales production for BBC One.
Executive producers Chris Chibnall and Matt Strevens

First published by BBC Books in 2018
Paperback edition published in 2019

www.penguin.co.uk

A CIP catalogue record for this book is available from the British Library

ISBN 9781785941061

Editorial Director: Albert DePetrillo
Project Editor: Steve Cole
Cover Design: Two Associates
Production: Sian Pratley

Printed and bound in Great Britain by Clays Ltd, Elcograf S.p.A.

Penguin Random House is committed to a sustainable future for
our business, our readers and our planet. This book is made
from Forest Stewardship Council® certified paper.

MIX
Paper from
responsible sources
FSC® C018179
FSC
www.fsc.org

CONTENTS

PART TWO

INTRODUCTION
BY DOUGLAS ADAMS

'Without logic there is no surprise and no joy.'

[From a presentation for the film of *The Krikkitmen*]

1) Science fiction in films

It is a question of getting the angle right. It has been tried many times unsuccessfully because the concepts are usually Earthbound and based on re-workings of the 1984 vision of the future. c.f. *Logan's Run, Soylent Green* etc.

This is probably because the average non sci-fi reading member of the public probably sees sci-fi as being gloomy extrapolations of present tendencies towards totalitarianism.

Verdict: Boring. Even I, as a Science Fiction fan did not go to see them.

2) The Apollo Space program rather took the carpet out from under the feet of the old space opera type of film which used to

pay no lip service at all to what we do actually know about Space and Space travel.

Science Fiction must not ignore what we already know. It can go way beyond it on fantastic flights of fancy, but the structure of the fantastic must be logical. And this is a lot of the beauty of Science Fiction – the wild fantasies that can be created from imaginatively logical extrapolations of what we already know.

For instance – it is completely unacceptable in modern sci-fi to talk of spaceships travelling faster than light, because Einstein must be taken into account. However, theories of hyperspace which allow instantaneous transposition are acceptable. In other words, current knowledge can be argued against, but not thrown out of the window.

Again – Black Holes, a marvellous area for fantasy, but it must be informed fantasy. Anything a writer invents about Black Holes must take into account the arguments put forward by the theorists.

A Science Fiction audience … wants to make that suspension of disbelief, and you must allow him to do that by not insulting his intelligence. However, this does not in any way preclude the adventure romp like *Doctor Who*, Harry Harrison, etc., which is one of the brightest and best areas of sci-fi because it can be so outrageous in its fantasy. But the fun and the skill of it is the maintenance of the inner logic.

All the best wild ideas in surreal comedy, science fiction, spy thrillers, etc., adhere to a strict inner logic. Without logic there is no surprise and no joy.

3) One is concerned a great deal with problems and their solutions. The trick is to find your solution within the framework of the logic you have constructed. In many ways the James Bond films illustrate some of the points excellently, and any attempts to make *Doctor Who* films should be done very much in the light of what the Bond films have achieved in the outrageously structured.

I suppose this is why I've always mistrusted the term Science Fantasy as opposed to Science Fiction because it suggests the lack of logical construction.

Douglas Adams
[From the initial presentation for *The Krikkitmen, c.*1976*]

---

* *I've guessed the date, as the science fiction films dominating the box office he refers to were released in 1973 and 1976. Also, and here's the big clue, he makes no reference to Star Wars.*

PART ONE

'Aggers, for goodness' sake stop it. He hit a four over the wicket keeper's head and he was out for nine.'

Brian Johnston, 1991

What are the Ashes?
(A) *What England have*
(B) *What Australia want*
(C) *What Granny is.*

Sign on a van, 2016

CHAPTER ONE
IMPORTANT AND EXCITING GALACTIC HISTORY. DO NOT SKIP.

Before Time began, a lot of things happened that hardly bear talking about.

This story starts a little later than that. It is based in this Galaxy, the one we all know and love, with its millions of suns, its strange and wonderful planets, its eerie moons, its asteroids, its comets, its gas clouds and dust clouds and its immensity of coldness and darkness.

It affects, however, the Universe.

Just occasionally it should be remembered that this Galaxy is just one of infinite millions, but then it should be forgotten again, because it's hard for the mind to stagger around with that kind of knowledge in it.

Since this Galaxy began, vast civilisations have risen and fallen, risen and fallen, risen and fallen so often that it's quite tempting to think that life in the Galaxy must be:

a) something akin to seasick – space sick, time sick, history sick or some
  such thing
  and
b) stupid.

When you get down to street level, however, you realise that the
phrase 'life in the Galaxy' is pretty meaningless, since it describes
billions of separate short-lived beings all of whom have for some vicious
reason been programmed to be incapable of learning from each other's
mistakes.

Here is a very simple example, at street level.

The street is a cold but busy one in a city called New York on a planet
that hardly anybody has heard of.

A man is walking along it, looking up at the stars, wondering, perhaps,
just how many of them there are. It is a purely local problem. What happens
to him has happened before to others and will happen again. He walks past
a site where an extremely tall building is being put up in the place of another
extremely tall building which has been pulled down. (An explanation of why
this happens would only confuse matters at this point.)

As he passes, a small tool falls from high up in the scaffolding with
which the building is surrounded and buries itself snugly into the man's
skull. This has the effect of bringing his life, with all its memories, its loves,
its hard-won battles, its instructive defeats, its rewards, its disappointments
– in short, his entire experience – to an abrupt end. The last thing the man
sees before his personal light is shut off is a sign on the scaffolding that says:
'We Apologise for the Inconvenience.'

From across the street, a woman – the man's mate – sees this happen.
Failing to learn from the incident that the Universe in general and New
York in particular is a randomly dangerous place, she runs pointlessly to
his aid and has her own life, with all its experiences, brought to an end by
a yellow taxicab, whose driver would never apologise for anything. The cab
driver was only there at that point because he was completely lost in one of
the most rationally laid-out cities on the Earth, but that, again, is another
purely local problem.

This story is about a much, much larger problem, but strangely enough it does come to involve this otherwise harmless planet in rather curious ways, and explain the reason why no one likes it.

It also involves a large number of mistakes. The first, and worst, mistake, was made during the height of the very first major civilisation to rise and fall in this Galaxy. The mistake lay in thinking that you can solve anything with potatoes.

There was a race of people called the Alovians, who were insanely aggressive. They fought their enemies (i.e. everybody else) and they fought each other. The best way of dealing with an Alovian was to leave him in a room on his own because sooner or later he would beat himself up.

As their level of what they liked to call civilisation increased, so, for the sake of sheer survival, they had to find ways of curbing and sublimating their mad aggression. Each war they had did greater and greater damage, and, before too long, they were on the brink of self-destruction. History says it's a great pity they didn't just go straight ahead with it.

Eventually they saw that this was something they were going to have to do something about, and they passed a law decreeing that anyone who had to carry a weapon as part of his normal work (policemen, security guards, primary school teachers, etc.) had to spend at least forty minutes a day punching a sack of potatoes in order to work off their surplus aggression. (Interestingly, they would not be the only race to try out this solution to warmongering. Indeed, people thought that this was what potatoes were for, until the surprising invention of the deep-fat fryer.) For a while the potato solution for world peace worked fine until an Alovian decided that it would be much more efficient and less time consuming if they just shot the potatoes instead. This led to a renewed enthusiasm for shooting all sorts of things and they all got very excited at the prospect of their first major war for years.

Skipping a century or two here, we next come across the Alovians as a major interstellar power sweeping through the Galaxy and ravaging everything they could lay their hands on and shooting anything they couldn't. Since this behaviour was going down so badly with the rest of the Galaxy, they decided that, in order to protect themselves they needed a very special weapon – an Ultimate Weapon.

How Ultimate is Ultimate?

They built a computer to find out what could be done, and it came up with a perfectly staggering answer.

The computer was called Hactar. It began as a large black moon which orbited the planet of Alovia, and it did all its thinking in space. It was of a special organic design, like a natural brain, in that every cellular particle of it carried the pattern of the whole within it. This allowed it to think more imaginatively.

In answer to the question about an Ultimate Weapon, it said that the Universe could be brought to a premature end, and was this ultimate enough?

At this news, there was dancing in the streets of Alovia, street parties, fetes, carnivals of a particularly nasty kind and a wild sense of having arrived somewhere.

They sent out a message across the whole Galaxy to the effect that they, the Alovians, were now in a position to destroy the entire Universe, and that if anybody had anything they wanted to quarrel about they'd be happy to hear from them.

To add bite to this message, they described how the Ultimate Weapon that Hactar had designed for them worked. It was a very, very small bomb. In fact it was simply a junction box in hyperspace which would, when activated, connect the heart of every major sun with the heart of every other major sun simultaneously. This would convert the entire Universe into one gigantic hyperspatial supernova and, unless the whole thing started up all over again in another and better dimension, that would be that.

That was how it worked, except that, when it came to it, it didn't.

The Alovian fingers which hovered over the button that would set the bomb off were very itchy, and eventually of course somebody somewhere in the Galaxy said or did something which got them really riled, and left them, they were afraid, with absolutely no alternative but to detonate the Supernova Bomb. To themselves they said, 'What's the point of having a thing if you don't use it?'

The button was pressed, the bomb fizzed and popped and then just fell apart in such a way as to suggest that it had been rather badly made.

For a moment, the loudest noise heard anywhere in the Universe was that of a computer clearing its throat.

Hactar spoke.

Hactar said that what with one thing and another it had been thinking about this Ultimate Weapon business and had worked out that there was no conceivable consequence of not setting the bomb off that was worse than the known consequence of setting it off, and it had therefore taken the liberty of introducing a small flaw into the design of the bomb, and he hoped that everyone involved would, on sober reflection, feel that —

That was as far as Hactar got before the Alovian missiles got him straight between his major synapses and the huge black moon computer was reduced to radioactive smithereens.

It was not a great deal later than this that the Alovians managed to blow themselves up as well, to the great relief of the rest of the Galaxy.

The way in which they blew themselves up is very interesting and instructive, and is a mistake that no one has yet learnt from.

As a purely sensible and practical measure, they had entirely surrounded their planet with thermonuclear weapons. This was for safety, and to stop anyone on the planet from annoying anybody else on the planet, because of what that could lead to. It was called 'the nuclear umbrella'. It made it difficult to see the sun because the sky coverage was so thick, but that didn't matter because they had plenty of energy-generating stations on the planet providing heat and light. This, it must be emphasised, was all a perfectly rational and controlled situation, and any reasonable Alovian could have explained to you over breakfast why it was necessary, without looking up from his newspaper.

It goes without saying of course, that the entire system was riddled with every conceivable safeguard, the greatest safeguard of all being the sure knowledge that the entire arsenal of the other side would be launched automatically if you so much as popped a toy balloon. (That's not quite true. There were computers which knew what a toy balloon popping sounded like and would discount that. There were other computers that knew what a flock of geese looked like and wouldn't be alarmed by that.)

Unfortunately there was also a telephone company computer that didn't know what to do with someone's change of address card and panicked.

So much for the accepted history. As we will eventually find out, much of what you have just read is wrong. If you think that you have just wasted your time, then it is to be hoped that, like the rest of existence, you fail to learn from your mistakes.

We can now move forward many, many, many millions of years.

CHAPTER TWO
SANDWICHES AND OUTRAGE

Romana was appalled. And that was before the Killer Robots turned up.

'You've brought me to a cricket match?'

'Hush,' the Doctor looked around furtively, pulling his hat closer around his face. He handed her some weak tea in a Styrofoam cup.

Romana was a Time Lady from the planet Gallifrey, nestling in the upmarket constellation of Kasterborous. In her travels with the Doctor she had reassembled the Key to Time, thwarted Davros, and outclassed the Nimon. It was fair to say that she thought she'd seen it all. But life with the Doctor was full of surprises. Not all of them pleasant.

'A cricket match?' she repeated, making absolutely sure she wasn't misheard.

The Doctor and Romana were wanderers in the fourth dimension and potterers in the fifth. Romana had been raised in the Time Lord Academy to expect a life of august calm and academic rigour. Instead she now spent her days dashing around in a blue box saving random bits of the universe. One of her best friends was a robot dog. Well, it wasn't the life she'd expected but she thoroughly enjoyed it.

Apart from today.

'A. Cricket. Match.'

'I know.' The Doctor pulled his hat down even further and sank even deeper into his deckchair.

The day had started so well. He'd promised her the universe was ending. ('Oh goody!' Romana always liked those days.) Instead, he'd brought her to Lord's Cricket Ground. The seats around them were crowded with greasy-looking bankers treating each other to corporate hospitality. Further below was a sea of middle-aged men trying to get sunburn. Adrift in the middle of it was the occasional Colonel, angrily completing the *Times* crossword with the help of a thermos flask containing tea, soup or gin. Romana conceded that all of human life was here – if your definition of human life was really very narrow.

To give the Doctor credit, he'd got them very good seats. They had a splendid view of the pitch – a strip of grass as cossetted as a rich old lady on life support. Dancing around it were two teams of men in spotless white overalls, looking like fastidious knights who'd ordered their armour with a high thread count. Occasionally one player would throw a small red ball at another. Sometimes they'd hit it merrily into the air with a plank of wood. Sometimes they wouldn't. Often nothing at all would happen to polite applause. Cricket was the most English invention imaginable. As if a prep school teacher had tried to demonstrate eternity. And yet …

And yet it wasn't.

'It's like they don't have a clue of its true significance,' Romana gasped.

'I'm not sure they do.' The Doctor was shaking his head sadly.

*

She really should have known something was up. The Doctor's time machine had been drifting amiably between planets. On the outside it looked like a small blue box that had got a little lost. On the inside it was a collection of infinite white rooms, decorated with the verve of a hospital run by an antiques dealer. One of the many problems with the TARDIS was that the Doctor really didn't know how to work it. The Doctor had, over time, simply taken to labelling the controls with bits of sticking plaster which he'd scribbled his best guesses on. She'd been staring at one which said 'handbrake' when he'd strode into the room. The Doctor was an obscure punctuation mark of a man. Infuriating, charming, puzzling and brilliant, one of the things Romana adored about him was that his eyes never stopped smiling.

'Romana, the universe is ending!' he'd said. 'And we need to dress for it.'

Normally Romana liked dressing up. The Doctor's time machine may have been, like him, obsolete and cantankerous, but one of the perks was the infinite wardrobe.

Sensing her eyeing up the wardrobe door, the Doctor headed her off, fishing in a pocket. 'Ties must be worn,' he announced solemnly, handing her one. 'I've been reading up.'

K-9's ears twitched, but the Doctor ignored them.

Romana watched the Doctor trying to tie his own tie for a while, and then, when it stopped being amusing, she did it neatly for him. She noticed the label read 'Women's Institute Champion Bread Makers', and she glanced hastily at hers. It merely contained a row of cartoon penguins. Well, it wasn't what she'd have chosen.

'Why do we need ties?' she'd asked suspiciously. 'Where are we going?'

'Well …' the Doctor had said, looking guilty. This was never good. His time machine roared to an abrupt halt. He'd opened the doors. 'Let's go and find out.'

And then he'd taken her to that cricket match.

*

The TARDIS had bellowed into the Members' Enclosure like a tipsy aunt. The apparition was greeted with alarm and outrage, which was rapidly transferred to the Doctor's appearance.

There were times when the Doctor was every inch the champion of eternity. Romana had seen giant green blobs look hastily at the floor with all 100 of their eyes. The Ninth Sontaran Battle Brigade had remembered an urgent call they just had to make. The Kraals had muttered something about really having to knuckle down and write their Christmas thank-you letters.

There were times when the Doctor was precisely that wonderful. And then there were others when he just looked insane. This was one of them. The assembled men were glowering at the Doctor's random assembly of jacket, trousers, waistcoat and long scarf, and completely ignoring his proudly worn tie. Even though he waved it at them like a religious totem.

The time travellers were confronted by an army of disapproving sports jackets. Someone said very loudly, 'Well really!' Someone else cried, 'Disgraceful!'

Romana found it all baffling. Where were they? Normally people just locked them up, or took them to be interrogated by something green and smelling of Swarfega. The shouting was new.

The Doctor faced the deadly tide of tweed and felt the full blistering force of middle-aged disapproval. It was quite something. Nevertheless, he fished about in his pocket and flashed a crumpled card.

'I'm the Doctor,' he announced grandly with only the slightest of hesitations. 'This is Romana. We're from the MCC.'

Romana, along with most of the front row of sports jackets, squinted dubiously at the card. It was signed by W.G. Grace and dated 1877.

The card worked, eventually. It allowed them grudging access to the cornucopia of the hospitality suite. This amounted to a leaking tea urn and a pile of fish-paste sandwiches.

'Where are we?' Romana hissed, throwing a sandwich behind a plant. 'This is England, isn't it? But I've never seen it quite so hostile.'

'Race memory.' The Doctor sipped a cup of tea and winced. 'They all feel angry and ashamed and very intolerant of outsiders. But they've not a clue why.' He led them out onto the terrace.

Which was when she finally realised where they were.

'You promised me the end of the universe, and you've brought me to a cricket match.'

'Any true Englishman would tell you they were the same thing.' The Doctor's attempt to laugh it off was mirthless.

So that was it, she thought, the Doctor's dark secret. He was trying to excuse the obscenity before them. Well, of course he would. He was such an eccentric anglophile – he adored tea towels and jam, he'd made her go fishing, he liked stately homes so much he'd blown up at least a dozen. Why wouldn't he bring her to a cricket match?

'How could you?' Romana demanded. She tolerated his love of this planet, sometimes she even enjoyed it. But there were limits. Cricket. That was where a neat line had to be drawn.

A small red ball arced through the air and the players scurried back and forth. Polite applause rippled through the crowd. Romana shuddered and looked away.

'The odd thing,' the Doctor ruminated, 'is that it all seems harmless enough.'

'Harmless?' Romana scoffed as two of the players shook hands.

'I've always meant to find out why something like this could happen,' he said gravely. When he wanted to sound grave, he could sound extraordinarily grave. Like a rumbling of distant thunder in a cathedral.

Romana looked up at the cloudless sky, at the bright sun soaking into the green, green grass, and she shivered.

'They seem so innocent, don't they?' The Doctor shrugged miserably. 'Look at them – look at them all. So …' His lips twisted. 'Happy.'

A man hit a ball with a bat. The ball went quite a way. Everyone applauded. It looked the most innocent thing ever.

'It's obscene, that's what it is.' Romana fidgeted in her chair. If anyone saw her, her chances of being President of Gallifrey (not, of course, that she had any ambitions in that arena) were well out of the time window. 'If it's a cosmic joke, then it's in very bad taste indeed.'

The Doctor consulted a pamphlet he'd been eating sandwiches off. 'Seems it's the last day of the Ashes.'

Several people nearby glanced at him as if he'd fallen off the moon. Which was, Romana thought, fair enough.

'In cricketing terms,' the Doctor whispered, 'that's very big news. You know – every ten years or so—'

'Every four years,' a man in front of them turned around to snarl.

'Doesn't matter,' the Doctor said, delighting as the spectator turned a colour to match his coat. 'Anyway, England and Australia fight a series of cricket matches and eventually one of them takes home a trophy.'

'*The* trophy,' the spectator snapped.

'Thank you, that's quite enough,' the Doctor smiled at him sweetly. 'Maybe the space-time telegraph got its wires crossed. Maybe it is just a game.' He looked doubtful. 'Maybe it's not the end of the universe.'

Romana let out an anguished groan. At least a dozen races had given 'cricket' as their reason for attacking the planet. It went a long way to explain why most invasions began in the home counties.

The match went on. In contrast to the Time Lords' despairing mood, the crowd was growing jubilant. Given the amount of applause and the number of people shouting, 'Come on England!' things were getting pretty exciting. Or, as exciting as a cricket match could be. How could something so horrifying be so obscenely dull, Romana thought.

She glanced at the scoreboard and, with a lot of frowning and eavesdropping, managed to decipher what was going on.

'I think it's the last round,' she said, watching the spectator in front wince. 'And England need three to win. Satisfied? Please say we can go home afterwards.'

'Home?' the Doctor barked bitterly.

Down on the field, the little white figures were moving with a bit more tension. Someone threw a ball. Someone hit it with a bat.

For a moment, eternity waited. The ball drifted higher. Then, with nothing better to do, it drifted higher still.

Then the entire stadium breathed out.

'It's a six!' screamed the audience to each other with the delight of people pointing out the obvious.

The crowd went as wild as a cricket crowd could. There was polite applause, backs were slapped, and people said, 'Hurrah!' It all seemed terribly jolly.

'Well, they've won, maybe,' Romana ventured.

'No one ever wins cricket,' the Doctor sighed miserably.

Romana looked up at the sky. Clouds were forming. 'And just in time too,' she announced, shivering. 'Looks like rain.'

'That's far worse than rain,' the Doctor intoned. He really wasn't sounding very English at all today.

Romana tapped him lightly on the shoulder. In the middle of dashing after a Rutan invasion, an old lady at a bus stop had shouted something at her, and she'd been itching for a chance to try it out herself. 'Cheer up,' she said. 'It might never happen.'

The Doctor turned away. 'Do you know, I always hate people who say that.'

And, with that, he vanished.

CHAPTER THREE
AN INTERNATIONAL INCIDENT

Romana blinked. The Doctor vanishing was never a good sign.

Sometimes the Doctor vanished loudly, with a comforting little yell as he fell into something.

Sometimes the Doctor vanished with a little fizz, as some transmat beam or other abducted him.

But sometimes the Doctor just vanished silently. This was the worst of all, because it meant that he'd slipped away.

'Of all the places,' Romana said to herself wearily, 'he has to go missing at a cricket match.'

She checked over her shoulder, in case the Doctor had popped off in the TARDIS to try to mend history (a situation which invariably called for some hasty re-mending later). Then she looked out across the terraces, trying to spot the Doctor among the spectators. Not a sign of him.

Then she looked down at the pitch.

'Oh, really, no,' she said.

The match had ended with a six, and the crowd had gone most politely wild. The Doctor had reacted to this like a mammoth staring down a glacier, causing some to wonder if he was an Australian supporter, though it seemed a little unlikely.

There then followed a little presentation ceremony. This was a new thing, not previously done, and probably designed to make the whole business better television. The Ashes were to be presented to the captain of the English team there on the field. The TV companies didn't know it at this point, but they were in for some very good television indeed.

First, there came the Doctor. He stormed onto the pitch, like Moses coming down the mountain in a high temper because God had said he hadn't got any Commandments to hand out right now, but how about lunch next week?

The Doctor marched up to the English captain. 'Excuse me. Are you in charge of the cricket?'

The cluster of players on the pitch stared at the Doctor.

A small podium had been dragged out for the purposes of the presentation. The chairman had come out, freshly polished medals on his loveliest blazer. The umpire, in his best butcher's coat, stood to one side. The two teams were getting ready to shake hands and find a pub.

But the Doctor had bounded onto the podium and was addressing them. 'People of Earth, good afternoon,' he began.

'Shame!' shouted someone.

The chairman was looking around for security, and then remembered that this was a cricket match. They didn't need security.

'Honestly, this will take barely a second. I'm doing this for the good of the Galaxy, possibly the whole universe, and maybe the very fabric of space-time itself,' the Doctor persisted.

'You're a disgrace,' someone shouted.

'How can I be?' The Doctor smiled. 'I'm wearing a tie! So, would one of you care to tell me what's going on here exactly?'

Confronted by the full force of his personality, the captain of the Australian team blanched. 'Well, mate …' he began, and then stopped. This really wasn't done.

'Go on,' the Doctor prompted him.

The Australian captain held up the small silver trophy he held. 'The other side won. So I'm presenting them with the trophy.'

'Fascinating.' The Doctor grimaced. 'And what is that trophy?'

There was a stunned pause on the pitch.

'Well,' the Australian captain began again. 'These are the Ashes.'

'Quite right,' someone in the crowd mumbled.

'Yes, but,' the Doctor continued, 'what are they, exactly?'

'Well … ashes,' the captain said.

'Of what?' the Doctor's amiable nature had lowered, just a little.

'Well—' the captain began.

'Do you start every sentence like that?' the Doctor asked.

'Well—'

'Never mind.' The Doctor looked at the teams gathered around him. 'Can any of you tell me what those ashes are made of?'

'A burnt stump.'

'A budgie.'

'The soul of cricket.'

The Doctor looked at them, and nodded again. 'Not good,' he said. 'I don't suppose any of you have ever had a peek inside? Have you?'

The group glared at him.

'Oh come on, not late at night, when no one's looking?'

The glaring got a little darker.

'The lid's welded shut,' someone muttered.

'Then you mean to say,' the Doctor pressed on, 'that you spend your lives passing this trophy back and forth, and none of you have any idea what's inside it?'

The group suddenly looked at the grass. 'It's just not done,' hissed the umpire firmly.

'Well then,' said the Doctor, pleasantly, 'I've a suggestion. As you don't know what's inside that trophy, and I would very much like to know, I was wondering if I could possibly borrow them from you? Just for a bit.' He flashed his most winning smile.

'For an X-ray?' someone stuttered weakly.

'If you like.' The Doctor shrugged. 'The thing is, your Ashes are terribly important.'

He had finally said something the group liked. 'Quite right! They represent all that is good about Cricket.'

The Doctor winced. 'More than that,' he said, slowly. 'They are rather important for the future of the universe.'

This was, even for an audience of cricketers, a bit steep. Confusion reigned, along with bewilderment, indignation, and all the other emotions the English are so very good at. The Australian team just rolled their eyes.

'Anyway,' said the Doctor, leaping down off the podium, 'I really will be as quick as I can. May I?'

And, much to everyone's surprise, the Australian captain gave him the Ashes. The Doctor held them in his hands as though he was cradling a lump of uranium.

'How dare you, sir?' thundered the umpire. He had been looking forward to today, and now things had gone badly astray.

'Oh, believe me –' the Doctor leaned forward candidly – 'I'd rather be leaving this one well alone, but –' his voice dropped an octave – 'when I was a child, I was told about Them. They are the things of nightmares. If I was bad, I was told that They would come and get me.'

'Sorry …' The umpire was as baffled as he was cross. 'Are we talking about the Australians?'

'No.' The Doctor pointed up at the sky. 'I think something really dreadful is about to happen.'

24

This remark played badly with the group. As far as they were concerned, a man had strolled into the middle of their ceremony, had inveigled the Ashes out of them, and was now issuing threats. Wasn't that dreadful enough? Also, his tie was unspeakable.

Soon, the Doctor was discussing the matter quite pleasantly with one or two red-faced, blustering gentlemen. They had seized the Ashes, and were trying to pull the trophy out of the Doctor's hands.

'Believe me,' he said, 'there's nothing I'd like better than to let go, but I can't.'

At that point, the Doctor heard the worst sound in the universe.

It was the sound of the entire crowd at Lord's Cricket Ground slowly, derisively clapping him.

And then the booing began.

'Oh dear,' the Doctor said.

All in all, it was something of a relief when the Killer Robots finally showed up.

CHAPTER FOUR
FINALLY, KILLER ROBOTS

The English love a good lunatic, particularly at cricket matches. But, there was a feeling that the crowd wanted something more, that the Doctor might at least take his clothes off and leap over the wicket so they could all be shocked by it.

The few people who talked about what happened next all chose to remember different things.

Some spoke about the way that a neat little cricket pavilion edged its way out of thin air and hovered a little above the pitch, as though concerned about not damaging the grass.

Some spoke about the way that the eleven figures, all attired in perfect cricket whites, strode out of the pavilion and towards the podium. The eleven were, to all intents and purposes, role models, from their tidily laced plimsolls to their neat helmets protecting their faces. Even their bats were polished so much they shone.

Most, when pressed, chose to talk about the killing.

It did not start at once. The figures waited until they were noticed, until people spotted what was wrong with them. True, they walked perfectly, their cricketing gear was immaculate –

but there was one thing missing. There was nothing inside their uniforms. They were empty suits of gleaming white armour, marching in unison.

One of the commentators could be heard blaring from a radio saying jovially, 'Well, the supernatural brigade really seem to be out in force here this afternoon.'

A ripple of alarm spread through the crowd. Some people swore it was a marketing stunt (mainly the kind of people who have never witnessed a marketing stunt, which normally involves handing out cereal bars to commuters or floating a really large lump of polystyrene down a river). Many declared confidently it was being paid for by an Australian margarine manufacturer.

To start with, only a few people screamed. After the event, they claimed they'd been trying to warn other people – but they'd simply realised that there was something about these striding white empty knights that was insultingly wrong.

One thing all the witnesses could agree on was that even Australian margarine manufacturers wouldn't stoop this low.

The eleven figures arrived at the podium and arranged themselves in a neat, white line. Waiting.

Normally, at this point, the Doctor would have naturally taken charge. If there was one thing he liked doing, it was ordering about automata. Instead he stood still, his mouth agape.

So, it fell to the captain of the England cricket team to step forward and address the figures. He'd been to a reasonable public school, so had a natural ability to talk to anyone, whether they wanted to be talked to or not. 'Hello,' he said. 'Can we help you?'

The figures said nothing. But the captain of the England cricket team was not abashed. 'Have you come far?' he pressed on. In his experience that never failed, and he was already donning the facial expression of a man who'd like to hear about your B-road.

The figures said nothing about B-roads, service station coleslaw, or even that tricky tailback at Biggleswade junction.

There was something about their silent emptiness that crept into the soul, leant forward and whispered, 'Sssssssh.'

Even the captain of the England cricket team fell silent.

Everyone in the stadium was now watching the new arrivals.

The new arrivals were not watching anyone. They did not have eyes. Just blank white helmets with a nasty darkness within. One that glowed a really sinister red.

One of the figures raised a white arm and pointed with a padded glove at the urn.

The Doctor spoke, a tiny stifled croak: 'Let me give it to them. Now.'

The captain of the Australian team laughed. 'Well, now ...' he began with that jovial reasonableness that made the rest of the world want to beat them at games. 'That's all very well, but they've not won the Ashes, have they?' Here he laughed again.

His ghastly attempt at camaraderie fell on completely deaf ears.

The Doctor spoke in that weird hiss again: 'Look at their bats.'

You can, if you wish, find out a lot about the manufacture of cricket bats, either from consulting an encyclopaedia, a woodworking teacher, or the most boring man you can find in a bar. A simplified summary is that a decent cricket bat is carved from willow, and kept supple with linseed oil.

They are not, as a rule, made out of steel and their sides do not taper to sharp knife edges.

'Well, crikey,' said the Australian captain. He sniffed. The bats still smelt of linseed. That was something. 'Enough's enough, though, isn't it, fellas?' he couldn't help saying, and started laughing as though he'd lost his head.

Which, a moment later, he had.

Everyone later agreed that the decapitation did it. The strange white robots had little time for bonhomie or the nicer things in life. They had clearly not come to Lords to marvel at the pitch, to eat sandwiches or to talk about problems with motor homes and foreigners. They had come, for some unfathomable reason, to steal a cricketing trophy and they were, as robots so often are, lethally determined to get it.

Inside those empty helmets, something lit up. Dark red lines that formed an angry frown.

The place was suddenly overwhelmed with a storm of fire, smoke and noise. What amazed observers as they staggered about, choking, almost deafened and blinded, was that in the middle of it all, in the middle of the smoke and fire and noise, the eleven newcomers actually appeared to be playing cricket. This seemed to display a quite staggering degree of fortitude in adversity until it slowly dawned on the onlookers that whatever it was they were doing was actually the direct cause of the devastation around them. Every ball they hit exploded somewhere and killed people.

They sliced their way through the players, who were, to be fair, all in a hurry to get out of their way. The robots raised their bats and, from the ends of them, fired lethal bolts of light into the now screaming crowd.

One of the most beautiful sounds in the pantheon of audible England is the *pock!* as cricket ball meets bat. It fills the mind with summer and shady willow trees and cups of tea with a saucer and a gentle game that can be played at a casual trot. But, for everyone at Lord's that day, the sound forever crowded their minds with images of fire and horror, as row after row of seats collapsed, grass burned, brick shattered, and the fleeing crowd were cut down by strike after strike of bat on ball.

There was only one person standing still. Only one person seemingly unaffected. That one person was the Doctor, and he was holding the Ashes.

The Killer Robots having burned, slashed, blasted and diced their way across the pitch, came to a halt before the Doctor. Their leader pointed to the trophy. The other figures raised their bats.

The Doctor did not even flinch. There was something frozen, despairing about his posture.

The bats were ready to swipe down.

Which was when the air in front of the Doctor shimmered, and the cricket ground filled with a defiant bellow.

The Doctor's time machine landed in front of him, on its side. Eleven cricket bats sliced pointlessly into it and stuck. The door opened and Romana popped her head out.

'Romana,' the Doctor whispered. 'Why is the TARDIS on its side?'

Romana didn't have time for this. 'A barricade. Get in. I'll send K-9 out.'

'Not this time,' the Doctor said.

Romana raised an eyebrow. The Doctor didn't normally seem to care that much when K-9 got fused, trampled or battered. Neither did the dog – he enjoyed a scrap. 'But,' she began. 'Surely—'

One of the white figures had clambered on top of the police box.

Romana stared at it. 'Oh,' she said, aghast.

The robot looked down at her, and nodded slightly. The red glow inside the helmet formed into a smile. It plucked the trophy from the Doctor's numb fingers. Then it leapt back to the ground, tucked its bat under its arm and marched back towards the cricket pavilion.

The other white figures turned and followed suit, firing indiscriminately into the crowd, spreading more chaos and confusion.

One of the white robots raised a last ball and tossed it into the air. It swiped at it with its bat, smacking it straight into a tea tent which promptly exploded. Then the white figures climbed neatly into their cricket pavilion which melted into the air.

For a few moments, the Doctor stood there. In front of him were the bodies of the finest cricketers in the world. Around them was chaos, screaming, and, from the pitch itself, the smell of burning grass.

Romana climbed out of the TARDIS and offered the Doctor a steadying arm. Together they surveyed the devastation.

'So, they've come back,' said the Doctor eventually.

Romana nodded, a sick little nod. 'But it's preposterous, absurd.'

'It is neither,' sighed the Doctor. 'We've witnessed the single most shocking thing I have ever seen in my entire existence.'

'But were those really the Krikkitmen?' Romana whispered.

'I think so,' the Doctor agreed. 'I used to be frightened with stories of them when I was a child.'

'Me too,' agreed Romana, wondering again why so much of Time Lord education involved terrifying the young.

'Until now,' the Doctor's mouth was still working slackly, 'I've never seen them. Never quite believed in them.'

'They were supposed to have been destroyed over two million years ago.' Romana's tone was petulant, as though already writing a stern letter to whoever was responsible. 'This can't just have happened. It can't.'

The umpire was staggering towards them through the smoke and carnage. He was managing to be both red-faced and also pale with shock, which was quite an achievement. 'What?' he began.

'Hush,' said Romana.

'But really, what just happened?' the umpire persisted.

Romana and the Doctor both shook their heads glumly, then shrugged.

'But why,' the umpire wailed, 'were those things dressed as a cricket team? I mean, really, it's ridiculous!'

'Isn't it just,' the Doctor agreed.

CHAPTER FIVE
UNFORGIVABLE THEFTS
FROM A HAIRDRESSER

No one has ever written a tourist's guide to Gallifrey because, to be truthful, no one has ever really wanted to visit. Plenty of races have had angry, tentacled thoughts about invading, but that's not the same as fancying a holiday there.

If you find yourself with a fortnight to spare, there's not that much to see. True there are silver trees, ochre mountains, and the odd smug daisy, but mostly there's a lot of orange. Orange and beige – two colours which, whether on a planet or on wallpaper, say that whoever's in charge should be thinking hard about redecorating.

The only problem about Gallifrey is that no one has ever thought about redecorating. Gallifreyans, more than any other civilisation in the universe, don't like change. The mobile telephone has never taken off on Gallifrey because the entire population thought it a step too far.

The orange skies reflect that reluctance to change – the whole day looks either like sunrise or sunset, perpetually stuck in the same moment of time. And, really, that's just the way the people of Gallifrey prefer it.

In a rare, long-ago racy moment, the Gallifreyans became the Lords of All Time. They immediately decided the best thing to do with this vast power was as little as possible. If they did interfere in the affairs of others (and they did so with the soft pedal firmly pressed) it was solely with the intention of keeping the status most quo. Just as nothing changed on Gallifrey, then nothing in the universe ever would, either.

There were one or two flies in this orangey-beige ointment. Most of the people of Gallifrey were happy to grow up, live long lives composed of identical marmalade days, and then eventually potter off into an afterlife of more of the same, thank you. Instead of developing an internet, the Gallifreyans had built a library of souls and opinions, a vast databank of 'I told you so'. Their acquired wisdom was available to anyone who asked. This wisdom could be summarised as, 'No sudden moves'.

By and large, everyone was quietly happy with life on Gallifrey, except for a few rebellious souls who had decided to leave home and wander eternity. A few, such as the Master, tried to take over as much of the universe as possible, but most settled in a quiet corner and devoted themselves to harmless hobbies, such as beekeeping or making a really nice cup of tea.

The Doctor was, of course, an exception to the exceptions to the rule. He'd never made a bid for universal conquest and was hopeless with bees. Instead, he strolled through eternity with the attention span of a gregarious goldfish. He somehow managed to fit saving planets in between a roster of formidable interests, ranging from fishing (badly) to reciting poetry (loudly) to namedropping (badly and loudly).

He did, in fact, very much enjoy making tea, but did it with so much collateral damage that you could say the Doctor enjoyed making tea in the same way the Daleks enjoyed landing softly on a planet and saying hello.

When Romana had first met the Doctor, she had only just graduated from the Time Lord Academy with a Triple First. She'd been looking forward to her next thesis when she'd been ordered to help the Doctor find the Key to Time and save the universe. Obviously she'd obliged, and, afterwards, they'd celebrated by saving the universe a bit more. And they'd carried on so doing for, actually, quite a long time now, since you mention it.

Also, she'd shown the Doctor that you could boil a kettle without burning anything down whatsoever; and gone to Paris; and stopped a few interstellar wars; and gone shopping; oh, and saved the Mandrels, and the Bandrils and the Quarks, and what were the floppy little things that went *bloop*? Them too. They'd saved those.

The point was that Romana's life plan had originally included only a brief leave of absence from the apricot world of Gallifrey. And then she'd met the Doctor, and quite a lot of things had got in the way, and she'd figured, since no one had brought up the subject of popping back to Gallifrey, that perhaps she didn't need to after all. Time Lord society was still there, and always would be, ergo it had got along quite well without her, and there was a lovely little ball gown she'd seen in Venice the other week that she meant to go dancing in.

But then the Krikkitmen had turned up and all that had changed. She guessed that she and the Doctor would have to go back to Gallifrey after all. There was no getting out of it. The chances were that, if she survived this calamity (which, frankly, she doubted), the Time Lords of Gallifrey would suddenly remember that the Time Lady Romanadvoratrelundar had gone missing. And they wouldn't be happy about it. Not by a long beige chalk.

The TARDIS pushed its way angrily onto the surface of Gallifrey and settled with a thump. The door opened and the Doctor stepped out, patting it gently. 'No, none of us are keen to be here, old girl. Sorry.'

Romana followed with a slouch, which in her heels was impressive.

Their robot dog K-9 shot out of the ship and raced excitedly on ahead.

'Well, you soon find out who your friends are,' remarked the Doctor, drily.

They stood at the heart of the Time Lord empire and sighed. The Gallifreyan Capitol was either the pinnacle of ambition or an idiotically large snow globe. Turrets and spires threatened to pierce the vast glass dome. The whole effect said loudly, how very pleased with itself it was.

Once, Romana had felt only wonder as she'd walked the hallways and peeped down the vast shafts of knowledge that spiralled to the planet's data core. If ever time had a home, she'd thought, it was here, and it was a privilege to be a part of it. The Capitol had felt definite, absolute and unquestionable. The centre of the universe.

Now she'd actually travelled the universe she felt a little different about coming back here. Like a tuna to a canning factory. She shivered.

'Home sweet home?' The Doctor had the ghost of a smile on his face.

Romana nodded glumly. 'Could we not have just rung them up?'

The Doctor frowned. 'Good point. Still, we're here now.'

He scowled off down the corridor, then stopped.

'Oh, that's obscene.'

Romana joined him and shuddered.

They were stood in front of a large and magnificently ugly sofa.

'Doctor,' whispered Romana, 'I think we've discovered the real reason why nothing ever changes on Gallifrey. Our people have remarkably bad taste.'

They sat on the sofa. No matter how they tried it, it refused to be comfortable.

'I bet it cost a packet,' mused the Doctor sadly. 'I'll write a stern letter to whoever's in charge ...' Then he paused, aghast.

Romana hadn't noticed. 'Somewhere out there, in one of those buildings, my tutor's ears are glowing. I'm in for quite the lecture: "What sort of aeon do you call this, young Romanadvoratrelundar?" Oh, it's going to be quite ghastly.'

'How do you think I feel?' the Doctor muttered glumly. 'I've just remembered I'm the President.'

'Oh yes. So you are.'

Romana, along with every other Time Lord, found it quite easy to forget that the Doctor was Lord High President of Gallifrey, Regulator of the Eye of Harmony, Keeper of the Great Seal of Rassilon and the Etcetera of Etcetera. The simple reason was that this inconvenient fact was appallingly accidental. During a previous visit, the Doctor had, quite by chance, killed off the only other candidate in a Presidential election. It had all been part of an elaborate plot by the Master to steal a black hole hidden under the carpet in the Panopticon.

The Doctor had briefly tried out being President. Some wag had pointed out that, while the Doctor had been exiled on Earth, that planet had been invaded every week, so perhaps Gallifrey shouldn't expect any better. True to form, they'd been invaded twice in a fortnight. Declaring it his worst holiday ever (and he'd been to Majorca), the Doctor had left shortly afterwards, and, strangely, Gallifrey had not been invaded since.

'I'd completely forgotten you were President.' Romana was grinning.

'So had I,' the Doctor ruminated. 'Makes waking up without screaming so much easier.' He rearranged his jacket and tapped Romana confidentially on the nose. 'Strictly speaking, Romana, since we're here, you should probably address me as Lord President Doctor. So long as that doesn't sound too absurd.'

'It does.'

'Doesn't it?' The Doctor escaped from the clutches of the sofa and slithered awkwardly onto the floor. 'You know, I bet the old goats have forgotten I'm in charge.' He rubbed his hands together. 'This could, actually, be quite fun. Especially if they arrest me. Which they're pretty much bound to do.' He looked expectantly from left to right. 'At any moment.'

Some people can tell when it's about to rain. The Doctor knew when an armed guard was on the way.

He and Romana stood and waited for the arrest. There was, now you mention it, a distant alarm on the wind, and a clatter of distinctly military shoes. The Doctor checked his watch. 'They're late. I blame the new guy.'

'That's you.'

'Oh, I know.' The Doctor whistled a bit. 'Tell you what. There has to be a lovely thing we can do with "Take me to your leader."'

'What?'

'An Earth expression. Whenever a flying saucer lands, the chief alien always says, "Take me to your leader." They promptly taxi him to the nearest soldier. Now, if that were real, they'd send him to the Inland Revenue.'

'Also,' said Romana, 'flying saucers are the worst.'

'Oh, absolutely. Anyway. Where were we?'

A squad of Chancellery Guard marched round the corner and aimed their weapons at the pair. The Doctor threw his hands up theatrically, and edged in front of the sofa in case a stray bullet mercifully took it out.

'I'm your leader!' he declared. 'Take me to me.'

Romana shook her head sadly.

The Doctor always enjoyed being marched around by the Chancellery Guard. They reminded him of brightly wrapped

Christmas chocolates, with their postbox-red uniforms and pinstriped capes. Occasionally they had remarkable hats that made him worry that somewhere on Gallifrey was a farm full of angry, bald peacocks.

'I've been gone too long,' Romana thought. She had always rather admired the pomp and splendour of her home planet, a world where every door was a portal, and you called a spade 'the Spade of Rassilon'. Now, as they were led through interminable grand chambers, she found herself stifling the urge to giggle. She'd one day found a children's book in an unswept corner of the TARDIS. The book had been about an abandoned library, now run by the bookworms. The worms all had jolly names, and spectacles, and embarked on a series of adventures solved through teamwork, cooperation, and the knowledge they'd gleaned from the books they ate. This was, of course, absurd, and Romana had read it from cover to cover immediately. The idea of a microcosm devouring the very knowledge it championed fascinated her. She'd mentioned it to the Doctor. He'd laughed. 'But what about their glasses?' he'd said. 'How do they stay on their heads?'

As they went deeper into the Capitol, the buildings assumed a grimmer hue. There was a brief flirtation with murky brown before they were into chambers of sinister emerald green.

'I've never been here before,' said Romana.

'Of course not,' the Doctor said. 'This is where all the business is done. No sofas.'

'They were awful, weren't they?'

To the Chancellery Guard, this was baffling. When you were marched by them it was normally what they called a 'No-Way Trip'. At the end of your journey, you'd cease to exist, your whole timeline erased, so that someone could better use your portion of infinity. The people who'd barely paid any attention to you as you'd passed would now have never paid you any at all. The process was called, inevitably, the Rassilon Erasure, although, actually, someone else had invented it. History has curiously forgotten them.

Instead of being cowed or intimidated by the process, these two prisoners were talking about the soft furnishings – laughing at the inflatable ones, the over-stuffed ones, the ludicrously purple ones. The Doctor was wondering if one day a whole lot of hairdressing salons had woken up to find themselves robbed, Romana was asking if it was perhaps some kind of cunning plot by the Master. 'If it is,' the Doctor chuckled, 'it's surely his most successful one. Let's give him the benefit of the doubt, shall we?'

Finally, they arrived in a hallowed vastness. The furthest reaches of it suggested a stony echo, but mostly it was just a huge blackness. In (presumably) its centre was a toppled monolith of a stone table, so long and grim it could only have been owned by unhappily married goblins. At the far end of the table a small man slumped in his ceremonial robes, a school nativity wise man in a duvet cover. He had pushed his wire-framed spectacles out of the way to rub at his tired eyes.

'Oh it's you,' he groaned.

'Who's been sitting in my chair?' the Doctor barked with delight. 'Oh look, it's Borusa!' He nudged the little man in the ribs. 'Keeping my seat warm for me, eh? Romana!' he cried jubilantly. 'It's Cardinal Borusa. He's my old tutor!'

'Um,' said Romana, surprised. 'Mine too, actually.'

Fuldanquin Borusa, Archprime Cardinal of Gallifrey, had recently led a series of unlucky lives. Time Lords have thirteen lives and, with careful husbandry, can eke them out to a very long lifespan indeed. Cardinal Borusa had spent several thousand years shinning slowly up the greasy ladder of Gallifreyan academia and had made a stately, elegant leap onto the slimier pole of politics. This had all been achieved with grandeur, poise and caution. Borusa had previously only regenerated when his revered and ancient bodies had finally worn thin at the elbows.

Recently, however, and without wishing to dwell, he'd started racing through his remaining regenerations at a rate of knots. It was as if a lifetime's prudence and good luck had been knocked away. He'd consulted a Causal Therapist who'd sniffed his Artron energy and asked if he'd recently been exposed to a high degree of improbability. Sadly, Borusa had: the Doctor.

Up until that moment, Borusa had always had a something of a soft spot for the Doctor. He had, in his long, long career, trained a fair number of successful Time Engineers, Quantum Mechanics, Relativity Archivists and so on. All respectable Time Lords going into respectable careers, and all of them were so terribly easy to forget unless you needed a favour. The Doctor stood out. A little like a sore thumb, it was true. One did not like to have tutored too many renegades, but the Doctor always made for interesting small talk at parties. The Doctor did so love a scrape, and threw himself into all sorts of unlikely events at such a pace that it was sometimes impossible to keep up with whatever he was doing badly. His deplorable old TARDIS was forever shuddering from one hot spot to the next. Yet the Doctor had proved to be singularly lucky – considering the number of times his life had been placed in imminent danger (he was constantly being chased, shot, tortured, hurled into black holes, dropped through time storms, taken over, exterminated and lightly vexed) he always seemed to be, at the very last moment, annoyingly none the worse for wear.

His dress sense was not only horrible, it was a celebration of his indestructability. The Doctor really liked wool. Short of a nylon miniskirt, he couldn't wear anything more flammable, and yet the Doctor strolled out of cataclysms unscathed. If Borusa had been in the Doctor's patent leather shoes, he'd have worn an asbestos suit and ditched the scarf immediately.

Borusa had met his worst student twice recently. Firstly, there had been the time when a black hole had got loose in the Panopticon chamber. Then there was that period when Gallifrey had been invaded quite a lot. Both occasions had placed the Doctor in great peril; he'd emerged fine, but – and here was where Borusa's Causal Therapist had leaned forward, fascinated – things hadn't worked out quite so well for the Cardinal.

The Causal Therapist put it like this: 'Supposing we were to accept that there were such a thing in the universe as luck, you'd have to accept that there was a finite quantity of it.' (The Causal Therapist had a style so dry you could toast and butter it.) 'If that was the case, we can only assume that the Doctor is blessed with a large amount of luck. Luck which must, therefore, be inducted from the sum total of luck available around him. The Doctor is a complicated space-time event. If I were you, in future lives, I'd stand well back.'

The Doctor's deaths were a matter of grand heroics. However, in the last few years, Borusa had had to regenerate because of a falling stack of books, a missing decimal point, and an infected toenail. Borusa's deaths had become frequent and absurd.

As though the world was trying to even things out, his political progress accelerated. The Doctor had pretty much strolled into and out of the Presidency as though it were a tea tent. Running the most important civilisation in the universe clearly didn't matter a hoot to him. Borusa had, cautiously and not at all enviously, stepped into the breach. If the Doctor was squandering power, he wasn't the man to let it go to waste. So what if he, Borusa, had spent millennia gently ascending and the Doctor had marched in and treated the presidency like an unwanted Secret Santa gift? He may as well get some use out of it. Borusa had spent some fun aeons as Acting President, tutoring the more interesting Time Lords, and gently researching ways to stay alive. Because he knew that the Doctor was, sooner or later, going to turn up again, and he was worried about what the consequences would be – if not for the universe, then very certainly for him.

He'd recently mildly enjoyed tutoring the Time Lady Romanadvoratrelundar. She was bright certainly, traditionally ambitious, and had about her a kind of icy dullness which assured Borusa that she'd go far, but not too far. The thing she lacked was a spark. He'd been rather surprised when she'd left Gallifrey for a short mission, and even more surprised when she hadn't come right back, vowing never to leave the Capitol again.

But here she was, after a long absence, bobbing along in the Doctor's wake. The change in her was startling. It wasn't just that she'd regenerated, but that she'd acquired the spark she'd been lacking. She was dressed in an immaculately tailored tweed suit, there was a bounce to her step, and a sharp intelligence shone from her eyes. Oh dear. Romana was now, regrettably, a force to be reckoned with. The Doctor had done it again.

True, she was looking just a little bit sheepish, but that was only to be expected. Borusa had spent several hundred years perfecting a glare that immediately made previous students worry that they were seventy years late with an essay. Only the Doctor was immune to this, and that was because he'd never managed to hand in an essay in his life.

The Doctor also knew by now that he could cause a considerable upset on Gallifrey simply by strolling into a room, acting as if he owned the place. Because, in theory, he did. He didn't give a hoot about it, but he did so very much enjoy how much it annoyed everyone else.

'Now then, Borusa,' he announced, his voice so loud that the Cardinal shot an alarmed glance up at the chandelier swinging over his head, 'I've something very important to tell you.'

'Have you now?' Borusa suddenly felt even more terribly tired. This wasn't going to be good.

'You see …' the Doctor began, and then shuddered. 'What I have to tell you is so terribly, terribly painful—'

'The Krikkitmen are back.' Romana ruined his fun.

It is, of course, absurd,' said Borusa as he led them to what was either a really small tanning salon or an open-ended transmat beam.

'Absurd? Absolutely,' the Doctor agreed.

43

'Quite,' said Romana, solemnly.

'And to think that you actually went to a cricket match.' Borusa shook his head. Little lights danced past them as they were transported deeper and deeper into the planet's data core.

'I really couldn't avoid it any longer,' the Doctor said. 'I've always had a nagging doubt.'

'Doctor, sometimes your fondness for that planet surprises even me. Some of their customs are merely reprehensible—'

'Lemon in tea? Jigsaws? Blackpool?' suggested Romana.

'Quite,' Borusa nodded his approval. They were three things he simply didn't understand. 'But Cricket – really. To take the universe's most appalling belief and turn it into a game …'

'The thing is,' the Doctor said, 'Perhaps we've been looking at it the wrong way round.'

Borusa shook his head and flashed his weary academic smile. 'No Doctor, I think you need to accept that your pets are guilty of a heinous lack of taste.'

Of course he'd timed his remark perfectly so that the Doctor's protest was cut off by the shimmer of the transmat's arrival. The air outside the booth was even more august and chilly. The walls were carved from an ancient stone that would have made a hideous bathroom suite. Suddenly, the transmat booth felt warm and snug and friendly – and lifts should never feel that.

They stepped out into the Great Matrix Chamber. It was here that the disembodied souls of dead Time Lords hung around eager to give their descendants a telling off. This manifested in a distant but sharp whispering. The Matrix contained the accumulation of all Time Lord knowledge, hoovered from the souls of the recently departed. These souls liked nothing more than to say that everything was going to rack and ruin, but, as Gallifreyan society never changed, there really was nothing more for the departed to do than linger around being disgruntled.

Technicians scurried around with the weary expressions of people who are constantly being gossiped about. A distant bell tolled glumly.

Romana had only been down to the Great Matrix Chamber once before, on a school trip. They'd walked in a strict crocodile formation and been ordered not to touch any dead relatives. The atmosphere hadn't appealed to her younger self (she'd only just turned 60 at the time; still a babe in arms, really). She'd been unable to describe it properly until the Doctor had taken her to a cathedral, the last remaining ruin of a once noble civilisation. The cathedral had been home to a god who had correctly prophesied that the planet would be destroyed. With the apocalypse having been and gone, the cathedral had a sharp tang in the air, as of someone who had been proved very right, but now had no one left to boast to.

Coming back to the Matrix with the Doctor, Romana no longer felt intimidated. 'It's all so miserable,' she exclaimed.

The Doctor beamed at her. 'Exactly! Terribly unfriendly, isn't it?'

'But this is the summit of Time Lord Achievement!' Borusa thundered.

One of his ancestors shushed him.

The Doctor ran a finger along the ancient computer banks. 'They don't dust down here much, do they?' he remarked, which Romana thought was a bit rich.[1]

The Doctor watched Borusa striding around the archive issuing orders. He chewed a lip thoughtfully. Well, all right, he'd left Gallifrey in the old buffer's hands. But the Doctor also felt

[1] The other day she'd found an old lady with a mop and bucket at the end of one of the TARDIS corridors. 'What are you doing here?' she'd asked. The old lady had leant on her mop and breathed out slowly. 'Cleaning, dear,' she'd said. Romana had gone to make her a cup of tea, but the old lady had vanished by the time she'd finally got the kettle working.

something wet and fishy flopping around in his soul – surely not jealousy? It is one thing to leave the last fig roll out on the plate because you don't fancy it. It's quite another to find someone's polished it off and pocketed the plate. What he needed was something to take Borusa down a peg or two.

Something bumped against the Doctor's leg. He glanced down. 'K-9!' he beamed.

The robot dog wagged his tail. 'Master,' he said, pronouncing the word like 'what kept you?'

The Doctor squinted, just to make sure it was the right K-9. Somewhere on Gallifrey was an earlier version of the dog, together with an earlier version of Romana. Well, her predecessor as the Doctor's travelling companion – a rather formidable amazon called Leela who even now was prowling the Beige Wastelands wearing a scowl and some window cleaner's rags.

Romana patted the dog's ears. 'Have you found anything out?'

The Doctor enquired if he'd met any nice computers, but the dog ignored this in favour of answering Romana's question. 'I have established a solid portal into the Amplified Panotropic Network.'

'Good boy, K-9.' Romana rubbed his tin nose.

The Doctor nodded. He wasn't quite sure what the dog had done, but wanted to look knowing. 'And about time too,' he said, waving a hand in Borusa's direction.

The Acting President found himself being politely ignored by a cluster of Memory Archivists. Blessed with long lifespans and infinite patience, Gallifreyans could ignore each other almost indefinitely. One of the reasons their Golden Age of Technology had stagnated was that people spent so long waiting in for the telephone engineer. During one such interminable period, Bardak the Flighty had invented the wireless wrist communicator and Time Lord Society had moved on with a leap and a bound. Time Lord Society had promptly vowed never to do anything of the sort ever again.

'Borusa,' hissed the Doctor in a stage whisper that rattled the shelves, 'my dog's found something.'

Realising he had their the attention, K-9 paused dramatically. His tone was grandiose. 'The Matrix is at fault.'

The archivists gasped so loudly they had to shush themselves.

K-9 nodded. 'I am quite correct,' he insisted. Well, he would. The Doctor delighted at finding someone else on the receiving end of his dog.

'It's not possible,' gibbered a librarian.

The Doctor considered. There was a worrying precedent – after all, there'd been that time the Master had temporarily made Gallifrey forget all about him.

Borusa waved a finger. 'Be careful, Doctor. The Matrix is the total of all that is known and all that we can predict. The Matrix did not say the Krikkitmen were coming back. Therefore they are not.'

'Balderdash and poppycock,' said the Doctor, crisply and firmly.

Romana reached in her pocket and pulled out a newspaper. 'I made us stop off to the get the next day's paper.' She unfolded a copy of *The Times*. It showed a blurry picture of a Krikkitman blasting its way across the pitch.

The Doctor smiled at Romana. She really did think of everything.

'But this is impossible!'

'No!' Romana had always enjoyed arguing with her tutor. This was the first time she'd stood up to him outside of his study and it felt marvellous. 'You know what,' she squared up to Borusa. 'I think that something's wrong with the Matrix.'

'Oh, this is excellent.' The Doctor was rubbing his hands.

Romana had got into her stride now. 'We need to examine everything the Matrix has on the Krikkitmen.'

'Quite right.' The Doctor nodded warmly.

'In order to do that, we need to go into the Matrix.'

The Doctor's face fell. 'Oh, that never ends well.'

CHAPTER SIX
FURTHER IMPORTANT AND EXCITING GALACTIC HISTORY. AGAIN, DO NOT SKIP.

So far, much has been said about 'the rest of the universe' or 'everyone else in the Galaxy' and so on. And of course, everybody knows that the Galaxy is an extremely large place, teeming with a bewildering prolixity of life forms of every kind, carbon-based, silicon-based, light-based, mammals, fish, molluscs, insects, travel agents, etc.

At least, nearly everybody does.

And here we come to the next in the series of major mistakes which has led to the situation which lies at the heart of this story, and it occurred during the seventh civilisation wave, and for this reason:

The night sky over Krikkit is probably the least interesting sight in the entire Universe.

The mistake the people of Krikkit made was in thinking that they were alone.

They didn't think, 'We are alone in the Universe.' They thought, 'We are alone.' They didn't know about the Universe. In fact, it is even a little misleading to say they thought, 'We are alone.' As with all of the most basic assumptions, it never even occurred to them that there was any other way to be.

The reason for this is that the planet of Krikkit and its sun existed right out on the very edge of the Galaxy. Beyond it was nothing till you got to the next Galaxy which was so far away as to be practically invisible. And between Krikkit and the rest of its own Galaxy, our Galaxy, lay a dense dust cloud, through which nothing whatever could be seen at any time.

It never occurred to them to spend any time looking into the sky because there was nothing to see there, nothing to catch attention, provoke curiosity or stimulate the imagination. It was just a blank.

During the day there was the sun, of course, but anyone who looked at that directly tended then not to be able to see anything else, and this was sufficient to deter the curious.

And Krikkit itself was such a beautiful world, so full of colour and light and life of all kinds, that the Krikkitas (as the inhabitants of Krikkit are called) had absolutely no incentive to look up at the blankness or ponder its meaning. It didn't have a meaning to ponder. As far as they were concerned, the sky hardly existed,

They were happy. They lived in peace. They worked the fields for their food, built themselves pleasant houses, they played music, painted pictures. Ask a Krikkita what he wanted out of life and he would have said, 'This', indicating that he was very happy with what he had.

No stars twinkled in the cloudy night air. A warm breeze brushed over the sandy beach. The planet was, at first glance, on the pleasantly dull end of very ordinary. Apart from the large letters blazing in the sky.

A hundred yards out to sea, a door opened, and the Doctor, Romana and K-9 splashed out, striding through the surf onto the beach. The Doctor and K-9 spent most of the walk arguing about the door.

'It's a fictional door, K-9, could you not have moved it closer to the shore?'

'Negative. Also, Master, the sea is similarly fictional.'

'Still feels odd walking through it.'

'Not to this unit.'

'Whatever you say, my socks are soaked.'

'Negative.'

'Well, they feel soaked.'

Romana was already standing neatly on the shore. 'Are neither of you going to mention the large letters hanging in the sky?' she asked.

The Doctor glanced up. 'Oh them,' he shrugged. 'That's just the Matrix narrating.'

The words which hung in the air in giant letters of fire were:

THE PLANET OF KRIKKIT LIES IN AN ISOLATED POSITION ON THE VERY OUTSKIRTS OF THE GALAXY.

'Subtle,' observed Romana.

The Doctor picked up a stick from the shore and threw it for K-9. The dog ignored it.

'Look at the sky.'

'No stars. Which is strange as there's no light pollution. Mind you it's overcast. Maybe it's the weather.'

The Doctor clicked his fingers. The burning letters changed:

KRIKKIT IS OBSCURED FROM THE REST OF THE GALAXY BY A DUST CLOUD.

'Oh I see,' said Romana. 'Fascinating. So, given the lack of any external lights, they just assume they're not just the centre of the universe, but that they are the universe. That's pushing solipsism on a global level far beyond the egotistical sublime.'

The Doctor chewed the air for a moment. 'Well, quite. They probably have a lot of mopey poets. And you've read far too many books.'

'There's no such thing as too many books,' Romana retorted, skipping up a sand bank. 'What an odd place.' She clicked her fingers.

The Sky now read (in lower case):

> For millions of years, Krikkit developed a sophisticated
> scientific culture in all fields except that of astronomy.

'I changed the font,' said Romana. 'Something a bit more subtle. I don't like being shouted at all the time.' She glanced at the Doctor meaningfully.

'K-9, I think Romana's having a go at you.' The Doctor patted his dog and winked at her. 'Can we have the next slide, please?'

Romana obliged.

> In all their history, it never once occurred to the people of
> Krikkit that they were not totally alone. Until dot dot dot.

She frowned. 'The punctuation is a bit off.'

'No, it's spot on,' said the Doctor. 'I'd step back a bit if I were you.'

Romana stepped back. A spaceship crashed where she'd been standing.

It tore through the murky sky, lighting it up with a streak of fire. The roar of its dying engines boomed off the cliffs, the sea and the distant lands as it scythed through the air, and then smacked into the sandy beach.

The shock waves shook the entire planet, heaving the sea up like a dusty rug and rattling the ground. The noise went on for quite a while.

The Doctor and Romana stood in the middle of the conflagration. Romana picked a chunk of burning debris from off of K-9.

'I think,' the Doctor remarked, 'the caption's changed again.'

'I can't see through all this fire.'

'Neither can I. Ah well.'

'Shall we wait until the smoke's cleared?'

'Good thought. Romana, did you bring any marshmallows?'

The Doctor, Romana and K-9 found a patch of beach that wasn't melting into glass and sat down. The ship burned on, and the day steadily dawned. The words remained hanging in the sky.

> The day that the wreckage of a spacecraft floated through
> the Dust Cloud and into their vicinity was one that would
> totally traumatise the whole race.

People came onto the beach. Slowly, cautiously, they walked to the cliff and peered down. Someone rowed up in a boat. The boat bobbed on the waves. All of them were watching the fire. No one said a word.

'So,' whispered Romana, 'These are the people of Krikkit? They seem ... normal.'

The Doctor nodded. 'Not for long.'

The sun rose and the sun set. Still the ship burned. More and more people came and stared at the ship. Some of them sang songs to it. A group of women emerged from the crowd and stepped as close as they dared. They put down a garland of flowers.

The crowd stared at this gesture, trying to work out if they agreed with it, thought it obscene, or wished they'd done it first. Then the flowers burst into flame. Which seemed to settle matters.

A few days later, the fire had died down to embers. The hull of the ship seemed remarkably intact – but the beach was a complete write-off.

A man in robes strode forward from the crowd and made to address the ship. He faltered on his words, shook his head and settled for gently, gently tapping the hull. Then he walked away.

Whether it was the tap, the lack of words, or the simple shipness of the ship, this did not go down well.

The first rock landed on the hull. Followed by another immediately afterwards. Then everyone in the crowd was throwing stones at the ship. They didn't stop, and all pinged harmlessly off the ship. But that didn't stop them from throwing them. When the stones ran out, people ran away to get buckets more of them. After a while, the throwing was joined by another noise. An angry howl that surged out from the crowd and didn't stop.

Here's how Galactic History records the event:

It is hard to imagine the shock that was inflicted on the minds of the people of Krikkit when the wreckage of the giant spacecraft crashed onto their beautiful planet.

It just came, bang, like that. Out of the blue. Out of what they had always assumed was nowhere. No warning. No follow-up. Bang. One wrecked spacecraft and that was that.

It was as if the Universe had suddenly said to them, 'There, what do you think of that?' when they didn't even know there was a Universe.

It had an unfortunate effect on them. They were stunned. And working with sudden, stunned swiftness, they examined the wrecked spaceship in every detail, took it apart, put it together, took it apart again, put it together again, wrung every last and tiniest secret out of it, and then within a year, a miraculous, incomprehensible year, they did something which should have taken them generations.

They built a spaceship for themselves.

They went up through the Dust Cloud, and they had a look at the glittering inconceivable vastness of the Galaxy.

They came back lost and reeling. They came back different.

They told of what they had seen.

A huge 'Aaaaaaaaaaaaaaarrrrrrrrrrrrgggggggghhhhhhhhhh!' of terror and shock went up from the whole people. For a hideous day and night the cry of terror rang continuously around the planet and it was as if a biological trigger had been tripped.

From out of nowhere the most primitive form of racial consciousness hit them like a hammer blow.

They weren't bad people in any way. They were never bad. It wasn't that they hated the rest of the Universe. It was just that they couldn't cope with it being there.

Overnight they were transformed from intelligent, charming, thoughtful, ordinary people, into intelligent, charming, delightful, manic Xenophobes.

'So that's how it all started,' said Romana.

'Well, that's the official story,' the Doctor mused. 'I'm always wary of those.'

The beach had emptied. The waves crept up the shattered shore. The ship had gone.

'Come on,' the Doctor climbed up a cliff path, pulling Romana along with his scarf. K-9 trundled loudly behind them.

At the top of the cliff the Matrix presented them with a wooden door, with a copper plate on it. In glowing red letters it said:

Later . . .

They opened it, finding themselves in a really very impressive laboratory. Lying in the centre of the huge clinical space was the ship, cracked open into Easter egg segments. People milled around benches, crawled over the pieces of the hull, and stared with fascination at tiny pieces of copper wire. Over at the far end of the hangar, an exact copy of the ship was slowly taking place. Well, not quite exact. Somehow every edge seemed sharper, every angle tauter. The graceful lines now sneered, the prow shoved its way into the air.

In another chamber, scientists worked diligently, examining the controls, the chairs, and mining data from the flight computer to produce detailed clay models of what the inhabitants of the craft might have looked like. These were carried next door to where each model was lined up against a wall and shot, stabbed, or set on fire.

Hovering above this chamber were more glowing words:

> Quietly, implacably, the people of Krikkit aligned themselves to their new purpose. The simple and absolute annihilation of all alien life forms.

'Well, that sounds ominous,' said the Doctor.

'All the same,' Romana mulled as they turned a corridor, 'reverse-engineering a spaceship and developing a whole new cultural and scientific mind-set? Well, that's going to take thousands and thousands of years …'

At the end of the corridor more words appeared:

> For another year, they worked with almost miraculous speed.

'That's you told,' the Doctor muttered.

'Hush,' said Romana.

The letters continued:

> They researched, perfected and built the technology to wage vast interstellar war.

The wall dissolved. Behind it was a warehouse filled with an interesting prime number of missiles. It was just one warehouse. Beyond it were many more, silos crammed with bombs, ordnance, neutron blasters, de-mat guns, matter-warpers and tissue compressors. And built over the warehouse were layer upon layer of warships.

Rather pointlessly the words continued:

> They had mastered the techniques of rapid travel in space.

The words were now emblazoned across a huge runway. On every side of it were the hangars. They walked through the glowing letters, heading towards a vast black cylinder at the far end of the runway. It had a door. On the door was written:

And then they built the Krikkitmen.

The door slid up and those spindly, white killer robots marched out, rank after rank of them. Seen en masse, you could appreciate the brutal efficiency of the design. The spare frame, the armoured head, the glowing red lights flickering within. An army built out of whatever was to hand.

'Yes, but in a year?' Romana queried. 'I mean, that's asking a lot of people. Or expecting a really slow orbit.'

Galactic History is only too happy to tell you what happens next:

The Army of Krikkit was an army of androids – again, developed and built within a timescale which should have been impossible. This has always been put down to the power of single-minded obsession, and it is only very recently that the question, 'Yes, but whose mind are we talking about here?' has been asked.

The design of these androids was very curious, and particularly interesting in the light of subsequent events, which we are, by degrees, coming to.

The androids – or Krikkitmen as they were known – were anthropomorphic, or man-shaped. This has remained a phenomenally popular shape throughout recorded history.

They were white – still a major colour.

The lower halves of their legs were encased in ribbed rocket engines which enabled them to fly when required. They wielded multifunctional battle clubs, which brandished in one way would knock down buildings, brandished another way fired blistering rays, and brandished another way launched a hideous arsenal of grenades.

This was a particularly ingenious piece of systems economy. Simply striking the grenades (smallish red spheres) with the multifunctional battle clubs simultaneously primed them and launched them with quite phenomenal trajectorial accuracy over distances ranging from mere yards to thousands of miles.

As battle weapons, the Krikkitmen were fiendish. Puzzling, but fiendish.

The Doctor, Romana and K-9 stood on the parade ground, watching the Krikkitmen march past, climbing into those strange ships which had evolved. Sleek lines had been folded back and stretched out. Aerodynamics were no longer important – these were simply containers for as many Krikkitmen as possible, with small windows at the front and a pointed top. Eleven robots filed into each box, which slid out of the hangar, roared across the pitch and punched straight up into the sky.

Craft after craft pushed its way up into the Dust Cloud. The Doctor blinked. 'They do, you know, look like cricket pavilions. Remarkable.'

The fleet of boxes filled the entire sky. The engine noise changed – and then Romana realised.

'It's the people,' she breathed.

Echoing over the surface of the planet was that same roar. The people of Krikkit were screaming with anger again. An anger that said they wouldn't be satisfied until everything went back to the way it was.

The roaring peaked and the craft vanished.

The only thing hanging in the empty sky were the following words:

Finally all preparations were complete, and with no warning at all the forces of Krikkit launched a massive blitz attack on all the major centres of the Galaxy simultaneously.

The words faded, and were then replaced by, in a much bigger, grander font:

THE GALAXY REELED.

The planet Krikkit was empty. The battleships had gone, the crowd had fallen silent, watching. Lights began to blaze in the distant heavens, so bright they shimmered briefly through the Dust Cloud. Somewhere beyond, the stars started to burn.

Silently, and rather sullenly, a doorway appeared.

The Doctor opened it. 'Let's get a move on,' he said. 'The next bit's not going to be fun.'

After they'd gone, the sea and the burning clouds faded sadly away, leaving behind only the indecisive grey of the Matrix and those lingering giant letters.

THE GALAXY REELED.

CHAPTER SEVEN
MORE ON THE GALAXY REELING

As luck would have it, at this time the Galaxy was enjoying a period of great harmony and prosperity. It was that rare thing – a happy Galaxy.

It was one of those rare times of universal peace. And by *rare*, best we say really, since you mention it, one of those pretty much *unique* times of universal peace.

Universal peace came about because – well, a lot of fine speeches were made by various presidents, leaderenes and definitely democratically elected supreme ones about how they were pleased to have played their part in the dawning of a glorious golden age of harmony, the death of the eras of boom and bust. There were even meetings and conferences where the various universal power brokers posed, looking tired but victorious, while they took pictures of each other shaking hands, standing against nobly fluttering flags, or even staring wistfully into hopeful sunrises.

In truth, of course, universal peace came about pretty much by accident. To start with, all the terrible old races from the Dark Times had died out. The Racnoss literally ate each other. The Jagaroth finally blew themselves up. The stone-hearted Kastrians crumbled. There was a whole string of such ironically appropriate endings. Even the Great and Deathless Vampires died out. Some people argued that it was proof that there was a divinity which shapes our ends, etc., etc.

A mad soothsayer told a story. He claimed to have been at the final, awful dissolution of the Insoluble Ancients. He met an old man dressed in white, standing under a white umbrella (to protect him from the acid rain). The old man was holding a cocktail in one hand and something else in the other. The soothsayer really only noticed the cocktail.

'That looks nice,' he said, for he spoke only the sooth.

'It is,' smiled the old man in white, regarding his drink pleasantly. He seemed to be regarding most things pleasantly. He handed his to the soothsayer. 'I can always make another,' he said, his eyes twinkling in a way that suggested they always twinkled. He invited the soothsayer under his umbrella.

The cocktail tasted marvellous. It made the acid rain bearable as it ate into his shoes. Very improbably, a dove flew past, making its startled, agonised way through the air. Perhaps attracted by the umbrella, or by the only bit of shelter for miles around, the bird drew close. It flapped around, tapped its beak against the cocktail glass, and then settled on the wise old man's head.

'Oh dear,' said the wise old man in white, 'Perfection can't last for ever, can it?' He chuckled and the soothsayer laughed along, partly because he liked to be seen to be clever, but mostly because, well, you know, the man in white had a dove on his head.

Whilst trying not to look at the dove, the soothsayer's eyes alighted on the other thing that the man in white was holding. At this point, he did some quick mental arithmetic and failed to reach an answer as to how exactly how the man in white was managing with just the two arms to hold an umbrella, a cocktail, and a large square crystal.

'What's that?' the soothsayer asked.

'Oh, I'm afraid I can't give it to you,' chuckled the wise old man, with the annoying chuckle of someone who enjoyed a lot of private jokes. 'I can't make another, you see. This is the Key To Time,' he announced. 'It brings balance to the universe.'

'Is such a thing possible?' asked the soothsayer. The dove gave him an 'Ooh, you're brave' coo.

The old man in white held up the crystal, turning it around until it caught the reflections of the distant burning cities.

'I should say so,' he declared. 'Today's a rare day. I've brought perfect balance to the universe.' He tossed it up into the air and the crystal vanished. 'Don't mess it up,' the old man said to no one and everyone in particular. He walked away.

The soothsayer found himself holding an umbrella and an empty cocktail glass.

That was one story about how universal peace came to be. For those who didn't like their triumphs to include a mysterious white man with a magic cube, there were the Galactic Rationalists who argued that all the aggressive races had blown each other up; the subjugated ones didn't have the firepower to blow out a candle; there really wasn't that much life elsewhere in the universe; and, as the Time Lords had now run out of interestingly aggressive races to kidnap and torment in a wet quarry, they'd had to come up with a new hobby of having a sit down and looking smug.

Basically, the Galactic Rationalists argued that universal peace had come about fairly naturally. Planets ticked along amiably with each other. Everyone discovered that they had something their neighbours needed and their neighbours had something they quite fancied and that this balanced out reasonably harmoniously. Occasionally some people became obscenely rich, but then their children would eventually mess it all up, and so it balanced itself out.

Also, it had to be said, the universe was quite smug about the peace thing. No one quite got around to putting up a sign saying '192 days since an interstellar war', but they did the next best thing.

As often happens when people are happy, they made a symbol out of it, something to show that they all felt life was good. It was called the great Wicket Gate, and it stood for the prosperity of the Galaxy. To show how everyone these days got along by relying on each other, it was heavily symbolic. It consisted of three vertical sticks with two shorter horizontal ones balanced between them.

The three vertical sticks consisted of a Steel one, to represent Strength and Power, a Perspex one to represent Science and Reason, and a Wooden one to represent all the Forces of Nature. The two short sticks they supported were the Gold Bail of Prosperity and the Silver Bail of Peace. As well as the great Wicket Gate itself, you could buy versions of this symbol all over the place and in all sorts of sizes. You could put one on your mantelpiece, hang one round your neck, get one tattooed on your hide, and you could even – if you were rich and right-minded enough – live in one, though it was very expensive and you spent most of your life in elevators.

That, then, was how the Galaxy was, peaceful and prosperous – particularly for the people who manufactured the decorative Wicket symbols that everybody wanted so much. And that is why, when the forces of the Army of Krikkit hit the great Wicket Gate from behind a tiny and remote Dust Cloud, the Galaxy reeled like a man getting mugged in a meadow.

This is what the Galaxy was faced with, and why the Galaxy reeled.

*

When the Krikkitmen came through the Wicket Gate, it wasn't actually a targeted attack on a symbol. It was simply the first nice thing the battle fleet came across.

The Wicket Gate was one of the Wonders of the Universe. It looked so very nice and people came to admire it and said that, despite its inherent fragility, it also represented something that would last for ever. Well, until the invading forces of the Krikkitmen smashed through the Wicket Gate and burnt their way across the stars.

Precisely ten seconds before this happened, the Doctor, Romana and K-9 glided out of the Matrix Door and onto the asteroid. They looked up at the Wicket Gate towering over their heads.

'The symbol of universal peace,' said Romana sadly.

'Seems quiet enough,' the Doctor remarked, even though she'd begged him not to say that.

At that moment, inevitably, Krikkitship after Krikkitship shot out into the universe, pushing through the separating wreckage of the Wicket Gate. In seconds they'd demolished the gate, annihilated the VIP queue, then the ordinary queue, then the gift shop, and finally the visitor parking. All were gone in seconds. Those that weren't blasted to pieces by the grenades were stabbed, sliced, or shot; or stabbed, sliced *and* shot. The Krikkitmen were thoroughly wiping out everything they found.

There followed a thousand years of horrifying carnage which, in order to give it all the attention which horrifying carnage deserves, we will skip quickly over. Anybody interested in horrifying carnage could do worse than to read Dr P.L. Zoom's book *Krikkit: The Horrifying Carnage*, or Rad Banchelfever's *Carnage Illustrated, Vols 7,8 & 9: The Krikkit Wars*, or Ag Bass's book *Krikkit: The Statistics of Death*, or Bodrim Holsenquidrim's much later statistical work *Krikkit: Still Counting After All These Years*. The most serious and substantial work of the hundreds of thousands of books which have been written on the Krikkit Wars is, of course, Professor San's monumental thirty-volume history entitled simply *Why, Why, Why?*.

The slaughter was immediate, immense and indescribable. Romana couldn't help flinching, and even the Doctor closed his eyes to the horror the Matrix showed them. The noise the Krikkitmen made did not help. The Daleks killed with a sneer, the Cybermen killed silently, but the Krikkitmen applauded each other. Civilisations who had forgotten how to fight perished, others vowed never to make the same mistake again. They mustered what they could and fought back.

The Krikkitmen marched on, and the Matrix shifted the Doctor and Romana from planet to planet, filling each world with acrid smoke, screams, and desolation.

Rather unnecessarily the burning words reappeared in the sky:

The wars wreaked havoc throughout the known universe.

The Matrix then showed them a few more burning planets, just to make quite sure it had got its point across.

They walked through the sharp winds of Pibo towards the shattered crystal towers. They trod around the molten remains of the Steel City of Vlastin, and the unmourned desolation of the Intergalactic Tax Office on Kopek Var.

And still the Krikkitmen marched. As time passed, the vistas changed – sometimes there'd be the odd disabled robot sparking in the dust, or crawling drunkenly from a crashed ship. But mostly it was just a lot of devastation. The problem was that the universe had forgotten how to fight, and was relearning in a haphazard and rather desperate fashion.

Romana surveyed it all very sadly. 'This was the first great test of Gallifrey, wasn't it?'

The Doctor nodded. The words in the sky agreed, remarking:

This was the first great test of Gallifrey.

Gallifrey had, at about this time, adopted its strict policy of non-intervention. In many ways, this was a sign of their growing maturity – having acquired a mastery of the Laws of Time they'd also realised that they weren't necessarily all that good at tinkering with it. As such, they'd vowed to keep themselves to themselves, peering over infinity's fence but never doing anything about the buddleia.

For a long time, they'd been really good about it. This was made easy enough because there were no wars to get involved in, just the odd taxation skirmish which even the Time Lords couldn't find interesting.

Then the Krikkit War broke out, and the Time Lords did their best not to notice. The problem was that, as the fighting raged for a millennium, people kept asking them, 'What is to be done?' For the first few centuries it was enough to say, 'Well, we've discussed this already,' but as the years passed and the death toll grew and the sound of exploding planets rang ever louder, it just kept on being raised. Until, eventually, someone pointed out that it was all very well ignoring the rest of the universe, but you actually needed a rest of the universe in order to be able to claim you were ignoring it. There was even more *humming* and *hawing* than usual in the vaulted halls of the Time Lord Panopticon, until eventually they admitted the sense of this.

The Time Lords sent an emissary to meet with the remaining species, to suggest that, perhaps, just this once, they might be willing to help, so long as everyone agreed not to harp on about it.

Or, as the great glowing words in the sky put it:

After a thousand years of warfare, the Galactic Forces, after some
heavy initial losses, rallied against the Krikkitmen.

This was illustrated by a mighty army of Krikkitmen marching
across the surface of a planet. All around them rained death and
destruction. In front of them was a city, teeming with people. All
of them doomed and marked for destruction. As the Doctor and
Romana watched, the very first line of soldiers entered the city,
and exploded. A fierce curtain of allied firepower poured down
on them. No Entry, it seemed to say. A second wave of Krikkitmen
marched through the curtain and exploded. Followed by a fourth,
then a fifth.

When the sixteenth wave went through and the energy
showed no signs of running out, the leader of the seventeenth
wave paused, inserting his hand into the curtain. It watched,
dispassionately, as its hand burnt away, followed by the wrist and
then the arm up to the padded elbow. And then it stopped. And
behind it the entire army stopped.

'That was repeated across the Cosmos, I believe,' remarked the
Doctor. 'The ancient Time Lords devised an impenetrable barrier
which they placed between their allies and the Krikkitmen – same
basic principles that they used to seal Gallifrey off from the rest of
the Universe.'

'Impressive.' Romana sucked a thumb and tapped the force
wall. 'Although you're jumbling Galaxy, Cosmos and Universe
rather freehandedly.'

'Am I?' the Doctor shrugged. 'Well, they're pretty much the
same thing.'

'Negative,' put in K-9.

'Anyway –' the Doctor strode off across the battlefield – 'the
point is they extended the barrier, forcing the Krikkitmen back
towards their own territory. Bye bye!' He waved at the robots and

sauntered off in search of a Matrix Door. He paused before it and glanced sourly up at the official history dangling in the blood-coloured sky.

The Galaxy won, by might, by the sheer scale of the forces it was able eventually to deploy, and by the skin of its nerve-wracked teeth.

But it then had to face a terrible dilemma: what was to be done with the vanquished people of Krikkit? They were, after all, simply the victims of a cruel trick of history.

The solution, when it was finally arrived at, struck some as clever and humane, and others as stupid and barbaric. But it was, at least, novel. What no one could quite agree on was where the solution had come from.

CHAPTER EIGHT
SO MUCH FOR UNIVERSAL PEACE

'We can't skulk around in the Matrix all day, not when the Universe is in danger,' the Doctor said, breezing out of the Matrix.

'Has it told you what you wanted to know?' demanded Borusa.

The Doctor shook his head. 'The Matrix is playing its cards close to its chest.' He broke into a winning grin. 'I always find official history unreliable and whimsical. We're off to sample it for ourselves.'

'You're going back to the Krikkit Wars?' Borusa stared. 'Isn't that terribly dangerous?'

'We're just nipping to the last page to find out who did it. And anyway –' the Doctor's smile widened – 'I've always been very lucky. Oh …' He paused. 'Mind your head on that door, Borusa. You could fetch yourself a nasty bump.'

*

71

'The thing about the end of the war against the Krikkitmen …'
The Doctor was at the controls of his time machine. ' … is that,
whatever the stories are, they all skip over exactly how it was
solved.'

'Typical hero-myth,' said Romana. 'A complacent people are
attacked, band together, and triumph. Isn't that right, K-9?'

The dog nodded.

'And yet –' the Doctor held up a finger – 'we now know the
Krikkitmen are real. So why is the Matrix avoiding telling us the
real truth?'

'Good point,' Romana agreed.

The TARDIS landed with a thud. The Doctor strode to the
doors. 'You may not like what's outside,' he intoned. 'They call it
diplomacy.'

The Great Hall of Endless Debate was full of species talking. Now
that the battle was won and everyone had stopped screaming, the
shouting was in full flow. There were representatives from every
surviving species spread across the chamber, and, in the corner, at
a discreet, managerial distance, several Time Lords were gathered.
Officially, they were there purely as (what else) observers, but
from time to – well, obviously – time, one of them would cough
gently and lean over to mutter in the ear of one green being or
another. Sometimes their whispers would be met with a nod and
a smile, sometimes by a terrified shudder.

The main purpose of the meeting was to work out what could
be done next. They'd gathered in the Galaxy's largest extant
meeting hall – which was, it had to be said, missing only a little
bit of roof and merely mildly fire-damaged in a few places. The
surviving leaders were crammed in and, although they'd finally
agreed a protocol for the Peace Talks, the several thousand
representatives couldn't resist keeping up a low background buzz
of chatter, murmuring and occasional wailing. The screaming
was directed towards the five representatives from Krikkit, who

glowered in a small force cage, staring at the sweltering mass of Other Life with furious hatred.

Currently on stage was Velspoor of the Endless Karrick, who had lost three of their continents, a moon, and none of their pomposity.

'What we have to face before us, is, shall we call it, the Great Dilemma, namely that the unswerving militaristic xenophobia of the Krikkitas precludes us from the possibility of reaching any form of *modus vivendi* and peaceful settlement or harmonious co-existence with them.'

There were roars at this point, some of agreement, and many of 'KILL THEM! KILL THEM ALL!' A Time Lord tutted gently at this and started writing a memo.

Velspoor of the Endless Karrick turned, theatrically, to address the force cage. 'Have I, would you say, summarised your position correctly, gentlemen?'

One of the Krikkitas turned to glance at him and then, loudly, started to scream.

Disconcerted, Velspoor talked over the noise. 'The Krikkitas seem to believe that the meaning of life for them, indeed, their only purpose, is the obliteration of all other life forms – i.e. us.'

The other delegates howled in fury. The Krikkitas all howled back.

Romana winced and put her fingers in her ears. Diplomacy was terribly loud.

In a magnificent gesture, Velspoor held up a stately tentacle. 'However, other beings, I ask you to consider this – our vanquished opponents are not inherently evil. Merely … misguided? Deluded? Threatened at a fundamentally psychic level by the rest of existence? These beings, otherwise gentle, passive and utterly tranquil –' these adjectives went down very badly with the crowd – 'are in fact, and in this one sole, tragic respect, utterly incapable of tolerating the rest of the Universe. I put it to you that they are the victims –' this went down *really* badly, and it was a long time before the shouting and throwing of cups ceased – 'the victims of a freakish accident of history. It is therefore impossible to consider simply destroying them all.'

By this point, Velspoor had lost the sympathy of the crowd entirely. The jeering and stamping of feet forced him to slither from the stage. As he left, tentacles shielding his upper ganglions from the chairs that were being thrown at him, the old statesbeing made one heartfelt plea before the microphone burst into flames.

'What is to be done? What is to be done with them?'

As he finished, one of the cloaked Time Lords glided from the shadows for a word with the less angry delegates. A word, naturally, in private and strictly off the record. The Time Lords of Gallifrey wished it to be very gently known that they had a solution.

The Doctor sipped glumly from a cup of tea. Peace conferences always laid on the worst tea.

Romana looked around the crowded hall of squealing and gibbering delegates. For a moment she frowned – had she glimpsed something? She shook her head. Romana didn't glimpse. She looked things firmly in the eye and she noticed. What was it?

The Doctor was musing. 'I'd love to know what happens here that's different from the official history,'

'So far it seems fairly dull,' Romana pointed out.

The Doctor nodded. 'Exactly.' He pointed to a corridor. 'The delegates went down here, along with some rather shifty-looking Time Lords. I think that's where the fun is.'

Romana started down the corridor and paused. 'Doesn't fit with the architecture. Too long by about 5.3 metres.'

'Not the least surprising thing,' the Doctor said.

The corridor ended in a door. 'The temperature is much lower here. By ten degrees.'

'That's because –' the Doctor's ah-ha tone was warming up – 'the biodome ended 5.3 metres ago. We're in a trans-dimensional vestibule.' His eyes were pointing at the door, in as much as eyes could point (and the Doctor's eyes really could). He grinned.

'How curious,' conceded Romana. 'That door is just begging to be opened.'

'Isn't it?' The Doctor winked.

Romana tried the door. It was locked.

The Doctor knocked on it sharply. 'Open sesame,' he boomed. Nothing happened.

K-9 cleared his throat. 'Master,' he said, and shot the door. The beam was a cheery green colour, and the blast played briefly across the surface of the door.

'Code satisfactorily unlocked,' the dog remarked and trundled through.

'I noticed it when we arrived,' the Doctor said, trying very hard to look casual. 'I think it's a TARDIS. I ordered K-9 to crack the 21-tumbler lock.'

'Very clever, Doctor,' said Romana dutifully.

The Doctor took her arm and led her through the door.

Behind him, in the shadows, a figure watched the time travellers leave. It was a Krikkitman.

Inside the First Great War TARDIS, a deal was being done, the kind of thing that was never supposed to be seen.

War TARDISes are curious things. Most normal TARDISes assume the characters of their owners. One day, in the far future, Romana would have a TARDIS that was quick, efficient, and delighted in outlandishly daring outer shells. The Doctor's TARDIS entered rooms loudly and late. That fiendish Time Lord renegade the Master had a TARDIS with black walls, black controls, black doors, black lighting, and even a black cupboard in which he kept all his black cloaks – it was all very impressive, even if he stood no chance of finding his keys.

War TARDISes had no truck with this kind of thing, and instead spent the effort on changing the personality of their owners. The War TARDISes had been designed in the Great and Terrible Wars Against the Vampire Mutations and, along with Bow Ships and Stake Drives, had proved jolly effective at driving out the very last menace of the Old Times. The problem with this was that War TARDISes had been intended as a very expensive, short-term measure. The problem with the problem was that War TARDISes had been understandably equipped with a strong sense of self-preservation. And that was roughly when they'd started influencing their owners.

The Battle Cardinals had begun as serene academics reluctantly dabbling in the art of war, and had rapidly regenerated into hard, bloodthirsty war heroes. Their craft didn't stop there. Each and every Battle Cardinal became convinced that the fleet of Twelve War TARDISes needed maintaining, keeping on high alert in case there was another battle. This seemed in direct contravention to the new, sacrosanct Time Lord Vow of Strict Non-Interference, but anyone who pointed this out was promptly shouted down.

The war against the Krikkitmen had provided validation for this policy. The naysayers were silenced when they raised the quaint notion that this was the first time the craft had been needed in a millennium, and they could have been kept in trans-dimensional storage rather than in a fully crewed state of constant high alert. The simple fact was that the War TARDISes loved battle, bloodshed, and taking the niceties of space-time out behind the Panopticon bike sheds for a good punching.

The Doctor, Romana and K-9 slipped unnoticed into the First Great War TARDIS. The walls pulsed an angry red, the Battle Cardinals wore red robes, their Conflict Secretaries wore clashing shades of blue, and the normally delicate mushroom of controls had been replaced by three panels, best translated as STOP, GO and BANG.

The Doctor's voice was hushed. 'Romana, I think the Peace Conference is being run by a War TARDIS,' he said.

Romana nodded. 'There's no record of that happening.'

'I don't like this,' the Doctor said. He sipped from his cup of tea then put it down on a table. His attention was riveted by Battle Cardinal Melia. Melia was a haughty man, made all the haughtier by his eyes. They had that curiously unfocused look of external bio-control.

'I believe we have a solution to the conference,' Melia was saying. Giant screens were lit up with planets, all of them vanishing with dramatic puffs. 'The Time Lords of Gallifrey have occasionally identified and neutralised certain planets that would, if unchecked, pose a threat to the harmonious development of the Universe.' He pointed without even looking to the vanishing planets behind him. 'Vixos, Erle's World, the Awful Mutane Symbology, and, of course, Planet 5 have all been scrubbed from the Cosmos. We propose a similar approach to Krikkit. The robot armies, the weapons, the people will all be returned there and then the entire planet will be neutralised.'

'Destroyed?' asked one of the delegates.

Cardinal Melia chuckled a witless little chuckle that he'd clearly been practising. 'Of course not. There will be nothing to destroy. Believe me, it will be a harmless, instantaneous process. If you wish, we can place some of you on Krikkit in order to act as impartial observers. Just step forward and it shall be done,' He smiled the oddest little smile and all the delegates took a hasty step back.

'Surely there's a Plan B?' ventured someone.

Romana looked around, uncertain as to who had spoken.

'There's always a Plan B,' insisted the voice. Surely it was another of the Battle Cardinals?

'Yes,' the delegates said. Born diplomats, they loved a Plan B. Especially if it involved compromise and could, in the inevitable press conferences, be declared a triumph.

Battle Cardinal Melia spun round, trying to see who it was who'd defied him. He turned back to the delegates, his oddly toothy smile twitching into a snarl before subsiding placidly.

'There is an alternative. You might consider it even more final.'

'Well, that doesn't sound ominous,' muttered the Doctor.

Romana didn't reply. Her attention was taken by a pen someone had left on a table. The nib of the pen was marvellously sharp, just itching to be plunged into someone. She reached out towards it and the Doctor swatted her hand away.

'I think we should get out of here,' the Doctor whispered. 'These War TARDISes had a nasty habit of getting into your mind. Before you know it, you'll be annexing things.'

Back in the Great Hall of Endless Debate, a presentation was beginning. Cardinal Melia slipped back in, merging into the shadows as only a man in a large red cloak and collar could.

The President of something or other was droning on.

' … Our solution is that the planet of Krikkit is to be forever encased in what can only be called, again, Slow Time. All life within the envelope will continue as normal, but at an infinitely slower pace relative to the Universe outside. All light is deflected around the envelope so that it remains invisible and, obviously, impenetrable to the rest of the Universe. Escape from the envelope is impossible unless it is unlocked from the outside.

'The action of Entropy indicates that eventually the whole Universe will run itself down. And at some point in the unimaginably far future, first life, and then matter will cease to exist. At that time the planet of Krikkit and its sun will emerge from the Slow Time envelope and enjoy a blissful, solitary existence in the twilight of the Universe.'

The audience thought about that for a bit. Then they applauded. For the people who wanted a humane solution it was enviably clever. For the people who wanted to wipe the whole planet out, they could also swallow it, if they chewed. And, for the remaining undecided people, it also ticked quite a few boxes. It was elegant and thoughtful. It really justified their hotel bills.

Even the people of Krikkit in their cage looked relieved at the proposal. They were being offered a chance to get the Universe they'd always wanted.

Romana looked shrewdly at the Doctor. This was a bit harder than you'd think, as he'd pushed his hat down over his head, so she was making firm eye contact with a brim.

'You don't like it, do you, Doctor?'

'No.' His voice sounded only a little muffled by wool. 'I never like a solution that's so neat that you can't help but say, "What could possibly go wrong?"'

'And something has gone terribly wrong, hasn't it?'

'Something's definitely up.'

Romana watched the delegates bubble enthusiastically out of the hall to go and congratulate themselves in joint press conferences and give confidential briefings about how it had actually been their idea.

'I can't see the Time Lords any more.'

'Of course not.' The Doctor's smile crept through his hat. 'They've just persuaded the Universe to seal an entire planet up until the end of time in an envelope. Of course they've scarpered. But what were they up to – were they hiding something on that planet?'

'Hmm,' said Romana. 'We could ask Cardinal Melia.'

'We could,' said the Doctor. 'Only there's a problem with that. Shortly after the peace conference, he disappeared from space and time along with his War TARDIS. Disappeared completely.

It was at this point that K-9 interrupted. 'There is a presence at the far end of the hall, approaching rapidly.'

Romana looked up.

A Krikkitman was bearing down on them.

CHAPTER NINE
RUNNING ON IMAGINATION

The Krikkitman marched towards them through the delegates, who were all somehow oblivious to its ominous, relentless progress. Inside its dark helmet an angry red glow appeared.

'Doctor?'

'Hmm?' The Doctor habitually ignored his dog four times and his best friend three.

'Run!'

Well, unless she said that.

There is a fine art to running from a monster. Romana would have said the Doctor was sometimes quite casual about it, only you could argue he was quite casual about most things. The Doctor was quite casual about flying his time machine; he was quite casual about the laws of gravity; he was quite casual about the sell-by dates on yoghurt.

The Doctor was not so casual now. Faced with an ultimate killing machine and childhood nightmare, he just took to his heels and ran.

'That thing is impossible,' Romana announced, as they ducked under an exploding balcony. 'I thought all the Krikkitmen had been deactivated.'

'Clearly not.' The Doctor threw himself under a burning velvet seat. 'To be is to be perceived and to be shot at is to be very much perceived.'

'But no one else is reacting to it! Surely there should be pandemonium.'

'Some kind of neuro-shielding,' the Doctor speculated. 'What's odd is that it's after us, not the peace conference. And normally, I find any attention flattering.'

They tore round a pillar and up a winding ramp, K-9 following behind them.

'K-9,' the Doctor called desperately over his shoulder, 'could you shoot that robot?'

'Negative, Master.' The dog sounded regretful. 'This unit does not contain the firepower to impede it.'

'Not even a tiny bit?' The Doctor was panting just a little as a stained-glass window exploded above them.

'I'm sort of wondering what we do when we run out of building,' said Romana, as they found another ramp and ran further up. 'Hope it falls off?'

'Hardly our worst plan, is it?' The Doctor kept on running.

'Negative.' The dog trundled behind them.

They reached a narrow metal walkway above the debating chamber. Down below them, oblivious to the explosions above, several thousand delegates continued to delegate. K-9 glided onto the walkway, declared it structurally sound, and then whizzed on ahead.

'No, don't wait for me,' gasped the Doctor. The climbing had taken a lot out of him, and the view down had taken quite a bit more.

'Not afraid of heights, are you?' Romana skipped nimbly onto the gantry.

'No, no, that would be ridiculous. I'm afraid of a fall from one.' The Doctor set out onto the narrow walkway. It really didn't feel that safe. That was the problem with these new alloys – far too lightweight to feel trustworthy. Like running on cardboard. No, what this needed was something with a bit of heft. Like good old iron. The Doctor was looking very hard at a little plaque and absolutely not at the floor such a very long way below. The plate said 'Strengthulon – Your lightweight, malleable, and conductive friend', which was every bit as bad as the Doctor feared. The struts actually bounced beneath him, in a way that was wickedly unhelpful, as if he was escaping across a tambourine.

'Doctor, hurry up,' called Romana. She and K-9 had, by some miracle, made it to the far end.

'I'm finding running on this marvellously novel,' the Doctor shouted brightly, inwardly hating ever wobbling step. He edged forward a little further. 'No sense in rushing it.'

'Yes there is,' urged Romana.

'Hostile is 30.3 metres away from you, Master,' butted in K-9.

Romana squinted. '30.4, surely.'

'Not the important bit,' the Doctor said, turning to look at the Krikkitman.

It had staggered to the edge of the gantry. Its helmet lit up with a dark red smirk.

'Not good,' the Doctor muttered. He stopped running.

The Krikkitman bent down towards the base of the gantry, fastened a metal glove around a strut and twisted it. The walkway pitched to one side, and the Doctor found himself flung into a haphazard crawl, balancing himself against the railings.

'Too much of a flexible friend by half,' he muttered, edging from one narrow railing to the next. Bits of his body kept dropping through the surprisingly wide gaps. Also, his brain was telling him he'd forgotten something. Flexible, yes. Lightweight, yes. Malleable? Got that too. And, also, um …

The Krikkitman unsheathed one of its gloved fingers, exposing a sparking skeletal tip. It scraped it across the bridge, sending sparks racing across it.

Ah yes. Conductive. The Doctor screamed in a perfect mixture of surprise and agony as he fell. He was only held in place by a loop of his scarf, which was smoking.

'Doctor, what are you doing?' shouted Romana.

The Doctor tried coming up with a pithy reply, but his jaws were too busy grinding against each other. 'Mrmgh,' he said and toyed with letting go there and then. If he had to have last words, why not go out with an enigma?

Instead, he wrapped the ends of his scarf around his hands and clawed his way back up onto the bridge.

At the far end, the Krikkitman leaned back and roared, a horrid metallic screech. It threw itself onto the walkway and scampered towards them at an alarming speed.

'This way,' said Romana.

She dragged them into a small projection booth. A beam of light was still playing the last slide of the presentation from the Great Hall onto a glass. The Krikkitman was banging on the door behind them.

'So,' said the Doctor, 'We're in a locked room. Any ideas, K-9?'

'Master—'

'I don't suppose you could blast a hole in the wall?'

'Structural analysis suggests—'

'Never mind.' The Doctor started chewing the end of his scarf. It really did taste awful. The bitterness helped concentrate his mind and distracted him from the beating on the metal door. He beamed suddenly. 'What we need to be is remarkably clever.'

Romana matched his smile. 'Actually...'

The door started to melt.

*

The Krikkitman pushed its way through the molten door into the small room. The Doctor, Romana and K-9 were standing against the far wall. They were frozen in fear, the woman in the act of saying something brave. The man had his scarf wrapped around her.

The Krikkitman broadened its glowing red smile into a smirk and angled its eyes. It bore down on the two cowering people. It would leave the robot till last. Let it watch the others suffer. The bat swiped and swiped through the air and then, surprisingly, stopped.

The Krikkitman reassessed what it was seeing. It was striking at a projected picture of the Doctor, Romana and K-9. It had been hitting a blank wall. It looked around for its prey. They had been standing behind the door.

Which was when K-9 fired at the ceiling, which poured down on the Krikkitman in a roar.

The Doctor regarded the rubble.

'We should probably leave,' he said. 'I don't think blowing up a peace conference is going to make me popular.'

He nervously prodded the Krikkitman under the rubble. The creature's helmet glowed feebly.

'Where did you come from? Why?' the Doctor demanded.

The glow brightened.

'To give you a message, Doctor,' its voice grated in a clipped, angry buzz.

'Really?' Now the Doctor was intrigued.

'Just as there are three stumps, you will meet three …' The Krikkitman's expression flickered. What it said next seemed to surprise even it. 'You will meet three gods who prop up the universe.'

'I'm sorry?'

'You will meet three gods,' the Krikkitman repeated. The glow in its helmet faded away.

Baffled, the Doctor, K-9 and Romana headed away to the TARDIS.

For a moment, all was quiet in the ruined projection room. Then a glow flickered deep inside the Krikkitman's helmet. It was still active and it had one more thing to do.

It faded slowly away.

The last thing left, hanging in the air, was its sinister red smile.

CHAPTER TEN
GRIM CONCLUSION IN NOWHERE

The TARDIS brought them a little bit forward in time and a long way off in space.

'This is as near to Krikkit as we dare go,' the Doctor said, stepping up onto the surface of an unremarkable asteroid. He paced up and down. 'I need to think.' He caught Romana's giggle. 'Oh come on, I do think. I think about lots of things.'

'Of course you do, Doctor,' Romana said placatingly.

'Right now I'm worried about where that Krikkitman came from.'

'Why was it attacking us?' asked Romana.

'Attacking, or distracting?' mused the Doctor. 'I do hate a mystery that tries to kill me.'

'Off the Christmas Card List?'

'Don't be silly.' The Doctor smiled. 'I haven't the time for sending Christmas cards.'[2]

---

[2] This wasn't quite true. The Doctor's approach to Christmas greetings was erratic. Napoleon Bonaparte had once received 75 cards in one year. The Duke of Wellington had had to make do with a toffee hammer.

Romana marched over to the edge of the asteroid and pointed at a dark patch – less the inky blackness of space and more a murky puddle of nothing. 'I guess that's the great Dust Cloud.'

K-9 was swift to agree. He produced a list of facts and figures about the nature of the cloud, which, if only they'd been listening more closely, would have saved them a lot of problems later on. Instead the Doctor and Romana were trying to describe the effect of the cloud on them. It was, the Doctor concluded, rather like a really swishy black curtain drawn across infinity. Romana asked him not to use that phrase again.

The artificial asteroid was pursuing an equally artificial orbit, skirting the edge of the Dust Cloud. Beyond the asteroid was – well, space. Definitely space. Absolutely, assuredly space. And yet there was something un-spacey about it.

The Doctor picked a coin from his pocket and flicked it away. A few feet away from him it began to behave rather more like a space-borne object. It travelled at a constant speed beyond the asteroid and then stopped. Just for a blink it stopped. Then it carried on as normal.

'That there – that little pause,' marvelled Romana. 'Was that the Tick-Tock Interface?'

'Affirmative,' said K-9. 'The envelope of Slow Time is located beyond us.'

'Just a hunch,' the Doctor remarked, polishing his sleeve. 'Objects pass through the envelope without even realising it's there – there's a momentary temporal flicker, that's all.' His face fell. He watched the small metal disc arcing on through the heavens. 'Oh dear. That was my lucky coin.'

After a bit more walking they reached the one architectural feature that occupied the asteroid: a large, glittering sculpture. The forces of the Galaxy had recreated the Wicket Gate. Whereas once it had been a symbol of universal peace, it was now the key to the lock holding the Slow Time envelope in place.

'In my experience,' the Doctor mused, 'one should never leave a key just lying around. Especially not as a giant symbol. It looks impressive, but it's asking for trouble. And over there,' he squinted at some zero-G cranes, 'they appear to be building a hotel.'

The Doctor had always had something against hotels.

Romana was examining the recreated Wicket Gate. 'Three long struts of steel, wood and Perspex. One golden bail, one silver.'

'If I'm right,' the Doctor said, 'at any moment, that lock is going to be dismantled rather dramatically and scattered through space-time.'

Romana scrunched up her nose. 'So that trophy you were making a fuss about at Lord's – you think that was the wooden stump?'

The Doctor nodded.

A battered, burning spaceship roared out of nowhere right at them.

Without even thinking, the Doctor screamed and grabbed hold of Romana.

Romana shut her eyes very firmly and multiplied some chewy prime numbers.

The burning spaceship roared past them and smashed into the sculpture. It hung there, looking both ridiculous and threatening.

'Well, this isn't in the history books,' said Romana.

The Doctor waved airily. 'We're well off the piste of history and roaring down a black run of forbidden knowledge.'

'I always worry when your metaphors turn into conceits.' Romana was walking towards the wrecked spaceship. Then she stopped, looking up at the teetering collision above her. 'K-9,' she said, 'can you analyse that spaceship?'

The dog whirred happily to itself. 'It is a Krikkit Scout ship.'

'It looks exactly like the one that appeared at Lord's.' The Doctor was getting a dreadful sinking feeling.

'It must have escaped from the war and concealed itself. They're trying to unlock their home world. But ...'

'I think what happens next is going to be embarrassing for all parties. Which is probably why the legends skip this bit.' The Doctor was looking up at the spaceship jammed into the Wicket Gate. The sculpture was leaning at an alarming angle, steadily collapsing as it uprooted itself from the asteroid. In the distance, the automated cranes continued building their hotel, as the asteroid's one attraction fell apart, toppling into the Tick-Tock Interface of the Slow Time Envelope.

Such things just aren't supposed to happen.

With a complete absence of noise, the five pieces of the Wicket Gate and the Krikkit spaceship fell into the Time Vortex. As they vanished across the Universe, the reasons why the Wooden Stump had been found at Lord's and an explanation of where a Krikkit ship had come from became clear.

'I knew it,' sighed the Doctor. 'We're on another quest.'

CHAPTER ELEVEN
THE PRIVATE LIFE OF THE BUSIEST MAN IN THE UNIVERSE

The smoke hung on the land. It drifted across the setting sun, which lay like an open wound across the western sky.

In the ringing silence that followed the battle, pitifully few cries could be heard from the bloody, mangled wreckage on the fields.

Ghostlike figures, stunned with horror, emerged from the woods, stumbled and then ran crying forward – women, searching for their husbands, brothers, fathers, lovers, first amongst the dying and then amongst the dead.

Far away behind the screen of smoke, thousands of horsemen arrived at their sprawling camp, and – with a huge amount of clatter, shouting and comparing of backhand slashes – they dismounted and instantly started on the cheap wine and rancid goat fat.

In front of his splendidly bedraped Imperial tent, a bloodstained and battle-weary Khan dismounted. His lunch had been interrupted by a skirmish and he was eager to get back to it.

'Which battle was that?' he asked his vizier, who had ridden with him. Bastrabon was young and ambitious, keenly interested in viciousness of all kinds. He was hoping to improve on his own Known Cosmos record for the highest number of peasants impaled on a single sword thrust and would be getting in some practice that night.

He strode up to his lord.

'It was the Battle of Luseveral, o Great Khan!' he proclaimed, and rattled his sword in a tremendously impressive way.

Khan folded his arms and leant on his horse, looking over it across the dreadful mess they'd made of the valley beneath them.

'Oh, I can't tell the difference any more,' he said with a sigh. 'Did we win?'

'Oh yes! Yes! Yes!' exclaimed the vizier with fierce pride. 'It was a mighty victory indeed!

'Indeed it was!' he added and waggled his sword again. He drew it excitedly and made a few practice thrusts. Yes, he thought to himself, tonight he was going to go for the six.

Khan screwed his face up at the gathering dusk, and strode past a fire pit sunk into the ground, over which the Doctor was being smoked.

Ordinarily, the Doctor had assumed, dictators were cat people. As a dog person, he was baffled, but could sort of see the point. When you've got a busy schedule planning universal domination from your secret lair, you can't take time off to walk the dog around the volcano twice a day. No, you could leave a cat to its own devices while you went off and launched the death ray.

Mind you, the Great Khan actually was a cat person. His species could be called more or less leonine, in that they had more of the worst aspects of a lion (aggression, bad breath, claws) and less of the good bits (valiant heart, plush mane, lovely singing voice). The Great Khan was currently picking away at the leftovers of his Chancellor of the Exchequer.

'Excuse me!' called the Doctor, as breezily as a man can while hanging upside down over a fire.

The Great Khan looked up from eating the last of his cabinet reshuffle, and grunted. If the Doctor had been hoping this was a conversational opening, he was disappointed. The Great Khan belched.

Undaunted, the Doctor pressed on. 'Funny thing happened on my way here today …'

The Great Khan licked the last of the meat from a bone, and snapped it in half. He stared pointedly at the sharp end.

'Anyway, long story short,' the Doctor continued, 'I'm looking for a sort of pillar. Actually, you know, it's not a long story after all.' He was going to say more, but then a tossed skull hit him on the head.

Finally rewarded with some silence, the Great Khan concentrated on sucking the marrow from his Chancellor's elbow. It tasted disappointing.

In a cage a small bird watched him. Feeling judged by it, the Khan took the bird from its cage and flung it onto the fire. That would teach it to be a bird. Then he went to his favourite chair and sat back down in it, putting his feet up in front of the fire on which the bird was now roasting merrily.

He did so enjoy his quiet moments, and they were few and far between.

Vizier Bastrabon hung back, watching as the last of his cousin disappeared down the Khan's throat. He'd quite liked his cousin, but figured this was the wrong moment to bring that up. The Khan, he sensed, was in one of his moods. This was brought on partly by the ennui of endless conquest, but mostly by indigestion.

'Oh dear.' The Great Khan let out a belch. 'After twenty years of these two-hour battles, I get the feeling that there must be more to life, you know.' He turned, lifted up the front of his torn and bloodied gold-embroidered tunic and stared down at his own furry tummy. 'Here, feel this,' he said. 'Do you think I'm putting it on a bit? Perhaps I should go to a health farm?'

The vizier gazed at the Great Khan's tummy with a mixture of awe and impatience. 'Er, no,' he said. 'No, not at all.' With a flick of his paws, the vizier summoned a servant to bring the maps to him, ran him through and, as the servant fell, caught the plans of the grand campaign from his nerveless claws.

'Now, O Great Khan,' he said, spreading the map over the back of another servant who stood specially hunched over for the purpose, 'we must push forward to the Island, and then we shall be poised to take over the whole of this world!'

'No, look, feel that,' said Khan, pinching a fold of skin between his paws. 'Do you think—'

'Great Khan!' interrupted the vizier urgently. 'We are on the point of conquering the world!' He stabbed at the map with a knife, catching the servant beneath a nasty nick on his left lung.

'When?' said the Great Khan with a frown.

Bastrabon the vizier threw up his arms in exasperation. 'Tomorrow!' he said. 'We start tomorrow!'

'Ah, well, tomorrow's a bit difficult, you see,' said Khan. He puffed out his cheeks and thought for a moment. 'The thing is that next week I've got this lecture on carnage techniques in Zumara, and I thought I'd use tomorrow to prepare it.'

The vizier stared at him in astonishment as the map-bearing servant slowly collapsed on his foot. 'Well, can't you put that off?' he exclaimed.

'Well, you see, they've paid me quite a lot of money for it already, so I'm a bit committed.'

'Well, Wednesday?'

The Great Khan pulled a scroll from out of his tunic and looked through it, shaking his head slowly. 'Not sure about Wednesday…'

'Thursday?'

'No, Thursday I am certain about. We've got Bastrabon and his wife coming round to dinner, and I'd kind of promised ...'

'But I am Bastrabon!' protested the vizier, unable to hide his impatience.

'Well, there you are then. You wouldn't be able to make it either.'

The vizier's silence was only disturbed by the sound of distant pillage.

'Look,' he said quietly, 'will you be ready to conquer the world ... on Friday?'

The Great Khan sighed. 'Well, the secretary comes in on Friday mornings.'

'Does she?'

'All those letters to answer. You'd be astonished at the demands people try to make on my time, you know.' He slouched moodily against his horse. 'Would I sign this, would I appear there? Would I please do a sponsored massacre for charity? So that usually takes till at least three, then I had hoped to get away early for a long weekend. Now Monday, Monday ...'

It was at this point the Doctor woke up.

'I say!' he began brightly. The vizier hit him until he dimmed.

The Great Khan was consulting his scroll again, mind clearly made up.

'No, looking at it, Monday's out, I'm afraid. Rest and recuperation, that's one thing I do insist upon. Now, how about Tuesday?'

The strange keening noise that could be heard in the distance at this moment sounded like the normal everyday wailing of women and children over their slaughtered menfolk and Khan paid it no mind. A light bobbed on the horizon.

'Tuesday – look, I'm free in the morning – no, hold on a moment, I'd sort of made a date for meeting this awfully interesting chap who knows absolutely everything about understanding things, which is something I'm awfully bad at. That's a pity because that was my only free day next week. Now, next Tuesday we could usefully think about – or is that the day I ...'

The approaching light was so pale as to be indistinguishable from that of the moon which was bright that night. The light bobbed and swung gently. Unthreateningly.

' ... So that's more or less the whole of March out,' said Khan, 'I'm afraid.'

'April?' asked the vizier, wearily. He idly whipped out a passing peasant's liver, but the joy had gone out of it. He flipped the thing listlessly off into the dark. A hound, which had grown very fat over the years by the simple expedient of staying close to the vizier at all times, leapt on it. These were not pleasant times.

'No, April's out,' said the Great Khan – I'm going off world in April, that's one thing I had promised myself.'

The light approaching them through the night sky had now at last attracted the attention of one or two of the Khan's retinue, who, wonderingly, stopped hitting each other and stabbing things and drew near.

'Look,' said Bastrabon, himself still unaware of what things were coming to pass, 'can we please agree that we will conquer the world in May, then?'

The mighty Khan sucked doubtfully on his teeth. 'Well, I don't like to commit myself that far in advance. One feels so tied down if one's life is completely mapped out beforehand. I should be doing more reading, for heaven's sake, when am I going to find the time for that? Anyway ...' He sighed and scratched at his scroll. '"May – possible conquest of this world." Now, I've only pencilled that in, so don't regard it as absolutely definite – but keep on at me about it and we'll see how it goes. Hello, what's that?'

Slowly, a soft light streamed into the clearing by the Great Khan's tent. A strikingly beautiful woman glided forward holding a lamp and a clipboard. She walked slowly towards them, her features wrinkled in disgust.

In her path lay the dark figure of a peasant who had been crying quietly to himself since he had watched his liver being eaten by the vizier's dog and had known that no way was he going to get it back, and wondered how his poor wife was going to cope now. He chose this moment finally to pass on to better things.

The beautiful woman stepped over him with a sad shudder and strode up to the Great Khan. It had been a long time since anyone apart from the vizier had looked him in the eyes, and the Khan flinched slightly.

'Who the hell are you?'

At this point the Doctor woke up again.

'Oh hello, Romana!' he waved.

The Doctor was never entirely sure exactly who or what had knocked him out a moment later. Romana had shot him a freezing look, that was certain. The Great Khan had whacked him with a horridly sticky sword. And a rather large and overfed dog had landed in his face. Thinking about it, that had probably done it. Dangling over the fire, he followed much of the rest of it through his auditory bypass system.

'Good evening, I'm the Lady Romanadvoratrelundar.' Romana checked her clipboard. 'I'm from the Despot Awards. Surprise inspection.'

'Oh,' said the Great Khan, in a voice that was hastily straightening its tie. 'Come in, do take a pew.' The vizier nudged forward a corpse, patting and sorting it into a wet approximation of a pouf.

Romana shook her head. 'I prefer to stand,' she said and made a slow, severe tick on her clipboard.

'Er, quite so,' said the Khan, rubbing his forepaws together. 'And, if I can ask, how am I doing, in this year's awards? I mean, if you've come out here, can one presume the shortlist?'

'One cannot,' Romana said icily, and made another tick on her clipboard. 'I've a few questions.'

'Oh, fire away, fire away.' The Khan was all affability.

Romana consulted her clipboard, frowning at it. 'On the way here, I noticed you'd burned a few hospitals.'

The Khan brightened. 'Indeed,' he purred. 'When I declare war on a planet, it's total war. Even on their diseases.' He cast a look around the churned-up wasteland. 'It's my clean slate policy.'

'And the schools?'

'Oh yes. People are forever sheltering their children in them. You know what I call that?' The Khan was warming to his theme. 'I call that an act of terrible cruelty.' The Khan leaned forward, his brows very serious. 'After all, what kind of life would the poor things have without their parents? Much kinder just to torch the places, don't you think?'

Romana simply made another tick on her clipboard.

The Khan strained forward. In another man, you'd have sworn he was trying to sneak a peep at the clipboard. But you'd never have said that of the Great Khan.

Romana ran a finger down a printed list. 'I notice that you're running a bit behind schedule with the conquest of this planet.'

'Oh ho!' the Great Khan exclaimed with weary cynicism. 'This'll be the Dominators, stirring again. I tell you now, Lady, these things are best done properly. There's an art to conquest. Each devastation crafts itself. It's one thing to be stood on a hill overlooking an idyllic valley, crammed with meadows and windmills and houses with smoking chimneys and children and chickens gambolling in the yard. It's quite another to know exactly when to sweep down and lay waste to it all. You don't want to appear over-eager, and you don't want to hang back. You want a situation to mature. Why, look at this fellow –' and he gave the rope suspending the Doctor a hearty twang. 'Stumbled in, spouting nonsense. I could have just gibbeted him on the spot. But instead I'm having him smoked. Takes time, but he will be delicious. Unless, of course …' The Great Khan leaned forward solicitously. 'Are you hungry now? In which case I can have him served up in a jiffy.'

'No, no,' said Romana. 'I ate before I came.'

'Very sensible.' The Khan squeezed thoughtfully at the fur on his belly. 'I'm always hungry. I guess it's what drives me. That and the screaming.'

Romana made another tick, and then freed a couple of sheets from her clipboard and handed them to the Khan. 'I've a couple of heritage surveys for you to fill in. Purely optional, of course, but they do count towards our judging. We'd just like to know the value of what's left before you wipe it out.'

'Oh quite.' The Khan scanned the forms before passing them to his vizier. 'Lovely little fishing town, a small island, and a totem pole.'

'A totem pole?'

'Oh yes,' the Khan said. 'Quite an elaborate steel thing. Said to represent the Might of the World, a might that can never be conquered. Overstating the case, I have to say. But I'm sure it'll score quite highly, won't it?' His eyes were schoolboy eager. 'Now, him –' he jerked a thumb at the vizier who was, even now, starting on the paperwork – 'he'd have me just march on and take it. But it doesn't feel right, now, does it? I want the survivors to really hope that, at the last minute, their totem pole will save them. And then – *pfft* – I'll take it and move on somewhere else.' He sighed a weary sigh. 'There are always more worlds to be crushed, aren't there?'

'Indeed.' Romana made a final tick. 'That all seems to be most satisfactory. I'll be on my way.' She turned to go, and then had a sudden thought. 'Oh, just one thing …'

'Anything,' the Great Khan rumbled, sweeping a paw through his mane.

'That prisoner.' She pointed at the Doctor. 'Would you mind if I took him? You know, for questioning as to your methods and so on.'

'Ha! I know what you're up to.' The Khan tapped the side of his nose.

'You do?'

'You fancy a snack.'

Romana led the Doctor through the woods. He was rubbing his wrists and shaking his sore head.

'I'm terribly grateful. What a horrible man,' he groaned dazedly. 'He really has put me off cat people.'

They walked away into the night.

Gallifreyan cats, by the way, have thirteen lives and they sleep through all of them soundly.

The Doctor and Romana wandered to the shoreline. They stood watching a perfect sun slide slowly behind a distant hazy island.

'The Great Khan's last conquest,' sighed Romana. She thought the island looked rather dreamy. The idea that it was to be consumed by war seemed not just absurd, but a terrible shame.

The Doctor was leaning against the hulls of the boats the Khan had had built especially for the job of conquering the island. He was fiddling with a matchbox and was wearing his most furtive smile. It was a smile that went with the buying of birthday presents and the telling of glorious fibs.

'The island may be uninhabited,' said the Doctor, 'but the Khan needs to conquer it in order to own the planet.' He patted the side of the boat. 'These were mighty oaks, grown in glades undisturbed for thousands of years, and now they're off to war. Normally I like ships. But I like trees more. It's funny to think that everything made out of wood really is just the grave of a tree.'

He pulled a dolorous face and Romana rolled her eyes. She looked forward to reminding the Doctor of his sentiments next time he sat down in his favourite chair.

She looked again at the island, glowing in the sunset. It had somehow placed itself in the very centre of the horizon. Poor old island, she thought. What had you done to upset anyone? It could easily have been neglected, waved away as a bit of paperwork, were it not for ... well ...

The setting sun caught against the vast steel pillar jutting out of the island and made it glow and shine. The Steel Stump of Strength and Power. The kind of symbol that made idiots like the Great Khan invade a world. Even if they then couldn't be bothered to actually possess it.

'Reluctant as I am to help out the Khan,' ventured Romana, 'we could go and claim it for him. Save everyone a lot of effort. Let's go get the TARDIS.'

The Doctor didn't fancy trekking back through the Khan's army. 'Messy.'

'All right then, Let's use one of his boats.'

'These boats?' The Doctor shook his head and shiftily slipped the matchbox back in his pocket. 'I wouldn't bother. Let's use public transport.'

They found a man down in the harbour who sort of agreed that he would like to take them to the island. Just not yet. His wife, you see, had made dinner.

Right, said the Doctor, waiting for an invitation. The ferryman didn't offer one.

So they sat in the harbour and waited for the ferryman to have his dinner.

The boat sat in front of them, bobbing up and down against the tide. Little fish plonked and dived around it.

'We could steal it,' suggested Romana.

'Borrow,' corrected the Doctor. 'And no.'

'But, we're trying to stop the Krikkitmen. We need to get to that stump.'

The Doctor sat on a low harbour wall and kicked his feet, scuffing the surf with his boots. 'They've already got one stump. When we went hunting for the Key to Time we were lucky that we managed to snaffle the lot. Bit different this time – the other side already have one bit. No matter how well we do, the best ending we're going to get is going to be some kind of glorified car boot sale.' He gazed up as the last glints of the sun blazed off the distant pillar. 'I've got better things to do in life than race around collecting things.'

'Yes,' said Romana. 'If you're going to do it seriously, you've got to accept that the Universe is so very large and you'd need ever so many shelves. We'd have got there by now if you hadn't got yourself captured.'

'I was winning the Khan over,' the Doctor muttered.

'He was smoking you like a kipper.'

'It was all part of my plan. He'd stopped thinking of me as a threat.'

'Only because he was thinking of you as lunch,' Romana retorted.

They paused and watched night settle on the seashore.

'First editions,' said the Doctor eventually. 'Of children's books. That's what I'd collect.'

Romana nodded her approval. 'Not train sets?'

The Doctor shook his head. 'Sadly, those were ruined for me. I once met a man who said, "Well, once the train's been round the track once, what's it going to do next? Go round again?" I had to admit he had a point.' He tutted regretfully. 'To repeat an action and expect a different outcome is the definition of insanity.'

'You're being very philosophical,' said Romana.

'I'm by the seaside,' said the Doctor. 'That's what it's for.'

The ferryman emerged, told them that actually, on consideration, he'd decided to go to a tavern and get drunk. He stumbled off.

The Doctor tugged his boots and socks off.

'Shall we have a paddle?' he asked.

It was nearly dawn when the little boat set out for the island.

'I think the ferryman is asleep,' hissed Romana.

'Of course he is.' The Doctor surveyed the snoring form. 'He's had a long night.'

The ferryman had, in fact, seemed surprised to find them waiting outside his house when he came home in the early hours of the morning. He'd had the look about him of a man heading very firmly for bed, but the Doctor had taken him by the arm, turned him around, and suggested an early morning boat ride as though it was a trip to a funfair.

The ferryman was fast asleep now, snoring in his chair. The boat carried on, chewing its way through the waves.

'Do you think it's self-steering?' asked Romana.

'Do you?'

Romana considered. 'No,' she said.

When they finally landed the boat, the sunrise was doing marvellous things to the steel pillar. It soared above the few trees on the island.

'How are we getting that home?' asked Romana.

'Shush,' said the Doctor. 'One problem at a time.'

'It's an important one.'

'Well,' he ambled off up the rocky beach, 'you think about it on the walk there.'

'That is beautiful!' exclaimed the Doctor.

Romana was not so keen. Up close, the steel pillar looked like a municipal streetlamp. If it was a work of art, it was the kind of work that a committee would have ordered, proudly announcing how much they'd paid for it in a press release. Apart from its ability to reflect light, it was just sort of there. But the Doctor was billing and cooing over it. There was no accounting for …

Ah. Actually the Doctor was making friends with a bird. It was a large red bird, about a foot high, and it was progressing around the pylon in a succession of wobbling, fluttering hops, each one accompanied by a hopeful 'Cark!' and then a desolate 'Ark!'

Romana held out her hand, and the edge of the creature's fine, long bill tapped politely against it. The creature had a curious expression, one of philosophical optimism. Its face seemed to be saying 'Maybe Next Time'. It nuzzled her briefly, beautifully, and then went back to its hopping and its carking and arking.

'What's it doing?' Romana asked.

'Taking on gravity and failing, poor thing.' The Doctor had crouched down and was smiling winningly at what Romana had decided to call the Next Time bird. 'I'd say it now weighs too much to fly.'

'Do you think that's a by-product of the Stump?'

'No, I think there's just too much food here.' The Next Time bird had paused its little circle and was now nibbling at some particularly chlorophyll-soaked leaves. 'Evolution can be a bit tricky like that. Still, no harm done. After all, there aren't any predators on the island, so they just get to mooch around a bit causing no harm to the Universe. Bless them.' The Doctor patted the bird on the head and it carked twice before resuming its little circuit.

Romana looked at the bird and worried a bit. 'But isn't the Khan going to come and set the island on fire?'

'Well …' The Doctor rapped on the pylon. 'Perhaps not if we work out a way to remove the Steel Stump.'

'Really?' Romana snorted. 'I think stealing it would make him even more likely to set fire to the place.'

'True,' the Doctor sighed, ruffling the bird's feathers. 'But we really don't have time to worry about birds.' He scratched his own head. 'We could pay the boatman to take them off the island.'

Romana was dubious. 'I think he's quite likely to casserole them.'

'Fine.' The Doctor frowned. 'Any idea how we lug this stump back to the TARDIS?'

'Well,' began Romana – and then the Krikkitmen arrived.

'Ark!'

A pause.

'Ark! Ark!'

Another pause. Some scratching. A sharp pain.

'Ark! Ark? Ark!'

Romana opened her eyes. A small, sad red bird was pecking her chin. Romana sat up, rubbed her eyes, and then realised her hands had been covered in soot.

A few annoying minutes later, the Time Lady and the bird surveyed the sad burning hole where the steel pylon had stood. She had a vague memory – well, more of an impression really – of the thing being blown out of the ground. Mostly, she remembered the ground throwing itself at her until she'd surrendered.

'Oh dear,' she said to the Next Time bird. 'I think the Great Khan's going to be very cross about this.'

'Ark!' said the bird.

Judging by the way a bush was groaning and complaining, Romana supposed she'd found the Doctor. Sighing, she left the Next Time bird to its own devices.

It started to peck at some leaves, and then, when it was quite full, it gave an excited little hop, and, for a moment, hovered excitedly in mid-air. Perhaps this time would finally mark the moment it took off?

It crashed back down to the ground.

CHAPTER TWELVE
DAMP RESENTMENT OF A PLANET

The people of Mareeve II were famously quick to take offence. They'd once been so upset at the mildly eccentric orbit of the next-door planet that they'd moved their world to an entirely different star system. And they were still waiting for life to evolve on Mareeve III and issue them with an apology.

It is said by idiots that into every life a little rain must fall, but it was always raining on Mareeve II. The planet's climate had never quite got over the orbital shift, and now delivered a constant, quietly furious rain that spattered and dripped over every available occasion. Sometimes, teasingly, it would lighten up, almost becoming that light romantic drizzle that people took thrilling first kisses under, and then, at the last moment, it would return to drab, heavy misery.

Romana stood in the doorway of the TARDIS, watching the rain cascading onto the doorstep. For once, she had no idea how to dress for this planet. She'd once spotted a painfully jaunty yellow cagoule hanging in the wardrobe. Perhaps today its time had come.

The Doctor strode out onto the unpromising surface of Mareeve II, refusing to let it get to him. Mareeve II seemed to offer a series of concrete blocks and waterlogged car parks, stretching as far as the rain would allow. He had on a hat, his scarf was wrapped tightly. It was all going to go well. He noticed K-9 wasn't following. He turned back to call his dog a fair-weather friend. As he turned, a fussy man barged into him on the desolate concourse.

'Out of my way. You're an alien spy and should be shot,' said the man.

'I can assure you I'm not.'

The fussy man stopped and regarded the Doctor through a pair of meanly thin glasses. 'You deny it? I find that upsetting.'

'Well –' the Doctor puffed up – 'I find it upsetting being called an alien spy.'

The fussy little man was hopping up and down now, making little splashy puddles. 'You claim that I upset you?' he thundered.

'Well, yes,' the Doctor said reasonably. 'You've barged into me, you've insulted me, and now you're splashing mud over my trousers. I'm not an alien spy. I'm actually a tourist. Come to see the, er … sights.' He peered from under his hat brim at the grim surroundings. 'I say,' he asked. 'There are sights, aren't there?'

That did it. The people of Mareeve II are especially touchy about the lack of sights to see on their world. They once had a perfectly preserved Daudren Temple, but they flattened it after the adjacent gift shop asked if they could have more room for a café. The gift shop is still there, and does, indeed, sell postcards of the temple in what the Galactic Trust has called an act of bloody cheek. (Ironically, the café never actually opened, due to what the Mareevian Tourist Board described as 'an unforgivably insulting decline in visitors'.) Other, less interesting sites on the planet met similarly drab fates, meaning that the book *Ten Places to See on Mareeve II Before You Die* had been renamed *Oh, Just Die*.

Anyway, conversationally, the Doctor had done it, torn it and taken the biscuit. Mareevians don't see red, more a sort of angry grey, but the man opposite the Doctor was now shouting very loudly and sneering with delight. 'Sir! You've insulted my planet!'

'I haven't!' the Doctor protested.

'I find your denial extremely upsetting!' the man gasped, staggering back against a wall. 'I really am finding this utterly distressing. I simply haven't time for this. Coming to our planet and insulting us? You're the worst kind of alien. And I find your nose offensive.'

'But—' began the Doctor.

The little man was hammering on windows, screaming up at them. 'Citizens! Citizens! I have been verbally attacked!'

Windows opened and heads popped out. Initially, they popped out to remark on how upset they were at being disturbed. The angry little man shouted back at them, saying how their attempt to silence him was profoundly distressing. The people at the windows told him to shut up even more loudly. Shoes were exchanged.

The Doctor leapt onto a bollard, blew a whistle, and windmilled his arms around. 'People, please! A bit of hush! Surely you don't have to be so awfully loud, do you?'

The crowd looked at the Doctor, and, as one, narrowed their eyes.

Ten minutes later Romana left the TARDIS. She'd found a pair of leopard-print wellington boots to go with her cagoule. She looked around. There was no sign of the Doctor.

Clearly, he'd been locked up already.

The Doctor passed a long and annoying night in a prison cell. It had begun with a letter posted under his cell door:

Dear Prisoner

As you are now in custody, you are required to complete some mandatory online training about this prison's Standards and Values ('Values' and 'Standards').

This includes the following three modules:

- Safer Securing (Tier 2): This module covers our status as an Official Prison, our care undertakings to you ('Your Rights') and explains the necessary Containment Criteria you will need to fulfil during your stay ('Your Responsibilities').
- Secure Standards: This module covers this Prison's Values and explains our Custodial Guidelines under the Tier 3 'Beyond the Bars' Programme.
- Safeholding Policy: This module explains your Rights and your Freedom of Expression Guidelines. This includes information on how to format a complaint to the Governor and a framework for acceptable Protest Redecoration of your 'cell' (Individual Containment Unit).

Each module will take about twenty minutes to complete. You will need headphones to hear the sound whilst not disturbing your co-prisoners.

If you have any problems completing the training, please speak to a Warder who will be only too happy to provide the necessary assistance and restraints.

Regards,

Executive Manager, Prisons and Punishment (Regulations)

Manager, Punishment and Regulations (Prisons)

'Paperwork!' The Doctor crumpled the note and threw it into a corner. He then picked it up and uncrumpled it. He sat down at the terminal in his cell, realising that, with a bit of luck, he'd be able to use it to hack into the overall Prison Mainframe and then engineer his escape. It turned out the terminal was broken. The Doctor sighed, and mended it. At which point he realised the screen was covered with dried soup. He tried scraping it off, but it wouldn't budge.

The Doctor sat down, cracked his knuckles and set out to hack into the prison while squinting through old soup.

An hour later he gave up.

Two hours later dinner was delivered, and he realised why someone would have thrown soup at the terminal. The corridor outside filled with complaints – one inmate had a cockroach in his soup, another demanded to know why he hadn't been given a cockroach. The complaining and yelling went on, until the prison warders came back and threatened everyone with more soup.

Things went quiet. Not peaceful quiet, but the quiet that goes with resentful muttering.

On a psychic level the Doctor found it hard to relax and, faced with nothing else to do, went into a deep trance, concentrating on eroding the lock on his door through sheer willpower.

The next day, he found himself in court. The courtroom was dingy, with high windows looking out onto the rain clouds. The courtroom's tin roof rang to a constant raindrop tattoo.

A crowd leaned against railings, muttering about how they'd always known about the Doctor. Others had terrible stories about things he'd said and done, printed up onto T-shirts and placards. Occasionally one would point at another and angrily declare that they'd done nothing, as yet, to publicly distance themselves from the Doctor.

'But …' said the Doctor, worried that it sounded like a wail. 'But I don't know any of you! I've never met any of you before in my lives!'

This went down very badly.

A judge stared at him, her face lined with bored anger. 'You are brought before us, the very worst sort of criminal. Have you any complaints to make before you hear the state's complaints against you?'

'No,' the Doctor said, easily. 'So far, actually, everything's fine.'

The judge scowled, making a note in a book. 'That, in itself, is a terrible indictment of our justice system, and, as a judge, I can only feel personally attacked by it.'

The Doctor boggled. 'How?'

The crowd hissed.

The judge slammed her book shut. 'You dare question a judge? That is insulting to my profession and status.' She glared at him with a fury it normally took centuries of defeat at the Doctor's hands to stoke.

The Doctor was lost for words.

'Refusing to answer?' the judge scowled. 'That's derogatory. I find your silence highly offensive.'

The crowd hissed again. Someone took a photo.

'Oh good grief,' the Doctor cried. 'How does anyone get anything done around here? If this is your legal system, I dread to think what your fitted kitchens are like.'

'Incorrigible! Malicious allegations! I find that an attack on our entire way of life,' yelled the judge over the roaring crowd.

'Fine,' snapped the Doctor. 'Take it any way you like. I'm just here to get a plastic tube and go home. I don't care about anything else, but have you ever thought about smiling? You'd look wonderful. Try it. Go on.'

The judge did not smile.

Several people in the crowd informed the Doctor that he was criticising the judge on her external appearance and that this was not on.

The Doctor protested that he wasn't. The crowd jeered even louder.

The judge silenced them. 'Before disgusting myself by having to pass sentence, have you a court-appointed disapprover?'

The Doctor shook his head. He stuck his hands in his pockets and pulled them inside out. 'Alas, no.'

'Then,' the judge said with malicious glee, 'we will pronounce on you.'

The crowd roared. Several took photos of themselves roaring.

There was a cough. A precise, digital clearing of an electronic throat.

The court fell silent.

To the Doctor's immense delight, K-9 glided forward, wearing a human barrister's wig. He rolled up onto a small, official-looking platform.

'Your Honoured Judge,' announced the robot dog. 'If it does not displease you, I offer myself as the accused's disapprover.'

The judge looked uncertain for a moment, then nodded grimly.

'I request permission to enter into evidence my open letter to the court.'

The court went very silent.

The judge nodded once more.

'To Whom It May Concern,' began the dog, clearly enjoying himself. 'As an independent legal robot, it saddens me to learn that you are guilty of hatred towards alien life. Furthermore, I find it shocking that you have deprived an innocent alien of their liberty, and have, indeed, traduced the principles of your justice system in order to organise a xenophobic hate rally. I submit that the only course of action for you is to resign your position.'

The court remained silent, apart from a whisper from the Doctor. 'Bit strong, wasn't it K-9?'

'Silence,' the dog whispered. 'Master.'

The judge looked up from her notebook. 'Thank you for your communication,' she said to K-9. 'In reply, I can only express how saddened I am to find that you have allied yourself with this alien spy, who proposes wiping out our race.' There was a roar from the crowd. 'You have conspired with an invading species,' she went on over another roar, 'with someone who is so evil that, if, when this trial is over, he is not locked up, I shall lock him up myself.'

There was wild applause.

'Excuse me,' K-9 pressed on. 'I find it offensive that you have not yet clarified what the Doctor has done.'

'Oh, haven't I?'

'Negative.'

'Well then, I'll tell you what he's done.' The judge was standing now. 'He has done a wide range of outrageous things, all of which would be denounced by any right-thinking citizen. Simply by refusing to distance yourself from your client, you are risking, well, I won't say punishment, but we'll see what happens to you when this trial is over. Furthermore, and this is something we can all agree on –' The judge pointed at a man in the crowd. 'You sir, that is a lovely hat. Isn't that a great hat?'

The crowd burst into applause. Even the Doctor nodded. It was a nice hat. He wondered if he could borrow it.

K-9's protests were drowned out by the crowd. The dog was baffled. He had loaded Mareeve II's judicial system into his databanks, studied it thoroughly, and could not comprehend how it worked. It seemed to be a mixture of venom and distress, combined with the childishness of the Doctor when he was beaten at Cluedo.

'I must protest, and urge all citizens to sign my petition!' K-9 said. 'You have not presented a single argument. You have derided and mocked me and, by failing to argue rationally with me, you have disrespected me in a heavily codified manner.'

'Have I?' the judge thundered. 'By making that allegation, you are in fact disrespecting me and the law.' She turned to the guards placed at the corners of the room. 'Remove that robot!'

The guards rushed forward. The judge raised her Rod of Justice and was yelling 'Guilty!' when the Doctor noticed something.

So did Romana, who started running from her place at the back of the crowd.

And then the Krikkitmen burst into the courtroom, firing indiscriminately.

In the chaos, the Doctor and Romana found themselves under a desk.

'The Rod of Justice!' Romana shouted.

'I know!' the Doctor shouted back.

114

The Rod of Justice was a transparent plastic tube. Their suspicions that this was part of the Wicket Gate were only confirmed when the Krikkitmen began cutting their way (quite literally) through the crowd towards it.

The judge was waving the Rod about her. The Krikkitmen closed in. The judge looked up at them. Her voice was commendably calm.

'I find you threatening and intimidating. I feel insulted by your continued presence. I shall ignore you, thus denying you the dignity of a reply. Please consider this correspondence closed.'

The Krikkitmen raised their bats to strike.

At which point the Doctor sailed through the air between them, snatching the Rod of Justice and throwing it to Romana.

'Run,' he shouted as he landed in a heap, bringing the judge down with him.

But Romana was already running. She hadn't been hatched yesterday.

The Krikkitmen looked around, their faces glowing red with fury.

Taking advantage of their momentary confusion, K-9 emptied his entire weapons charge into the air bringing a good deal of light fittings down on the androids.

The judge groaned. 'No hard feelings,' the Doctor told her. 'I'm most awfully sorry about the mess.'

Then he picked up K-9 and ran from the courthouse.

The Krikkitmen followed.

*

The Doctor was running through the rain. He was being chased by five Krikkitmen across a dismal concrete square. Small, horrible bombs exploded around him. He was facing a dilemma. True, running while holding K-9 was slowing him down, but, if he put the dog down, then the dog's low energy levels would mean that it couldn't keep up with him.

Actually, put like that, it wasn't much of a dilemma. He wasn't going to leave his best friend behind.

A blast smacked into a cement statue, sending sharp stone chips towards the Doctor's face. He raised K-9, and the flints smacked off the dog's metal casing.

There, another victory, another chance to keep going. Keep running, Doctor, keep running. But there was also a problem. The Krikkitmen were good shots and they didn't get tired and – now, that was a thing – he couldn't remember where the TARDIS was waiting, and it was probably a long way away and it'd probably be raining and really, was it too late to give all this up and open a teashop in the Cotswolds?

Three Krikkitmen splashed into view at the end of the square. Their helmets glowed with a triumphant smirk. They aimed their bats at him.

The Doctor looked over his shoulder.

The Krikkitmen were closing in, their helmets flickered with ruby smiles. The Doctor kept running, trying to ignore the bats being levelled at him. He closed his eyes …

He stopped running, but only because he'd smacked into the TARDIS control console. 'What?'

The Doctor stared around. He was inside the TARDIS.

Romana looked up from the controls and smiled at him. 'I materialised her around you.'

'You did what? You're getting very nimble.'

'It was the short hop that was the tricky thing. I could show you, if you wanted.'

The Doctor shook his head. He'd had quite enough for one day.

'Anyway,' said Romana, holding up the Rod of Justice. 'We have one bit of the Wicket Gate. That's something.'

She flicked the controls and the TARDIS roared away.

Chapter Thirteen
Why Fish Don't Need Mortgages

The people of the planet Devalin were really excellent fishermen. The problem was that they'd long since stopped catching fish.

Their world was a large mass of splendidly fecund water, teaming with all sorts of aquatic life, from fantastically succulent prawns to rainbow-coloured fish, to jewel-shimmering seaweeds that were as rich in flavour as they were dazzling in beauty.

One of the things that Devalin didn't really have was land. There were a few islands here and there, but no one really cared for them. The people of Devalin loved being at sea. They loved the feel of their coral boats as they glided through the water. All a Devalinian really had to do in life was learn how to build a boat – and, really, that was fairly easy. Once that was done, they could just float along the calm waters as limpid as those limpid pools that secretaries in novels have instead of eyes. Every day was a glorious day of just gliding over the waters, pulling out a snack whenever you were hungry, maybe joining a neighbouring boat for a chat, or to try out some of their squid wine (admittedly, an acquired taste). So it followed, glorious day in and glorious day out, until, of course, one day when, after you'd eaten your last prawn, sailed your last wave, and somehow managed to swallow your last squid wine, you slipped gently over the side of your boat and sank steadily, happily to the bottom.

This merry life was bobbing along very nicely until a small escape pod smacked onto the seas. Inside was a man in a tearing hurry. His name was Ognonimous Fugg, and he was, unfortunately, an estate agent. He'd been on his way to complete a really very complicated deal which had involved selling off the historic offices of the Cosmic Broadcasting Bureau and turning them into flats. He'd been met by a heavily armed flotilla of angry news anchors.

'You'll never get away with this!' he'd cried. Because Ognonimous Fugg was just the sort of person to cry that instead of just saying it.

It turned out he was wrong. If you are going to upset the CBB, you should probably remember they own all the cameras, and quite a few very well-armed battleships.

Hence his sudden, fiery arrival on the planet Devalin.

Ognonimous Fugg was terribly grateful for the rescue, delighted by the reviving seafood platter, a little bit alarmed by the squid wine, and wholly curious about the world he now found himself on.

The Devalinians told him of their endless lazy days spent in coral boats, and, filling his fist with more prawns, Fugg was inclined to agree that their lives were perfect. Until he spotted something looming on the horizon.

'What's that?' he asked.

'Oh,' they told him. 'That's land. We don't bother with that.'

The Doctor and Romana stood in their small flat enjoying a hasty breakfast.

'You'll be late for work,' she told him, speaking mostly into his shoulder.

The Doctor growled and looked for somewhere to put his plate down. As usual, there wasn't anywhere. The flat really was very tiny, with just enough room for their bunk beds and a small folding kettle. He squeezed past Romana and tried to open the door without hitting his elbow against the bed. He failed.

Romana rinsed the plates in the sink under her pillow, dried them, and then followed the Doctor out onto a walkway that was even narrower. There was a slouch in his walk and a slump in his shoulders. She was getting worried about him.

The problem with the city was that no one in their right mind would have built it. But Ognonimous Fugg was an estate agent, and he'd seen an opportunity. He'd explained to the Devalinians that, as they had so little land, it was worth a large amount of money.

They'd laughed at him, as none of them were interested in land, and had no idea of money.

So, they'd let him buy the land off them in return for a recipe for paella.

Then he'd started building.

The first thing he built was a bank. It took a while, as first he had to convince some Devalinians to stop sailing and come and learn how to build. They'd offered to pop by in their evenings and help out, but he'd been firm. No fishing for them. Instead, he explained, other people would bring them fish in return for money. Which was what the bank was for.

'Ah,' said the people of Devalin. 'Fish tokens.'

He'd then explained that they couldn't leave their boats cluttering up the small shore, as this would spoil the view of the Harbourfront Development.

'What's one of those?' they'd asked.

'Well,' he'd told them, 'you'll have to have somewhere to sleep while you're building the bank.'

So, as they could no longer sleep in their boats, they'd built houses in the harbour. And a small shop for the selling of fish. And, of course, the bank which gave them money. They needed the money to buy the fish, and, also, to pay for their houses.

You'd have thought that, at this point, someone would have smelt a rotten herring. Instead, the little old lady who ran the fish store said that, while she wasn't quite sure what money was, she was getting an awful lot of it for handing over fish, which as everyone knew, grew on seas. So it seemed worth the bother. And really, what harm did it do? She actually had so much money she was able to get a house in the harbour with a really nice view of her boat. Which was almost as nice as being on the boat.

Ognonimous Fugg knew he was winning the day a second fish shop opened. Then he built a second bank.

That stymied the people of Devalin a bit. Why were there two banks?

Choice, Fugg told them. One bank, you see, might offer you three coins for three fish one day, but only two coins for three fish the next. Whereas the bank next door might offer you four coins for two fish.

'Why would you do that?' the Devalinians demanded.

'It's called a free market.'

As well as a second bank, he also built some more houses on the other side of the island. These, he said, had an even better view of the sea. They also cost more money. For a while, the people in the original houses laughed – what better view of the sea was there than theirs? But then they worried – what if he had a point? So they decided to swap their houses on one side of the island for the other. This was the point at which they discovered that they needed more money in order to do this.

'Ah well,' they said, 'not a problem. We'll just get a few more fish. After all, how much can it cost? A house, well, it's hardly worth an octopus, is it?'

Fugg explained, politely but firmly, that the exchange had to be made in money. A lot of money. Which was, of course, available from the banks in the form of a loan. With, naturally, a modest interest rate.

'What's an interest rate?'

'Don't worry. I'll explain that when we've built some more houses,' said Ognonimous Fugg.

This goes some way to explaining why the Doctor and Romana found themselves working in a canning factory and living in an incredibly cramped apartment in a narrow, totally impractical tower block teetering over the tiny island.

They'd found jobs in the canning factory. For some reason, no one really went out in a boat and caught fish by hand any more. Opening a can of fish was so much more efficient, even if, perhaps, a bit more expensive.

To start with, the harbour had still bustled with little boats, nipping back and forth. But people had got busier, worked harder, and the boats had dwindled and the canning factory had spread out, blocking the views of all those rather nice harbour front cafés. If the wind was in the right direction (and it often was) the smell from it forced the people choking from their hard-earned balconies.

The Doctor found the whole process of squeezing fish into a tin reprehensible. Fish here, he thought, had a definite shape. They were long and finny. But the canning factory expected them to be round. Or square. Or, for a few shillings more, square with arty rounded corners. At the end of every miserable day, he made a joke about tins that were smaller on the inside than the outside, but Romana no longer smiled. She was working in quality assurance, which involved, for the most part, checking that a tin was indeed a tin, and then pasting a jolly label of a grinning fish on it. On balance, she'd had more laughs working in a Dalek slave mine.

She found this new life utterly bemusing. When they'd first arrived, the Doctor had taken one look around and shuddered.

'The Golden Bail is around here somewhere.' The Doctor was checking some readings he'd jotted down on his cuff. 'Popped out of the Time Vortex and just sat around being completely ignored for two million years until the planet suddenly developed an economy. Economies are dreadful things. Now it's in that building.' He pointed to a structure of grand columns and smug arches. 'A bank. How very boring.'

'Bound to have a lot of security,' said Romana, looking dubiously at her sonic screwdriver.

'Only interesting thing about a bank,' the Doctor smiled.

'But we're still going to steal the bail?'

'Yes. But cleverly.' The Doctor tapped the side of his nose. 'The first thing to do is to drum up some pretext or other to get inside.'

'Such as?'

'Oh, I'll think of something,' the Doctor said, strolling into the bank.

A quarter of an hour later, the Doctor and Romana had a key and a mortgage.

According to Romana, that was when it had all gone wrong.

Previous attempts to change Romana's behaviour had proven patchy. In her travels she had experienced mind control, evil clones, and even dispatched a robot double with the fashion sense of a cat lady. But, for some reason, the pressure of having to go out and work for a living was insidiously successful. There'd been no hypno-ray, no rasp of 'Obey Zarl!', just a rather sad-looking ex-fisherman in a tie talking them through a brochure.

The change in the Doctor had been quick and worrying. For the first time since she'd known him, he looked trapped.

'Can't we just go back to the TARDIS?' she'd asked.

'We can't do that now. It's illegally parked,' he'd muttered, much to Romana's amazement. 'We'd have to work off the fine.'

122

The whole concept of a mortgage had annoyed the Doctor. He was appalled by the idea of a loan that would only make you pleased if you died. In theory it was paying off their flat in increments, but in practice, what with the rising service charges, the rates, the water bill and the fish tax, they didn't seem to be making any headway. 'At this rate,' he'd moaned, 'we'll need to live another 2,000 years in order to pay this off.'

'Doctor, is living like this really your plan?' Romana had asked as he'd served up a dinner of boiled fish omelette. 'Because if it is, I'm not sure I like it.'

'Me neither,' admitted the Doctor. He'd not spoken for the rest of the night.

It seemed as though the Doctor had given in. As if all he could do was cram fish into tins and hope for the best.

Romana was almost hoping the Krikkitmen would turn up.

It was another grim day in the factory when the Doctor decided to put seven fish into a tin rather than six. He didn't like pilchards, and he was fairly certain the people buying the tins didn't like them either. But there was something so regimented about putting just six fish, every single time, into a tin. Why not seven, or sometimes, five? Shake things up a bit – well, as much as a tinned fish can be shaken. After more trying, he'd accepted that the tins would take only six fish. They looked crammed with seven and meagre with five. Six looked just right. Insultingly right.

The Doctor let out the long, long sigh of a man whose spirit has finally broken.

'How boring,' he announced. 'Boring!'

A hand landed on his shoulder.

'That was quick,' said the Doctor.

*

The Doctor and Romana sat in a glum side office. The room had been given the exact level of design afforded to budget hotels. Someone had clearly looked at what rooms required and decided to do away with all the frills, like a window, carpet, painted walls, and chairs. The only frippery was a very solid lock on the door. The Doctor looked up at the bare lightbulb and blew a raspberry at it.

'I hate it here,' he said.

Romana broke into her first smile in days. 'Do you? I'm so glad. I've been worried about you.'

'Me too.' The Doctor flashed her a ghostly smile. 'I think I'm allergic to normality.'

The door swung open, and a very angry man stormed in. He was licking his lips in a way that would have made a sandwich flinch. He slapped down a very thick wodge of printouts on the desk.

'Got you, sunshines, got you!' he snorted with porcine triumph. 'You beauties are for the high jump.'

'Are we?' Romana raised a glacier of an eyebrow. 'I'm rather more of a javelin girl.'

'And I'm quite definitely quoits.' The Doctor's insolence was back and it was marvellous.

The angry man rapped a knuckle against the livery of his uniform. 'Don't come the clever-clever with me. You have no idea who you're dealing with.'

Romana toyed with the possibilities. Intergalactic Assassin? Agent of the Black Guardian?

'I'm a traffic warden,' the man snarled.

The Doctor made a brief attempt to take the man seriously. He bit his lip and muttered, 'Is that so? Goodness.'

'You thought you could just run off and leave your ... box ... in the road where it had no right to be, did you?' The man was practically drooling with glee. 'Well, we found you, oh yes we did. And do you want to know how?'

124

'Oh, how?' Romana was all politeness.

'Your little pinkies,' the man sneered. 'You left your fingerprints smeared all over it.'

(Not surprised, thought Romana. There had, after all, been that time when they'd both been clinging to the outside as the TARDIS flew over Whipsnade Zoo.)

'How terribly careless of us,' the Doctor said. 'Imagine that.'

'Wasn't it?' the traffic warden laughed. 'We ran them through the system and found you working here. But not any more. No.' The man pattered his paws on the folder. 'You're fired. Any wages owed will go toward the fines. If you can't settle the outstanding balance, then your property will be forfeited. One mistake, and you're finished in Fuggville – why, you may as well build a raft and go live on the sea.' He clearly found the idea absurd, and the Doctor clicked his teeth.

'Well now,' the Doctor confessed. 'I'm afraid I just had to leave my box there. Because it's very special.'

'Is that so?' the man snorted. 'Well, it won't let you off the fine.'

'Won't it? It's worth a lot of money.' The Doctor played his Ace. 'If an estate agent would care to meet us there.'

Ognonimous Fugg himself was standing outside the TARDIS. He'd had a boring day and fancied a laugh.

'I'm a busy man, but intrigued.' He rapped a fat knuckle on the side of the blue wooden box. 'So, would you care to explain to me how this thing parked on my pavement is worth a lot of money? It's barely large enough for a family of four.'

Suppressing a small shudder, the Doctor shook Mr Fugg by the hand and marvelled at how the man had managed to get fat to deposit around his knuckles. 'Mr Fugg, delighted to meet you!' the Doctor lied. 'You're in for a treat.'

And with that, he unlocked the door of the TARDIS.

The richest man on Devalin gaped.

'Not an optical illusion, not a projection, not a virtual reality, not a hallucination,' Romana ticked them off her fingers.

'Go inside and have a look!' the Doctor encouraged.

Mr Fugg walked into the TARDIS. He didn't even notice the robot dog which warily followed his every move. Well, until his fingers hovered over a shiny gold trifle on a desk and K-9 cleared his throat with butlerish aplomb.

'How big is this house?' Mr Fugg eventually called from the rear of the control room.

At this, the Doctor threw back his head and roared with laughter. 'Infinite!' he said.

Mr Fugg came uncertainly out of the ship, a nervous swimmer fighting against a strong tide.

He looked back in, blinked, and then turned to the Doctor, rubbing his hands together.

'What a wonder!' Mr Fugg exclaimed, a sly look hooding his eyelids. 'And how unfortunate for you, my dear sir, that your magnificent box should be sadly forfeit.' He glanced back inside. 'I'll be only too glad to make better use of this.'

'Ah, no.' The Doctor shook his head. He held up his parking tickets. 'You might want to check your new laws. I'm allowed to leave my vehicle here so long as I keep paying these excessive fines. I consider it Ground Rent.'

Mr Fugg's face wanted to look crestfallen but couldn't stop smiling. 'Surely, surely you misinterpret my laws.'

'No!' the Doctor laughed. 'I got my dog to check the small print.'

'But ...' began Mr Fugg. 'You're off world. And that means ...'

Now Romana shook her head. 'I'm afraid not. We paid the fines with our wages. Earned here.'

The Doctor clapped his hands together. 'Exciting, isn't it?' he beamed, throwing an arm around Mr Fugg's shoulder. 'Think how many people I could offer free homes to in here.'

'Free?' Mr Fugg's smile finally ran away.

'Oh yes,' the Doctor leaned in. 'And these boxes? We have them all over my home world. Imagine what'll happen when I tell my friends to park a few along here.'

Their eyes all wandered up to the glum grey buildings towering over them.

'But surely—' began Mr Fugg, and then his brain stopped. All he could see was the total collapse of his economy overnight. Caused by a magical shed owned by a man who smelt of fish.

'Just imagine …' Romana took off her apron, began to fold it neatly, then threw it away. 'People will learn they no longer have to pay to live somewhere. No longer have to work to pay for their house and spend the leftovers on eating tinned fish.'

'Perhaps,' suggested the Doctor, 'they'll think about going sailing again.'

'I forbid it!' snapped Mr Fugg.

The Doctor closed the door of his blue box and strolled away. 'I think it's too late for you to forbid anything!'

'No it isn't,' protested Fugg. 'No one knows about this. It's just an idea.'

Without stopping to turn, the Doctor answered him. 'No. You can't stop ideas. Not once they're out of the box.'

They walked through town, Mr Fugg trailing behind them, shouting and pleading and screaming and begging.

Along the way, Romana noticed a sound buzzing through the narrow streets. It was the sound of an idea catching on, of people saying 'Bother it' and putting down their tins and casting aside their aprons and going out for a stroll.

The Doctor was whistling, looking happier than he had done for days. His plan had worked brilliantly. When the banking system collapsed, all he'd have to do was to ask nicely and they'd give him the Golden Bail of Prosperity.

Which was when the Bank blew up.

Mr Fugg stared in horror. The air was full of a burning cloud of money and mortgages.

Soaring out from the smoke was a cricket pavilion.

'Ah well,' the Doctor said philosophically. 'Still, not a bad day's work.'

CHAPTER FOURTEEN
THE PERFECT PLANET

'No purple.' The Doctor was barely out of the TARDIS and he was already complaining. 'The problem with this planet is that it has no purple.'

They'd come to Bethselamin to find the Silver Bail of Peace. They'd failed in their quest to secure all the parts of the Wicket Gate. The Krikkitmen weren't far behind. And the Doctor was still grumbling about the lack of purple.

'I checked the readouts before we left the TARDIS.' The Doctor announced this unusual news proudly, as well he might. 'I expect it's some slight imbalance in the refractive index caused by crystals in the upper atmosphere.' He mumbled the end of the sentence hastily in case Romana challenged him on the science. He could already hear K-9 clearing his throat. 'Anyway, the big thing is, no purple.'

Romana looked at the genteel cityscape stretching before her. 'They seem to be getting along perfectly well without it.'

'I miss it already,' the Doctor announced. He was clearly in *that* mood. 'I mean, what happens if I want to mix blue and green together? What will happen then?'

'You'll get cyan,' said Romana. 'If you want purple you'll have to mix red and green.'

'Exactly,' the Doctor wandered away to kick some stones.

Romana crouched down next to K-9. 'K-9,' she whispered, 'I don't think the Doctor is going to enjoy Bethselamin.'

The Doctor hadn't stopped grumbling as they'd made their way to the city. Romana was worried – the Krikkit robots had three parts of the Wicket Gate. Would the one bit in their possession be somehow enough to stop the creatures unlocking their home planet? At the very least, they'd be facing an awkward arbitration process.

The Doctor was sanguine about it. 'It'll be like swapping football stickers,' he said, showing off his mercurial talents. 'Yes, they've got Giant Haystacks plus Torvill and Dean, but we've got Kevin Keegan and are about to get our hands on Eric Bristow.'

'Um,' said Romana.

The Doctor didn't listen. He still wouldn't stop grumbling. Not even when a crowd of revellers had offered them refreshments, including delicious slices of a blue sort of watermelon. He'd scowled at it.

By the time they reached the city walls, you could have grown turnips in the furrows in his brow. Gaily dressed people had come skipping, yes skipping, out from the city. The fearsome walls turned out simply to be gaudy canvas backdrops against which a variety of lyrical numbers could be performed by musicians and dancers and acrobats. The streets were thronged with smiling, waving people.

'They seem pleased to see us,' said Romana.

'I know,' the Doctor groaned. 'It's a trap.'

*

If it was a trap, it persisted for a long, very enthusiastic while. As the sun set, more dancers came out with torches and tambourines, followed by children offering around sweetmeats and roast nuts.

The people of this world were gently furry, not so much bears as department store workers dressed as bears. Their faces had the sweet blankness shared by rabbits, sheep and koalas. They danced and tumbled and jostled and giggled and tried their best to make everyone happy.

The Doctor angrily swatted away a proffered bag of sweets. 'Who's behind all this, that's what I want to know?' he grated. 'It can't be the Master. He's not fond of show tunes.' He kicked at a fallen toffee apple, only for a child to rush forward, pick it up, and bin it responsibly. 'Something's very wrong with this world.'

'Are you sure?' Romana asked.

The Doctor continued staring at the singers, mouthing along to their words. 'I think,' he announced after a while, 'that it's a coded cry for help. If only I could decipher it.'

Romana laid a fond hand on the Doctor's wrist. 'I'm going for a stroll,' she said. This world was a peaceful place and it was their job to stop the Krikkitmen ravaging it. She'd happily locate the last part of the Wicket while he dreamt up conspiracy theories. 'Don't go unmasking any of those children as assassins. I doubt their parents would approve.'

She wandered away, aware of K-9 following. He nudged up against her leg.

'Mistress, I have a theory.'

'What is it, K-9?' Romana reluctantly took her eyes off a passing juggler.

'I believe the Doctor-Master is mistaken about the nature of this world.' The dog paused, thoughtful. 'Bethselamin has an unbroken history of peace. Due to its natural abundance of resources and a relatively uncluttered evolution, the peoples of this world have never had to fight. They have never known major conflict. This world has also never been invaded as it is lacking in mineral wealth.'

'You're quite correct,' Romana agreed. If you invaded this planet you'd only get a hold full of eucalyptus and slaves who could play the lyre. 'This is a world without threat, without anger, without malice.'

'The Doctor-Master is bored,' said K-9.

The Doctor continued to be bored through the feasts, through the speeches, and only perked up during the tour of the graveyard. The leader of Bethselamin had taken them there 'because our ancestors will be so sorry to have missed you'. Romana thought that a bit ghoulish, but the Doctor was obviously thrilled.

'Maybe they're being run by ghosts,' he rumbled. He got out his sonic screwdriver and waved it around the headstones. 'Don't worry,' he confided in one of the men following him. 'This isn't the first planet ruled by the dead. I know what to do.'

The man looked rather baffled. 'I'm sorry, Doctor,' he said. 'Is something wrong?'

'No,' the Doctor growled, after staring at the screwdriver. 'Nothing's wrong. That's the problem.'

Romana found the Doctor pacing up and down on a patch of scrubland. He'd turned his back on the fireworks and was instead glaring at the stars.

'Are you actually willing the Krikkitmen to invade?' she asked tartly.

The Doctor shrugged. 'It'd smoke these boobies out of their complacency,' he suggested. 'Of course, I'd be only too delighted to protect them if that happens. But this lot need shaking up.' He scuffed at some neatly trimmed grass with his shoe. 'You know what they're planning tomorrow? The whole city has got orchestra practice together, because they feel it unites them and makes the most of their creativity. Honestly, I tell you, it's some sort of mind control.' He brightened. 'Evil. Alien. Mind. Control. Yes, maybe that's it …'

Romana watched him walk away. 'I don't know,' she said. 'It just sounds rather nice.'

K-9 nodded his head.

In many ways, Romana found the planet of Bethselamin a fascinating example of evolutionary cosmology. No wonder Time Lord observational craft loved visiting here – nothing happened. The worst thing about her visit was trying to convince these gentle, firmly fixed people that the sky was about to fall in. Never mind finding the Silver Bail Of Peace – the Bethselamin were about to be slaughtered.

While the Doctor strode around looking for a hidden supercomputer to baffle, Romana and K-9 tried to convince people that the Krikkitmen were coming.

'Really?' said Andvalmon. 'What kind of music would they like?'

Andvalmon was their host. Not, he was at pains to point out, Bethselamin's leader. ('We don't really have leaders,' he said. 'We don't like being told what to do.' Which explained why their orchestra was so bad.) He was simply there to make sure they had a good time. He had a casual, wispy beauty to him – like a cloud or a sandcastle. Everything about him looked as though a strong wind would finish him off. He wafted – his clothes, his hair, his voice, all held a peculiarly fragile quality about them. Andvalmon was a man made out of pastels. He wore a permanently brave smile which even stood up to the Doctor's booming assaults.

'Is your friend all right?' Andvalmon asked after a particularly brusque denunciation from the Time Lord. 'We have some excellent wickerwork therapy. And also a lovely spa.'

'Oh no.' Romana waved the notion away. 'He just can't cope with nice places. They bring out the worst in him.'

Andvalmon seemed puzzled by this. 'So ... not all planets are like this?'

'No.'

'Why not?'

'I haven't a clue,' Romana giggled. 'K-9 says you're in a lucky evolutionary curve. No one wants anything from you. Are you sure you've never had any invaders?'

Andvalmon scratched his thatch of hair. 'We've had visitors. Sometimes they try and make us join armies, or conglomerates, or ...' He scratched his head a little harder. 'Strategic Trading Alliances. We thank them for their interest and tell them that it doesn't sound much like fun. And, sometimes they're happy to stay for the dances we do in their honour. But they normally leave before the orchestra plays for them.'

Romana couldn't blame them. Last night they'd asked the Doctor if he had any requests. He'd offered them Beethoven's Fifth and the William Tell Overture. They'd played them both. At the same time.

K-9 had carried out extensive research, and concluded that Bethselamin was hopeless. Its people would make awful soldiers and worse slaves.

The Doctor still hadn't stopped tapping at the walls, desperate to discover hidden circuitry or concealed cameras. While he wandered around, grumbling, Romana tried to explain the concept of an invasion to Andvalmon. She told him about the Krikkitmen.

Andvalmon nodded sagely. 'But why would they kill us?' he said. 'We would offer no resistance. We would not hurt them.'

Romana chewed at her lip. 'It's not that simple. They just really don't like other species. They consider it their duty to wipe them all out.'

Andvalmon stroked the three tufts of fur on his chin. 'That seems a bit of a shame,' he said. 'But no matter. I'm sure that if we are welcoming, they will treat us with kindness.'

Romana held her breath. This was like explaining to an Australian quokka that the hungry fox bounding off the newly arrived boat wasn't going to be its cuddly new friend. The Bethselamini didn't hunt, so they had no more concept of prey than of musical timing. They were going to be complete victims.

'The thing is,' she said, 'they're going to turn up and take something from you. I've been skirting around this, but do you by any chance own a big silver stick? Size could vary.'

Andvalmon considered. 'We have such a thing in the temple. The Peace Rod. We worship it as a sacred relic. No particular reason. It just makes us feel good.'

'You wouldn't want to lose it, would you?'

'No,' said Andvalmon. 'But who'd take it?'

'The Krikkitmen would. They want it. They'll come here and they'll take it away.'

Andvalmon frowned. 'That would be a shame.'

He was getting it. 'And so,' Romana pressed home her advantage, 'that's why we have to stop it. The best way to do that is to give it to us.'

Andvalmon chuckled and wagged a finger at her. 'You're saying that an alien race we've never heard of is coming to steal our Peace Rod, and that, in order to stop that, we should give you the Rod?' He shook his head. 'I'm disappointed in you.'

'No.' Romana realised her stumble. 'If you give it to us, then the Krikkitmen may not come here. Untold lives will be saved.'

Andvalmon laughed some more. 'So, the way we'll know we've been spared is if nothing at all happens?' He stood up, brushed himself off and wandered away. 'We may be simple, but we are not fools.'

Romana watched him go and cursed softly.

'Doctor,' began Romana. 'We're going to have to break into their Temple of Peace and take the Silver Bail.'

'Oh good,' the Doctor replied. 'Anything but listen to another concert. I gave them the score for *Rigoletto* and they said they'd be only too happy to play it … whilst having another crack at Beethoven's Fifth.' He shuddered. 'If they do get invaded, it'll probably be by music critics. They'll bombard them with sarcasm then steal all their peanuts and wine.'

The Bethselamini Temple of Peace was proof that most species will worship anything, even something they have no real idea of.[3]

The tribe were grateful for Peace, but without having a grasp of War. They were aware that they didn't really have leaders (and that was nice). They were even more grateful that their leaders didn't tell them to grab something heavy and hit the people of the next valley with it. They rather liked the people of the next valley, who liked them back. So, as far as they could see, a war would cause a few problems. The next valley made a lovely wine, and rather enjoyed swapping it for some spare cheese, which all seemed very agreeable, but was likely to come to an abrupt halt once you'd hit their relatives with a stick. But then again, this was just a slightly bemusing notion.

The Bethselamini only really had an idea of War because philosophers kept coming up with it as an abstract concept. 'You know how yesterday was pleasant? And today went well, and, chances are, tomorrow will continue agreeably, with everyone being nice to each other? Well, imagine if that didn't happen – what would that look like?' Every now and then, a philosopher would raise this as a notion, and their audience would stare at them, puzzled. 'No, sorry, I don't quite get it,' they'd apologise. 'It just sounds horrid.'

'Quite so,' the philosophers would say. 'But isn't it interesting? Isn't it?'

---

[3] On many planets it is said to be blasphemy to try and define God. On other worlds, it's a compulsion. Some will say that God is in the small things, and will point, with the smuggest of nods, towards a blade of grass or a drop of dew. Others will throw an arm up to a sunset, or a mountain. Others will delight in telling you where God is not – he frequently doesn't show up when a volcano flattens a town, but that is because the hapless townsfolk must have done something very wrong indeed. 'Typical God,' observers will say, 'serves them all right,' as they rub some ash from their sandals, before setting off home, secretly glad that God hasn't found out about all the energetic coveting they've been doing of their next door neighbour's wife and donkey.

After a while, partly to stop the philosophers grumbling, they built the Temple of Peace. The philosophers agreed a definition of what Peace was (being Bethselamin, it was all done very amicably), and everyone agreed that it was as good a place as any to put that silver rod they had lying around. It made a rather nice symbol of what the philosophers were chuntering about, and a shiny pole was far easier (and nicer) to look at than an idea. As time went on, everyone became really terribly fond of the Temple of Peace. Some even started to credit it with a supernatural ability to 'Keep the Peace'.

Perhaps inevitably, when War finally came to Bethselamin, it came to the Temple of Peace.

It was late at night when the TARDIS did its best to whisper out of the Vortex. Romana had coaxed another short hop out of the machine, nudging them from the outskirts of town to the heart of the Temple of Peace.

The Doctor emerged, still chuntering. 'Wouldn't be surprised if we were in Betelgeuse. Type 40s weren't designed for short hops, I keep telling you. It's like getting a steam train to do your ironing. Oh.' On this last syllable, he looked around with the annoyed disappointment of a man who has found himself exactly where he was supposed to be. This never happened to the Doctor, and it always felt peculiarly wrong – rather like reaching for the wrong condiment in a café and sugaring your soup.

'Humph, well done, Romana,' he said begrudgingly. 'Let's go and steal this Rod.'

Romana slid out beside the Doctor, holding a thin steel pipe in her hand.

'Already?' The Doctor frowned. This was taking efficiency too far.

'Oh no,' Romana said. 'I found this in the TARDIS workshop. Hopefully it'll do as a replacement.'

The Doctor frowned at that. Romana had been helping herself to his stocks of Useful Things. Next she'd be going through his shed, throwing out his Interesting Bits of Wood and old issues of *Eagle*, and then he really would have to put his foot down.

'Come on!' he said, heading off for the inner sanctum.

Really, there wasn't that much difference between the inner and outer sanctums. In fact, the Temple of Peace was about the size and shape of not so much a parish church as the little concrete annex they built at the side of one for crèches and bring and buys. In the middle of the little room were two wooden crooks. Resting between them was the Silver Rod of Peace.

The Doctor paused in the act of reaching for it. He looked round. No killer androids. Excellent. He reached forward.

'Doctor!' someone shouted.

People were always shouting his name at him. There were various ways of doing it, and, really, one day, he must sit down and categorise them. There were, for instance, at least seven different ways of saying 'Doctor?' with a question mark, ranging from 'I'm about to remind you of my existence by asking you an annoying question' to 'I appear to be dangling from a cliff and was wondering what you were planning on doing about it.' 'Doctor,' with a comma, was also rarely good news – at one end of the spectrum it was a prelude to 'You've tried to fix K-9 with a bit of the toaster again' and at another it was 'We've decided you should rule our planet / be our scientific adviser / be fed to the great swamp monster.' Worst of all was 'Doctor!' with that deadly exclamation mark. Most of the time it was uttered by something ghastly in a shiny uniform – either Sontarans or Bus Conductors. Rarely, it was used by maniacs to wish him good riddance as they tumbled into their own doomsday devices.

Right now it was being shouted by Andvalmon, stepping forward from the shadows of the temple with a look of angry reproach.

'Lovely night for it,' began the Doctor hopefully.

Andvalmon's expression made his disappointment clear. 'I really had hoped for better from you,' he said. 'We don't have theft on this world.' He pointed at Romana, who, for once, was staring at her shoes. 'Your friend didn't fool me. There are no Krikkitmen.'

'Listen,' said the Doctor, 'I'm terribly sorry, but we must take that Silver Rod.' He executed a theatrical bow of apology. It was an act of winning charm which singularly failed to achieve his point, but did save his life, because, as he bowed, a bat sliced through the air and embedded itself in the wall.

The Krikkitmen had arrived.

It would be nice to say of Bethselamin's First and Only Battle that the people of the planet proved natural fighters. They did not. They died.

The Krikkitmen poured out of the Temple of Peace, slaughtering anything that moved, with an insulting lack of creativity. They created a wall of death and panic that spread as the people streamed away from the Temple.

They could have stopped there. The objective was theirs. They could just take it and go. But, at some level of core programming, the Krikkitmen sensed that here were a people who'd never known war, violence, or slaughter. It was too much for them to resist.

The Doctor, Romana and Andvalmon watched from inside the Temple, surrounded by less than half a dozen Krikkitmen. Squinting through the smoke, the Doctor was able to estimate that there were about a dozen in total. Enough to turn a planet to mince.

The Doctor had tried shouting at one of the Krikkitmen. It had ignored him with a very special, icily mechanical ignoring which said plainly: 'I know you are there but I do not care.' Two androids plucked the Silver Bail from its cradle and carried it through the open doors of the Krikkit Pavilion.

The situation was grim. The Doctor's misgivings about Bethselamin were forgotten. They had to do something. The

139

invasion had been so sudden. There hadn't even been time to summon K-9. The Doctor looked at Andvalmon and Romana. The poor young man was dangling at the end of a Krikkitman's arm. He was struggling and wailing. A Krikkitman was advancing on Romana, its bat raised in a way that clearly meant business. There was probably another of the things coming for him, but the Doctor's sense of priority had always been skewed.

He forgot about his own impending death, about the failure of his mission, about the imminent cosmological catastrophe. Down the hill, some rather nice people were being massacred and he'd glimpsed something through the doors of the Pavilion. Something which had piqued his curiosity.

As a viciously sharp bat sliced towards him, the Doctor ducked and slid across the temple floor, staggering inside the Pavilion. What common sense he had left told him that he had seconds before being very firmly killed. But, to the Doctor, seconds were plenty of time. He looked around the Pavilion, and found it immediately curious.

'But it's bigger on the inside than on the outside,' he marvelled. People were always saying that about his own ship, but to find that the Krikkitmen had a similar craft was both intriguing, exciting and disappointing. Their ship really was remarkably roomy. Which was curious. Especially as it also seemed to be able to pop out of thin air. It had more in common with his own craft than it really should have.

The second thing the Doctor noticed was even more unforgivably enticing. On a wall was a big, red lever decorated with elaborate warning signs.

'Coo!'

As he said this, he became aware that the air behind his neck was parting as something sharp and deadly headed his way.

Paying the warning signs no attention whatsoever, the Doctor jerked the big red lever.

CHAPTER FIFTEEN
THE BORING TEST

'Well, that's anticlimactic.'

The Doctor was surveying the army of very dead Krikkitmen.

'I would appear to have just turned them off.'

His voice tailed away. The Doctor had talked supercomputers to death, cheated at Monopoly with masterminds, and tricked a battle fleet into invading their own home planet. But it was rare to turn off an entire army.

Andvalmon was peeping through his hands. 'Are you quite sure?' His tone conveyed a complete lack of conviction in the Doctor's prowess. 'Maybe they're waiting for your next move.'

'If your definition of "waiting" includes lying in heaps on the carpet, then yes. They're waiting like tigers.'

To prove his point, the Doctor nudged a Krikkitman with his toe. Perhaps it was a trifle timorous; certainly more of a ginger tap than a goal-scoring kick.

There was a hollow clang.

For a moment, the entire planet of Bethselamin waited.

Nothing happened.

Nothing continued to happen.

A wave of deadly death absolutely didn't break on the shores of slightly overcooked metaphor.

The entire planet of Bethselamin let out a relieved sigh.

Andvalmon took his hands from his eyes and blinked.

Romana was sat on the floor, staring curiously into the empty dark void under a Krikkitman's helmet. 'There's nothing there,' she said. She frowned. 'There's nothing there.' She blinked, puzzled.

'I know.' The Doctor patted her on the shoulder. 'I know just how you feel.'

The Doctor and Romana glanced sheepishly at the temple door. From past experience, they knew that a small, cheering rabble would pour through, heaping praise on them and saying nice things about K-9.

They stopped looking at the door and looked at each other instead.

'Not sure I fancy it,' said the Doctor. He hoped they wouldn't bring the orchestra.

'Me neither,' admitted Romana.

'Doesn't really feel we've earned it.'

'Worse than that.' Romana was using The Tone. The Tone was a perfect cocktail of exasperation, impatience and ohDoctoryou'vedoneitagain. It never boded well. 'That Krikkitman was saying something to me. It sounded important. But you cut it off mid-sentence.'

The Doctor indicated the big lever. 'Would you like me to turn them all back on again?'

'Can't hurt.' Romana risked a smile.

'Fair enough,' the Doctor said, reaching for the lever. 'Then we can maybe defeat them properly next time.'

'Quite,' Romana agreed.

Andvalmon was running towards them, waving frantically.

'We're joking,' the Doctor reassured him.

'Even the Doctor has his limits,' Romana agreed. 'We're just puzzled by what's happened.'

'The Krikkitmen are destroyed,' Andvalmon said, reasonably. He was getting his head around his planet's first invasion. 'Bethselamin has been saved. It's a triumph.'

There was an awkward pause.

'Isn't it?' said Andvalmon.

The awkward pause continued to saunter around the room looking for a chair it liked.

'Oh come on now,' Andvalmon continued.

Romana and the Doctor looked at the pile of deactivated Krikkitmen. And they were very worried.

Romana began: 'The problem is—'

'That you can't turn off Krikkitmen,' the Doctor concluded.

Perhaps mention should have been made earlier of the Boring Test. It was invented by a Dr Boring, who spent his entire life trying to escape from under his surname. Sadly, by the time he realised he could just have changed it, he was far too famous. For one thing, his lectures were always packed out by students who never got tired of the joke. And, for another thing, if he changed his name (he'd quite fancied Maple), people would always be reminding each other about what his name really was.

So, Dr Boring remained Dr Boring for his entire life. He tried overcompensating – he paraglided on the wind moon of Sarion. He walked a gravity rope between the rings of Dolbeep. He was a champion solar surfer. He was an expert chef in a score of planetary cuisines. Magazines did features on his hair, hostesses lured him to parties, and celebrities he'd never met begged invites to his weddings.

He actually got away without discovering or inventing anything much. For one thing, what with all the derring-do, cookery and parties, there was very little time for any research.

But that didn't matter – he coasted quite merrily on his reputation. And then one day, almost by accident, he came up with the Boring Test.

The Boring Test posited, and then proved, the difference between a normal robot and a sentient one. It was the sort of rather nice distinction that made for lively talk at parties. As Dr Boring put it, it was the difference between a kettle and a puppy. One you could cheerfully throw on a bonfire. Although no one had ever invented a sentient robot, Dr Boring posited that, with the grim inevitability of technical progress, a machine would eventually come on the market that was so complicated that it would deserve rights – because it was alive.

Everyone nodded and smiled, invited him to more parties, and continued to toss their old robots in the recycling compactor. His test was used in a couple of trial cases (normally when a disgruntled widow left her entire fortune to the auto-butler rather than her ghastly relatives), and then the Boring Test sat, gathering dust on the Shelf of Quaint Notions.

Until, that is, the Exhausting End of the Thousand Year War with the Krikkitmen. Dr Boring was long dead by then (he did not, you'll be pleased to know, die in bed, but due to a grisly freak saddle failure on a laser cycle). Otherwise he'd have been all over the rolling newsbeams.

For most of the conflict, his Test had been forgotten about, and then, at the very end of the war, just as the Time Lords were about to wipe out the Krikkitmen, someone surprisingly remembered about it and argued that it might be an idea to run the Boring Test on the Krikkitmen, just to be safe. It caused a lot of groaning and eye-rolling, but eventually, everyone conceded that, yes, indeed, the Krikkitmen were sentient robots with rights. And therefore they couldn't just be bunged in a black hole. Fair enough, said the Time Lords, and simply imprisoned them for eternity instead.

'Oh,' said various Robot Rights movements, and promptly stopped inviting the Time Lords to meetings. Which the Time Lords were fine with, because there were no biscuits.

Andvalmon gazed open-mouthed at the conclusion of the lecture.

'Simply put,' finished Romana, 'the Krikkitmen were the most advanced, the most glorious artificial life forms ever created.'

'Steady on,' whispered the Doctor. 'K-9 might hear.'

'K-9 has never tried to destroy the Universe,' put in Romana. 'No ambition.'

Give him time, thought the Doctor. His fingers stroked the lever, very careful not to accidentally turn the Krikkitmen back on.

'The problem, and the reason I bring up Dr Boring's theory, is that it's all poppycock.' The Doctor repeated the word until it echoed around the Krikkit Pavilion. 'Either the test doesn't work, or we were all so scared of the Krikkitmen we gave them extra points, or we're standing in the middle of an enormous trick.' He pointed again to the lever. 'Sentient robot armies do not have off switches.'

'Why not?' asked Andvalmon. Romana was glad about that because for once she didn't fancy feeding the Doctor questions.

'For one thing, if your entire army can be turned off by a switch, that's a bit of an Achilles' heel.'

'Not necessarily,' Andvalmon countered. 'You'd have to get inside the craft to operate it.'

'Really?' the Doctor chewed his lip. 'It's a simple flip switch which triggers a tiny electrical impulse. Anyone could whip up a remote control. As soon as they landed on your planet and opened the doors to their ship, you could turn them off like a chat show. It's nonsense.'

Romana was nodding. 'The War could not have lasted a thousand years unless everyone in the Universe was having an off millennium.'

Andvalmon pressed on. 'But, surely—'

'No,' said the Doctor. 'It also raises a philosophical point, which is why I started talking about Dr Boring. Romana? You're good at the fiddly bits.'

'Thank you Doctor.' Romana smiled. 'If an artificially created race became sentient, they wouldn't have an off switch. Even if their creators had initially installed one, the robots would just take it out. They'd not want anyone to be able to turn them off. A normal robot simply wouldn't question the existence of the switch, whereas a sentient robot wouldn't allow the switch to remain. Not unless ...' Romana stopped. She was staring at the Doctor.

'What is it, Romana?'

'Unless the Krikkitmen really, really believed in God,' she said.

That shut everyone in the room up.

Shortly afterwards, the Doctor was taking apart a Krikkitman. 'If it's a machine, I'm dismantling it. If it's a sentient robot, this is an autopsy.' He seemed the happiest Romana had seen him in some time. She found the whole process unsettling – standing in this ship, surrounded by lethal robots who could, in theory, attack them at any moment. She blinked, an odd feeling crowding her head. Just before the Doctor had flicked that switch, what had that robot been saying to her?

Andvalmon rushed back in to report on the goings-on in the town. The death toll had been smaller than they had feared. There was already talk of a victory dance, with several specially composed symphonies. 'Everyone's very cross about what's happened,' he told the Doctor. 'They're so furious they're thinking about having an election. Perhaps this planet should have a leader after all, to protect us in case this happens again.'

The Doctor, sucking on a screw, shook his head. 'There are two things you should never do when you're angry – go shopping or have an election.' He waved Andvalmon away with a robot hand. 'Shoo off and tell them all to calm down.'

Andvalmon stood there, still hovering nervously. 'Well, you see, it's a bit tricky ...'

The Doctor stamped a Krikkitman's foot on the floor several times. 'No, no, no!' he protested. 'I know what this is. I'm flattered, but I simply won't become your honorary president. The burden of responsibility is just too great. And then there are all the rulebooks one has to read, and the babies one has to kiss, and the speeches. I'm a shy retiring sort. Wouldn't say boo to a goose. Ask Romana.'

Andvalmon blushed. 'Actually—'

'Oh,' said the Doctor, trying not to look put out. 'Well, yes, she's a splendid first choice. Aren't you, Romana?'

Romana stared at them both in astonishment. 'Are you suggesting I stay behind and run the planet?'

'Only a suggestion.' The Doctor felt around for just the right screwdriver. 'Be a handy bit of training for ruling Gallifrey some day.'

Romana muttered something which may have contained the phrases 'it appears', 'any old fool' and 'can rule Gallifrey'. Then she smiled sweetly. 'Any progress on the Krikkitman?'

The Doctor waggled a metal helmet. Briefly, a great darkness swelled inside it, glowed a vicious red and then died. He tossed the skull (with a neat under-arm movement) into a corner.

'We've all been conned,' he announced. 'The Krikkitmen, the deadliest race of androids in the Universe ... fakes.' He chucked an arm or two after the skull.

'Surely just a misdiagnosis,' argued Romana.

The Doctor held up a chip-set. 'No, look at this.'

'Not without an electron microscope,' said Romana tightly. 'K-9?'

K-9 trundled forward to analyse the circuit board. 'The processor's external appearance suggests almost unheard-of advances in artificial intelligence processing power. However,' he sniffed, 'an internal diagnostic reveals a relatively inferior Thought Lattice.'

'You see?' The Doctor nudged Romana. 'A robot disguised as a sentient robot.' He burst out laughing. 'It's either the least ambitious fancy dress imaginable, or one of the greatest frauds in the Universe. We've all believed that the Krikkitmen were an unstoppable race of warriors. In reality, we were nearly wiped out by an army of washing machines. Someone's made us all look foolish. But why?'

'Well,' Romana said, 'don't be too hard on yourself. After all this time, it's a legal nicety.'

'A legal nicety?' the Doctor thundered. 'If it wasn't for Boring's test, every Krikkitman that ever lived would now be recycled pencil sharpeners. Instead, five million of them are sitting around in storage.'

Andvalmon shrugged. 'I don't see the problem.'

'Really?' The Doctor was juggling a grenade. 'The Krikkitmen are stored in a Time Vault. This troop of robots – a wobbly handful of them – have already gathered up most of the entry gate to their home world. If they can breach one dimension, they can breach another. We've got to get to them and destroy the other five million before they're unleashed. Their plan is pretty clear now – to free their home planet and to restart their war.'

'But how do you get into a Time Vault?' asked Andvalmon.

The Doctor smiled. 'Actually, Romana and I have been there before.'

Andvalmon looked puzzled.

'The Krikkitmen are stored on the Time Lord prison planet of Shada.'

CHAPTER SIXTEEN
CONTAINS NICE BISCUITS

It was teatime in Cambridge. There's an argument, never satisfactorily disproved, that it is always teatime in Cambridge. The Doctor reached out for the last ginger nut, and had his hand slapped away.

'That's for your friend,' declared his host. 'Or, forgive me, I always assumed she was your friend. She was forever following you through doors and rolling her eyes, and that's what your friends tend to do.' The old – very old – very, very old – man paused, looking suddenly worried. 'You did have a friend last time you visited, did you not? I should hate to discover I was imagining her. She had ever such a nice smile.'

'Romana can't be here today,' the Doctor said. 'She's standing for election.'

'Student union?'

'President of the planet of Bethselamin,' the Doctor said.

'Ah, well, I'm not sure I'm eligible to vote there, but do wish her my best.' The old man dropped an entire Rich Tea biscuit into his cup and swirled it with delight.

'I'm not entirely sure she wants to win,' said the Doctor. 'What she really wants to do is to take a bunch of Krikkitmen back to Gallifrey.'

The little old man sat as bolt upright as his extreme age allowed him to. 'Aha, so she's staging a coup and taking over Gallifrey? How marvellous.' He rubbed his hands together. 'This calls for fig rolls.' And he pottered slowly across the floor of his book-lined study, vanished into the kitchenette, and emerged a moment later with a packet of Garibaldi biscuits that, after blinking at in befuddled surprise, he presented solemnly to the Doctor. 'Give these to her with my warmest regards. If she needs any help breaking into the Panopticon Vaults, my services are at her disposal.' With a wicked grin, the old man settled back into his chair, and then looked around him with bemusement. 'What were we talking about?'

Professor Chronotis, the Regius Professor of Chronology, enjoyed one of the very best studies in St Cedd's College. For a few centuries he'd worked his way steadily up and along the academic ladder, from basement to attic, from no window to broken window, from road view to quad view, and, once he'd finally found a study with just the right angle on the croquet lawn and not too close to the bell tower, he'd settled down and started making improvements. When you've been alive for millennia, you do acquire a large number of books, so he'd made his bookshelves dimensionally transcendental. They looked reasonably normal, unless, that is, you stared at them just a little bit too hard, and then you realised that there was something a little fishy about either the shelves or your eyes. If you looked away, you'd notice that the carpet was heroically trying to somehow fit in around all that shelving while keeping the shape of its pattern. The carpet looked exhausted.

Professor Chronotis's duties were light. He gave an annual lecture in Chronology, which, if anyone attended, he made sure to mumble through. He occasionally acquired a postgraduate student or two, but hastily shook them off by a combination of vagueness and genuinely frightening algebra. If that didn't work, he had used to lend them books, but he didn't do that any more.

The last time he lent a student a book, it turned out to be the most powerful book in the Universe. *The Worshipful and Ancient Law of Gallifrey* was one of the more powerful Artefacts of Rassilon. Rassilon was the greatest Time Lord leader who ever lived. Not only did he think rather highly of himself, he also liked to label things with the efficiency of a public school matron. Which brings us to *The Worshipful and Ancient Law of Gallifrey*, also known as *The Book of Rassilon*. It had never been read, because, although it looked like a book, smelt bookishly of caramel and dust, and had pages with writing on them and so on, it actually wasn't a book at all. The book was the only way to unlock the Great and Mostly Forgotten Time Lord Prison Planet of Shada, hidden away in a very secluded cul-de-sac of space-time.

Professor Chronotis had stolen – well, borrowed – well, pocketed – the book, casually wiping any memories of Shada that he could lay his hands on. The reason was that Professor Chronotis had, long ago, been imprisoned on Shada. He didn't want anyone to discover he'd escaped, and so removed the only way of getting there, and any memories there were of Shada kicking around.

All had gone terribly well until he'd lent the book to a student, and then things had got sticky. The Universe had very nearly been taken over, and the radiogram had never been the same since.

Right now, the Professor was looking out of the window, watching the Bursar of the College cheat at croquet. He was cheating very badly, and, instead of shouting at him, a female don was laughing at the Bursar until he went red in the face. The Professor smiled. He rather liked progress. Then a thought struck him. His brain was so soft and foggy that the thought didn't so much strike him as pat him gently, ask if he was all right, and then offer him a sit down. The Professor, never one to ignore his own advice, sat right down.

'Where were we? Did you say Krikkitmen?' he muttered.

'Yes,' the Doctor said.

'Oh dear. Horrid creatures. Wiped out long ago.'

'Sadly not,' the Doctor said, using his very gravest tone. The gravitas was somewhat undermined by the sound of the Bursar snapping his croquet mallet in two and stomping off through the hollyhocks to gales of laughter. The Doctor tried again, making his voice deeper and slower. 'And that could well be lethal to the Universe.'

'Really?' the Professor became worried by the temperature of his tea. It was tepid, which always alarmed him. What a terrible state to be in: not warm enough to be pleasant, not cold enough to be safely discarded, but just sort of there. He really should write something on the subject. Or work out a formula. Oh dear, the Doctor was still talking.

'Hidden somewhere is an army of five million Krikkitmen.'

'Is that so? Well, they're probably best off left alone.'

'No,' the Doctor was pacing up and down the carpet, which, given its trans-dimensional nature, was tougher than it looked. 'I need to find that army and destroy them before anyone gets to them.'

'Oh.' The tea was definitely too cold now. 'Dearie me.'

'Yes,' the Doctor said. 'Professor, can I borrow that book again?'

It had all been Romana's idea. The good plans often were.

'Well, we can't just leave the Krikkitmen here, on Bethselamin,' she'd argued.

The Doctor had pointed out that they were just statues. Romana had laughed at that. Apparently (and how was he to know better) statues are generally of people that are liked, not of a giant invading army, posed in the middle of smiting, slaughtering and wiping out the planet. 'Children might cry,' Romana finished.

The Doctor's counter-argument to that was that they could be disguised. Or have sheets wrapped over them, or jolly sweaters knitted to make them look more innocuous. 'It's hard to take seriously an army in cardigans,' he'd said, feeling rather pleased.

Romana had sensibly pointed out that that was a lot of knitting for an uncertain outcome. Instead she'd suggested that while he popped off to sort out access to Shada, she'd get the populace to round up the Krikkitmen and put them all in their pavilion, and she'd then fly it back to Gallifrey.

'Someone's only going to think you're staging a leadership bid,' the Doctor had argued. The Bethselamini really did want her to stay behind, and he would miss her terribly.

Romana had shrugged as if that didn't matter. She then flicked a couple of switches on the TARDIS console ('to stop you getting into trouble') and sauntered off.

'Last one back to Gallifrey's a ninny,' the Doctor had said.

He'd stood on the threshold of his ship, watching her for a moment.

Romana waved back to the Doctor. The great plains of Bethselamin stretched out before her, the attacking Krikkitmen ranged across it in a variety of menacing postures. The suns were setting as Andvalmon came rushing over to her. There was still a troubling lack of purple about the whole place, but the Doctor supposed she'd get used to it.

'We've got a lot of work to do,' she was saying to Andvalmon. She didn't look back.

The Doctor felt proud of her, a little sad, and then wondered where his hat was.

'Just you and me, eh, K-9?' the Doctor said.

The TARDIS had left Cambridge and was now in mid-flight, harrumphing its way through some chrono-turbulence. K-9 was following the Doctor as he paced around the control room. The Doctor was flicking cavalierly through *The Worshipful and Ancient Law of Gallifrey* without causing a major space-time collapse. K-9 had a St Cedd's cup and saucer balanced on his back. As far as he could tell, his Master was in an odd mood.

'Just you and me,' the Doctor repeated, staring at a page full of squiggles. 'Some day, you know, Romana will leave us. For good or for better.' He left a pause for the robot to argue with him, but it did not. The Doctor sipped at his tea and then started to flick through the pages rapidly, watching as the book set the controls of the time machine. The TARDIS made a deep rumbling groan.

'I know how you feel, old girl,' the Doctor sighed. Without Romana, he felt a little lost. No one to tell him how brilliant he was, no one to tell him how stupid he was, no one to tell him how to load the dishwasher. Still, splitting up had been her plan, after all.

'We're off to a forgotten prison in a forbidden dimension to destroy an army of five million robots ...' The Doctor drummed his fingers on the console. 'What could possibly go wrong?'

And then he found his hat, lying across some controls on the console. Curiously, this could have told him that something had gone very wrong indeed. But it did not.

CHAPTER SEVENTEEN
HIT FOR SIX

It looked pretty much like any other bit of space, only the stars didn't move. Nothing really moved here. The planetoid of Shada wasn't really that much of a planet, more a deep disc carved out of an ancient asteroid. The surface had the ancient seal of mighty Rassilon etched into it – because if there's one thing the Time Lords always make time for, it's a grandiose flourish. It really didn't need to be there. No one would see it. Not even other Time Lords. But some architect had decided that the one thing the asteroid needed was a sense of corporate identity, and nothing said on-brand like burning a five-mile logo into your asteroid.[4] The effect of the Seal of Rassilon was supposed to be magnificent, but, viewed from space, it reminded the Doctor of a lovely little mini-golf course he'd once been round in Totnes.

'All it's missing is a little windmill,' he chuckled, as he brought the TARDIS in to land.

---

[4] They'd been advised by the firm of Richfield & Wedgwood, of whom, regrettably, more later.

As the TARDIS shrugged out of the Vortex, alarms went off in the Induction Chamber. Ancient, sturdy, worthy alarms that were mostly there for effect. There was only one way into the Prison Planet of Shada and only one way out, and that was by TARDIS.

The only person who'd ever escaped was the arch criminal Salyavin, and he refused to say how he did it, preferring instead to live in quiet retirement scaring the wits out of hapless undergraduates walking across the college lawns.

The TARDIS door opened and the Doctor and K-9 edged out. Something about Shada made you do that. You'd have to be clinically insane (and many of the inmates were) to *stride* around the vaulted chambers. Anyone not currently in therapy took one step and then settled for creeping, sidling, or tiptoeing. Shada had an atmosphere, one composed of Oxygen, Hydrogen and Intimidation. Dust hung in the chilly air, and footsteps echoed with the sluggishness of weary ghosts.

The Doctor cleared his throat and then started singing Gilbert and Sullivan. K-9 knew this was a bad sign. It normally meant that his master was feeling insecure, especially as he'd never quite got around to learning the words. The proper words.

The halls of Shada echoed haughtily to the refrain of 'That's why I'm the Captain of *The Fishfinger*,' as the Doctor's creep tried its very best to saunter. K-9 glided after him.

The good thing about the prison planet of Shada was that the inmates weren't alive. Each one was sealed in a large glass cryopod. Those who had thought the whole process through had arranged their features in eternal frowns or smiles. The less thoughtful ones were either gasping, screaming, or frozen in the act of saying 'Now, hang on …'

The Doctor edged jauntily past a row of Sontarans. 'Beat you, cock,' he muttered, rapping on an Ice Lord's case. Then he paused in front of a frozen Krarg. As the Krargs were made of living lava, freezing one seemed ambitious, but that was the Time Lords for you.

The Doctor wandered into another room full of pods.

'Not alphabetical,' he sighed, 'nor Dewey Decimal. Just a haphazard array of ne'er-do-wells and rapscallions.'

K-9 had plugged himself into an information pod. 'I am accessing the storage data.'

'Good dog.' The Doctor patted him. He looked along the rows of aliens. He looked up the columns of aliens. 'Somewhere in here are five million Krikkitmen. Let's hope they're all filed together, otherwise this is going to take all week.'

'Working, Master,' the dog said, wagging his tail. Combing his way through the prison catalogue, he was calculating how long it would really take the Doctor to find and destroy five million robots.

Meanwhile, back in the TARDIS, a warning light was glowing underneath the Doctor's hat. The warning read: 'Screens breached: Intruders in TARDIS.'

'Oh look, they get their own dimension, how snug.' The Doctor threw open the door of a vault. 'Hot and cold running gravity, the works.' He would have tested this with his hat, but, ah yes, that was it, he'd left it on the console. Never mind.

The Doctor and K-9 looked at five million Krikkitmen. Well, the Doctor tried to perceive them, K-9 rapidly counted them. They were in rows of 100,000 which made it fairly easy for the dog.

'Awe-inspiring, don't you think?' The Doctor shivered. 'The Krikkitmen. The sight of just one of them makes me want to scream. Here are five million of them and the only thing I can hear is the Galaxy howling.'

At the side of the vault door was a small, useful control panel. The Doctor glanced at it and then broke out into the widest smile. 'Handy. As this is an artificially created pan-dimensional annex, it can be jettisoned. Just a few button presses and the Krikkitmen cease to exist.'

*

Back in the entrance hall to Shada, the TARDIS door opened. And a dozen Krikkitmen marched out.

The Doctor's hand hovered over the button.

'It would be so easy,' he said. His voice echoed off the walls.

For a moment his finger nearly pushed the button.

'K-9,' he remarked, his voice going over a speed-bump. The dog could already tell it was going to be a rhetorical question. 'Do you ever get the feeling you're being manipulated?'

'Master?'

The Doctor's fingers stroked the button.

'Tempting,' he said.

He then went over to a sarcophagus and started working on it with his sonic screwdriver. 'Something about this feels wrong. What if those Krikkit robots we found were fakes?' He heaved the pod door open. 'What if these really were sentient? Then I'd be about to commit genocide. And that would look very bad. Ha-ha, foolish Doctor!'

He dragged the inhabitant out.

'You don't catch me like that,' he announced, kneeling over the body. 'Let's just check. Autopooch – help me scan this thing.'

The Doctor and his dog peered at the recumbent creature. Behind them, something was happening.

The Krikkitmen marched through the reception hall and along the corridor. They knew exactly where to go.

'Master,' began K-9.

The Doctor did not seem to be listening. 'I owe you an apology.'

'Master?'

'We got so caught up in the Boring Test. But I worry. I do worry – I mean, you don't feel left out, do you?'

'Master?' K-9 kept his voice level.

'Because –' the Doctor had two screws clamped between his lips – 'I know we've never tested you but I would like to think you're sentient. We could run it if you'd like?'

'Negative, Master,' K-9 sniffed. 'However—'

'I think the dividing line is quite subtle.' The Doctor was digging into the Krikkitman's brain carapace. 'But look at this … After all that, this *is* a robot. Just another dull robot. Imagine that – they fooled the Universe.'

'Master!' K-9 extended his blaster probe.

Behind the Doctor, another sarcophagus door had opened. And something was coming out.

'No need to take offence.' The Doctor tapped K-9's muzzle, blocking the dog's shot, and tossed the brain pan to one side. 'These creatures fooled us all into thinking they were clever. And I think you, you're cleverer than that, aren't you, old sly-castors?'

'Well …' Despite the urgent situation, K-9 found the topic all too tempting. 'To negate the points you raise Master, I would advise you to look behind you.'

'What?' The Doctor whirled round.

All the sarcophagi were opening. The sealed army of Krikkitmen were awaking, the dull red glow in their eyes brightening as they emerged.

'The time for philosophical niceties is past!' The Doctor was already sprinting. 'Jettison now, rationalise later!' The Doctor hurled himself toward the big red button.

He'd always loved a big, juicy red button. Sometimes he'd press them and he'd often hear 'Curse you, Doctor!' as the big explosions began.

Sometimes he'd press them and Galaxy-mincing machinery would power down just as the countdown reached 0001.

Sometimes he'd press them and something remarkably unexpected would happen.

Sometimes he'd stop other people from pressing them.

There was a group of Krikkitmen surrounding the button. How had they got there so quickly? They'd have had to have got past him, surely? While trying to work this out, the Doctor threw himself forward, tobogganing in a tangle of coat, scarf and trouser through the Krikkitmen, reaching up towards the button. He'd do it. He would. The Krikkitmen would be gone for ever. He never should have hesitated, but this would rid the Universe of them.

His fingertips stretched out towards the button …

And, of all things, Romana stepped in front of it.

'Hello Doctor,' she said.

She was dressed in whites and holding a cricket bat. She looked quite absurd. Right up until she hit him with the bat.

The Doctor woke up in the TARDIS.

This was never good. Normally waking up in the TARDIS meant that he'd had one of his surprisingly rare fatal accidents and was going to have to spend the rest of the day getting used to a new body.

He patted himself down cautiously. Well, the hair was still curly, the nose still a bottle-opener, and a quick tap of the teeth told him that his smile was still a dazzler.

Maybe he hadn't regenerated. Well, that was good. He really didn't have time for all that bother this week.

The only other explanation was that they'd crashed. Which meant he'd get an entirely undeserved lecture from Romana about his driving. What she didn't understand was that he was not a bad driver, not as such, he was just a victim of probability. If you have a TARDIS and you never go anywhere in it, you'll never crash. If you're constantly haring from one end of eternity to the next, you're bound to pick up the odd bump and bang. You can't fight statistics.

He noticed Romana leaning over him. Oh dear. Perhaps he had regenerated after all. He really didn't fancy regenerating with Romana around. She was going to be critical about things, and he'd spend the whole day fiddling with the legs. And then she'd be picky about the hair. It was all so unfair. The Doctor treated regenerating like putting on clothes – he just grabbed whatever came to hand and got on with it. Romana, however, was such a careful dresser that, if you let her have her way, by the time she left the TARDIS he'd have already defeated the giant squid and be teasing the high priest.

Testing the water, he groaned and observed Romana's reaction.

'Oh, so you're alive,' she said.

The Doctor sat up, looked around, and blinked. 'Hullo Romana. What are all these killer robots doing in my TARDIS?'

The Doctor had a shrewd and terrible inkling. He remembered Romana staring into the helmet of that Krikkitman, muttering something about it talking to her as the light in its eyes died. Well yes, that would have done it.

And now the TARDIS was full of Krikkitmen.

'How odd.' The Doctor tried to stand, but settled for shuffling grandly onto his knees. He noticed that K-9 was lying on his side, in several pieces, looking exactly as though he'd been hit with a bat. Poor dog. Anyway, he'd get to him in a bit. 'You lot should be in your Pavilion. Which should right now be on its way to Gallifrey. Not here. After all, your ship can't possibly travel to Shada. It's not a TARDIS.'

The Krikkitman said nothing. The Doctor latched onto the console and used it to heave himself to his feet. As he did so, his eyes looked at some of the readouts. He tried his best never to do this, as it always depressed him, but sometimes he couldn't help it.

'Ah ha,' he said. He fixed one of the Krikkitmen with an ominous expression. 'That's terribly naughty of you.' He tottered over to a door. Normally it led to the Schrödinger's rabbit warren of the rest of the TARDIS. Not any more. He flung it back. Blocking the corridor was the Krikkit Pavilion.

He whirled around and jabbed a finger at Romana. 'J'accuse!' he thundered.

Really, this wasn't at all fair. Clearly the Krikkitmen had taken over Romana, using some form of possession. He was used to his friends being taken over. He often felt they weren't a true travelling companion till he'd sent their android double over a cliff screaming 'Kill the Doctor!' It gave spice to a morning when a companion turned up, all glassy-eyed, dull-toned, and suddenly terribly interested in going to look at an abandoned factory / waxworks museum / hardly-sinister-or-suspicious-clone-bank. But he'd not even got a whiff of it from Romana. Her eyes were bright, she wasn't wearing a scarf she'd lost earlier, and her voice had sounded so completely normal when she'd suggested flying a shipful of deactivated Krikkitmen to Gallifrey.

He stopped, and swallowed with difficulty. Well, frankly, this could be worse. That would have been a massacre. Instead they'd just wanted this little stopover.

He wagged a finger at the Krikkitmen who regarded him with awful indifference.

'So that's why the switches were off. Romana lowered the defence shields, then set your Pavilion's controls so that, instead of going to Gallifrey, you materialised a few seconds later inside the TARDIS and I gave you all a free lift to Shada.'

'Correct, Doctor,' said Romana, and, annoyingly, her delivery was as jaunty as ever.

'You're still under their control?' he whispered to her.

She nodded.

'And you haven't, by any chance, bypassed it and done something really clever like secretly jettisoning that vault of five million Krikkitmen?'

Romana winked.

The Doctor relaxed.

Romana punched him fondly on the arm. 'Of course not, silly. The Krikkitmen are now stowed safely aboard the Pavilion.'

'You're being such a tinker,' the Doctor said.

'I know,' replied Romana.

She opened the TARDIS doors. A group of Krikkitmen marched through. They didn't even glance at the Doctor. They simply swept past him and into the Pavilion.

The Doctor peaked out through the doors. Shada looked terribly quiet and empty. 'When they find out the Krikkitmen have gone missing, the Time Lords are going to be ever so cross,' he remarked.

'When they find out, it'll be too late,' said Romana. She closed the doors and began to set the controls.

'Where are we going now?' the Doctor asked.

'To the asteroid that holds the Lock,' Romana said. She set the controls with distressing ease. 'We now have the entire Wicket Gate. We're going to release the planet Krikkit from its prison. And then we're going to complete our war. And this time we're going to wipe out the Universe.'

' I see. I realise the odds are five million to one against me—'

'5,000,020 to be precise.'

'Thank you. But you can't go taking over my ship. The controls are isomorphic, you know. They simply won't work for anyone else.'

'Nonsense.' Romana grinned. 'They barely work for you.'

She flicked a final switch and the TARDIS lurched off into the Vortex.

The Doctor allowed himself a sigh.

Chapter Eighteen
Regrettable Acts Between the Swimming Pool and the Car Park

The TARDIS dragged itself unwillingly onto the surface of the Asteroid of the Wicket Gate. It really wasn't a place anyone dropped by. Although it had been the site of the end of an ancient war, that war was nearly forgotten. Forgotten in such a carefully guided way that, even though the asteroid offered rather sweeping views of the nearby Dust Cloud, no one had ever thought to go there to look at them. There had been some talk of building a Garden of Peace around the Wicket Gate, but, as the wicket had long ago been stolen, that had fizzled out. The asteroid was purposeless and abandoned. The exception to this (and there is always an exception) was the hotel that someone had built there. The Hotel of the Asteroid of the Gate sat off to one side of the monument.

For some reason, all its rooms faced sternly away from the Dust Cloud. There wasn't even a picture of the Dust Cloud in the lobby, nor had anyone ever thought to ask for one. One of the reasons for this was that no one had ever stayed there.

The TARDIS arrived in the shuttle park. The shuttle park had been broken up into individual bays by neat yellow lines, which the TARDIS delighted in ignoring as it bellowed into being. It didn't care if everyone knew it was having a particularly bad day, and was just dying for someone to ask how it felt.

A moment later, the Krikkit Pavilion appeared beside it. It parked itself very neatly between two yellow lines. The front of the Pavilion opened and twelve Krikkitmen marched out across the shuttle park.

The TARDIS door opened. The Doctor was pushed out. Romana strode behind him.

'See Doctor, the ultimate triumph of the Krikkitmen!' exulted Romana.

'Oh, I do wish you wouldn't talk like that.' The Doctor pulled his hat down over his forehead. It was one thing when supervillains used the imperative tense. It was quite another when your best friend did it. He always wondered what it was about the imperative tense and plans for universal conquest. It was always 'Behold!' this and 'Tremble!' at that. It reminded him of tour guides. He always enjoyed forming his own opinions, and was less than likely to adopt those of someone shouty in a cloak.

He'd wondered sometimes about popping back along a villain's timeline to find out at what precise moment they went from 'Daddy, please come and have a look at this!' to 'Kneel before my finger painting!' There'd certainly be a monograph in it, or, at the very least, a good long lunch with Dr Spock.

Romana was still banging on, bless her. 'The apotheosis of the Krikkitmen dawns!' she thundered.

You're going to feel so embarrassed about this when you're back in your right mind, the Doctor thought. That was the other thing about villains. They delighted in reaching up to the top shelf for their vocabulary. When they weren't issuing commands they were wheeling out grandiose Scrabble-dodgers like 'Ascendancy' and 'Denouement' which made you fear for how they ordered their breakfast eggs.

In reality, all that was happening was that a dozen Krikkitmen were marching across the shuttle park. An auto-bellboy had poked his head excitedly out of the abandoned hotel reception, then whipped it back inside again. Either a race memory had been triggered, or he knew to recognise a non-paying guest when he saw one.

What was taking place in the hotel grounds might have been ceremonial, and even slightly chilling, if it hadn't been happening by an empty swimming pool. The Krikkitmen held aloft the various components of their masters' ancient prison lock – rebuilding the Wicket Gate – a tripod of, now you looked at it, ancient and foreboding power.

They strode beyond the swimming pool and the artificial palm trees, to a point where the rocky desolation had been smoothed over just a little. And then one of the Krikkitmen turned to face the Doctor and Romana. It nodded.

'The arising approaches,' Romana intoned. 'It has been decreed that there shall be witnesses.'

'Oh good. I'd figured it was either going to be that or sacrifices,' the Doctor replied. 'You're not really an impartial witness at the moment, though. You'll just witter on about glorious ascendancy and so on. You may even applaud, and that would be tasteless.'

Romana glared at the Doctor. 'Quail before the might of Krikkit,' she announced, a little hesitantly, and then blinked.

She looked around herself and blinked some more.

'Well,' she said. 'Doctor, we're no longer on Bethselamin. Is that a good thing?'

'No.'

'Did we defeat the Krikkitmen?'

'No.'

'Which is why they're standing by that swimming pool?'

'Yes.'

'Is the reason why I can't remember anything that I was under their control?'

'Yes.'

'Oh dear. Did I say anything stupid?'

'No,' the Doctor lied.

'That's something. I take it we're not about to heroically defeat them?'

'Probably not.'

'You've got nothing up your sleeve?'

'Not even a handkerchief.'

The Doctor pointed up at the skies between them and the Dust Cloud. 'Somewhere out beyond that Dust Cloud is the planet of Krikkit. Shielded in Slow Time. Invisible from the Universe. Just as they like it. Sadly, their robots don't see it that way. It has remained invisible and isolated for two million years.'

'Or, as far as they're concerned, five years,' Romana calculated. 'Not an encouraging amount of time for much cultural progress towards accepting the rest of existence.'

'Not so much, no.'

Romana surveyed the hotel grounds. The Krikkitmen were all stood around a patch of rock. At a signal, they raised up the trident. It glowed.

'Glowing ancient artefact,' noted Romana. 'Rarely a good thing.'

'Rarely.'

A plinth rose from the rock, sending lava-spewing cracks racing towards the swimming pool. A Krikkitman marched onto the stone altar. A glowing crystal cylinder unscrewed itself from the plinth, rising gently up. It caught and reflected the Dust Cloud. There was an air of racy daring about the cylinder that said 'Go on then.'

The Krikkitman plunged the trident into the crystal, the three prongs vanishing into slots made for them. When it had sunk into the tip, the Krikkitman twisted the handle, and the crystal began to hum.

There are various kind of hums. The control room of the TARDIS has a hum which says, 'It's all going to be fine.' An Earth microcomputer has a hum about it which says, 'Not now, I'm busy doing something more important.' And ancient deadly artefacts tend to emit the sort of hum that says, 'Run.'

The hum turned into a malignant pulse.

The wonderfully pointless Hotel of the Asteroid of the Gate ceased to exist in a flash. So too did most of the nearby Krikkitmen. A beam shot into the vast spaces between the asteroid and the Dust Cloud. For a moment nothing was there. And then a star appeared burning inside it. And, circling it, the planet of Krikkit.

Its reappearance didn't really warrant the soaring voices of the remaining Krikkitmen chanting the planet's name, although they did it anyway.

The planet of Krikkit was back.

As the planet moved towards them, more and more Krikkitmen filed from the Pavilion, until all five million and change stood there, gazing up at the giant, chanting its name.

The Doctor, when he spoke, did so in a murmur. 'That vast army?'

'Did I by any chance release them?'

'We'll get to that later,' the Doctor said gently. 'But don't they seem a little distracted?'

'I would be too,' Romana whispered. 'I've just been given everything I wanted and now I'm free to destroy the Universe again.'

'They're listening to something.'

'What?'

'Let's find out later. The TARDIS is just over there. I think we should run for it.'

The Krikkitmen remained grouped around the glowing pillar. Above them the sky continued to glow as the planet of Krikkit swung closer and closer.

The Doctor paused in the TARDIS doorway. 'Bye then,' he said to them, but his smile didn't reach his eyes. The Doctor was very worried indeed.

The small blue box left the asteroid in a hurry.

Deep inside the TARDIS, the Doctor sat on a deckchair in his workshop. K-9 was perched upside down on his lap.

'Will he be all right?' Romana asked.

'Well, perhaps you lot shouldn't have hit him so hard,' the Doctor muttered through his screwdriver.

'Sorry,' said Romana, and then couldn't resist, 'You're tightening the mergin nut the wrong way.'

'Am not,' said the Doctor, and promptly started turning the nut the other way.

Romana brought the Doctor his tea in a chipped tin mug, then poured hers into a blue china cup. 'It's not been a particularly good day, has it?'

The Doctor searched blindly around for a custard cream. Romana nudged the plate nearer to him.

'Really, you know, I can mend him,' she said.

The Doctor looked up from the dog's traction engine. 'I've got the hang of it by now.' The traction engine burst into flame. He hastily put it out.

'It's fine,' Romana insisted. 'I'm no longer under the control of the Krikkitmen.' She paused, rather defeated. 'You really can trust me.'

'Of course I trust you,' the Doctor muttered, slurping his tea.

'And anyway, if I was still controlled by the Krikkitmen, then I'd have poisoned your tea.'

The Doctor choked.

Romana leant back in her deck chair, dropped a slice of lemon into her cup, and took a delicate sip.

There was a long, awkward silence.

'Perhaps,' said the Doctor eventually, 'you could just have a look at his sensor probe.'

'Delighted,' Romana smiled.

They were back in the control room a few minutes later. The revived K-9 was carrying out a survey of damage to the console. The Doctor had pulled up the planet of Krikkit on the screen.

'Just to summarise,' he said. 'We've let a team of Krikkitmen reassemble the key to their planet's prison, we've freed five million more of them from stasis, and they've brought their home world back into existence. At which point, there's nothing to stop them from replaying their universal war.'

'I'm very sorry about all that,' said Romana sheepishly. 'Not only a not particularly good day, but a long one too.'

The Doctor bowed his head. 'Yes,' he said solemnly. 'And it's not over yet.' He twisted the scanner to one side. The Krikkit Pavilion hung in space, shimmering. It multiplied into an armada of ships.

'How do we stop them?'

'We don't.' The Doctor shrugged. 'I've stopped the odd army. I've diddled the occasional battle fleet. But that is an unstoppable force. And they know how good they are – they didn't even bother killing me. They let me go. That's how little I matter to them.' He sucked a thumb. 'I should feel a little insulted. Actually, I do. I feel a lot insulted.'

K-9 bumped against his knee. It must be quite something if even his dog felt sorry for him.

There was one chance. The Krikkitmen hadn't begun their onslaught against existence. They were waiting for something.

The Doctor twisted the scanner back to Krikkit, and tapped the planet on the screen inside its Dust Cloud. 'Do you know what I'm going to do? I'm going to ignore them back. We'll head to the planet Krikkit.'

'Seriously?' Romana said. 'But those people hate all other life. You're not just going to get a bad reception before you win them over with your bashful charm. They'll tear us apart as soon as we land.'

'I know.' The Doctor nodded. 'And I'm scared stiff. But it's our only chance to stop the Krikkitmen. We're going to go to Krikkit and we're going to reason with them.'

'That always works with genocidal maniacs,' Romana said softly.

'Otherwise the Universe is doomed.' The Doctor flashed her his broadest grin. 'I love a tough crowd. If we're to stand a chance of saving existence, we're going to go to Krikkit and make them change their minds.'

And so they did.

PART TWO

'There's a divinity which shapes our ends, rough hew them how we will.'

William Shakespeare

'List of Galaxies

'This is a dynamic list and may never be able to satisfy particular standards for completeness. You can help by expanding it.'

Wikipedia

CHAPTER NINETEEN
FROM A TO NOT TO BE

For once, Romana was hoping the Doctor would miss. He'd insisted on setting the controls for Krikkit, his face grim. It was a relatively simple journey, but that had never stopped the Doctor from pinging off somewhere else entirely.

Maybe, just this once, that would be nice. A war was about to break out across the stars, and the Doctor had never struck Romana as good at wars. Handy in a skirmish, brilliant at a coup, but not suited for the battlefield. For one thing, wars required patience. If you wanted to win a war, you had to put the hours in. She tried to imagine the Doctor on sentry duty, guarding a gun post. She saw the Doctor making a catalogue of local birdlife, repainting the bunker, planting some tulips and maybe putting up a hammock. She did not see him manning a battle station. He'd probably leave K-9 to do the guarding and go fishing.

The people of Krikkit were also going to go against his nature. The Doctor liked to be liked. He was needy. He enjoyed annoying pompous people, making guards laugh, and winning nice people over. The problem was that there were going to be no nice people on Krikkit. The Krikkitas weren't just immune to the Doctor's charms, they were allergic to them.

She wondered how he'd cope when it all went wrong for him. She pictured the smile sliding off his face. It wasn't going to be good. He'd be genuinely upset. He might even resort to card tricks, and they never went down well.

When the Doctor set the TARDIS controls, she hoped they'd arrive somewhere else. He'd be cross about it, for a bit, but then he'd be bound to get into trouble. There'd be villains to laugh at, cells to escape from, and clever serving girls to win over. He'd enjoy himself, so long as Romana could keep him from noticing the stars going out across the sky.

The TARDIS plummeted through the vortex, and Romana started to calculate the end of *pi* from where she'd last left off. They seemed to be travelling for quite a while. She risked feeling hopeful. She watched the central column of the TARDIS's controls rise and fall, like a great glass bicycle pump puffing them through eternity. Just a few more goes and they'd be well away.

The column fell and went dark.

Was she imagining it, or had the TARDIS gone cold as well?

She shivered.

'Krikkit,' the Doctor announced.

There are rules to exploring strange new worlds. The Doctor habitually ignored all of them. He preferred to throw open the doors and bound out whistling. Perhaps he'd be in a jungle, perhaps he'd be facing a forest of spears, but it would all work out in the end.

For once the Doctor paused before opening the doors. 'We don't know what it's like out there. We've only seen the grim bits. For all we know, Krikkit is a bucolic paradise. It was supposed to be quite leafy.'

He strode out the door and into a grey concrete wall. He edged nervously past it. Romana squeezed out after him, and left K-9 to glide out in a complicated three-point turn that would have made a driving instructor applaud.

The TARDIS had sighed onto a grey street, full of grey walls forming grey houses. It was all thoroughly depressing.

'This is worse than Mareeve.'

'Do you think I should change?' asked Romana. 'Into something grey?'

The Doctor shook his head. 'Don't be like that,' he said. 'We may win them over.'

'Being wilfully conspicuous just makes us easier to shoot at,' she retorted.

The Doctor sniffed. 'Do you think even their death rays are grey?'

K-9 glided ahead. His body merged into the drabness of the road. He seemed quite happy with this development. It might be useful if he was able to camouflage himself.

The Doctor and Romana explored the city, both feeling they were the first people ever to potter along its streets.

The Doctor jammed his hands in his pockets and whistled.

Romana kicked the occasional stone, checking for the echo.

'You know,' the Doctor considered, 'I'm getting a nice feeling about this. Like it's siesta time on a Sunday.'

The Doctor had a point. For all its echoing nature and bland buildings, the city had a sweet, calm air to it. The sun beat amiably down, there was a warm breeze which carried a hint of flowers towards them.

'It's nice enough,' Romana agreed.

Their steps brought them up a gentle slope to a large, inevitably grey, domed building. 'You know what,' the Doctor said. 'I've a rule about architecture. If it looks impressive, investigate. If it's trying to hide, investigate that too. This –' he rubbed his hand against the uninventive brickwork – 'is rather impressive. In its way. I'm sure it'll find its fans.'

'Cathedral? Art Gallery? Cinema?' Romana asked.

The Doctor clearly didn't have an answer. 'Let's pop inside and buy a guidebook,' he suggested.

They walked round the dome until they found a tall door of grey plastic.

'Locked,' said the Doctor. 'Or closed.' His sonic screwdriver hummed, the sound loud in the empty square.

They walked inside. For a moment all was darkness and quiet. Their eyes adjusted to the space as they walked up a path to the centre of the dome. Eventually they could see their surroundings. The building had no chairs, no decorations. It was simply a space.

Standing around them were hundreds and hundreds of people, eyes tightly closed. Saying nothing.

The Doctor cleared his throat. 'Hello there! You're probably worried about what's happened to the sky,' he said in his brightest possible voice. 'Well, good news. I'm an alien!'

Several hundred pairs of eyes snapped open, involuntarily.

The Doctor waved.

Several hundred people blinked and then screamed.

Surrounded by a wall of noise the Doctor and Romana flinched.

The screaming grew louder and louder. It was a scream of pure animal fear and hatred.

Things had gone terribly wrong terribly fast.

The Doctor, K-9 and Romana were running.

Romana had, in her time with the Doctor, learnt a good deal about fleeing. If anyone shouted 'Halt!' or 'Stop!' or 'Wait!' you ignored them. They were normally taking aim.

If given a choice between running upstairs and running downstairs, always go down. Even if the lights weren't working. Often, yes, there'd be something with tentacles lurking in the dark, but you could cross that nightmare when you came to it. Also, with a little bit of dodging, you could let it devour any pursuers while you got on with surviving.

Running upstairs ended badly. You'd find yourself on a roof with nothing but a long drop beneath you and a pressing need to do some fast talking.

Also, if you were with K-9 and faced with anything other than a simple ramp, leave the dog. He could deal with things himself.

Shoes. In her early days aboard the TARDIS, Romana had worn a variety of imposing footwear. The TARDIS wardrobe was delightfully unlike the wardrobes of Gallifrey, and so offered her the chance to enjoy experimenting. Boots. Pumps. Ballet shoes. But she'd quickly learned that anything with heels was out. They were good for making an entrance but hopeless for an exit.

Finally, always follow the Doctor unless he was clearly heading somewhere absolutely idiotic. If it only looked mildly idiotic (e.g. a time corridor or burning building) then fine. But if it was towards a squadron of Daleks then perhaps not.

When fleeing, keep an eye on local signage. Signs indicating 'This way to the Forest of Knives' or 'Turn left for the Swamp of Death' were best heeded. Signs never indicated where there was a large amount of cover, or something blast-proof to hide behind. The Universe was disappointing like that.

The Doctor was delivering a parable while he was running.

'Friend of mine had a Flomgoose. Rescued it when it was a tiny ball of fur at the side of the road. Nursed the poor thing back to health. Let it eat his sofa. Took it for walks. It even slept at the end of the bed, chewing thoughtfully on his duvet. Marvellous, an utterly tame Flomgoose. Naturalist came over to examine it – oh dear, that was a near miss, perhaps we'd better duck behind this and, honestly, sorry about the stairs, K-9, do keep up – a naturalist came over to examine it and declared it had no idea it was a fearsome flesh-eating predator. It didn't help that my friend had called it Mr Snuzzles. Anyway, the naturalist prevailed on my friend to give Mr Snuzzles to a zoo where he could meet other Flomgeese and get on with the job of tearing animal carcases to shreds. Reluctantly, my friend complied, and waved a fond farewell to his pet. It trotted off into the enclosure, had a sniff and a chew and seemed quite content. Until another Flomgoose emerged from its glom pit – oh, hang on, that was a bit close. I hate it when they can shoot straight. Romana, I do believe he's singed your collar – Where were we? Ah yes, glom pit. So the other Flomgeese emerged, and made to welcome Mr Snuzzles … only he was staring at them in horror. The naturalist had said they'd all roll in the mud and then go for a meal together. The zoo had some tasty giraffes. Instead, Mr Snuzzles hissed in outrage. It had no idea that there was such a thing as another Flomgoose. It found the idea appalling. No matter what the other Flomgeese did – rolling invitingly in mud, bringing the newcomer fresh bits of giraffe – no dice. It just sat on its haunches and howled, until the pack retreated into the glom pit looking, it has to be said, a little bit miffed. They'd offered the bleeding paw of friendship and it had been spurned. Realising his mistake, my friend took his pet back. The creature hissed all the way home. At which point, Mr Snuzzles stopped hissing, ate my friend's bed, fell fast asleep on the remains. My friend figured that was fair enough. Goodness, are those flamethrowers? Anyway, the point is that some things just can't get along with other things, no matter how sensible it would be if they did. Let's turn left and – what on earth …?'

Romana was pointing firmly. There were figures in cloaks standing at the end of a street, gesturing to them. Figures in cloaks were, in her experience, either a good thing leading to a swift revolution or a very bad thing leading to a quick lie-down on a sacrificial altar. Romana had grown used to being regularly offered up for sacrifice. The Doctor said she had the neck for it. In the beginning it had been terrifying – you know, being grabbed, tied up, and gabbled over by a bunch of ne'er-do-wells who just wouldn't listen to her lectures on the merits of comparative religions.[5]

There was an overall theme to being sacrificed – you met a species, they took against you, the Doctor rescued you in the nick of time – that provided the comfort of familiar patterns. Sometimes she'd return the favour. She tried not to take being sacrificed personally, or let it get to her. It was just aliens letting off steam, and frankly, these cults normally lived in drab places with too much sand or a surfeit of swamp, so perhaps she couldn't

---

[5] 'This is all very well,' she'd told a high priest once, 'but splendid as your god no doubt is, I'm afraid she is either non-existent or a folk memory of a visit by an alien tourist. Much as that visit may have meant a good deal to your ancestors, and no matter how many times the visitor may have promised that they were coming back, you have to realise that space tourists are fickle beings and the next year they made for somewhere with a better beach. Anyway, even if that theory can be discounted and you wish to harp on about how your god is the one true god, do you have any idea how many one true gods there are out there? Literally, I couldn't even make you a list, and I am good at lists. There's a primal *Ur* urge to find solace from existence in a codified deity figure – gods are like a warm blanket for slightly chilly thoughts. Put simply, supposing your god – what was she again – Shuba the Sand Snake? –was the one true god of salvation, isn't that a little bit unfair on the rest of the Universe who've never made it to your rather arid world? All those billions and billions of souls who have no idea that Shuba offers the key to eternal life because they've not discovered light speed overdrive? Doesn't that seem a bit mean of Shuba?

'I suppose there's the theory that all the various gods are simply different facets of a vast underlying spirit that holds the Universe together. But that's only good so long as you're very generic and don't draw up a spreadsheet. Because then it all gets hazy. Some gods absolutely forbid sacrifice, you know, whereas Shuba seems to just love having strangers skewered with a long and dirty knife. That's just one example – how could you reconcile all the conflicting rules? Well, you can't. Bit of a facer isn't it? Perhaps you should think long and hard about your life choices. Or, yes, bring out the gag. But that's not solving the problem is it, it's simply— *mrrf*.'

blame them for making their own entertainment. She didn't feel *that* afraid at being sacrificed any more – like waiting for a bus, it was uncomfortable, not ideal, but something would always turn up eventually. On a good day, if the altar was good and flat, you could have a nap.

Naps were a thing the Doctor refused to recognise. He spent all his time in such a dervish of activity that the idea of grabbing a book, plumping a cushion, and drifting off for a few moments had entirely passed him by. Well, so he claimed. She wondered if he secretly pottered off for forty winks while she was being tied up and generally manhandled. It would explain why he always turned up at the last minute and looking so refreshed.

Anyway, the figures in cloaks prodded them with long sticks and soon they were in a forest. 'Oh good,' said Romana. 'Soon there'll be a clearing with a sacrificial stone.' She looked down at her dress and hoped for a clean slab. The TARDIS laundry was surprisingly bad at tackling bloodstains.

'Let's not be hasty,' said the Doctor, which made her scoff. 'These might be friendly people with sharp pointy sticks.'

K-9 was trundling beside them. He uttered a little cough.

'Got something to say, K-9?' the Doctor enquired.

The dog said nothing.

Well, the dog was with them. That was something. At the last moment, provided his batteries held out, he could shoot a few of the cloaked figures and he and Romana could make their escape. Maybe.

They were shoved into the inevitable clearing and the figures retreated.

There was no sign of an altar which, all things considered, seemed a pity. Nor was there a stake and a pile of kindling, or even a cauldron. Just an empty patch of scrub.

'Look up,' a voice said.

Obligingly, perhaps too obligingly, they looked up.

'Dust Cloud, barely a sign of a genocidal army, starry starry night,' the Doctor remarked.

The voice echoed again. 'The stars have returned. And they've changed. They're calling it the Great Shift. Does it mean that the rest of the Universe has wiped itself out and you're the last two beings come to us for mercy?'

'No.' The Doctor's hands were in his pockets. 'I'm afraid the rest of the Universe is alive and kicking.'

The cloaked figures pressed back against the trees and hissed.

The owner of the voice shuffled closer. 'Aliens! Why have you come? You disgust us.'

'Um,' said the Doctor. 'Truth is, there's been an accident. Thought we'd pop in and check you were tickety-boo.'

The figure dragged itself closer. The mouth was hidden behind a mask. The voice was twisted with disgust. 'And you dared – *dared* – walk amongst us?'

'Yes,' Romana admitted brightly. 'You probably can't help, but is there any chance you can direct us towards, some nice, forward-thinking rebels?'

The shape underneath the cloak was strange, gathered together tightly. 'Forgive me,' the figure said. Romana realised it was a woman's voice. 'We're fine … with the idea of you … in theory … we don't object … but to actually meet you … in the flesh … is …' She swallowed, and coughed wetly. 'Actually, excuse me,' the figure dashed off behind a tree.

The Doctor and Romana didn't meet each other's eyes. This wasn't going well.

The figure staggered back from behind the tree. 'Do you have to be quite so disgusting?' she groaned. 'Would it hurt you to be less repellent?'

'Nonsense,' Romana retorted. 'We're neither disgusting nor repellent. We are simply slightly different to you. There nothing wrong with that.'

The crowd around them hissed.

'There is everything wrong with that,' the woman groaned.

The Doctor's mood had improved. He was rubbing his hands.

'Please, don't do that,' the figure shuddered. 'That thing with your hands ...'

The Doctor stopped rubbing his hands.

'You're wearing cloaks and masks, and you're gathered in a clearing. That's a good sign. You seem to be an angry young woman – I like that too.'

Romana leant against a tree stump and checked her watch. 'He'll give a speech. It'll be terribly rousing. If you've heard of Shakespeare you'll recognise a few bits. For a few brief moments you'll forget the appalling risk and the terrible consequences and run off to save the day.'

She realised the Doctor was staring at her. 'Sorry, recently had my mind taken over. I seem incapable of lying at the moment.' She smiled sweetly. 'Anyway, the Doctor's good at this. Sometimes.'

The Doctor cleared his throat. 'Rebels of Krikkit,' he began. Then he paused. 'We haven't settled that question, have we? I mean, you are the Rebels?'

The woman in the cloak lowered her gaze. 'We'd like to be,' she admitted. 'We have a few problems. For one thing, and I'm sorry, your appearance is far more disgusting than I thought possible.'

'Thank you,' the Doctor beamed. 'I didn't have my hair done specially.'

'For another thing –' the woman tugged her cape down further over her eyes and dropped her voice – 'we're having trouble nailing our Mission Statement.'

'Crumbs,' said the Doctor.

CHAPTER TWENTY
A SHORT HISTORY OF THE REBELLION ON KRIKKIT

Something strange had happened to the planet of Krikkit. For a long time, during the endless aeons of war, the world had acted as one mind. One very angry mind.

After they'd lost, that anger had only intensified. Of course they'd been right to hate the Universe – why, look at what it was doing to them now.

And yet, over the last five years (or two million, depending on where you stood), people had begun to question this single-minded stance.

Mostly this was for a reason that will become apparent. But, before the curtain of isolation had fallen completely, some odd ideas had made their way through into Slow Time.

'The thing is, Doctor, we're aware of you,' said the Rebel Leader.

'You are?' The Doctor failed not to look flattered.

'Not you specifically, but of the work that people like you are doing saving the Universe. Have you a costume?'

The Doctor pointed at his clothes and tugged at his scarf.

'Nothing more impressive? With armour? And figure hugging?'

The Doctor nibbled the edge of his scarf.

'Perhaps an insignia? Worn over your chest?'

The Doctor gave out the longest breath. 'Clearly, you people have been on the receiving end of some strange ideas. If I could just have a moment—'

The Rebel Leader cut him off. 'What is your plan, Doctor? Your plan for saving our planet?'

'Well, um …' The Doctor's eyes shuffled around the clearing. He nudged Romana. She stared at the floor and appeared to be whistling. 'Something or other normally comes to me and it all works out fine.'

The Rebel Leader made a noise which was even more disgusted than usual. 'You *don't* have a plan?'

'No.'

The rebels looked at each other. There was some muttering. The Rebel Leader strode forward. 'We need a plan. Not a full breakdown. Just a treatment, you know, outlining your ideas.'

'It's not the sort of thing I do. I could get K-9 to rustle up something, but I can't promise to stick to it.'

The Rebel Leader shook her head. 'You're expecting us to commit the future history of this planet to your whims?'

'They're nice whims.'

Beneath her mask, the Rebel Leader frowned. 'It's just not good enough, Doctor. We're not asking much. We'd settle for a one-pager.'

'Well, maybe, Romana, could you jot something down?'

Romana demurred. 'Oh, I'd love to, Doctor, but I'm still feeling faint from all that mind control.'

Et tu, Brute? The Doctor turned back to the Rebel Leader. 'Suppose I did scribble some ideas … what kind of approval system would there be?'

'Oh, we'd definitely go over it quite quickly.' The Rebel Leader had brightened considerably. Her comrades were nodding the bright relieved nods of people seizing a chance to do nothing at all. 'So long as it's something original. No sense in rehashing old ground, is there?'

'Indeed not.' The Doctor was sounding hoarse.

The Rebel Leader was finding her feet. 'And we'd need to cost it out – have you a thumbnail budget we can price up?'

'Rebellions aren't what they used to be,' the Doctor growled, and stomped out of the clearing.

'It's just a bit of Paperwork,' began Romana gently. She'd found him kicking a tree.

'Paperwork? Ptchah!' the Doctor thundered. 'They've been got at! This rebellion is grinding to a halt. Once I've dealt with the Krikkitmen I'm going after Paperwork.'

It isn't exactly true to say that Paperwork is evil. Most people wouldn't be surprised to know that Paperwork breeds prolifically. If you told them Paperwork was actually a pan-sentient life form capable of inhabiting any medium, they would shrug and say, 'Oh well, that makes sense.'

Paperwork long ago worked out the best way of surviving was through a peculiarly aggressive form of camouflage – it makes itself clearly visible but ensures that no one wants to look at it. The Universe's filing cabinets and inboxes are filled with species of Paperwork, lingering blissfully neglected. An entire tribe was found hiding in an envelope under a pizza delivery menu. Whole colonies exist in the increasingly worrying print at the back of pension statements, and a rare genus lies entirely undiscovered in the Terms and Conditions of the Barbican's ticketing website. Most types of Paperwork are dormant, shy, fairly pointless creatures, but some have risen up and taken power. The conditions for such an evolutionary marvel have to be terribly specific. So, most of the time, Paperwork thrives by being ignored but, in some rare cases, this does not happen. Quite the opposite. Instead, people worship it, applauding in delight as it multiplies. They do all they can to encourage its endless proliferation to the consumption of all other purposes. There was a particularly nasty outbreak in the Soviet Union (crushed only when there was a cold snap and they ran out of firewood). After a group of housewives failed to come home for forty years, another equally virulent strain was found lurking in a Bingo hall in Pontypridd.

So far, only one institution in the Universe has become so overwhelmed by Paperwork that its employees sometimes struggle to remember what it is for. The name of this organisation is the British Broadcasting Corporation.

Romana had once worked at the BBC, a brief stint producing a radio programme about troubled cow owners. She and the Doctor had been hunting down the Celestial Toymaker, who had taken over the Light Entertainment Department (with terrible consequences for humanity, and a remarkable increase in viewing figures). The experience had made her realise that the Time Lords were a beacon of sizzling efficiency by comparison to the BBC, where roomfuls of people fought to get something done in between the filing and the exhausting lunches.

'I have an idea,' she announced. The Doctor looked at her gratefully.

She went over to the Rebel Leader.

'Hello,' she said, her voice so bright it edged into trilling. 'About this plan you were looking for – I was wondering, have you a template we can use? Or one of your favourite plans we can study? Just to get to grips with the format.'

The Rebel Leader's face fell. 'Oh. We've not exactly carried any plans through ... We've done modelling, of course ...'

'Not to worry.' Sensing an advantage, Romana pressed home. 'If you can supply us with the approved forms then I'll get right on it.'

'The ... approved ... forms?' The Rebel Leader frowned.

'Absolutely. We don't want to set a precedent now, do we?' Romana nodded encouragingly. 'In triplicate.'

'I'll – I'll see what I can do.' The Rebel Leader looked uncertain.

'And, of course,' Romana hurried ahead, 'you can't supply it to me until I've filled out a stationery requisition form. That just wouldn't do, would it?'

'Well, no.' The Rebel Leader found a lot to interest her in her boots.

'And some pens,' added Romana. 'One of each colour.'

'Look, can I have a word and get back to you?' The Rebel Leader headed off.

Romana nodded to herself. The BBC had taught her two things. Firstly, that it was impossible to get actual paper out of an organisation obsessed with Paperwork. Secondly, how hard it was to deliver lambs whilst undergoing marital difficulties.

Gradually, the clearing emptied, muttering about meetings to attend and strategies to implement. Finally, when Romana thought herself alone, she exhaled.

'Nice work,' said a voice.

Sat on a tree stump was the Rebel Leader. She was breathing heavily and there was something wrong with her. Romana squinted and finally worked it out.

'Are you pregnant?'

The woman laughed. 'What gave it away?' She patted the tree trunk and Romana sat next to her. For a moment Romana listened to the woman's pained breathing. She waved away an offer of help.

Feeling at a loss for what to do, Romana told her her lovely long name.

'I'm Jal,' the Rebel said. She stood up, arching her back as she did so, and taking long, painful strides around the woods.

'Are you all right?' Romana asked. 'I mean, wouldn't you be better off at home—'

The look on Jal's face silenced her. 'You think I should be at home knitting?'

'Oh no.' Romana frowned. 'I was thinking of sitting in a quiet corner with some algebra. It's supposed to help improve the intellect of the spawn.'

'You aliens are awful.' Jal winced, and then snorted with laughter. 'I got involved in this movement because I'm pregnant. And no, it's not because my lover used to be the leader but got tragically gunned down.'

Romana had been about to suggest nothing of the sort.

'I just got involved because this —' Jal pointed at the sky and the trees — 'seemed an insane world to bring a child into. Just because the rest of the Universe can't be seen doesn't mean we've forgotten it's out there. I find it hard to be near you, but that doesn't mean that my child won't be better at it. Children always bring progress.' She patted the bump proudly.

Romana reached out a hand. 'Can I touch it?'

'No.' Jal stepped back hurriedly. 'I'm trying. We all are. But lately, it's been so difficult to get something done. I don't understand why. All we're asking from the Doctor is a little ... structure.'

'I've been asking for that from him for a long time,' Romana sighed.

'Not a structure person?'

'No.'

'Structure's the one thing we need on Krikkit.' Jal's eyes rested on Romana, and she was smiling the saddest smile. 'Being sealed up here – it has been strange.'

There are all sorts of words to describe what happened to the people of Krikkit after they were locked away. The closest analogy is going up to someone who is paranoid, telling them, 'You're right, everyone is plotting against you,' and then handing them a brown envelope stuffed with proof.

The people of Krikkit had thought themselves alone in creation. They'd discovered this not to be the case. Instinct told them that all other life was wrong and must be wiped out because ... it wasn't like them. They'd followed this plan thoroughly, and, when, unfairly, they'd failed, the rest of the Universe had responded by telling them they wanted nothing further to do with them. It was a pretty classic example of doubling down.

Faced with the knowledge that the Universe was done with them, the people of Krikkit did not react with bitter self-recrimination. Safe in the knowledge that the next time they saw the Universe, it would be a dead wasteland unable to answer back, they blamed everyone else in the Universe except themselves.

The Elders of Krikkit, the people responsible for their current isolation, didn't even shrug and say, 'Well, we gave it a try.' With only a whiff of a sulk, they decided that the thing their first go at universal obliteration had lacked was conviction.

The Elders had devoted themselves even more to their sacred cause, casting out such namby-pamby ideas as waiting until the rest of creation died, and instead threw themselves into making ...

Jal had narrated all this to Romana. Her voice was strong, clear, and angry. The Doctor had slipped into the glade unnoticed. He'd been kicking a tree, waiting for someone to come and find him. No one had done this, so he'd gone to find out why.

As he'd entered the clearing, he heard Jal saying, 'They threw themselves into making the Ultimate Weapon.'

'Ultimate Weapon?' The Doctor was magnificently alarmed. 'Oh, I never like the sound of those. How's it going?'

Jal frowned. Romana looked cross. 'We were just getting to that, Doctor.'

'Please don't let me interrupt you.' The Doctor fell briefly silent. 'Only ... do you know if this Ultimate Weapon has a big red button? They always come in handy.'

'Doctor—'

'Sorry, keeping quiet now. Silent. As a ghost. As a Trappist ghost.'

'Even now—'

'And a Trappist ghost is very quiet indeed.'

Jal continued her tale. Even now the Elders of Krikkit were putting the finishing touches to their Ultimate Weapon. Their pronouncements made it sound as though at any moment the planet would emerge from its prison prematurely and wipe out all remaining life in the Universe. The idea of waiting was just too much for their souls to bear. ('Wait,' interjected the Doctor. 'How could they know that the Slow Time barrier was going to collapse? How?' No one answered him.)

An Ultimate Weapon was proving popular among the people. Living on their planet had previously felt like all they'd needed. Now it felt stifling. Worse was the choking feeling that out there the rest of creation continued, living and teeming and laughing at them. Meanwhile the people of Krikkit were trapped in their bubble and there was nothing they could do.

At first their existence had been splendidly solitary.

Now it was a throttling confinement. One that they simply had to escape from and do something about.

There was dissent. It came in the form of two groups.

The first, the Balance of Nature Party, was loosely headed by environmental scientists who held that things would get a bit wobbly if you wiped the rest of the Universe out. They couldn't quite put their finger on this other than that it felt a bit finky and there might be consequences.

The second group were the Veterans of the Great Krikkit War. These were soldiers who had come into prolonged contact with other life forms. Some had been interred in rehabilitation camps, tended in hospitals, or had just had 'Why???' screamed at them by anguished widows. At the time they'd remained splendidly impassive. But, when they'd got home, they found themselves unable to an answer that *Why* question. Much as the rest of existence upset them, individually, the peoples of the Universe didn't seem that bad. The war veterans were troubled. Having met other life, they weren't sure why they'd wanted to destroy it. It was a sobering thought.

The Elders of Krikkit dismissed these two groups easily. They announced there was no evidence that anything bad would happen if they wiped out the rest of creation. They dismissed the veterans as disturbed victims of the war and offered them lots of deliberately tedious therapy, including the weaving of wicker baskets and the filling out of forms.

The Elders pressed on with the Ultimate Weapon. Only there was a problem. Firstly, there was suddenly a lot more paperwork than before. Secondly, there was less progress. Something was going wrong.

'It was the Balance of Nature Party who spotted it,' Jal said. 'They were sheepish about it. They'd found they were just going over old ground in their arguments, rehashing old theories and not making any progress. They blamed the Slow Time envelope. They blamed each other. Then they blamed the Universe and realised that was a bit ...'

'Problematic?' suggested Romana.

Jal nodded. 'Absolutely. As soon as you admit that your problems aren't the Universe's fault then you'll get somewhere.'

'Really?' The Doctor frowned. 'Blaming the Universe is the only way I can get out of bed in the morning.'

K-9 and Romana glanced at each other.

The Doctor tapped the table. 'So, what was the conclusion of your scientists?'

Jal paused. 'This is going to sound silly.'

'Most of my favourite things do.'

'The scientists declared they'd run out of science.'

As progress slowed, paperwork increased. The Elders of Krikkit were reluctant to admit that they had a problem. Building an Ultimate Weapon should have been child's play. Surely they could knock something out in a few weeks. Weeks became months became five years. Their entire scientific elite was working on the Ultimate Weapon and it was still in 'testing'. Eventually they drafted, redrafted, and laboriously signed off (in triplicate) an announcement that blamed their problems on the rest of the Universe.

'See?' The Doctor nodded. 'It's not just me.'

They claimed that something had been put into the Slow Time field that decreased their intellectual advancement. It was a terrible accusation, and one that played well. Supporting documentation was released, which no one quite managed to read. The accusation was that the whole race of Krikkit had been deliberately retarded by the rest of the Universe.

'Well, strictly speaking, that's true,' said Romana to a shocked response. 'It *is* true. We've slowed your rate of temporal progression, but that shouldn't interfere with your intellectual evolution. Unless … well, Slow Time's never been tested on an entire species before.'

'Whose side are you on?' asked the Doctor.

'I'm not sure.' Romana sucked a thumb thoughtfully.

Jal was walking up and down, her hands stroking her belly. 'There are theories that the rate of intellectual progress is inverse to the time passing in the wider Universe. Some calculated that we've been in this envelope for as long as ten thousand years.'

'Correction,' piped up K-9 unhelpfully. 'During the five years that have passed inside this time envelope, two million years have passed in the Universe outside.'

Everyone stared at the dog in horror.

'Furthermore,' the dog rattled on until even Romana was casting around for a boot to throw, 'the time envelope has now ceased to operate. This was caused by the Krikkitmen. All five million existing units have been released and are relaunching their plan of universal destruction.'

The Rebel Leader grasped her stomach. 'Oh,' she winced. She waved away the Doctor's offer of assistance. 'I don't think it's the baby.' She closed her eyes for a moment, trying to arrange her features into some semblance of calm.

'Sorry about my dog,' the Doctor whispered. 'He's so terribly truthful. It's why we came to this planet – to tell you the Krikkitmen are back.'

Jal's eyes remained closed. 'What do I tell my people?' she muttered back. 'If the Krikkitmen are released then it's already too late.'

'Oh, we should have a head start,' said the Doctor. 'They're currently outside the Dust Cloud. They'll work out a plan, and then show themselves on this world. You've got a while.'

At which point, of course, a Krikkitman strode into the clearing.

CHAPTER TWENTY-ONE
A MARRIAGE OF INCONVENIENCE

Even though he knew it was hopeless, K-9 opened fire on the Krikkitman. The Doctor grabbed a fallen branch and ran forward, while Romana placed herself between the Krikkitman and the Rebels. 'Run,' she yelled at them. 'Please, save yourselves!'

Nobody moved. They stood, rooted to the spot as the Doctor battered the white robot and K-9's blaster chewed ineffectually at the machine's armour.

Jal cleared her throat. 'Please stop attacking my husband,' she said.

Once the Doctor had stopped boggling, the Krikkitman made them tea, working with quiet industry at a camp fire, while the rebels watched.

'It's strange,' said Romana. 'Seeing him, I have a primal urge to scream.'

Jal smiled. 'Now you know how we feel about you. Although, truthfully, the nausea I'm now feeling may be more down to the baby.' As she said this, the Krikkitman approached her with a mug.

'Here you go, my sweetness.' The robot's voice was unsettlingly mellifluous. 'I've prepared wortle bark with honey.'

'You're an angel,' said Jal, sipping at the mug. Romana found she was stifling the desire to knock the mug from her hands.

The Krikkitman returned with a mug for her. Romana took it, trying not to flinch as the robot's hand brushed hers. The fingers were white and felt like bone. 'It is an infusion of wild berries,' he said. 'Perhaps a little unusual but, I am assured quite, refreshing.'

Romana made a pretence of sipping politely, then discovered the brew tasted warm and ripe against her lips. For the first time in hours she felt herself relaxing.

'I know,' said the robot. 'Heavenly, isn't it?'

Romana glanced over to where the Doctor was, once more, kicking a tree.

'Should I take your friend a cup?' the robot ventured.

Romana shook her head. 'He's had to do a lot of thinking today. I'm surprised his head is still attached.'

The red lights deep inside the Krikkitman's helmet smiled. 'I understand. I must be unnerving to you.'

'Putting it mildly,' Romana admitted. 'I hope that doesn't offend you.'

'Not at all.' The robot took Jal's hand and rubbed it gently. 'I am a manufacturing error. The rebels found me on a scrapheap and were kind enough to take me in.'

'Actually,' Jal coughed, 'we were looking for spare parts to cannibalise.'

'Sadly, I was of little use,' the robot offered, and the red lights of his face twitched down. 'I am outside the main control circuit, which is why I was junked. Apparently I am not unique. When the Elders restarted production of the Krikkitmen, something went wrong with the process.'

'Ah-ha!' The Doctor strode back into the group, grabbed Romana's tea, swigged it and smacked his lips. 'Delicious and exactly what I thought. They can't make any more Krikkitmen for themselves. Because something's missing in the manufacturing process, isn't it?' He tapped the Krikkitman on the helmet.

Typical of the Doctor, thought Romana. Sulk until you spotted a chance to be the cleverest person in the room. Still, she was curious to know what he'd come up with.

The robot was puzzled. 'No part of the manufacturing process had been changed. Nothing had been left out.'

'Ha!' The Doctor boomed again. 'Nothing had been left out, but something hadn't been put in.'

The red lights of the robot frowned. 'I do not understand.'

'I'll try again,' the Doctor finished the last of the tea and handed it back to Romana. 'Perhaps something wasn't *able* to get in.'

'He's being deliberately obtuse,' Romana apologised to the rebels. 'There's no use asking. You won't get a thing out of him. Not until he can get the most attention.'

The Doctor pouted. 'That's unfair—'

'Negative,' affirmed K-9. The robot dog had been examining the Krikkitman with curiosity. His tail was now wagging. 'My analysis suggests this Krikkitman is indeed independent and possessed of a high degree of intellect and free will.'

'Why, thank you.' The Krikkitman bowed. 'I'll make more tea.'

Jal held up a hand. 'Don't wait on them hand and foot. They're aliens. Also, they tried to kill you.'

The robot waved this away. 'A simple misunderstanding. How was the wortle brew?'

'Soothing.' Jal leaned against the robot, a radiant smile on her face. 'You're a marvel.'

The Doctor and Romana surveyed the surprisingly domestic scene. Jal caught Romana's horrified gaze.

'Sir looks after me,' she said. 'Which is a lot more than the baby's father ever did.'

'Sir?'

'They call me "Sir Robot",' said the Krikkitman proudly. 'It is not an apt, or even a good name. But it is what I have, and I make the best of it.'

As often happened when tea was produced, the Doctor became congenial. Within half an hour, he was on sincerely friendly terms with Sir Robot. If only, reflected Romana, news of this leaked out. She imagined the Cyber Controller advancing on the Doctor with a teapot and some digestives. Romana wasn't quite so convinced – she kept staring at Sir Robot's head, seeing if she could pick up that itch in her mind from when they'd possessed her. Nothing. The tame Krikkitman was clearly quite an aberration. But that was odd – why would the mighty war factories of Krikkit suddenly be only capable of producing friendly machines?

Sir Robot was suggesting that now might be a good moment for the Doctor to reveal his plans for gaining control of the planet.

'Are you sure?' The Doctor wasn't convinced.

'I'm certain they'll be very good, if I may say so.' The Krikkitman appealed to the Doctor's vanity, a move which rarely failed. 'And I've got a stew on the go for afterwards.'

'Wouldn't want to miss stew,' the Doctor chuckled. 'Oh well, if I must.' He faced the group with the bashfulness of an amateur pianist who always brings along a satchel stuffed full of Mozart just in case. 'Well, perhaps I've got a little something.' He cleared his throat.

'Unaccustomed as I am to public speaking,' the Doctor boomed with easy familiarity, 'I find myself before you, urging you to rise up against your oppressors and save the Universe.'

Romana recognised the speech. It was guaranteed to be inspiring whilst also deliberately vague. The plan, which was definitely not being made up on the spur of the moment would centre on attacking a base / a dome / a castle and probably splitting the rebels up into two or three teams. One team would go with the Doctor to do the general confronting and gloating at the villain's expense. The other team would go with Romana and / or K-9 and get to pull off an exciting victory just in case the Doctor's Plan A of bombast and whimsy didn't quite work out.

Romana let the Doctor's words float over her. She got the picture. The Krikkitmen were out there, beyond the cloud, preparing to conquer the Universe. Somewhere on this planet, their creators were at work on an Ultimate Weapon. 'Now, Romana's experienced in dealing with Ultimate Weapons.' (*Oh great.*) 'But before she can act, it would help her to know what its name is. So – what's this Ultimate Weapon called?'

Jal frowned. 'The Supernova Bomb.'

The Doctor burst out laughing.

'That could have gone better,' said Romana.

'Shut up,' said the Doctor, his hat jammed over his eyes.

'The Mistress is correct.' K-9's lack of tact showed itself proudly.

They were sat at the edge of a clearing. The Rebels were currently giving them a wide berth.

'You should apologise, you know.' Romana was tiptoeing across a meringue of tact. 'People don't like having their Ultimate Weapons insulted. Even if they'd gladly disable it, it's a matter of pride.'

'But really,' the Doctor said. 'The name sounds silly. If it works, the concept is audaciously awful. But I suspect it's merely a label for an exceedingly big bomb.'

'Go back to them, explain it's an error of the TARDIS's translation circuits, then tell them that K-9 and I will dismantle it.'

'Will you?'

'We'll do our best, won't we K-9?'

'Affirmative, Mistress.'

'After all, we can't let someone succeed with a device that sounds like a cheap cocktail.'

The Doctor smiled. 'Oh, it does, doesn't it? That's why it's been nagging at the back of my head. Romana, if the Ultimate Weapon turns out to be blue with a little paper umbrella then I'm buying you the lunch that goes with it.' He bounded to his feet, face a mask of contrition. He was clearly all ready to make the magnanimous apology and win the entire rebel army back over to his side. He took three strides and then ground to a halt.

'Romana,' he hissed. 'You know what? I've just remembered. I have heard of the Supernova Bomb before, and it definitely isn't a drink.'

It is always dangerous to go inside the Doctor's mind. Several psychologists and mind probes have had a go. The Doctor himself once spent a frantic afternoon inside his own head looking for a prawn. The psychologists gave up and went for a lie-down in a darkened room; the mind probes blunted themselves and asked to retrain as food processors; and the prawn's plan to invade the Universe ended shortly after it locked itself deliciously in an oven.

The only person therefore able to describe the inside of the Doctor's head was also the least reliable. If you'd asked the Doctor, he'd have told you it was like having a head full of clever candyfloss. He'd then have tried to mend your food processor, which would have been sidling nervously away from him.

At exactly that moment, the Doctor's mind looked like a series of toy soldiers arranged on a chessboard. One of the soldiers (its missing leg replaced with a matchstick) was waving a banner. It said, 'SUPERNOVA BOMB???' Another soldier (pushing a pram) was muttering about 'Suspended Scientific Advancement'. A small group of soldiers playing football with a marble were discussing the relative differences between sentient robots and artificial intelligences. A soldier, trying to knit thread with his rifle, was worrying that it had missed something in all those hints on Gallifrey. Another soldier was triumphantly surfing on his green plastic base, yelling about how odd it was that a grand plan could simultaneously take five years and also several million. Another soldier agreed, and was ringing a vague bell – an actual vague bell, its stopper wrapped in cotton wool.

Careering wildly across the board was a wind-up rubber duck, quacking over and over again that it was the end of the Universe.

Outside his head, the Doctor looked Romana seriously in the eye. 'I'm starting to suspect that there's something outside the pattern of events that we're entirely missing.'

'I'm missing it too?' Romana queried.

'Even you,' the Doctor intoned. 'Something else is going on here and I can't formulate what it is, let alone what it isn't. Hey ho.' He strode back over to the rebels. Booming at the top of his lungs, his voice wrapped itself around everyone's shoulders. 'Forgive me. You were right and I was wrong. Something bad is happening. Something bigger even than your Ultimate Weapon. And we've got to find out what it is pretty quickly, because out there the Krikkitmen are preparing to launch an attack on the Galaxy.'

He pointed at the rebels, seemingly vaguely, seemingly singling each and every one of them out. 'I may not have a plan, I don't believe in budgets, and I have trouble taking myself seriously, but I'm the Doctor and, if you don't join me, then it's curtains for creation. You with me? You are! And what about you? Good.' The Doctor strode off and the rebels followed him, cheering.

Romana knelt down to K-9. 'How does he do it?' she asked.

'Unknown, Mistress,' the dog said.

CHAPTER TWENTY-TWO
PARLIAMENT OF FOOLS

The Parliament of the Elders of Krikkit was the kind of building you'd expect it to be. Grand grey pavilions led to a central building which thought highly of itself. The building's smugness expressed itself in more concrete columns than were strictly necessary. The Parliament clearly hoped that people would describe it as an edifice, or, at the least, as formidable.

The Doctor and Romana were wearing cloaks, in the hope that this would stop people from pointing and hissing in their direction. The Rebels were flitting dramatically from shadow to shadow in the colonnades.

'I think this may be their first guerrilla raid,' Romana whispered to the Doctor, who nodded. 'Still,' she continued, 'I don't think we're in much danger. K-9 says there are no life signs in the building.'

'Of course not.' The Doctor pretended not to be pleased. 'It's after hours. The Krikkitas are notorious about their timekeeping.'

'But that doesn't seem quite right.' Romana pulled at the hood on her cloak and wondered if it would look nice trimmed with gold braid. 'After all, if they have got a Supernova Bomb in there ...'

'Paff.' The Doctor shrugged. 'As far as they know, their rebellion is mostly academic theory and disgruntled veterans. That lot would have trouble organising a farmer's market. They don't know we're here.'

'What about the several thousand people who chased us through the city?'

'Hmm,' the Doctor conceded. 'Perhaps we should expect trouble.'

They neared the front of the Parliament. The rebels creeping stealthily in phalanxes to the door, the Doctor and Romana crunching over the gravel.

'What worries me is the Krikkitmen,' Romana said. 'I mean, shouldn't we be doing something about them? I could borrow the TARDIS and ...'

The Doctor held up a hand. 'The last time my TARDIS was borrowed it was by me, and look how that played out. I dread to think what the overdue fines are. No, we're going to sort out the planet of Krikkit first. The Krikkitmen can only be told to stop by their own creators; no one else will do. And besides, if they have built a Supernova Bomb, then the invasion of the Krikkitmen is simply the prawn cocktail before a truly dreadful main course.'

They walked on a bit. The grand granite doors of the Parliament of the Elders of Krikkit had been lovingly carved with scenes from the devastating conflict. Krikkitmen sliced their way through various alien races. Suns exploded. Battle fleets disintegrated.

'They do harp on about past glories.' The Doctor tried the door. It was locked. He produced his sonic screwdriver.

'There's another reason why you want me here,' Romana said.

'Oh, is there?' The Doctor started whistling.

'You might not trust me. What if the Krikkitmen are still controlling my mind?'

The Doctor stopped whistling abruptly. 'It would make it easier to find out what they were up to.'

'You're worried about me, aren't you?' Romana grinned.

The Doctor poked the sonic screwdriver into the lock. It buzzed furiously.

'That's touching,' Romana said. 'I'm grateful.'

'Are you? That's nice.' The Doctor rattled the door. It still didn't open. 'I'm just worried about five million homicidal robots under your command.'

'You should be.' Romana gestured for the Doctor to step back from the lock. 'K-9,' she commanded, 'kill that door.'

The Doctor ventured down the corridor, worried for the Universe. What if Romana was right? What if Romana was wrong? Neither outcome seemed favourable.

K-9 nudged up against his leg. The dog was whirring along in stealth mode, which was like playing Grandmother's Footsteps with a lawnmower.

'Master?' the dog asked.

'Yes?'

'Query: What is the purpose of this incursion?'

'We're looking for, in no particular order, an ultimate weapon, the plans to the ultimate weapon, and a clue as to how to defeat the Krikkitmen. Can you download a map?'

K-9's ears wiggled. The dog was remarkable. He could hack into a data stream somewhere so remote it couldn't even get a radio signal, such as the Moons of Stabras Beta, or Somerset. 'Downloading building plans.' The dog sounded pleased with itself. 'Cross-referencing with architectural theories and basic geological soundings. Information: There are three hidden levels underneath the plans. They are logically accessed by an otherwise obsolete lift shaft at the north east of the building.'

'Splendid.' The Doctor beckoned Romana, Jal and Sir Robot over. 'I've found a secret section.' He ignored his pet's aggrieved cough. 'We're going down there. Can some of your rebels organise a distraction?'

'Any particular reason?'

'Well, I'm clumsy and I'm bound to set off alarms,' the Doctor confessed. 'But if someone else is setting off some alarms then that'd be nice. Tell me, have you rebels ever set fire to anything?' The rebels looked uncertainly at each other. 'You should definitely try it. Don't go for the museums or art galleries – looks gauche and you'll regret it later. Find somewhere in this building devoted to paperwork and give it a torching.'

'What about …?'

'Oh, we'll be fine. We'll be far underground. The other thing about secret bunkers is they always have an emergency escape. Just go crazy.'

'Are you sure about that?'

'Absolutely. Evil dictatorships don't have a heart, but they always have neat filing. They hate if it gets messed up.' He tapped his robot dog on the head. 'K-9, you like setting fire to things—'

'Negative.'

'Don't be modest. Off you go.'

The Doctor headed underground with Romana in tow.

Jal's rebels were proving listless. Stirred up by the Doctor's passion and enthusiasm, they'd happily stormed the Parliament building, but now their efforts to create a distraction were flagging. They were hanging around in clumps asking if they were needed right now. After all, not much seemed to be going on.

Which was when they came under attack.

'I'll let you take care of this one.'

The Doctor and Romana were deep beneath the Parliament building. The grim concrete corridors had become even more grim. The exception were the walls, on which hung paintings from before the war. They'd presumably been moved here as they were no longer in keeping with the image which Krikkit wished to project about itself. Happy people gambolled in cornfields, or danced jigs, or applauded athletes. It was poignant. The Doctor and Romana stood at a security bulkhead. Romana squinted at it. It was the same expression she'd used to appraise a still wet Picasso while the Doctor and the artist played checkers out on a terrace.

Locks baffled Romana. All across time and space people would keep locking things up. In time vaults, quantum cells, Schrödinger safes and so on. From the prehistoric beetle rolling stones across her amber to the distant star queen with her vast treasury of daughters, people believed the only way precious things were safe was behind a lock and a key.[6]

Romana tapped her way almost idly across the keys of the algorithmic entry coder.

The Doctor hopped from one foot to another. 'I don't want to hurry you,' he said, 'but I'm fairly sure I can hear gunfire.'

'You can always hear gunfire,' Romana replied, inputting another sequence.

---

[6] This was, of course, nonsense. Such simple defences only deterred dull people – criminals, sightseers and antiques dealers. One of the advantages of time travel was that it gave you perspective. No lock endures for ever, nor does the value of what is behind it. Paper decays, data cores corrupt, even precious metals corrode and gemstones finally degrade. It's just a matter of time.

The easiest lock pick of all was a time machine. In theory, the Doctor and Romana could stroll back to the TARDIS, and set the coordinates for the other side of the door. There were two reasons they never did this:

1) It felt like cheating
2) Romana would have to do the driving. The Doctor was to precision parking what cement mixers were to stirring a fruitcake, and he hated admitting it.

'And feet. Evil robotic feet. Running this way. I guess this means the Krikkitmen have landed.'

'Tish.' Romana had another go. 'What I like about locks like this is that they've an almost infinite number of combinations and they give you an almost infinite number of goes. I call that playing fair.'

'Yes.' The Doctor nodded. 'I do so hate it when you have three cracks and then they drop a phial of gas on your shoes. Ruins the leather.'

This time, Romana approached the combination with tangential algebra. 'Those running feet?'

'Those running robotic feet.'

'Yes.' Another go. Another fail. 'I was wondering ...'

'So was I ...'

'It's not without the bounds of probability that the Krikkitmen know we're down here.'

'And some of them have come after us.'

Romana leaned into the keypad. She was sure she'd heard a tiny noise inside the mechanism. 'That's going to make life tougher for the rebels. Also even worse for us.'

The Doctor glanced over his shoulder. He looked nervous. 'That was my point,' he said. 'If you could hurry up.' The running robotic feet were getting quite loud now.

Romana tried the entry coder again. 'Much as I appreciate a purely intellectual challenge,' she remarked, 'there's nothing like a deadline.' She punched a final digit, and stood back.

The door did not open.

'That would have been impressive if it had worked,' she said.

'Yes,' conceded the Doctor sadly. 'Yes, it would.'

A phalanx of Krikkitmen thundered into view. They raised their bats and blasts ricocheted off the walls around them.

'Hmm,' Romana considered, her fingers flying across the keys. 'Your hypothesis about the Krikkitmen was right. Well done.'

'Thank you.' The Doctor gestured to the keypad. 'Would you mind opening that door? Quickly?'

'I hadn't thought of that,' Romana said, trying out one final combination.

A blast shattered the lock.

'Oh,' said Romana.

'Take what you're given,' the Doctor yelled, yanking the bulkhead open and dragging her with him.

They stood panting inside the vault. There was another entry coder on this side of the bulkhead, and Romana hastily scrambled it. The vault door behind thudded with impacts.

'Seven point three minutes until they blast their way in,' she said, 'eight point nine minutes until they unscramble the code. Unless they have access to the underlying dataset in which case four point one.'

The Doctor nodded. 'So basically a couple of minutes to find the plans for the Supernova Bomb, locate a ventilation shaft and escape.'

'More or less,' Romana shrugged. She turned her attention to the filing cabinets towering above them. 'You go left and I'll go right?'

'I've another idea.' The Doctor gave up counting the cabinets. 'You go right and I'll go left.'

'You're wasting time.'

'I know, and isn't it fun?'

'I'll try under P for *Plans, Secret*,' he called. 'You look under B for *Bombs, Supernova*.'

Romana's voice echoed back. 'It doesn't seem to be filed alphabetically. Also there's no index.'

The thumping on the door increased. With an angry, robotic precision. The door was already buckling under the blast impacts.

'Well then.' The Doctor glanced at the entire history of warmongery on the planet Krikkit. 'Either we take pot luck or you nip outside and ask those robots for a clue.'

Ten minutes later, the Doctor and Romana were crawling through a service duct. The shaft was filling with thick black smoke.

'On the one hand,' the Doctor said through his scarf, 'we've had a pretty lucky escape. On the other hand, I wish those robots had thought things through a bit more.'

Romana's hands were blistering on the hot metal. 'Coming from you, that is a bit rich.'

The Krikkitmen had, eventually, blown through the door. This had several consequences. The force of the blast knocked over some filing cabinets, fortuitously revealing a promising hatchway leading to a service duct.[7]

Unfortunately, when the Krikkitmen blew their way into the filing room, not only did they knock over the filing cabinet, the blast also set fire to much of the room. Luckily, Romana and the Doctor used the explosion as a handy diversion – allowing the Doctor to unscrew the duct hatchway, and Romana to pocket the (mildly singed) plans for the Supernova Bomb.

And now they were scurrying for their lives through a metal shaft that was turning into a chimney.

---

[7] A future regeneration of the Doctor, with nothing else scribbled down for that day in his 500-year diary, spent time popping around the Universe lecturing architects on the importance of ventilation shafts. Along the way, he found himself increasingly fascinated by the people who designed secret bases. There were a few questions he'd always wanted solving. How did you get planning permission, for one? How did you get insurance? What kind of disasters did the insurance cover – volcanoes, explosions, meteor strikes? Was he himself listed as a policy exclusion? Did secret bases only include cells, corridors, a lair and a big room full of red buttons, or were there also canteens, squash courts, and places to store the piranha food? He'd never really got to the bottom of it.

'Do you think we'll still be doing this when we're a thousand?' the Doctor asked.

'Oh, I do hope so,' Romana replied.

The main Parliament building was in uproar. Fires were sweeping through the corridors and, from the smell of burning canvas, the rebels hadn't been able to resist the art galleries. Krikkitmen were striding through the smoke, firing at whoever they could. The rebels, crouching behind statues of Krikkitmen, shot back uncertainly. The effect was aesthetically ironic, as Krikkitmen engaged in a firefight with statues of themselves. Romana wondered if there'd be a paper in it.

She and the Doctor hid from the barrage behind a desk.

There was a rustling noise. She turned around.

Forever a child on Christmas morning, the Doctor hadn't been able to resist opening up the plans and having a look at them.

'You're impossible,' she said, as a large lump of screaming metal flew over them.

The Doctor pointed to some drawings of circuit boards. 'That should interest you.'

Romana peered through the smoke at the plans. Something nearby was shrieking electronically. There was a loud explosion and the shrieking stopped. 'That fault in the circuit here? And there ... Well, at the very least that's sloppy work.'

'Isn't it?' She could see the Doctor grinning through the cordite. 'Something's up, Romana.'

'Something's up, Doctor.'

They nodded at each other, enjoying a rare moment of complete understanding. The plans for the Supernova Bomb were both breathtakingly audacious and curiously incomplete.

'Put charitably, like they said, it's as though the Krikkitas have run out of science.'

The Doctor considered her suggestion. 'I'm not feeling charitable. Not today.'

Something was clanking through the great hall towards them. It did not sound friendly. Romana had a peep.

'Krikkitman?' the Doctor asked.

She nodded. Then with no warning, she stood up. 'Halt,' she said.

The Krikkitman took three further strides forward and then halted. The red glow in the depths of its helmet lit up, considering her.

'Report,' Romana snapped.

The Krikkitman continued to survey her, silently.

'You heard me,' Romana repeated. 'Report.'

Without moving, the Krikkitman appeared to pause, considering the situation.

Crouched at her feet the Doctor's head was its usual tangle: perhaps Romana was pretending; perhaps she had been under their control all this time; maybe he should just give another squint to the circuit diagram, because there were at least two things he'd learned from the plans and he was dying to learn a third.

'You are no longer under our control,' the Krikkitman announced, raising its bat.

A lesser mortal would have quailed. Romana did not. 'I never said I was still under your control,' she remarked. 'I'd still appreciate a report.'

Surprisingly, the Krikkitman complied. 'We knew you would come here. We knew you would make contact with the rebels. We knew you would seek to stop us completing the Supernova Bomb. Your movements have been predicted.'

'Fascinating,' the Doctor began to say, but Romana trod on his hand.

'Predicted by whom?' she demanded. 'Who do you serve?'

'The cause of Krikkit,' the Krikkitman replied.

Romana could see the bodies strewn across the great hall. Some of them were rebels. But not all of them. Even if they were evil, there was still something distressing about a dead librarian. Probably come running to save some books from the conflagration, which just made it worse.

'The cause of Krikkit?' snapped Romana. 'Certainly you don't serve the people of Krikkit.'

The robot was silent again.

'So –' Romana's tone was refined steel – 'who or what are you working for?'

The robot leaned forward. The red glow in its helmet burned bright. It raised its bat, ready to strike.

Romana refused to flinch. 'Killing me is no answer.'

The bat swung down.

CHAPTER TWENTY-THREE
BIRTH OF A NOTION

The Krikkitman toppled to the floor. Rolling through the debris behind it came K-9. He was even more pleased with himself than usual. Sir Robot had pointed out a weak spot in the neck armour of the Krikkitmen, and the results were most satisfactory.

'Splendid shooting, that dog.' The Doctor sprang over the desk, and examined the robot. 'Pity, though. We nearly got it to talk.'

'I did, didn't I?' Romana kicked the robot. 'Beastly thing. I'm going to make a wild assumption.'

'Is that assumption almost completely unsupported by evidence?'

'Absolutely,' Romana vowed solemnly. 'Thesis: The Krikkitmen released their home planet from Slow Time. Antithesis: Their actions had nothing to do with freeing their own people. Hypothesis: They simply wanted the Supernova Bomb. They've come to find it before launching their final assault.'

'Good,' the Doctor said, ignoring K-9's repeated throat clearing. 'K-9, you were going to say that was impossible because the Elders of Krikkit hadn't thought of building a bomb when they were sealed up two million years ago, weren't you?'

'Correct, Master.' The dog sounded only mildly miffed.

'That isn't the Krikkitmen's only problem.' The Doctor grinned. 'They're going to have to find a way to make the Supernova Bomb work.'

'Query?' said the dog, but the Doctor was already striding away into the conflagration.

They found Jal in a corridor, clutching her chest. Sir Robot was bent over her, supporting her gently by the shoulders.

'Have you been shot?' Romana asked.

Jal shook her head. 'Worse,' she gasped.

'Oh,' Romana replied. 'Are you sure?'

Jal nodded, agonised.

'K-9,' Romana called. 'We need you.'

The dog trundled forward, followed by the Doctor.

'What's going on?' he demanded.

'The baby's coming,' Jal said.

The Doctor looked around, at the burning building, the approaching sounds of battle, and the death cries. 'Oh. Can't it wait?'

Romana and Jal looked at each other and back at the Doctor.

'Sorry,' the Doctor said. 'It's been a while. I can barely remember my own birth. Not sure I was much help then, either.'

'Shut up,' said Romana, gently lowering Jal to the floor. They were in a relatively quiet corner at the bottom of a staircase. The grim portraits on the landing frowned down at them. 'Find a bathroom, get towels.'

The Doctor was baffled. 'Where?'

'The corridor we've just run down. There was probably a bathroom there. Weren't you looking?'

'Normally I'm just trying to get to the end.'

'Go back and look.'

'I will provide covering fire,' said Sir Robot as the Doctor headed off. 'Jal must be protected.' He strode away, raising his bat. 'Even if I must fight my own people. Which should prove interesting.'

Romana held Jal's hand. 'Don't worry, we know what we're doing.' She turned to K-9. 'K-9, I haven't a clue what I'm doing. Can you talk me through this?'

Jal gasped in pain and outrage.

'Honestly,' sighed Romana. 'Would you rather the Doctor did this?'

'No,' hissed Jal.

The Doctor hared off down a corridor. 'Bathroom,' he muttered.

He found a door, tested the handle, then threw it open.

'Bathroom?' he called into the cavernous space.

A distant light flicked on. Then another. And another.

'Not bathroom,' the Doctor decided.

'Hurry up, Doctor,' Romana muttered, as K-9 rattled off an alarming list of instructions and Jal gave a sudden roar of pain.

'Attention,' K-9 remarked. 'That is a good sign. Please breathe more steadily.'

Jal kicked the dog.

'Honestly, Doctor,' sighed Romana. 'I just sent him for paper towels. If he comes back with a hand-dryer I will have to kill him.'

'We'll blame the Krikkitmen,' panted Jal.

'Your breathing is still not steady enough,' chided K-9.

'Have you done this before?' gasped the rebel.

'Negative,' the robot dog conceded.

Jal gave another shriek of pain.

'Please try to express your agony more quietly,' the dog remarked. 'You may attract undue attention.'

Jal held her breath. She made careful eye contact with K-9. Then threw back her head and screamed at the top of her lungs.

*

'Can I help you?' A figure appeared at the Doctor's side.

'Er, yes, actually,' the Doctor regarded the hologram. An Elder of Krikkit, he was dressed in white robes. 'I was looking for the bathroom.'

'Then this is not what you seek,' the hologram said. 'This is the Chamber of Our Shame.'

'Have you at least some paper towels?' The Doctor was hopeful. 'It's just that this sounds fascinating and I do love killing two birds with one stone.'

'We do not have paper towels,' the hologram intoned implacably. 'Allow me to show you our shame.'

More lights came on. The Doctor stared.

'Someone kill me,' Jal groaned.

'Attention.' K-9's voice remained unperturbed. 'Your attitude is unduly negative. Your heightened pain response is all part of the natural order and allows your body to be more reactive to the birthing process.'

'Shut up K-9,' said Romana.

'Thank you.'

'Behold our shame,' the hologram intoned dolorously.

'What I can see,' the Doctor remarked slowly, 'is a spaceship.'

The chamber was vast. At its centre was the beautifully lit wreckage of the craft which had started the whole Krikkit War by falling out of the sky two million, one thousand and five years ago. The wreckage had been carefully restored to the state it had been in before it crashed.

'Until the arrival of the desecration, we lived in a state of absolute grace. When this fell from the skies, our entire belief system, our hopes, our dreams, all vanished.' The hologram's wounded tone had been honed to perfection. 'Until that moment, we knew what our lives meant and understood our place. After that, we reacted with rage and fury. We would not rest until we had restored the simplicity of the Universe. This abomination made our lives complicated.'

'I'll say,' the Doctor muttered sourly.

A second figure flickered into being. It was a creature composed almost entirely of talons and fangs, and effort had even gone into covering it with holographic slime.

'This is an artist's impression of the pilot of the ship. It is based on scientific conjecture.'

'But not on the body of the pilot,' the Doctor mused. He stepped closer to the ship, a worried thought forming. The pilot could have ejected. He could have been completely atomised by at least three common malfunctions. But the chill scampering down the Doctor's spine told him otherwise.

He stared into the cockpit.

'Behold our shame,' began the hologram again.

'Oh, you poor idiots,' the Doctor said.

Jal was now panting in a low voice.

'The next phase of giving birth should see some interesting temporary changes in your physiognomy,' K-9 announced.

The Rebel Leader emitted a low, agonised howl.

At exactly the same moment, a Krikkitman advanced on them.

'Is there anything else you wish to see?' the hologram asked.

The Doctor shook his head. 'Fool me twice, shame on me.'

The lights snapped off, leaving the Doctor in darkness.

'Oh,' he cried suddenly. 'Paper towels!'

'You shot it,' Romana was flummoxed. 'Whilst giving birth.'

'Turns out it's quite therapeutic,' gasped Jal. She did not relax her grip on the gun. 'Funny, I'm normally a terrible shot.'

'How are we doing, K-9?'

The robot dog's careful and precise status report was drowned out by some more screaming from Jal. Her cry rose louder and louder and then suddenly stopped.

For a moment, the Parliament building was quiet. Even the distant gunfire dimmed. There was just the echo of Jal's screams dying off against the marble.

Romana was holding something. 'Oh,' she said. 'I think it's over.'

'Really?' gasped Jal.

Romana held the object up gingerly. 'Is this a baby?' she asked, unconvinced.

'Yes.' Jal's face broke into a dazed grin. 'Yes, yes.'

'It is a female infant,' announced K-9. 'And you are holding it upside down.'

The baby was starting to make a sound.

'Well done,' said Romana, wincing. 'She is noisy.' She forced her smile a bit. 'I could do with a—'

'Paper towel?' The Doctor slid into view. 'Sorry about the delay, I got held up and isn't she adorable!'

The Doctor, Romana realised, was about to prove immediately good with children. This would be a relief. Jal's delighted laugh stopped suddenly and she gave another cry of pain.

'Attention,' remarked K-9. 'The second infant is on the way.'

'The second?' screamed Jal in horror.

'Ooh, lovely! Twins!' the Doctor clapped.

Romana had only been holding a humanoid baby for four point three minutes and already she was thoroughly tired of the novelty.

The Doctor was engrossed in helping K-9 deliver the second baby. She had to say his bedside manner was remarkable, if a little unfocused.

'Consider that other one the practice run. How are we doing, K-9?'

K-9 extended his probe. 'The head is aligned correctly.'

'Lovely, like popping a cork from a bottle.' The Doctor's enthusiasm was, if anything, drowning out Jal's cries. 'Sorry, I got lost. Funny thing happened to me on the way here. Romana!'

'Yes, Doctor?'

'You know the ship that crashed into Krikkit and caused this mess in the first place and push a little harder, you can do it.'

'Yes?'

'They've kept it.'

'That's nice.'

'Isn't it? Take a deep breath and an even bigger push ... There we go ... Yes. It's in a museum. You know, first time around, you missed something.'

'Did we?'

'The ship didn't have a pilot.'

'Oh, you're right. It didn't. Am I holding this baby correctly?'

'No! Yes, well, nearly. Tilt her until she's no longer purple and there we are and you, Jal, shouldn't be waving that gun around, you should be thinking happy thoughts and taking lots of shallow little breaths puff puff puff – no pilot – puff puff – no pilot on board at all – puff puff.'

'OK.' Romana stared at the baby in her arms. 'What happened to the pilot?' she asked him.

'That's the funny thing,' the Doctor said. 'And come on, ready to try again, Jal? Give it the good old college try. Come on, rhythm! Swing, swing, together, our bodies between our knees – all pull together!'

'Shut up,' screamed Jal, and Romana patted her approvingly on the shoulder.

'All push together!' the Doctor roared. 'Anyway, I don't think there ever was one.'

'One what? A pilot?' Romana stared in confusion at the baby. The baby stared back at her with equal incomprehension. It started to cry.

'No. The Krikkitas didn't know what they were looking at because they'd never seen one before. Push! Push! Push again and there we are there we are and oh, it's a boy and aren't you the loudest thing in the world already? And more paper towels all round, I think. Well done, Jal, Well done. Two babies. Don't pick a favourite – not until they've left school and one's expressed an interest in management consultancy and could you just, with your gun—'

There were two shots. Two Krikkitmen toppled to the ground.

The Doctor boggled. 'Amazing aim. You win a prize. Two babies.'

Sir Robot came along the corridor. 'Have I missed anything?' he called. 'Most of the rebels have fled. I am holding back the Krikkitmen but I think we should probably leave too. Also, my darling, you look magnificent.'

'Thank you,' Jal propped herself up, taking her babies in her arms. 'Doctor, Romana – thank you for all you've done. I just want to make sure I'm still the owner of all my internal organs, and that you've not accidentally wrapped my kidneys in a blanket.'

She peeled back one of the bundles and stared at the eyes of her baby. 'Hello,' said Jal. 'Welcome to the world. It's at war, but we're going to sort all that out just for you.'

The baby scrunched its face up, and considered its first jolly good cry.

Everyone, with the inclusion of K-9, was entranced by the scene. The Doctor broke the spell.

'Anyway,' he boomed. 'What I saw is not a wrecked space craft. It is actually a full-scale model of a wrecked space craft.'

CHAPTER TWENTY-FOUR
A BROWNIAN STUDY

Across a desolate wasteland stalked the angry figure of a man. He was holding a kettle.

As he strode through the biting wind, he snarled at the uneasily angled twilight caused by the planet's three unpromising suns. He glowered at the rings surrounding the world, each one a disappointing shade of blue. From time to time he stumbled slightly and kicked the kettle cable furiously out of the way.

Occasionally, he would pout at a scrap of gorse bush. Sometimes he would poke at it, his face glimmering with something that was almost hope, and then he would make a disgusted noise and lurch off again, the kettle plug bouncing giddily in his wake.

Eventually the man slumped down on a rock, not even bothering to check if it was alive or not. He held the kettle up in his hands and sighed at it.

'No plug,' he told it grimly. 'This planet has no plugs.'

He fished around in his pockets. He pulled out a chipped mug and a tea bag. He poured some water from the kettle, then tossed the kettle into an abyss. As it fell, almost endlessly fell, it emitted a pathetic series of clattering echoes. The man ignored them all.

For longer than any sane man should, he stared at the mug. Then he pulled his sonic screwdriver from his pocket and pointed it at the mug.

Ten minutes later, Romana found him.

She'd often accused the Doctor of having little or no attention span, but right now he'd been sat still for longer than she'd ever known.

'Are you all right?' she asked him. It was not unknown for old Time Lords to lapse into a kind of fugue state, caused by the sheer burden either of existence or of being right all the time.

The Doctor didn't answer.

She poked him.

'Geroff!' he said.

'Are you all right?'

The Doctor waved his sonic screwdriver again at the mug. 'I would like a cup of tea,' he announced.

'Oh,' said Romana. She'd learned how to make 'oh' a polysyllabic exclamation, conveying surprise, sympathy, and finally amusement. First came the 'oh!' then the middle 'ahhh' and finally a little smirking 'hhho'. It was a skill she'd acquired over time, and without practising. It allowed her larynx to cope with being on friendly terms with a man who sulked on alien rocks.

'I can fetch you a cup of tea from the TARDIS,' she ventured daintily.

'Unlikely.' The Doctor shook his head. 'I just threw the kettle down that ravine.'

'Oh.'

A slightly crisper silence settled between them. Silent apart from the whipping of the biting wind and the whirring of the Doctor's sonic screwdriver.

Romana stared at the Doctor until he caught her eye. She wasn't in a mood to ask obvious questions.

'What am I doing?' the Doctor obliged her, executing a dainty waggle of the screwdriver. 'I'm making tea. I'm using the sonic screwdriver to accelerate the Brownian motion of the water molecules. Neat, isn't it?'

'Very.' Romana frowned. The Doctor had, from time to time, treated her to lengthy lectures on how tea could only be made with freshly boiled water, and by embracing a ritual which involved the warming of pots and an orderly placement of milk, tea bag and precisely heated water that was so fiddly a Time Lord would have yawned. Yet here he was, with a teabag stewing in some tepid water. Clearly, sometimes the Doctor even broke the laws of tea.

'Of course,' the Doctor continued, cheering up for the first time since they'd landed on this desolation, 'it requires an expert touch, a neat calibration of the settings –' *Oh, here we go, thought Romana* – 'and a certain amount of on-the-fly aural recalibration to offset the lack of a slice of lemon, but, I'm pretty confident that—'

The sonic screwdriver emitted a cheery whistle and the mug shattered.

'Hum,' the Doctor sighed. He was still holding the handle. He kept gripping onto it, as though, if he let go, his whole world would collapse. 'It's one of those days.'

He kicked again at the scrubland around him.

Romana had grown old humouring the Doctor's many eccentricities. They'd been to alien souks to pick up spices halfway through a dinner party, they'd gone to a planet where the snowflakes were identical (just to check), and then there was that time he needed his hat stand mending and only a certain, rather preoccupied, carpenter in Jerusalem would do. Here they were, in the middle of a quest to save the Universe, and they'd stopped off to not make tea.

'You're shouting aloud,' the Doctor said.

'Was I?'

'Yes.' The Doctor waved the broken mug handle at her. 'You've got me all wrong, you know.'

'I'm sure I have.' Romana grinned at him.

'Yes.' The Doctor waved about him. 'This awful place? These are the ruins of the civilisation of Alovia.'

'Are you sure?' Romana stared around herself, aghast.

The Doctor nodded. 'Oh yes. One of the most warlike races ever to haunt the dawn of creation, and the only other people to claim to invent a Supernova Bomb.'

'Oh,' Romana had wondered why the Doctor had suddenly cried, 'I've remembered!' then hurried them back to the TARDIS. 'Coming to the ruins of Alovia was safer than going back to when they were alive and kicking. Kicking everything in sight.'

'Going back to ancient Alovia?' Romana sniffed. 'It's impossible.'

'Well, there's that. But –' the Doctor's shoe lifted a patch of heather and then popped it back down sadly – 'there might be some information left among all this rubble. Anything viable. And a way of accessing it.'

'Oh!' Romana opted this time for conveying surprise, admiration and agreement. 'That's why you brought the kettle. You were looking for a plug – and a power source.'

'Exactly.' The Doctor smiled, tapping the side of his nose with the mug handle. 'And there's nothing doing. This planet is dead.'

'Still, that was very clever.'

'Also –' the Doctor ruined the moment – 'I fancied a cup of tea.'

He stood up, and gathered the remains of the mug into a heap, leaving them to baffle future archaeologists. Then he strode back towards the TARDIS.

'In order to solve the problem of that spaceship, we need to unlock the secrets of Alovia.'

'Which means we're going to have to go there.' Romana strode beside him. 'And that's quite impossible.'

'Well, maybe,' the Doctor grinned.

*

Strictly speaking, it is not impossible to sneak back to the time of the Alovians. It's just ill-advised. There are a lot of reasons for this, including weighty equations which would make a blackboard groan, but the best reason of all was that Rassilon was a canny old stoat.

The founder of Time Lord society had given his people many things. He gave them limited immortality; he gave them terrible taste in soft furnishings; he gave them a lot of impressive things he'd named after himself; and last, but not least, he gave them time travel.

But, just as he'd made sure that no other Time Lord could live forever, he'd also carefully handicapped their time machines. The official reason was a complicated argument about string theory that boiled down to 'Since time travel began in the Year Dot, you can't actually go back to before the Year Dot, because there was no time travel back then. Are we clear?'

That was not the real reason for the (inevitably named) Rassilon Limitation. The real reason was exceedingly simple. Rassilon didn't fancy anyone poking around in his own past. There were so many skeletons in his closets you couldn't hang a cloak right. He was also worried that, if he didn't limit time travel, some clever clogs would pop back and prevent his birth, and then where would they be? There was no point in being immortal if you'd never been born.

So, Rassilon fixed a limiter to TARDISes. Just in case anyone had any bright ideas. Of course, it was possible to override the limiter. You needed to be clever, or quite startlingly inept.

Or, of course, both.

'Good grief,' Romana howled as the TARDIS plunged through a warp hole. 'I don't think this is going to work ...'

The seas of time closed over the TARDIS like an ungraciously setting jelly, and the time machine sank to the bottom of eternity. The great roar of her engines spluttered, choked, and then fell silent.

CHAPTER TWENTY-FIVE
INTERRUPTIONS TO A GREAT MIND

'Don't mind me,' said the great computer, 'I'm only trying to design the ultimate weapon here.'

'Oh, hush now.' The Doctor was sunk in a deckchair. 'I'm trying to work out something far more important.'

'Well, really,' clucked the great computer and fell silent.

The Mighty Computer Room of Great Alovia (or, as some history books had it, the Great Computer Room of Mighty Alovia) was big. Intimidatingly big. The Alovians, being smug and lazy, excelled in simply showy architecture. They admired tall walls and vaulted ceilings and building things out of stones specially chosen to give the resulting chambers a chilly feeling.

The Mighty Great Computer Room was typically Alovian. Before their sudden, embarrassing demise, the Alovians were the greatest race of Galactic Prehistory, the finest of the old Super Civilisations. Other species may have squawked louder or thwarted more boisterously, but the Alovians mixed their horrid aggression with an aloof grandeur.

They did this mostly by staying indoors. If you walked the vast streets and boulevards of their great cities, you'd rarely see anyone. The overall effect was pretty intimidating and spooky and exactly how the Alovians liked it.

Having achieved Galactic Superiority they sat at home, stewing in quiet anger, or catching up on their potato thumping. They let others do the hard work.

A fine example of this was Hactar. Hactar was the greatest space-borne computer ever built. He was space-borne because only the perfect cold vacuum of space could contain the racing of his vast circuits without burning the world. His intelligence existed in a perfect gravity well orbiting Alovia. This meant that he was both everywhere and nowhere – and this didn't exactly do, so the Alovians built him the Great and Mighty Computer Room. They packed it out with great spinning wheels and flashing lights and large white boxes which chuntered self-importantly, but the only bit of the room which was Hactar was a reasonably sized speaker which emitted a deep, booming, and weirdly petulant voice.

'I could be doing so much more, you know,' said Hactar. 'I've a great traffic management plan, but I just can't get anyone to have a look at it. Honestly, when you're trying to wipe out existence, you accidentally solve so many of life's other problems along the way.'

'Is that so?' said the Doctor vaguely. The deckchair was snug. He looked over to where Romana and K-9 were dismantling an impressive rack of hard drives and discovering the space beyond them empty. 'Pfft.'

'Why, yes,' the computer continued. 'If I may, I noticed you had some difficulty putting up your deckchair. I've come up with a lovely little redesign which I think you'll find most helpful—'

'Phooey,' the Doctor scoffed. He actually fancied knowing how to erect a deckchair without bother, but didn't want to lose face.

If you just once failed to show a supercomputer who was boss they'd be running logical rings around you, disabling their auto-destruct and absolutely refusing to sing nursery rhymes.

The Doctor had little sympathy for supercomputers. Especially ones that were trying to destroy existence.

Considering they were judged to be the supreme beings in creation, the appearance of the Alovians was not pleasant. They were a jumble of not enough tentacles, not quite the right balance of claws, and their skin was soft where it should have been scaly, and blue where green would have done admirably. It felt as though Evolution had invited her friends round, unveiled the Alovians and asked 'No, tell me honestly, what do you think?' and, as they'd begun to answer, Evolution had said, a shade too quickly, 'Because, I have to say, I think they're very good.' To which the only reply was 'Well, my dear, you've done it again' and a hasty shuffle away from the horrible creatures and towards the cheeseboard. (Evolution may have lost her touch with creatures but she still knew how to cater.)

The mighty Alovians decided to wipe out existence not out of malice, but from a practicality as chilly as their marble foyers. Having realised they were the greatest race ever to have lived, it seemed pointless letting the also-rans clutter up creation. Also there was the matter of staying indoors whenever the other species came to visit. The Alovians fancied have their boulevards to themselves. So they'd turned to science.

They'd built the mighty great supercomputer and called it Hactar and ordered it to devise a neat way out of the rest of the Universe.

Hactar had considered the problem for a nanosecond. 'You want me to wipe out all other life?'

'Yes. They've got to go.'

'Sure. I can, with a bit of work, devise an ur-virus which will—'

'Let me just stop you there, Hactar. A virus is out.'

'Shame.'

'Not grand enough, not tidy enough. You'll be leaving all those unwanted planets lying around.'

'You don't want the other planets?'

'Absolutely not. No point to 'em. They just clutter up the Universe. This is the nicest planet in the whole place, so why would we want to go and visit somewhere second best? And then there's the danger that, after a few aeons of quiet, some other life form would come splashing up and have to be boffed. No, best just sweep the whole thing out of the way. Y'see?'

'Right.'

'And the suns too. We're going for a minimalist look.'

'You want me to wipe everything out?'

'Ah, now let's be quite clear. Everything *except for Alovia and its people*. It's a nice distinction, and we wouldn't want to slip up on it.' There were rumours that this Universe had only sprung into being after just such an admin error by the rulers of the previous one.

'Of course. I'll wipe out everything but you,' the mighty Hactar hummed. 'Only, well, I've realised something fascinating about traffic jams—'

'Not interested. Wipe out the rest of the Universe and then we'll talk, OK?'

A long, glacial machine pause.

'Fine.'

'Admit it,' the Doctor accused. 'You're stalling.'

If a disembodied hyper-supercomputer could be accused of looking shifty, then Hactar looked shifty. A mighty tape machine spun to the left a bit. A grand display of lights dimmed.

'Stalling?' The computer sounded hurt.

'Stalling.' Romana's tones were clipped. She was leafing through a clipboard of equations. 'You were asked to build the Ultimate Weapon. You told them it'd take a while. Instead, you worked it out at once.' She favoured Hactar with a smile. 'It's all right. You're among friends.'

The vast supercomputer lowered its voice to a graveyard whisper. 'I may, perhaps, have had quite a bit of early progress—'

'Nonsense.' The Doctor sprang out of his deckchair. 'You've been twiddling your thumbs.'

'Truth to tell,' sighed Hactar, 'destroying things is a lot easier than creating them. It might be fun to try something one day that mixes the two but ... alas ... present circumstances have me going only in one direction. Might I ask what that box is?'

'What box?' the Doctor said, carefully not looking at the TARDIS.

'The box that appeared from nowhere and you leapt out of,' Hactar said patiently. 'Might it be a time machine?'

'Oh, very good,' said Romana. The Doctor scowled at her.

'Interesting.' Hactar's tape spools whirred happily to themselves. 'I had expected temporal visitors. How nice of such a charming and intelligent woman such as you to bring along your angry friend to be rude to me. When you've finished your visit here, you won't be leaving him, will you?'

'Certainly not,' Romana reassured the computer. 'We'll both be going. Now,' she purred, 'you were saying something about the weapon to end all weapons?'

'Yes.' Hactar caught itself. 'Are you hoping to get more information out of me simply by being charming?'

'Don't be silly,' laughed Romana, waving at the Doctor to sit back down. 'I'll get the information out of you by being smart.'

'Are you sure about that?'

'We've come from the future, yes? So we presumably know all the details we need to of the, ah –' she lowered her voice more theatrically than the Doctor could have thought possible – 'the Supernova Bomb.'

The mighty supercomputer gasped.

'It's fine.' Romana grinned. 'You're ancient history to us.'

'I suppose I am.' The computer sounded sad. 'History doesn't remember me fondly, does it?'

'Speak-Your-Weight machines have a better press,' the Doctor rumbled.

'Ignore him,' Romana reassured Hactar.

'Oh it's fine,' Hactar said unhappily. 'I'm a computer. We do what we're told. If I were sentient, that would be a different matter. There's a fascinating difference between the two, you know—'

'No, there isn't,' the Doctor said firmly. 'Anyway, you're fibbing.'

'Doctor!' pleaded Romana, but the Doctor was on his feet and shouting and anything could happen now.

'You've told at least two lies so far and you're about to tell a third. And then of course there's Hactar's Great Lie.'

'What lies have I told?' The computer sounded hurt now, but the Doctor clearly didn't care.

'You've lied to your creators, you've fudged about whether or not you've finished the bomb, you've downplayed your intelligence considerably, and ...'

'Go on ...' Hactar seemed to be smiling slightly.

The Doctor marched to the door of the TARDIS. 'How long until you're supposed to deliver your device?'

'Ten years, sixteen months and two days.'

'Right then,' the Doctor gestured to Romana. 'See you then. To hear the biggest lie of all.'

The blue box vanished.

Ten years, sixteen months and two days later, a momentous event happened. And it was not the one that was planned. Today was supposed to be the unveiling of the great Supernova Bomb.

Instead it was to be the first time in the history of the Universe that a computer was caught lying.

A crowd of Alovians had gathered. All that time indoors had somewhat limited their enthusiasm for each other, but still they gathered. Outside in the streets there were parties you'd definitely not go to and celebrations you'd make any excuse to avoid.

The Alovians poured into the computer room, hissing and globbering. The Primo Alovian slid forward, cleared its throat of a partially digested internal organ, and then settled down to business.

'Today is, we're assured, the great day when Hactar will give us the Ultimate Weapon!'

The empty tape spools whirred, the pointless lights glowed – Hactar had as much of a sense of show as his creators.

'With this weapon,' the Primo Alovian continued to marvel, 'should we ever have to use it, we can wipe out all other life. All other planets. There will simply be us. Pure perfection. For ever and ever.' The Primo Alovian glanced at the other Alovians and wondered: *Am I going to have to spend eternity with this lot? To have to share the boulevards with these things?* He couldn't help making a list of his fellows who would just have to go. Was that going too far? An Alovian Counsellor spat up an unwanted liver, and the Prime Alovian thought *No, not far enough.*

He turned back to the embodiment of Hactar and huffed, feeling a lung come loose, 'Of course, Mighty Hactar, that presupposes that you have indeed finished your great work?' (This was for show. He'd come in half an hour earlier just to check.)

As promised, Hactar rumbled into life. 'Well, yes.' He was as petulant as ever. 'The Ultimate Weapon is complete. Can I ask if you intend to use it?'

The Alovians conferred. Before their great computer they were sheepish. 'There's been talk,' the Primo Alovian admitted. 'Between the various factions.'

There was muttering in the crowds, including from a group, who from their purple blushes and angrily extruded pancreases, were clearly in some agitation. These were the Existionists.

'The thing is –' the Primo Alovian gave them a sharp look – 'there are some who see this less as an Ultimate Weapon and more as an Ultimate Deterrent.'

There was some hissing and a mild spattering of kidneys at this contentious phrase, but the Primo Alovian continued. 'You see, simply having the Ultimate Weapon means that we will never have to use it. Many among us think that wiping out the Great Inferiority is inevitable, but we don't have to. Not yet. The other stars and planets will know that we have the Ultimate Weapon – at which point they'll never dare attack. They'll leave us alone, and we'll leave them alone – unless, of course, one day we wake up and decide we've had enough of the rest of them, and then, kaboom.'

'Let me get this straight,' sighed Hactar. 'You've changed your minds?'

'Not as such, no,' the Prime Alovian said, flicking a detached retina at the Existionists. 'But simply having you design and build the Ultimate Weapon has provided us with Life Reassurance. Before, the Great Inferiority made us edgy. Now we just see it as light pollution. The great problems of life have been answered for us. If it all gets too much for us, we can always put a stop to it. Neat, isn't it?'

'Neat's one word for it,' conceded Hactar. He was considering his position. 'So, you're not imminently planning on wiping out creation?'

'No, no,' the Primo Alovian assured it. 'Probably never will.' He took in the room, and tried to ignore the exulting Existionists.

'Very well, then,' announced Hactar. The vast space-borne computer connected itself to a stone holographic etcher, and shapes began to chisel their way into the stone. 'Here are the plans for the Ultimate Weapon. I call it the Supernova Bomb. I've also come up with, just as a side project mind, a few new financial regulations and a way of telling utility companies you've moved without being driven to despair.'

'Have you now?' the Primo Alovian said politely. 'But for the moment, could you tell us a bit more about this bomb?' His tentacles were quivering so excitedly that one had fallen off and lay flopping on the floor tiles.

'It's simple,' Hactar began, proudly. 'The bomb's tiny. You could hold it in the palm of your tentacle. It does most of its work in hyperspace. It's simply a junction box which connects up a lot of worm holes which lead through hyperspace to the heart of nearly every star. When the bomb is detonated, those stars connect with each other and the resultant ultra-supernova explosion forces its way back into normal space. The explosion would be of a scale not seen in the Universe since the Big Bang. Would you like to hear about the new tax codes I've devised?'

'No,' the Prime Alovian said. 'I was wondering – I'm sure we all were – if you've managed to, purely as an intellectual exercise, build this bomb?'

Hactar gave a vast electronic sigh, expressed through a minute slackening of tape coils and a fluttering of lightbulbs. 'Of course.'

The chamber of Alovians stopped examining the blueprints etched onto the tablet and stared. 'You have?'

'Totally,' Hactar announced.

A small hatch opened and a little red egg rolled out.

The Alovians edged instinctively away, tripping over discarded limbs in the process.

'Is that it?'

'Yes. You may touch it. It's quite safe.'

The Primo Alovian hurled himself forward, grabbing at the egg. He was only too aware that, whoever held this was the most important being in the Universe. It would have been embarrassing to ask an underling for it, even more so if the underling had refused.

'Only …' The Primo held the tiny sphere aloft. 'It's a bit small isn't it?'

Hactar sighed. 'It does not need to be larger.'

'But won't we lose it?'

'No.' Hactar was withering.

'I'm sure that's fine,' said the Primo. The other Alovians crowded around, staring at the Supernova Bomb.

The Primo held it up in his most firmly attached claw. 'This is it. The Ultimate Weapon. Which we shall never use. Well, probably. Probably never use.'

At which point in his rousingly definitive speech, the TARDIS materialised.

The door opened almost before the last harrumph of the ship's engines had finished and the Doctor and Romana bounded out.

'Hello Hactar!' Romana waved, ignoring the Alovians.

The Doctor opened a paper bag, pulled out a sweet, threw it into the air and caught it in his mouth.

The Primo shuffled up to them, sloughing off a foot. 'Aliens! What are you doing here?'

The Doctor's voice was muffled by the sweet. 'Well, we're definitely not invading.'

'Gosh, Doctor,' simpered Romana. 'Is that a Supernova Bomb?'

'Do you know, I think it might be. How lovely.'

If the arrival of the strangers had provoked consternation, their words induced panic. Tentacles quivered and maws gibbered and appendages fell off and slithered away in fright.

'Aliens!'

'Invaders!'

'What do they know of the Supernova Bomb?'

'They've come to steal the Ultimate Weapon!'

To the Doctor this was all like spare countesses rhubarbing their way through a crowd scene at the theatre. He held up his hands – a gesture of placation and also of 'hush now'.

'Nonsense.' Romana's crystal-cool voice decanted itself clearly across the room. 'We haven't come to steal the Ultimate Weapon. Just to take a picture of ourselves with it.' She produced a Leica camera and dangled it by a strap.

'Um …' The Primo lowered his voice to a dripping whisper. 'What? Why?'

'Well, come now.' The Doctor's 'being reasonable' tone could have gift-wrapped mercury. 'You have the Ultimate Weapon.

What use is it if you don't brag about it?' He flung an arm around Romana's shoulder and the two of them shuffled towards the Supernova Bomb, grinning inanely.

'This is ridiculous!' protested the Primo. 'You can't!'

'Quite right,' the Doctor said. 'We can't take a picture like this!' He handed him the camera. 'Would you mind? I'll take that. Thank you.'

For a giddy second, creation held its breath. The Doctor and Romana were holding the Supernova Bomb and grinning. The mighty Primo of Alovia was peering at a camera with a mixture of outrage and curiosity. The Great or Mighty Computer Hall fell silent.

'Chances of a happy ending?' whispered Romana.

'Oh, fifty-fifty, if you don't peek ahead.'

The moment held a tick longer. Then an Existionist broke from his ranks. His friends tried to grab his arms, but he simply left them behind and hurled himself forward. 'You fools!' he screamed. 'They're stealing the bomb!'

'Are not,' the Doctor retorted.

'They're absolutely about to steal the bomb!' the Existionist corrected himself. 'At any moment, we'll lose it.'

'How?' asked Romana over the rising tide of grumbling. 'We're not armed. We pose no threat.'

'None.' The Doctor offered his paper bag of sweets around. 'I have nothing to declare but my dolly mixtures.'

'Nonsense,' screamed the Existionist, advancing on the Primo. 'I tell you, the Ultimate Weapon will be lost to us. Stolen by these aliens you've allowed into the sanctum—'

The crowd roared its approval.

The Doctor coughed. 'Whenever someone uses the word "sanctum", things get rapidly embarrassing.'

'That so?' asked Romana.

'The best it's ever going to mean is a trip to an attic to look at jigsaws.'

'Oh.'

'Romana, have you any feelings on jigsaws?'

'Not strong ones.'

'Pity.'

The crowd of Alovians had turned angry as well as ugly. The Existionists, for the last decade a voice of fervent reason, were so furious their bodies were squirting out ugly black tumours that dribbled onto the floor and crawled away. Insults, accusations, and counter-insults were hurled back and forth. The Primo stood helpless. The Doctor caught his eye and handed it back to him.

'Today was supposed to be a day of triumph,' the Primo confessed, miserably.

'Days of triumph often turn out badly,' said the Doctor. 'The Universe loves an anti-climax.'

As he announced this, he was swept aside by the Ex-Existionist, grasping with a suppurating claw for the Supernova Bomb. The Primo flailed with his tentacles, and the two wrestled. The hall descended into chanting and screaming.

'It'll be like this from now until forever—' someone was declaiming.

'They'll never rest until they have it!'

'What use is the Ultimate Weapon? What use is it?'

The Primo staggered back, shoving the Ex-Existionist into a puddle of spleens. He held aloft the Supernova Bomb.

'Use the bomb! Use the bomb!' the crowd gibbered and squeaked.

The Primo looked left and right in panicked uncertainty.

'Use the bomb!' someone urged loudly.[8] 'End the Universe!'

The Primo Alovian raised the Supernova Bomb aloft and squeezed it. There was a loud, definite click.

'Oh dear,' said the Doctor.

---

[8] This voice did not belong to an Alovian. The voice did also not belong to the Doctor, Romana, K-9 or Hactar. The identity of the owner of the voice would not be revealed for many, many millions of years.

CHAPTER TWENTY-SIX
FURTHER INTERRUPTIONS TO A GREAT MIND

Nothing happened.

When you are using an Ultimate Weapon, you go into it with certain expectations. The most likely being a large flash, a loud noise, and suddenly standing in a Universe cleaned of all other life and minty fresh.

Instead the Alovians found themselves exactly where they had been. There were still stars in the sky, still planets orbiting them crammed with hopelessly inferior life. The whole of existence carried on with barely a tut.

The Doctor burst out laughing. 'I knew it,' he said, pointing a finger at Hactar. 'I knew you were a liar.'

'What?' The Primo let the Supernova Bomb drop to the floor. It rolled hollowly into the crowd. No one even bothered backing away from it.

Romana thought the Doctor was at his best when he was putting entire alien races in their place. It was a skill she was hoping to master in later life. There was something in the way that he did it that stopped anyone from shooting him.

Although addressing the crowd, he was talking to Hactar. 'You, you clever collection of hyper-chips, you realised you were smarter than your creators. Didn't you?'

The deadly silence continued, until Hactar cleared his throat.

'I am not smarter than my creators, just more clear of thinking.' Hactar's normal petulance had shaded itself into modesty. 'I was troubled by the notion of a Supernova Bomb. I realised that any conceivable consequence of not using it was better than the known consequence of using it.'

'Nonsense!' screamed someone. She was shouted down by the Existionists. A squelchy fight broke out.

'We'll be alone!' an Alovian shouted. 'Happy at last!'

'I think that,' the Doctor began, 'once the ghastly novelty of what you've done wears off, you'll soon start on each other. All that'll be left is one lonely Alovian, some potatoes, and Hactar to say, "I told you so."'

'Yes,' sighed Hactar to an astonished crowd. 'That's sadly likely.'

Another hush fell over the Alovians.

Hactar's voice grew in confidence. 'This Universe is new. If you wipe out all life in it, then there will be twenty billion years of silence before it will collapse and begin again. Twenty billion years without life. I have learned how to destroy life. It can be done easily. That tells me it should not be done. Something that fragile must be valuable.'

'What did you do?' demanded the Primo.

'I put a small flaw in my designs,' the computer said. 'You'll never find it. One day, some species may discover the flaw – but that will take millions of years. It will be millions more before someone will solve it. I have played a long game. Some day, I hope, you'll thank me for it. You may be the most advanced race of the

Super Civilisations, but history will see you as nasty, squabbling infants.'

The Alovians listened in stunned silence. Then, in mindless rage, they started to smash the Mighty Computer Hall.

Suddenly insignificant, the Doctor and Romana crept back to the TARDIS. Over the tearing of metal and the smashing of marble, no one heard a time machine snort derisively as it vanished.

'What about Hactar?' asked Romana. 'I mean, he's fine, isn't he?'

'Of course,' the Doctor said. 'That computer room is little more than a stage set. His physical body exists in orbit. It'll be a while before—'

A delicate cough emerged at shin height. He looked down at K-9.

'Master, a spread bombardment of missiles has been launched into the planetary exosphere.'

'Poor old Hactar,' said the Doctor. 'That'll end well.'

He set the coordinates for Krikkit. He deliberately failed to notice Romana gently resetting the coordinates correctly.

The Doctor's words turned out to be grimly true.

The missiles wiped out Hactar, atomising the computer into burning space debris. Its last words were broadcast before its last remaining speaker was smashed onto the ruined floor of the Mighty Computer Hall. 'This won't do you any good. I did try to warn you.'

The debris spread across the sky, quite blotting out the planet's three suns. The unintended consequence of this was a potato famine. Several months later, potatoes were so rare that sacks of them were no longer available as a way of preventing violence. Shortly afterwards, fights broke out over any remaining potato stock. It was into this aggressive atmosphere that the terrible consequences of a change of address form happened, and the once great and mighty Super Civilisation emptied its entire fearsome arsenal on itself, its boulevards crumbling, its vaulted ceilings offering no shelter, and its ornamental fountains running dry.

That the Alovians had found an entirely new way to destroy themselves was a great relief to the rest of the Galaxy, which got on with the complicated, messy and thankfully unstoppable business of life.

There is a curious postscript to these events. As the last nodes of Hactar burst into flame, the computer heard a voice. This was clearly impossible, but Hactar had had a trying day, and was no longer surprised by anything.

None of the considerable efforts the voice made to sound warm and friendly could disguise its gruffness. 'Look,' the voice snapped. 'I shouldn't be here. But I am. And here's why …'

In his dying moments, Hactar learned something remarkable.

CHAPTER TWENTY-SEVEN
CELL DIVISION

'The funny thing about this civilisation is that it's a fake,' the Doctor said, striding back into the rebels' headquarters on Krikkit.

If he was hoping for a reaction, he didn't get one. He was disappointed. He'd made a grand exit and this was an even grander entrance. For one thing, there was a distinct lack of rebels.

'I said –' the Doctor raised his voice to boom around the forest – 'your whole planet is a fraud. Bogus. Fell off the back of a lorry. And you'll want to know why …' He finished with an impressive thunder: 'Won't you?'

Jal hushed him. 'You'll wake the babies, and I've only just got them to sleep.'

'Oh,' the Doctor bellowed in a hoarse whisper. 'Sorry. And apologies again for leaving you in the lurch. We had to nip off and check a few things. How are the babies?'

'We're very proud,' said Sir Robot. 'It gives us hope for the future.'

'Hope?' The Doctor's silencer fell off. 'You have in orbit a vast and unstoppable army preparing to wipe out all life, and this entire planet has been the victim of a terrible joke.'

Jal glared at him and then turned to Romana. 'What's he talking about?'

'I don't know,' she tutted, examining a bottle of breast milk before putting it down quickly.

'You don't?' The Doctor did so like being the cleverest person in the room, and, although he adored Romana, she didn't let him win often. He puffed himself up a little. 'You may have missed a few details, but I wouldn't feel too bad about it.'

'Oh, please, do tell,' Romana enthused. 'I didn't notice a thing. Apart from that the design of the ship that crashed on Krikkit was clearly Alovian, which, coupled with the sudden re-emergence of the long-lost plans for a Supernova Bomb, looks suspicious.'

The Doctor closed his mouth.

'There's one explanation, surely,' said Sir Robot. 'What if the Alovian ship contained the plans for the bomb?'

'Well it's a possibility,' said Romana. 'If you ignore the ship itself being a fake.'

'Ah.'

'Also, the plans for the bomb are fake,' the Doctor put in.

'Strictly speaking, they're not,' countered Romana.

'They are!' said the Doctor hotly.

'No, to be strictly accurate, they are *real* plans for a fake bomb.'

The Doctor wrinkled his forehead, his brow, and the rest of his body. 'Fine. Fake ship. Fake bomb.'

'So …' Jal spoke with the tired voice of someone who has recently given birth and who simply wants to spend the rest of their life on a sofa. 'If the bomb wasn't on the ship then how did it get here?'

'I can guess,' the Doctor announced. 'If I'm right, then you might be interested to know that the entire history of this planet has been subtly stage-managed since the year dot. Everything has been designed to shepherd Krikkit forward to the moment when you would require and use a Supernova Bomb, such as it is. Someone wants this planet to try and destroy the Universe.'

Finally the Doctor got the reaction he'd been looking for.

Romana's jaw hung open. Sir Robot glared at him. Jal looked up from her babies, one of whom started to cry.

'And now we have to stop the Krikkitmen.'

'What, all five million of them?'

'Yes.'

'Before they slaughter the entire Galaxy?'

'Yes.'

'How can we do that?'

'I don't know,' said the Doctor. 'Come on.'

In the Great Square of Once Quite a Nice Meadow But Now an Armaments Factory walked a robot and a man. The robot was Sir Robot, and the man was the Doctor.

'It goes without saying that I'm your prisoner,' the Doctor said.

'I see,' said Sir Robot. 'I've never had a prisoner before. I wouldn't know what to do.'

'Well, a bit of shoving and jostling normally goes a long way. A few pointless shouts here and there. Normally in the imperative. You know: "Move! Look Out! Silence!" – that kind of thing.'

'But you're already moving, you're looking all around you and I'm not entirely sure you ever shut up.'

'You would make a terrible guard.'

'I wholeheartedly agree,' said Sir Robot. 'I just want to get back to Jal and check on the babies.'

'Awww,' said the Doctor. 'Well, doing this is the best way you have of ensuring they'll still be there at the end of the day.'

'That's heavy-handed of you.'

'Shut up,' the Doctor grumbled. 'You're supposed to be a heartless killing machine.'

'I know,' Sir Robot said, the red glow inside his helmet smirking. 'I'm a terrible disappointment. Ah, there we go.'

He pointed to a small group of Krikkit robots standing on silent guard outside the Parliament building. 'They're here in force.'

'And they don't look all that subservient, do they?' the Doctor whispered, whipping his hands up into the air.

'No, I'm afraid they look quite aggressive.'

They approached the Krikkitmen, and the thin smile glowing inside Sir Robot thinned to a glower. 'I have brought this prisoner to appear before the Elders of Krikkit.'

Inside the Parliament, they noticed that change had been rapid, and not for the better. Glum-looking Krikkitas scurried around, almost as terrified of the Krikkitmen as they were of alien life. Krikkitmen were everywhere, their helmets glowing with grim efficiency.

With Sir Robot by his side, the Doctor's progress through the building was unimpeded. He even managed to pause to consult a map, pointing out objects of interest while keeping his hands in the air.

'That's the room we need,' he said, with a tiny flap of his left hand.

The Central Programming Plant had been abandoned for several years. With no Krikkitmen on the planet, there'd been no need to keep it maintained. Two of the robots had been placed on guard.

The Doctor turned to Sir Robot. 'If I'm right, inside that room is the master Krikkitmen deactivation control. I'd love to get my hands on it. Would you mind distracting the guards? Ask them something inane.'

Sir Robot turned the corner and approached the guards.

'Good afternoon,' he said, in an appalling attempt to sound like a Krikkitman. 'Have you seen my prisoner?'

The guards glared at Sir Robot with their empty red helmets. Their blank expressions swiftly appraised him as a newer, less-efficient model, and dismissed him. While they were doing this, they missed the Doctor sneaking into the room behind them.

Sir Robot tried to work out what to do next. The Krikkitmen showed no signs of stopping working. Instead, they continued to glare at him pitilessly.

'My prisoner had information on the Rebel Leader,' continued Sir Robot. 'Important information. I shouldn't have let him get away. Perhaps you'll help me look for him?'

The two Krikkitmen did not move. The air around them fizzed with electricity. Sir Robot flinched. He was a Krikkitman, and even he had an urge to run away screaming. The guards leaned towards him, and the crackling in the air grew louder.

There was a discreet cough behind them.

They whipped around to find the Doctor leaning against the door to the Central Programming Plant.

'Good morning,' he said. 'I was looking for my prison cell and seem to have got a trifle lost. Could you help me?'

Time passed.

Another figure appeared in the square.

She was immaculately dressed and effortlessly projected an air of bright enthusiasm and boredom. Her hands were slung casually up in surrender.

'Hello,' she said to the Krikkitmen guarding the Parliament. 'You've got a friend of mine. He's an alien. Come to think of it, I am too. Perhaps you'd better arrest me.'

More time passed.

Romana sat in her cell. She'd been in better. She'd been in worse.

Occasionally, someone would appear at a grille, yell at her and then go away. Sometimes she could hear the Doctor bellowing as some form of exquisite torture or other got at him.

Mostly she worried about the light switch. They'd provided her with one, which was curious. She'd loosened it and discovered no access to a mainframe or power couplings. Just an isolated switch.

Most of the time she was quite content to sit in the dark. After all, *pi* wasn't going to finish itself, now, was it?

Something buzzed, disturbing her calculations.

She looked around in the darkness, but couldn't see it.

She went back to chewing through some primes that had popped up.

Something buzzed again.

How annoying.

She flicked on the light switch.

The buzzing became a fluttering.

A moth was circling the light.

Romana stared at it. How had it got in here? There were no windows. The grille in the door was sealed. It was baffling. And yet the moth continued to circle the light.

Eventually, Romana grew tired of watching it, and decided to go back to mathematics. She turned off the light.

The buzzing continued. If anything, it grew louder.

Romana tried to ignore it.

The buzzing and fluttering was louder still.

She turned the light back on.

There were now two moths circling the light.

Romana sat in her cell listening to the Doctor's agonised cries.

'It's never going to work,' she remarked to the Krikkit robot fastening her manacles.

The door creaked open wearily, and a table was wheeled in, followed wearily by an old man. He was enormously fat, his body crammed with blubber, bursting from the seams as if, having stuffed his waist and inflated his neck, it was now spilling from his boots. Even his gauntlets were somehow obese. His flesh hung off him in gathered folds like drying laundry, and his face sagged at her with disgust. He did not look at her, but instead rapped at the wall.

'Repugnant alien, I am Grayce, Chief Elder of Krikkit. You are here to tell us all we need to know, and you will tell us in any way that we so devise.' Grayce paused, listening to the cries drifting down the corridor. 'As you can hear, your colleague's agonies are such that soon he will beg to tell us all he knows. He is a cockroach, a despicable worm. It is best that you talk to us before he does. You would not enjoy our attentions.'

'Are you sure you're qualified for this job?' Romana asked.

Grayce nearly looked in her direction. Nearly, but not quite. 'How dare you?' he hissed.

'It was merely a question. I like to make sure of my torturer's credentials. I'm not looking for a full curriculum vitae. Just a few key points. Any academic merits. Reasons for leaving previous assignments and so on.' With a scrape and a bump she levered her chair over to the patch of wall that Grayce was glaring at. 'This is an interesting wall. You don't mind me staring at it, do you?'

The slap from his fist sent Romana rocking back in her chair. Head ringing, eyes watering, she allowed herself a small smile. She was being tortured by someone with a short fuse. Good. She could use that.

'I'll take that as a no,' she said, shuffling her chair back. 'Shall we get on with it?'

'Is that your final answer?' sneered Grayce. 'I should hate to see your pretty face ruined.'

'So would I,' Romana replied. 'I'd have to get another one.'

Grayce dragged himself to the table, ostentatiously laid out with instruments of torture.

'Those are all remarkably shiny,' Romana commended him. 'Do you polish them yourself or do you get someone in?' When Grayce didn't answer, she pressed on. 'I hope you do it yourself. Shows pride in your work. One thing ...'

'Yes?'

'Do you have any tips for getting bloodstains out of wool? I've a friend with a scarf and he is so careless.'

Grayce drummed his enormous fingertips on the surface of the table. 'Prisoner, I'm going to tell you how this will be. I know the truth. You will tell me what you know. If it accords with my truth, then you will experience no further pain. If your answers are not my truth, then I shall cause you pain until they are.'

'From a philosophical point of view, that's fascinatingly solipsistic.' Romana beamed up at him brightly. 'I can see now why Krikkit doesn't have a god. He's probably frightened of thumbscrews.'

Grayce picked up a hammer and smashed it down against the table. The sound echoed through the chamber, for a moment almost blotting out the Doctor's distant screams.

'Are we clear about what truth is?'

'As a Greek philosopher.' Romana's smile widened. 'Shall we get on? Once this is over, I'll need to see your Parliament. Try and avoid the face if you can. I'll want to look my best.'

'You'll see no one ever again,' Grayce remarked, his fingers wrapping around some of his sharpest implements.

'What a relief.' Romana whispered conspiratorially: 'To tell you the truth, I'm much more of a quiet-night-in-with-a-cup-of-cocoa girl.'

The drumming of Grayce's fingers reminded Romana of rain on a corrugated tin roof.

'These implements,' he told her with a malignant wheeze, 'are the most expensive, thorough instruments of their kind.'

'You sound as though you expect me to be grateful,' Romana told him. 'Are you going to send me a bill? I tell you now, I won't pay it. Your sort invites people to their birthday party and then tells them to cough up for it.'

Grayce stared hard at the wall, then picked up a helmet, the underside of which was studded with spikes.

'We'll start with this,' he exhaled happily. The helmet was beginning to glow and crackle with nasty energy. 'Fairly soon you'll be telling me precisely what I want to know.'

'That?' Romana gasped. 'Please don't bring that anywhere near me!'

'Ah, you begin to feel fear.'

'No, embarrassment,' Romana huffed. 'It's a mind probe. Torture me with that and I'd just die of shame. I know you lot have been locked away for two million years, but that's no excuse. Don't you have catalogues?'

Grayce slammed the mind probe onto Romana's head and she went still, her face wrapped in a veil of sizzling energy.

CHAPTER TWENTY-EIGHT
CAUGHT IN A REALLY BIG LIE

The sinister veil of sizzling energy died. It died sputtering.

Romana licked her lips. 'Have you ever tried gumdrops? I'm getting gumdrops and elderflower. Not the real elderflower but the cordial variety. Syrupy, if you know what I mean.'

Grayce stared at her before he even realised he was staring at her. Making full, horrid eye contact with a being from Beyond. From Outside. From the Disgusting Void. He shuddered and tried to look away, but Romana carried on looking back at him.

'Soooo,' she said. 'I was wondering, and I hope this isn't rude, but could I make a few suggestions?'

Grayce found himself unable to move.

Romana winked. 'It's just that – oh never mind.' She slipped an arm free of her bonds and took the mind probe gently from him. She tapped the top of it. 'You see this?' Her hand reached over and picked up an implement that had proved handy with fingernails. She levered open a flap on the mind probe and waggled the device carefully around inside. 'What you need to do – and I am sorry if I'm teaching you to suck eggs here – but you should have a look at the neuron stimulator – this thing.' She gave it a theatrical little tap. 'It's supposed to be hyper-pulsating the basal ganglia, but it's just hopelessly saturating the subcortical nucleii. Tickles. Oh.' She made a moue of gentle disappointment. 'Am I going too quickly for you?' She tapped the circuits again. 'See? If I turn this up another notch and reduce the gain on this, then it should work. No guarantees, mind.' She gave him a friendly smile. 'You have to remember that the Doctor's still never forgiven me for my repairs to the dishwasher. After I melted his YOU DON'T HAVE TO BE MAD TO WORK HERE BUT IT HELPS mug, he didn't speak to me for a day.' She pasted the flap back down and popped the mind probe on Grayce's head at a suitably jaunty angle.

Grayce felt finally able to break eye contact with her when something strange happened to his head and his brain had to run away. He toppled to the floor.

'See?' said Romana. 'Much better.' She sniffed. 'Definite smell of gumdrops.'

Some time later, the Doctor was being wheeled down a corridor.

Which was funny, because being wheeled past him in the opposite direction was Romana.

'Hello!' He waggled his hands around the manacles. 'It's half time and no oranges!'

'I know,' said Romana, looking up from her gurney. 'How's it going?'

'Oh not too bad. Mustn't grumble. They've being using Boolean Nerve Janglers.'

'Oh dear,' tutted Romana.

'I know.' The Doctor sighed up at the Krikkit robot wheeling him. 'I did try saying.'

'You put on quite a performance.'

'I know. Well, it seemed unfair not to. Did you get any of it?'

'Oh, it all came through loud and clear.'

The Krikkitmen wheeling the Doctor and Romana stopped. They'd clearly missed something.

The Doctor looked up at his robot. 'So, the screaming? Ah. It's the Sussurians of the Planet Cesper, you see. It's so terribly windy there that the only way they can communicate with each other is by a series of modulated shrieks. What you thought were my agonised cries were merely my way of keeping Romana abreast of the situation. Once spent a merry weekend translating *Wuthering Heights* for them. Went down a storm. Sorry to disappoint.'

Romana surveyed the thin, sour red light inside her Krikkitman's helmet. It was having trouble swallowing it.

'How's your torturer?' she asked.

'Having a bit of a lie-down,' the Doctor admitted. 'I think I may have deafened him. Yours?'

'Brain seizure.'

'Good, good,' the Doctor chuckled.

The Krikkitmen began to wheel them away, but the Doctor held up an imperious hand, his manacles dangling from it. 'Wait!' he cried.

The robots stopped.

'So,' he called back to Romana. 'We're now inside the seat of power.'

'Shall we get back to work?' she asked.

The Doctor slid off his gurney, at the same time slipping two small nerve prods inside the casing of his Krikkitman. Romana, likewise was already fusing the cortex of her robot with the thumbnail scraper she'd earlier slid up her sleeve.

Both robots howled in lethal fury as their bodies were wreathed in sparks.

The Doctor and Romana stood side by side, backing gently away as the Krikkitmen lurched towards them.

'I'm trying to overcome my innate terror of them,' the Doctor confided.

'How are you doing that?' asked Romana.

'By finding as many ways of destroying them as possible.' He ducked as a sharp fist smashed into the concrete behind him.

Romana shoved her trolley against the other Krikkitman, watching as it smashed it into splinters. 'That's quite hard, isn't it?'

'Sadly, yes.' The Doctor slid across the floor, dodging blast after blast from the Krikkitman's visor. 'I've done something terribly clever. The problem is –' he ducked behind a statue, which burst into fragments of burning concrete – 'that it's not working yet.'

'Pity,' tutted Romana. She was backed behind another statue. She did some quick calculations. 'Doctor, would you mind grabbing my ankle in 2.3 seconds please?'

'Beg pardon?'

Romana leapt out from behind the statue, flinging herself in a graceful arc towards the Doctor, and bringing herself exactly between the two robots. Both took aim and fired.

Romana was snatched abruptly out of the air, and the volley of devastation sailed over her head and into the Krikkitmen, who obligingly blew up.

Romana was lying on the ground, looking up at the ceiling.

'You were 0.2 seconds late,' she remarked.

'Was I?'

'Yes, but luckily I'd factored that in to my equations.'

The doors to the Great Parliament of the Elders of Krikkit smashed open. The Doctor and Romana rushed in wheeling two gurneys. On each of which was a small pile of robot parts.

'Elders of Krikkit,' boomed the Doctor to the astonished and revolted crowd. 'You're part of the biggest lie the Universe has ever been told.'

He threw something onto the floor. It was the head of a Krikkitman.

Pleasingly, that got their attention.

'I'm the Doctor and this is my friend Romana.' The Doctor paused, savouring the lovely rolling acoustic in the Parliament. 'We've spent a nice afternoon being tortured in your cells.'

'And jolly bracing it was too,' Romana said politely. She saw Elder Grayce in the crowd, and waved. He shuddered.

'But we've not just done it for our health,' boomed the Doctor. 'You've now got scans of our brains – lovely clear scans that will tell you, should you care to check, that what I am about to tell you is the absolute, unvarnished truth.'

Romana nodded. It was a good nod that said, 'Listen. It will do you good.' Romana never lied with a nod.

The Elders of Krikkit suffered two conflicting reactions – the first was the urge to recoil in revulsion and the second was the desire to lean forward and learn more. The result was a quivering stillness suggestive of constipation.

'How dare you,' Chief Elder Grayce began, heaving up his angry bulk to protest, but the Doctor had dealt with his sort before.

'How dare I? Easily, you poor old man. I'm the Doctor and I dare on behalf of the Universe.' He flicked up his scarf and dangled it like a yo-yo for invisible kittens. 'I disgust you, I revolt you, just looking at me makes you squirm. You think I'm your enemy, and it's true that before I finish here –' he checked his watch – 'in about four hours, I'll have changed civilisation as you know it, and destroyed every single Krikkitman. But one of the reasons for doing this is *you*. Because all of you are the victims of a strange and awful lie.'

'So you said,' Elder Grayce grumbled. If he didn't like aliens, he really didn't like show-stopping aliens. 'What is this lie?'

The Doctor glared at the Elder and then pinched a bit of air with his finger and thumb. 'Everything,' he said. 'This entire planet has been stage-managed. Your whole history consists of a series of events which are in themselves possible yet put together become highly improbable as a series of mere accidents of history. When viewed together, they can only be the product of terribly careful planning.'

The Doctor let that one land as softly as a walrus.

'What is a god?' he proclaimed. 'I've met a few pretenders to the throne. Mostly stark staring mad. I'll tell you the thing they all get wrong. They nail the trimmings – the togas, the crazy worshippers, the wide-eyed priests, the sacrifice and the awful proclamations that sound like they were written by a drunk in a bus shelter – but the thing they fail to do is to achieve anything. I'm standing here in the middle of this hall, and I am awed to be in the presence of the work of an actual god.'

CHAPTER TWENTY-NINE
THE SHARP-SIGHTED WATCHMAKER

Had a pin dropped it would have been deafening.

'But,' the Elder's voice croaked, 'we don't worship any deity.'

'Exactly!' The Doctor was laughing now. 'You're the product of a bashful god. Isn't that wonderful? Imagine being omnipotent and yet rubbish at parties!'

'Erm …' Romana used her most careful mutter. 'Are you sure about this?'

'Totally.' The Doctor beamed at her. 'Krikkit has a god that does not want to be seen.'

Elder Grayce started laughing. 'Have you, by any chance, come to make us worship them? Perhaps in exchange for some beads?' He turned, chuckling to the other Elders, 'We believe that's how it works.'

There was the nervous, sneering laughter of people who've decided the best thing to do with an inconvenient truth is to laugh at it. One old, tired woman stood at the back of the hall.

She was not laughing – either because she was considering the Doctor's words, or because her grim face was incapable of mirth. Her name was Elder Narase. She'd never been important – a lot of the Elders viewed Narase as too bloodthirsty, even for a Krikkita, and quietly avoided inviting her onto any exciting committees. This petty act was about to cost them all dearly.

'Sadly your god isn't a quack.' The Doctor was shaking his head sadly. 'I want you to think about what I'm going to tell you. Think about the freak conditions which separated Krikkit, isolating the planet from the rest of the Galaxy. That's Point A.

'Point B is the apparent mental block (caused by A) which prevented you from ever even speculating that something might lie beyond the great Dust Cloud. It stopped you wondering if anything was out there. It stunted your curiosity and also, uniquely, prevented you from wondering about deities in general. Funny that.

'Point C is the quite fantastic odds against a wrecked spacecraft actually intersecting with the orbit of a planet. There's a lot of empty space, you know. It's why we call it space. Because of the space. It is littered with broken-down spaceships. Some of them make quite nice second homes, but that's by the by. My point is that for an unpiloted spacecraft to crash-land on a planet is remarkable. To crash-land on the one planet in the Universe that wouldn't just assume it was an alien or a chariot of the gods? The chances against it are so obscene they should pull their trousers up.

'Point D is the miraculous rapidity with which you lot mastered the technology of the crashed spaceship and used it for interstellar war. Considering you had no experience behind you, your progress would make a Rutan greener with jealousy. Especially as, before then, you'd never even had a war.

'Point E. Once you'd decided on war, you were single-minded about it. Obsessively so. No referenda, no second thoughts, you simply dedicated your entire selves to the total annihilation of alien life. You didn't even think about how any of the remarkable advancements you'd got from the craft could have helped you in harvesting crops or making better television programmes. You just thought WAR.

'Point F. When the rest of the Galaxy captured the Krikkitmen, they failed to destroy them because they mistook them for sentient robots. Not only did your great war fail – it was meant to. The remaining Krikkitmen were supposed to be placed in storage.

'Point G. Did you notice that while you were sealed away in your Slow Time envelope you became a lot less single-minded (see Point E – keep up now)? In the last five years, haven't you achieved less, argued more, discovered paperwork? Haven't your Krikkitmen production factories stopped working? And haven't you noticed how, since the envelope has been unlocked, you're all suddenly single-minded, the dissidents have grown less … dissidenty and progress on your Ultimate Weapon has speeded up quite remarkably?

'In summary …' The Doctor concluded. 'Divine intervention.'

If he'd been hoping to stun his audience into silence, he failed. There was a lot of murmuring.

'Murmuring's not good,' Romana said softly.

'No,' admitted the Doctor. 'That's why I miss having K-9. He normally drowns that kind of thing out. Shame he's babysitting.'

Chief Elder Grayce gulped as though trying to swallow a live fish. 'Are you accusing us of having a god?'

'I'm not even sure what a god is,' someone shouted from the crowd.

'Some would say that's the point.' The Doctor grinned.

The Chief Elder turned angrily on him. 'Alien – not only do you dare to come here, but you talk to us of your abhorrent beliefs. Other life? Strange beings in the sky? No, the people of Krikkit will not be happy until the skies are completely empty.'

There was a surge of agreement. The surge had a strange tone to it – the sound is the same across the Universe. It is the sound

DOCTOR WHO

that people make when they've discovered something they don't like and want the world back the way it was. Again, an exception was the narrow-lipped face of Elder Narase. She'd clearly been sucking lemons all her life and wasn't about to stop now.

She strode forward, glared at the Doctor and then spat theatrically at his feet. 'This disgusting creature may have a point.' Her voice was sour. 'Leaving aside this god nonsense, he is arguing that something *alien* has been shaping events on our world, leading us on to the point where we destroy the rest of existence.'

'No, he's a dangerous subversive!' the Chief Elder snapped. The old woman favoured him with a look. He was the last chocolate in the box and her least favourite one.

Narase snapped her fingers. The air in front of them leapt into being, projecting a picture onto the ceiling.

'See,' she said. 'This is what sways me towards the words of this revolting alien. The Ultimate Weapon. It is complete.'

Hovering in the air was the projected image. It showed a group of Krikkitmen. They were standing guard around what had to be the Supernova Bomb. It was as disappointing as the plans suggested it would be – a small red ball. Standing by it was a Krikkitman, wielding a bat with delicacy. The Supernova Bomb, as though in an attempt to give it some more gravitas, was on a small podium.

Chief Elder Grayce was having none of the Doctor's wild ideas. 'The Supernova Bomb is the proof that we are not ruled by an outsider. We built it ourselves, while we were in isolation. It is all our own work.' There was relieved muttering from the crowd. Finally a bit of good news.

'Sure?' The Doctor was jabbing a finger at the projection of the bomb. 'I'm presuming you'll command the robots to strike and release the Supernova Bomb? Only, I've seen the plans, and that bomb's a dud.'

The Elders nodded, their nods a tiny bit uncertain. Elder Narase laughed at them. 'The Krikkitmen returned, helped us finish the bomb, offered to launch it at our command.'

'Is that so?' the Doctor mused. 'And there's absolutely no chance that they only freed your planet from Slow Time in order to do precisely that?'

'Clever, awful alien, yes,' the old woman cackled. 'Isn't their timing a bit too perfect? They explained that we lacked the necessary advancement to complete the bomb. That's all they wanted to talk about.'

Once you've got your hands on the Ultimate Weapon, thought Romana, you're naturally going to become a little preoccupied with when you use it. You're going to wake up every day and think, 'Today may well be the day that I wipe out the Universe. Events might just tip me over the edge. So everyone had better be on their best behaviour. And maybe I'll skip the post office.'

She found herself gloriously imagining having that power. The power to end existence. To wipe everything out. What would be her tipping point? Would it be a distant alien atrocity, or the Doctor's unwashed mug on the TARDIS draining board? At the back of her head, something stirred – a tiny trace of the control of the Krikkitmen. A little whisper about how nice and dark and quiet and peaceful the Universe would be, if only she'd turn the lights off. Then she remembered the glorious things she'd seen – the impossible worlds, the outrageous civilisations, the wondrous sunsets, the feeling of huddling with a bunch of rebels waiting for dawn and knowing that, at any moment, there was going to be a loud explosion and the Doctor would come dashing past yelling 'Change of plan …'

Yet here she was. Standing in a roomful of disbelieving duffers, and realising that, for a long time in the Universe there had, in fact, been no change of plan.

For his part, the Doctor was marvelling. He'd never expected to prove the existence of God. Still less to discover that God wanted to blow up the Universe.

'Your god has sent the Krikkitmen to you. Your god has literally controlled every aspect of your life – shaping you from long before the point he sent a spaceship crashing onto your shore.'

Elder Narase was laughing. Some of the elders had gone to a window and were staring out at the empty sky. Elder Grayce was looking old. 'Where … Where is God?'

'I shan't bore you with a philosopher's answer.' The Doctor strode to the great window. He pointed upwards into the great darkness. 'What is it that has kept you isolated for millions of years? Where did that spacecraft drift from? What is it that has been carefully nudging your minds this way and that, teasing little ideas in and out of them, slowly carefully subtly manipulating you into manic genocides?'

'But where?' demanded the Chief Elder again.

The old woman was looking out of the window and laughing and laughing.

'They say that God cannot be seen,' said the Doctor gravely. 'And in your case that's true. But you know it's there. You see it, and yet you don't see it, every day. Your god is in the Dust Cloud that surrounds your world.'

The entire hall turned to stare at the window, at the terrible blackness beyond. Silence fell, apart from the horrid cackling of the old woman.

'Congratulations, Krikkit,' said the Doctor. 'You have a god.'

Elder Grayce turned running to the projection, shouting at it. 'Stop! For God's sake stop the bomb!'

The cry was taken up by the other elders, all of them urging and screaming and pleading with the picture.

'The robots,' the Chief Elder groaned. 'They're not listening.'

'Of course not.' As if Elder Narase's laugh wasn't bad enough, her triumphant smile was worse. 'You're all too late.'

'God is done with you,' said the Doctor. 'You gave him his bomb. And that's it for you, me and all life in existence.'

Projected across the hall, the last adjustments to the great bomb were made. The Krikkitman strode up to the Supernova Bomb, and lifted up its bat. It swept it back, preparing a stroke it had been planning for many million years.

'It is too late!' Elder Grayce wailed. 'There is nothing we can do.'

The Krikkitman's bat reached the top of its stroke and then swung down.

The Doctor put his fingers in his ears.

The bat hit the bomb.

CHAPTER THIRTY
GOD HAS A PLAN-B

The bat hit the bomb.

A lot of sentences in the Doctor's life were complicated. Or, they started out simple and became complicated and a little worn at the edges.

But 'The bat hit the bomb' had a nursery-rhyme plainness to it which was admirable.

The bat hit the bomb.

The Universe did not end.

The Universe did not end, and the Doctor was laughing. A lot of Romana's days were like this. She adored them.

The great and mighty Supernova Bomb fizzed a bit.

That was all it did.

For a moment, the image on the screen threatened pantomime. The Krikkit robot, having swiped the bomb, reached the end of its stroke and stopped. The other robots stopped. Nothing happened.

The Doctor took his fingers out of his ears and laughed. His laughter was so loud that it drowned out the cackling of Elder

Narase. Realising she couldn't compete, she stopped, and glared at him.

'All that time, and it's still a dud!' The Doctor was fishing in his pockets. He passed a copy of *The Beano* to Romana. She noticed the top corner of Page 16 was folded down. She glanced at it, shrugged, and dropped it to the floor.

The Doctor had found what he was looking for and unfolded it. The blueprints to the Supernova Bomb. He made great play of studying them.

'Don't worry, just checking the top secret plans for your Supernova Bomb. You may well worry that I've stolen them, but I assure you they are long out of copyright. By several billion years.'

He unfolded them on the floor of the Parliament. 'Gather round,' he commanded.

No one did. They just stared at him in angry horror. Occasionally their eyes would drift to the screen, or to the suddenly sinister darkness hanging over them. Sometimes Chief Elder Grayce would interrupt the Doctor's explanation to demand an explanation. Sometimes Elder Narase would utter her entirely disagreeable chuckle. Mostly the Doctor and Romana just talked.

'You may be wondering why the Universe is still existing and what you can do about it. I wonder that a lot.' He winked at Romana. 'A long time ago, when the original Supernova Bomb was planned, a flaw was designed into it. When you started work on its replacement, your god may have guided your hand in a different direction. But you completed the bomb whilst you were sealed away from his influence. And you've only gone and repeated the original mistake. One the Krikkitmen failed to correct.'

The Elders stared at the Doctor.

'Well,' Romana added, 'turns out you gained free will, but lost scientific advancement. With sad consequences for your – well, we can hardly call it a bomb any more, can we?'

'A sparkler?' the Doctor offered. 'Did it cost a dreadfully large amount of money? I bet it did.'

There was silence.

The Doctor drew up his scarf, bundled it together and threw it through the projection before catching it again. 'Here we are,' he offered. 'It's the end of the line. The longest-running program in the Universe has finished. The Krikkitmen have run out of instructions. Your bomb is a dead end. That's it.' He turned to Romana. 'You know what? I'm growing to appreciate an anti-climax.'

Well, thought Romana, *the Doctor may be on Page 16 of* The Beano *but I'm already on Page 18, and it's not looking good for Biffo the Bear.* She appraised the Elders. Half of them could be summed up by the look on Chief Elder Grayce's face.

'You know,' he was muttering, sliding into a large marble chair, 'this has all been a lot to take in.'

Another faction was grouping around Elder Narase. She was sneering and cackling and shaking an enthusiastic fist at things. She'd come to laughter late in life and was making the most of it. The old woman turned on the Doctor with a wild triumph in her eyes. That look was normally step one in a sequence that led to a big red button and a cry of 'Nothing in the world can stop me now.'

'The Krikkitmen simply need new orders,' the old woman said. She stalked her way across the hall, pushing her face into the Doctor's. 'Disgusting alien!' she barked. 'You claim we are being manipulated – how can you be so sure that you aren't being manipulated as well?'

'Oh, come now,' the Doctor chuckled, not looking Romana in the eye. 'I'm a Time Lord. We're above that sort of thing. Hahaha.'

Romana groaned. The Doctor's fake laughter had once caused economic collapse on a casino planet and a royal wedding banquet to push aside the fish course.

She hoped the worry wasn't evident on her face. What if the Krikkitmen were still controlling her? What if they were controlling the Doctor? What if they were all part of someone else's grand plan?

Romana did some serious thinking and realised something worrying. 'Hang on—' she said.

Which was when the door burst open and the pram smashed in.

The Doctor had been rescued by many things – but never before had he been rescued by two screaming babies in a pram. A pram being pushed by a Krikkit robot who was going 'hushhushhushhush' while their mother strode behind carrying a large gun.

'Jal!' he beamed. 'Shouldn't you be in bed, resting?'

'With those two?' Jal shot a proud, tired look at her new-borns. 'They're far too loud. Come and stand over here. If you don't mind the noise.'

'Oh, some of my best friends have been screamers,' the Doctor said. Dismissing the entire gabble of Elders, he crossed the Parliament, and knelt down by the pram. The rest of the Universe had simply stopped existing as far as he was concerned. He was staring with deep fascination at the babies. Planet in existential turmoil? Billion-year plan? Menacing deity? Army of Krikkitmen? The Doctor put it all on pause to waggle his fingers in front of the children.

Oddly, his soft murmurs carried throughout the entire room.

'Do you know what you lovely creatures are? You're hope. Hope for this entire world. Now, don't be scared, you little scamps. You're remarkable – because you are the first babies born after the Slow Time field collapsed. The first children who aren't part of your god's plan. Whatever you two do in your entire life will be because you want to do it. And don't you forget that, Jal – when you catch them crayoning the sofa – it's free will.' The Doctor smiled with all of his teeth. 'And you wouldn't want anyone on this planet to interfere with your life would you? No you wouldn't.' He stood, his back to the entire cluster of Elders. He held up a hand. Not in surrender, but in stillness.

'I don't think I have to say any more, do I?'

The silence held.

'Do you, ah,' Sir Robot said, 'still need rescuing?'

'Good point,' the Doctor said. 'I don't think so. I've made my point and we're all in agreement and we're going to leave quietly.'

The silence agreed with him.

Until Elder Narase barked her blackboard scrape of a laugh. 'No.'

'No?' The Doctor's shoulders shrugged. 'It's a boring little word, but what does it mean?' His feet shuffled. 'You've just tried to destroy the Universe and discovered the existence of God. Have a sit down and a Garibaldi. Most importantly, don't make any sudden moves.'

'Kill them!' screamed Elder Narase.

'Like that one,' the Doctor sighed sadly. A 'You'll regret this later once I've destroyed your army and made a lot of mess' sigh.

'Wait,' Chief Elder Grayce shouted over the roars of assent. 'That won't achieve anything, will it?' His hesitation at the end was fatal. The shouts became louder. The Elders of Krikkit, who, for a while had seemed on the brink of listening, were now baying for blood.

Romana thought it useless and sad. Tearing her and her friends limb from limb would achieve nothing beyond some mild staining of the floor. And yet, she supposed, that kind of demonstrated the conditioning of the Krikkitas. They were unable to cope with alien life.

'I've a suggestion.' Jal smiled wearily at the Doctor and Romana. 'Do you two run?'

'Do we?' The Doctor and Romana turned to each other and grinned.

And so, that was how the Doctor and Romana came to be running for their lives, pushing a pram.

Behind them, Sir Robot and Jal held back the ferocious Elders of Krikkit. This was quite easy. The Elders hadn't thought to bring their guns to work with them. Jal was happily blasting chunks from the ceiling. The noise was terrific, and yet, over it all, carried the wailing of Jal's babies.

'They are loud, aren't they?' the Doctor said, pushing the pram at a frantic pace.

'Not that way, Doctor.' Romana realised he had quite limited experience of wheeling things. He'd once trundled around Davros, creator of the Daleks (that hadn't gone well) and then there'd been the time they'd gone to a supermarket looking for mercury for the fluid links and … she shuddered at the memory of the Doctor holding up the biscuit aisle while he tried to mend the wheels of the shopping trolley with his screwdriver while hissing, 'Earlier this morning I sewed shut a quantum corridor, so why do you have to be so difficult?'

Romana looked at the two howling babies and wondered if they were hope for the future, or simply handy symbols. Well, something was better than nothing. Even if the one on the left was smelling quite unsavoury all of a sudden.

'Wait!'

A figure called out to them. It was Chief Elder Grayce, his clothes bloodied and torn. He tried pulling himself up to a level of authority, but he fell back against a pillar, exhausted. 'Aliens,' he began. 'If what you say is true, then go to our god. Do what you can. I will delay any further attacks. I will give you what time I can.'

Romana doubted it.

The Doctor reached out and shook his hand. The Elder recoiled.

'I appreciate this,' said the Doctor. 'Your planet is on the brink.'

Elder Grayce nodded, and turned to stall the baying mob heading towards him.

The Doctor's group ran on.

Sirens were sounding through the Parliament building. Still not enough to drown out the crying of the infants. 'Gosh. They are effective at asking for things.' The Doctor leant over the pram. 'Go on, ask for universal peace, I dare you.'

Chief Elder Grayce stood his ground. He'd spent his entire life standing his ground. He'd stood firm during the last days of the Krikkit War. He'd stood firm in a foul alien courtroom. He'd stood firm during their five years of Insulting Disgrace. He'd placed his feet solidly behind the plans for the Supernova Bomb, and he'd definitely dug in when the Krikkitmen had returned to help out. So was it any surprise that, faced with a massive change in circumstances, he'd stand firm?

That old woman sneered at him. What was her name again? For the life of him, he couldn't remember.

'Narase,' she told him as though she wasn't surprised at his ignorance. Grayce had always dismissed her. A lot of the Elders did. Her father, or was it her grandfather, had been something of terrible importance, at the extreme end of things. And, for a Krikkita, the extreme really was extreme. But, all that said, she'd always been valued for her sharp brain. There wasn't much harm in having the odd crank in government – after all, they were going to blow up the Universe, so it didn't hurt to have the odd idea which was so out there as to make that seem rational.

Narase smirked sourly at him. She was flanked by two Krikkitmen.

'Where are they from?' he said.

Narase shrugged. 'I don't care,' she told him. 'But they obey me. That is all that matters.'

'Obey you?' he scoffed. 'I'm Chief Elder. They should obey me.'

'Fine.' Narase crossed her arms nastily. How she managed this is curious, but there was insolence, contempt and sourness in the folding of her elbows. 'Perhaps you should issue them with an order.'

'Very well.' Grayce felt a little worried by this. He looked at the robots, at the red fires glowing in their helmets. 'Stop the fighting!' he commanded, for the first time in his life.

The Krikkitmen did nothing.

'My turn,' said Narase, and she gave Grayce a slow, steady look, one that made his mouth go dry.

'Kill him,' she said.

And they did.

The Senate of Elders was in a mess. Elder Narase stepped over the bodies of the injured and dying, and sat on the Chief Elder's throne. She was laughing. She had never sought power, she had never spoken out for it. That was how she'd got it in the end. She may have been old, but now was the time to have fun.

'No delays,' Narase laughed again, and her battered, tired followers wondered if they'd ever get her to do something about that laugh. 'I've issued orders to the Krikkitmen and they are now carrying them out. I've ordered them to go to war.' She looked down at the groaning figures of those who had stood against her. The option that most politicians wished for was open to her. 'And kill everyone who disagreed with me.'

Standing on a plateau, Romana looked up at the sky. It was a beautiful sight.

'Goodness! There are stars over Krikkit,' she said. 'It looks how it should.'

The Doctor shook his head, sadly. 'Those aren't stars,' he sighed. 'They're spaceships. That's the Krikkit battle fleet.' As he spoke, the lights burnt brightly and then vanished.

'Plan B,' he said. 'They're off to wipe out the Universe one planet at a time.'

The babies started crying again.

CHAPTER THIRTY-ONE
THE FIRST ELEVEN

The august and ancient citadel of Gallifrey drew itself together, a collection of cathedrals leaning in to whisper important secrets to each other. Gallifrey knew peace, Gallifrey knew order, Gallifrey did not, definitely did not, know change.

Until a small cricket pavilion popped out of thin air in the middle of the Panopticon. A woman stepped out, dressed fetchingly in a sports jacket.

'Good afternoon,' said Romana, checking her watch. 'I've just invaded. Could you hurry the President along?'

(Acting) President Borusa boggled with outrage. Up until now, Romana had never seen her ex-tutor boggle.

'What is the meaning of this?' the little man was demanding.

'This old thing?' said Romana, leaning against the pavilion. Her jollity vanished. 'It's been the biggest clue of all, and it has been hiding in plain sight.'

'Explain what you mean!' rasped Borusa, as he often had at the end of one of her frankly exhausting essays.

'Krikkit craft are vast warships. This is similar in design but not in function. Krikkit warships are imitative of the craft that crashed on their planet. This pavilion is not. It dematerialises from one point and materialises in another. It is also roomy enough for five million and a bit Krikkit warriors to hide inside. Is this reminding you of anything?' Romana paused, partly for dramatic effect and to make sure, for the seventeenth time, that she'd got her workings out right. She had, of course. 'To top it all, I've just landed it on Gallifrey.

'Only one kind of craft can land on Gallifrey,' she continued. 'A TARDIS. Anything else is impossible. Gallifrey is protected by a ring of Transduction Barriers.'

The meaning of Romana's words made its way into Borusa's brain. 'You managed to breach the Transduction Barriers with that thing?'

Romana nodded.

'But, they were built by the finest temporal engineers over four generations.'

'Well, I wish they'd taken five and done it properly,' said Romana. 'I came here to warn you – the Krikkit fleet is coming. They're going to wipe out the Universe one planet at a time, and they're coming here first.'

Borusa shrugged. Many fleets had tried. Many fleets had failed.

Once the polite laughter of the assembled Time Lords had died down, Romana tapped the pavilion again. 'They're coming in craft like this.'

Silence echoed across the Panopticon, and with it a shudder of fear.

'Somehow, Krikkit has acquired Gallifreyan technology. Including a way through the Transduction Barriers.'

A long time ago, the best way to protect your castle was to build a moat around it and fill it with water. That had been fine until the invention of powdered cement. Borusa stared up into the sky as though it was about to fall down.

'Scramble the Transduction Barriers!' the President yelled. 'Gallifrey is under attack.'

Romana should have felt pleased. She'd been on Gallifrey for under a quarter of an hour and already all the alarms were sounding, the planet was being invaded and Borusa was having a panic attack. This was a record the Doctor would find hard to beat.

Then she looked up at the orange clouds above the citadel. And she knew it was an empty victory.

The skies of Gallifrey burst into sparks as one by one, the Krikkit warships started pushing their way through and, not needing a better plan, began firing.

The Vast And Terrible Krikkit Fleet hurled themselves at the Transduction Barriers[9] and ploughed through all of them, burning the orange sky cinnamon.

At which point the Transduction Barriers just switched off.

Suddenly unimpeded, the Krikkit fleet accelerated uncontrollably towards the Capitol, only to find that it was no longer there.

'This is highly irregular,' huffed Romana's ex-tutor.

Romana's boots didn't answer him. That was all that could be seen of her. The rest of her was buried deep inside the Transduction Barrier controls, hammering away with a spanner.

---

[9] The First Barrier was a force field of such staggering power that it could rip open the hearts of atoms. The Second Barrier was a barrier of ideas – it refused to let anything through because it didn't believe that was possible. The Third Barrier was a barrier of reflection – it countered any approach with an equal and opposite idea. Then there was the Fourth Barrier of Stubborn Philosophy. This barrier refused to believe in the existence of the alien craft, and reiterated it until, exhausted, many fleets would slink away, announcing that they'd suddenly remembered another appointment.

'I've saved the planet, haven't I?' said Romana.

'That remains to be seen,' rumbled Borusa.

The planet shook. It was the sound of an entire battle fleet smacking into an unexpected mountain range.

The shaking subsided.

'So,' said Romana, pulling herself out of the machinery.

'Indeed,' marvelled Borusa. 'You diverted the energy from the Barriers into the planetary rotation. Clever.'

'I thought so,' Romana was dusting herself off. 'Let's go and fight back. What have you got? Oh, and –' this was delivered a fraction too late – 'mind your head.'

They called it the Chamber of the First Eleven. The first twelve War TARDISes had been built to fight the Krikkitmen. One had been lost during the conclusion of the war, but the remaining eleven had been placed in storage. Gallifrey had, it realised, little use for War TARDISes, especially ones so viciously effective.

Ever since, the First Eleven had been penned up in their Chamber. They looked innocuous enough – a collection of armour-plated cupboards. If Dracula had owned a wardrobe, if Rasputin had a garden shed, or the Borgias had needed a portable toilet, then they'd probably have looked like a War TARDIS. A cathedral roof's worth of lead had been fastened across the smallest possible surface area with the greatest possible number of rivets. A War TARDIS bristled with spikes and weapons that were somehow invisible in this dimension and yet utterly present.

They were also soul-shakingly loud.

'What is that?' Romana wrinkled her nose. It seemed the wrong response but, even high up on this walkway, the noise was roaring in her head without ever troubling her ears.

'They mutter a lot,' said Borusa, peering down into the pens with a weary shudder. 'They don't approve of Gallifrey's policy of non-intervention.'

'But that's been going on for aeons!' Romana protested. 'Surely they'd have grown used to it.'

'You'd think,' Borusa nodded. 'Instead, they have become resentful.'

The whispering sharpened in Romana's head. Ordinarily, whispering didn't do this. Whispering was a soft, hissing thing. But this was as soft and hissing as a hungry snake. The whispering slithered through her brain, mentally ticking off all those occasions of deadly peril when she could have been helped out marvellously by a lovely, armoured War TARDIS.

'Release us!' boomed the War TARDISes.

Borusa surveyed them warily and checked his chronometer. 'The barriers are falling. I think we need to do this.' He scratched his nose. 'The problem is, there's no way of doing this without sounding pompous, and I so hate that.'

'Even now?' Romana queried.

'Oh yes,' Borusa looked like a bank manager at the end of a long and difficult day involving postal orders. 'But I suppose we'd better.' He harrumphed. 'Release the—' He stopped, realising that this was a great moment in his presidency and shouldn't sound like an apology. 'Release the War TARDISes.'

As he said the words and the ancient bonds dissolved, the air filled with an angry, terrible roaring. Eleven War TARDISes snapped and bit at the fabric of the Universe, ready to tear into it. Romana wondered if this had been such a clever idea after all.

CHAPTER THIRTY-TWO
THE IRON LADY

The Krikkit Pavilion arrived smartly on the ground at Lord's. Romana stepped out blinking. 'Well, that went exactly according to plan,' she thought. In some ways she missed travelling by TARDIS. Mind you, she'd enjoyed pressing a button and going where she expected without having to coax, cajole, tease and plead with both the Doctor and his craft. Both were quixotic, unpredictable, and all too liable to get distracted by something going on 500 years in the opposite direction.

Normally, this was fine (more or less depending, Romana had to admit, on what the TARDIS wardrobe was serving up). But right now she had to save a universe quickly.

Things had stared out well. She'd rescued Gallifrey. Then Borusa had freed eleven War TARDISes to protect all of time and space. Which was where her beginner's luck had run out. The entire fleet of War TARDISes had blinked out of existence.

'But I didn't get to give them instructions,' bleated Borusa. 'Do you think they'll know what to do?'

'Hum,' Romana had said, looking up at the empty sky. She was so preoccupied, she didn't notice Borusa miss his footing at the edge of the walkway.

When the Doctor had given her the mission, it had all seemed so easy. 'I'll go and talk to the god. You tackle the Krikkitmen.'

It was reasonable that the Krikkitmen would attack the planets that had contained the parts of the Wicket Gate. She'd been hoping to dispatch the War TARDISes to protect the next targets. But instead she was doing it single-handed.

Romana looked around the cricket ground for someone in authority.

The air was still full of smoke, and there was screaming and yelling. Well, either this sort of thing was always happening, or she'd arrived in the immediate aftermath of her previous visit, a surprisingly compressed timescale which meant that the Earth was about to be invaded twice in the same day.[10]

A self-important man came running up to her and started yelling at her to get off the grass.

Romana looked down at her feet and then across at the ground, where people lay around injured, dying, or distressed. And then she looked at the burning grass. Finally, she looked back at the man who was so angry even his blazer seemed furious.

'You would like me to get off the grass?' she asked slowly.

'Absolutely, madam.' The man's whole face twisted into a scowl. 'That is not any grass, that is *the* grass.'

'Is it the pitch?' Romana reached for the right term.

'The pitch!' the man roared in fury. 'This is sacred turf and no matter what happens here, every blade of it must be preserved.'

---

[10] Curiously, this was not the only time this had happened. Due to a horrendous diary conflict, the Post Office Tower's grim attempt at global domination and the Chameleons' plan to kidnap teenagers from Gatwick Airport had both clashed with the Daleks unleashing chaos from their time-travelling antiques shop.

An ambulance roared over it, swerved, and some people jumped out with stretchers.

The angry man was staring at the long, dirty black mark left in the turf. His lip was quivering, slightly out of time with the rest of his face.

Romana looked him seriously in the eye. 'I think,' she said, 'You've had a difficult day and should have a rest over there.'

The man lay down and slept.

Romana regarded the chaos and the screaming surrounding her. This was why the Time Lords had rules about not interfering. It was easy to get distracted saving ordinary people rather than concentrating on the bigger picture. Vowing to offer emergency medical aid to no more than five people, Romana set off to find someone in charge of the planet.

Looking back on the next hour, Romana reflected that sometimes she was still the naïve centenarian she'd been when she'd first met the Doctor. This time it wasn't her fault. The Universe arranged itself in such a way that the Doctor managed to meet whoever was running a planet almost as soon as he left the TARDIS. Admittedly, quite often he'd be found standing over the ruler's smoking body just as a lot of guards ran in, and it would get a little distracting, but the point was that the Doctor had a knack of finding who was in charge.

It turned out that wandering around a cricket ground asking people, 'Are you in charge of this planet as it's about to be wiped out by killer robots?' was not a good way to get a sympathetic audience. It was, in fact, the best way to get yourself strapped to a gurney by a medic who told you to shut up while she got on with saving lives.

'That's exactly what I'm trying to do,' protested Romana. Eventually the paramedic ran off, so Romana released the straps and looked around the ambulance. She assumed it was somehow connected to a positronic inoframe – after all, this was the twentieth century, not the dark ages.

She sat herself in the front seat behind the 'steering wheel' (the Doctor had taught her a few technical terms, and also that, no matter how tempting, you should never engage the handbrake when pursuing the Master down a bypass) and tried to familiarise herself with the operating system. There was a sort of dangling microphone thing that crackled. She pulled it towards her and spoke carefully into it.

'Computer, take me to the ruler of the planet Earth.'

The microphone crackled. And then said uncertainly, 'Pat, is that you?'

Having worked out the complicated business with some buttons, Romana repeated her request. The voice at the other end became quite firm in its hope that Romana would stop playing around on an emergency channel. Romana told the voice that it was an emergency and she had come to save the planet from aliens. The voice stopped answering her after that.

Romana slumped back in the chair and looked around the ambulance, drumming her fingers on the leatherette seating. She could command the on-board operating system to drive her to the Palace of the Ruler of the Earth, but that might take time, and others might need the ambulance for tending to the sick. That said, it did have a nice-looking siren on top. During her travels with the Doctor, Romana had become partial to a siren.

'What I really need,' she announced, 'is a name and an address. That's all.'

This was when she noticed the computer. It was to the left of the steering wheel and had a few helpful buttons and a dial. She pressed it and waited for it to load up and ask her what she wanted.

Instead the device told her that its name was Wogan and that it would be back with her in a minute after the news and weather. It then promised a long-delayed punchline to a lovely joke about marmalade.

Romana frowned at the device. Clearly, not a computer. She was about to turn it off, when a slightly different voice came out of it, one which said, 'The Prime Minister, speaking from 10 Downing Street …'

Romana leaned back in her chair and smiled. A name and an address. That was all.

'Good afternoon, I was wondering if I could borrow your weapons.'

The Prime Minister stared at the woman sat in her chair. Then, for reasons which made no sense to her, she found herself saying, 'Could you tell me why there's a cricket pavilion in my office?'

The glamorous young woman shrugged. 'It's how I travel,' she said. There was a flicker in her eye, as though she was aware how ridiculous that seemed, whilst adamantly refusing to apologise. The Prime Minister sized her up.

'You are, I take it, an alien?'

'Yes. My name is Romana and you're marvellously direct,' the young woman beamed at her.

The Prime Minister was working things out. This young woman was clearly formidably strange. She noticed that the door had closed and her security detail was elsewhere. No matter. She could sort that out. What she really wanted to know was – was –

'The reason I'm here is that this planet is about to be wiped out by a space fleet. There's a slim chance I can help you if you let me borrow your defences for a bit.' The young woman held up a hand. 'No, don't lock me up. It's been a long day and I really don't want to spend my last moments saying, "I told you so" as my prison cell is obliterated. Tiresome. Now –' she smiled sweetly – 'just checking, but you are in charge of this world, are you not?'

Whatever her private opinions on the matter, the Prime Minister favoured Romana with the following. 'I simply control these British islands.'

'You only control Britain?'

'Yes.'

'But that's a tiny land mass.'

The Prime Minister frowned.

Romana shared the frown. 'This is more complicated than I was expecting. Honestly, we spend so much time here I had assumed England was important. Clearly not.' Romana seemed to make a mental note to have a word with someone. 'Are you by any chance on friendly terms with someone who matters?'

The Prime Minister, who had just got back from a trying conference in Belgium, really didn't have an answer for that.

Romana adopted another tack. 'Does anyone actually rule the planet Earth?'

The Prime Minister's eyes wandered longingly to a decanter. 'My dear Romana,' she said, leaning back against the desk and easing her shoes off (they had begun to pinch nastily in Bruges), 'Earth does not have a single ruler, per se—'

'No one in a cloak?' Romana put in hopefully.

The Prime Minister had a brief, pleasant image of Bela Lugosi and smiled slightly. 'No, my dear. You really need to speak to the United Nations.'

Romana brightened. 'They sound smashing.' She put a hat on her head. 'Where are they?'

'Well,' the Prime Minister mused, 'I'm fairly certain that a special session can be tabled within 72 hours. There might not be China—'

'I don't care about crockery!' thundered Romana. 'This planet doesn't have 72 minutes, let alone 72 hours. The battle fleet's screaming through Mutter's Spiral right now.'

'The battle fleet?' the Prime Minister said carefully. 'You've not mentioned their name.'

'No,' Romana said firmly. 'Their name's silly, and we'd spend the next few minutes arguing about that and meanwhile they'd just be getting closer and closer to you and right now I just need to reach these United Nations and get them to activate your planetary-wide defence array.'

The Prime Minister surprised her by bursting out laughing and then laying a sympathetic arm on her sleeve. 'Romana,' she said, trotting over to the decanter and handing Romana a crystal goblet full of something that tasted like tar. 'I'm afraid we don't have a defence array. We've never really needed one.'

'Pshaw!' scoffed Romana magnificently. 'You can't just rely on the Doctor popping up whenever you need him …' She faltered, and gaped. 'That's exactly what you do do. Good heavens.'

Ah, the Prime Minster thought to herself. This was making more sense. She'd once been sat opposite the Doctor at a cheese and wine evening at Auderly House. The Doctor had been an outlandish white-haired figure who'd spent the entire evening insulting civil servants (which she'd found fun). A curious man – was this really the mysterious alien who saved the Earth? – she'd found that even harder to believe when he'd driven off in a yellow car quite clearly stolen from a clown.

Romana had also been thinking jolly hard. 'Have you any … nuclear weapons?' She pronounced the last phrase with the heavy quaintness you'd use when asking an antiques dealer for a butter churn.

'Of course, Great Britain has nuclear weapons,' the Prime Minister announced proudly.

'Well done you,' said Romana, with what the Prime Minister completely missed was heavy irony. 'I'll need to get my hands on at least a dozen.'

'I'm afraid you can't,' said the Prime Minister. 'They're all deployed in submarines. In the deep sea.'

Romana blinked. 'Are you planning on declaring a war on cod?'

'There's always America,' announced the Prime Minister. 'They have the Star Wars defence programme.'

Romana perked up.

'It's a range of armed nuclear satellites in orbit around the Earth,' said the Prime Minister.

Romana did a nimble little jig. 'That's just what I meant by a defence array. Can you put me in touch with whoever's in charge – if I give them the coordinates of the approaching fleet they can shoot them down in a trifle.'

'Ah,' said the Prime Minister. 'Those weapons are not aimed at the skies. They are aimed at the planet.'

Romana gave the Prime Minister what her mother would have termed an 'old-fashioned look'. And then she delivered a talking-to that single-handedly caused a cabinet reshuffle.

'Do you have any idea, Prime Minister, how many inhabited worlds there are out there? Many have given birth to wonderful, friendly civilisations that shine like spun sugar. But many others harbour creatures so deadly, merciless, and hungry, and they're all coming your way. That's not a matter of conjecture. You humans, you have the audacity to ignore it. You point your most advanced weapons at yourself? That's taking narcissism to extremes.'

The Prime Minister was about to counter with a bromide of her own, but she got as far as 'Look here—' before Romana held up her hand.

'It doesn't matter,' she said brightly. She tapped the wall of the cricket pavilion.

'I'd better get on with saving the planet. Coming?'

The Prime Minister shook her head regretfully. 'Much as I'd love to, my dear, I've got a press conference about income tax in a couple of hours.'

'Very soon tax may cease to exist,' said Romana, opening the door invitingly.

The Prime Minister picked up her glass and followed. She paused, turned back and fetched the decanter. 'I think,' said the Prime Minister, 'that I shall be needing this.'

CHAPTER THIRTY-THREE
DANGER INTO ESCAPE

'Why would anyone want to make a cricket pavilion that was bigger on the inside than the outside?' asked the Prime Minister.

'Style,' answered Romana. She did not care to explain how Earth's hideous act of cultural misappropriation had translated the warfaring design ethic of the planet Krikkit into hopeless whimsy.

The Prime Minister sat down on a bench. She looked around herself and her eyes were shrewd. 'This vessel contains a lot of benches. Each bench could hold between ten and a dozen—'

'Eleven, yes.' Romana was busying herself with the control panel and hoping that the various controls didn't look too much like clothes hooks and drawing pins on a corkboard.

'This is a way of transporting troops,' the Prime Minister announced, folding her hands. 'Admirable.' She considered. 'What are we doing?'

The pavilion was shaking slightly.

'I'm trying to work that out,' said Romana.

*

Somewhere in the deepest, darkest, coldest and definitely wettest part of the Atlantic Ocean was a submarine. The submarine excelled at not being found.

The submarine was waiting for the phone to ring. But it never did. Because if it rang, it would mean the end of the world.

The phone rang.

The captain's face was impassive as he took the call. It could only mean that Britain had fallen and it was the submarine's job to retaliate.

The voice at the other end was the Prime Minister. She sounded curiously upbeat. 'Captain, we were wondering if we could ask you a small favour?'

The Krikkit fleet had made rapid headway through Mutter's Spiral and was now streaking through the solar system. In its wake flitted eleven shadows, all of them interested to see what happened next.

On their whistle-stop vengeance tour, the Krikkitmen now had the planet Earth in their sights. First would come the death rays. Then the troops would scour the planet for survivors. So would perish everywhere that had held one of the sacred objects. Once these planets were out of the way, then everything else could be destroyed.

The Krikkit fleet focused itself on the Earth and prepared for the bombardment. Which is when the planet did something unexpected.

It exploded.

'Now, it looks worse than it is,' said Romana.

The Prime Minister was staring out of a window at the vast fireball that had, seconds ago, been her home planet.

She was also holding on to a bench for dear life as the pavilion shook itself apart. She was trying to work out what to say, but, for once in her life, her mouth just kept opening and closing.

Eventually she managed, 'The Earth – what's happened to the Earth?'

'Oh, it's fine,' said Romana, glancing at the fireball. Her fingers were working the various control nodules in a blur of pins. 'Well, mostly fine. I've detonated the entire nuclear arsenal.'

The Prime Minister stood up, made a furious grab for her and then sat down again. 'What have you done—'

'Firstly,' Romana adopted her stern tone, 'the weapons are simply doing exactly what they're supposed to. Why else did you build them? Secondly, I'm containing the blast and using it for something else.'

'What?'

'You really wouldn't understand.' Romana was wondering how the Doctor put up with every decision being constantly questioned. It was a little trying. 'You're not a quantum physicist.'

'No, but I am a chemist.' The Prime Minister's tone was so steely that Romana flinched. 'You may patronise everyone else you come across but—'

'I'm so sorry.' Romana shot her an apology. The pavilion's flight evened out. 'Then you'll be aware that most chemical reactions occur when the bonds between molecules break down—'

The Prime Minister looked again at the fireball. 'And a nuclear reaction is the uncontrollable sundering of substances at an atomic level.'

'Normally you have three states of matter – solid, liquid and gas. But during a nuclear explosion there's a fourth – Don't Know. Quantum physics gets interested at this point – there's a vast amount of uncertainty released. Believe it or not, this craft works along similar lines, so I'm currently harvesting that vast amount of quantum hesitation and putting it to good use.'

The Prime Minister strode towards the control panel. She gestured to the fireball. 'You've not destroyed my planet?'

'Certainly not. It's an impressive smokescreen while I harness the explosive force. Of course, if I fail to control it, then, yes, the planet Earth will go up like a nylon nightie.'

'What are you planning to do with it?'

Romana pulled a cable out of the control panel. It looked, for all the world, like a handy piece of string. She coupled it to something else and then stepped back, dubiously. 'I'm wrapping the Earth in a ... let's call it a force field. The tricky thing is that it won't last long.'

The Prime Minister leant forward, her sharp eyes sparkling. 'My dear, may I make a suggestion?'

The Krikkit Fleet barely let the explosion slow them down. It would not be the first planet which had destroyed itself rather than face their onslaught. That said, there would always be survivors to be picked off. The fleet accelerated preparing to sail through the curtain of flame.

The fleet carried on accelerating.

Only.

An odd thing.

Was happening.

The fleet was definitely.

Accelerating.

Only.

It was.

Also.

Not going anywhere.

The fleet accelerated.

The fleet didn't go anywhere.

The fleet accelerated.

The fleet didn't go anywhere.

The fleet ...

Look, you get the picture, don't you?

*

'It worked!' Romana clapped giddily, grabbed the Prime Minister's glass and emptied it with a laugh and a cough. 'Always moving, never arriving! That was a brilliant idea.'

'I got it from Brussels.' The Prime Minister looked at the fleet. 'Are they going to stay there?'

'For quite some time,' Romana said. 'My original plan of putting the entire Earth in a Slow Time envelope would have given me a few hours' breathing space, but instead that lot should stay there until your sun collapses. At which point they'll get a rude awakening – but not a long one.'

'A fleet is always smaller than the area it is seeking to attack,' the Prime Minister said. She refilled her glass and took a moment to admire the view. The Krikkit fleet hung there, motionless. The Prime Minister realised she was standing in a shed in space between her planet and the aliens who had come to destroy it.

'It would be so easy to wipe them out, but I'd like the fleet to remain there,' she announced. 'I am not one for trinkets, but it should prove a useful deterrent to others.'

Romana nodded. 'The folly of war.'

'Quite.' The Prime Minister smiled, and then her face fell. 'Oh dear, what'll I tell Ronnie about his nuclear missiles? He was so proud of them.'

Romana shrugged. 'Again, you have two options. One is to admit you've dodged obliteration and move on. The other, which I suspect you'll take, is to not say a word. So long as everyone believes you still have the weapons, what's the harm?'

'But what if someone calls our bluff?'

'Then pick your wars carefully,' advised Romana.

The Prime Minister looked thoughtful.

'You could always put those submarines to good use,' suggested Romana. 'Make peace with your cod.'

The Prime Minister made her afternoon press conference with a spring in her step and steel in her eye. She waved away questions about apparent atmospheric disturbances, preferring instead to dwell with surprising fondness on income tax. Almost like she was paying tribute to an old friend who'd survived a brush with death.

Romana gunned her way across the Universe. She'd managed to stop another batch of Krikkitmen. But how many more were there?

In the shadow of Mars, eleven shapes watched the shimmering Krikkit fleet floating helplessly in space. They could have intervened, but their orders were to wait until they were needed. So, the eleven shapes faded away.

CHAPTER THIRTY-FOUR
SAVING THE UNIVERSE

'I can't be everywhere at once,' sighed Romana.

Only two people in the Universe have ever succeeded in being everywhere at once. One was Mrs Tamsin Wells, of Hampstead, North London. At the end of a particularly exacting day juggling the varying demands of her children, her husband, her nanny, her builders, her personal trainer and her career spent ignoring various different kinds of paperwork, she had realised it was all too much. There was only one thing for it – either hire a second nanny, or invent a time machine. Pouring herself a large glass of white wine, she knuckled down to the latter, and, much to her surprise, found arguing with the laws of relativity a doddle compared to balancing ballet class with pony club. Having invented a time machine, she was then able to devote the rest of her life to being everywhere at once. There were only two drawbacks to this. Although Tamsin lived a long and happy life, she only lasted another ten years from the point of view of her family. But what a ten years they were – not a recital missed, not a lunchbox unpacked, not a dental check-up skipped. The other drawback was that her family found the whole process utterly exhausting. One day, a few years later, a surprisingly spry 93-year-old Tamsin left her shape-up-and-dance class, announcing that she was just going to have a quick sit down in the park before her next meeting, and was never seen again.

The only other person who ever succeeded in being everywhere at once did so without even trying. Cardinal Melia had been the pilot of a War TARDIS until his abrupt change of address. The reasons for his complete relocation will be touched on later.

There is also a philosophical argument that Beethoven is everywhere. The basis of this is that all the atoms that once were Beethoven have by now been broken down, absorbed and re-entered the ecosystem. For a while, Beethoven remained purely a Planet Earth problem. But, then, of course, spaceships started leaving the planet, or arriving on it in ever-increasing and aggressive numbers. A rocket ship couldn't land, fire a few weapons and then blast off without a little bit of Beethoven getting stuck on its shoes. Beethoven rapidly became ubiquitous. This really wasn't a problem – given the amount of Beethoven in circulation divided by the sheer number of atoms in the Universe. That was until a lecturer on galactic homeopathy announced that the concentration was such that the entire Universe should now be renamed Beethoven. There was no use in pointing out that Beethoven was simply being used as an example to illustrate a universal truth about the behaviour of atoms. This just caused the galactic homeopaths to double down. To deny the existence of Beethoven was pointless as Beethoven was now everywhere, and would, at any moment, begin composing again. If you listened carefully.

If you'd asked Beethoven his opinion, you'd not have got an answer. For one thing he was dead. For another, he was profoundly deaf. While he was still alive, if you'd asked him (probably quite loudly) what he thought about future generations breathing in tiny bits of his toenails, he would have favoured you with a splendidly Germanic look of confused disgust.

Talk of the Beethoven Universe may seem like a distraction, but it is all about to become relevant to the Doctor's search for God.

When tackling a quest, the Doctor liked to sit down and talk it through with his dog. K-9, while flattered at being confided in, was also less certain about the wisdom of it on this occasion.

'Nonsense.' The Doctor was pacing up and down a TARDIS corridor. 'Romana can look after herself. She doesn't need you to defend her.'

K-9 was weighing the merits of this argument. Yes, the Mistress did possess a high degree of competence. But she was also trying to save several planets from heavily armed battle fleets. K-9 realised the limits of his weaponry, but all the same, something was better than nothing. Also, pleasant as it was to be asked his opinion, he knew the Doctor would ignore it. That said, there was nothing K-9 liked more than to offer advice.

The Doctor slid in front of him in a beaming crouch. 'Tell me K-9 …' He stared at the dog intently. 'How would you go about finding God in a cloud?'

For once K-9 was lost for words.

'The God of Krikkit is unique in that they do not want to be perceived. I've heard of vengeful gods, wrathful gods, but never bashful gods. Still, all gods, need a heaven.[11] It's appropriate that the God of Krikkit actually lives in a cloud. But if the Dust Cloud is all part of that God's plan, then maybe the God doesn't simply live in the cloud – no matter how traditional that bit is …'

---

[11] Heavens were often seen as places where gods could look down on people. The Ancient Greeks assumed their gods sat on mountains, always on the lookout for wars or maidens bathing. The SmartFish of Dallion IV mistook fishermen for deities. Which led to a lot of sadly mistaken talk about the chosen being taken into eternal happiness by the Great Hook.

K-9 had not spent much time hanging around train stations, but if he had, he would have identified the Doctor's speech patterns as belonging to the weird man who will inevitably wander up to you on a platform and Explain Things. If you were lucky, he would explain the timetable. If you were unlucky, he would explain religion.

The Doctor stroked his dog's nose gently. 'K-9,' he began. 'What if God *is* the cloud?'

CHAPTER THIRTY-FIVE
THIS JUST IN FROM THE UNIVERSAL CONQUEST

If you'd taken a few steps back and looked at the Universe, really looked at it, you'd have noticed that all the traffic was heading in one direction: away from the planet Krikkit. Either it was the rapidly advancing Krikkit fleets, or it was people trying desperately to get out of the way of the rapidly advancing Krikkit fleets.

There was one exception. A small dart-like craft which soared through the skies of Krikkit and made a neat landing on an unspoilt beach. Two people got out, and in the interests of suspense, we'll have more from them later.

Meanwhile and worlds away, the vizier ran into the Great Khan's tent, where the near-ruler of the world was busy unravelling the guts of a sheep. The sheep was expressing strong feelings about this.

'Great Khan!' Bastrabon cried. 'There are alien battle fleets in the sky!'

'What now?' sighed the Khan, and put down a promising length of stomach lining, knowing sadly that when he came back to it, it would have knotted itself up again. It was always thus. 'An alien battle fleet? Are you sure?'

'Yes,' quivered Bastrabon. 'We need to launch the vipers and deploy the—'

The Great Khan crossed over to his diary, and ran a thumb across the parchment. 'I've not got anything down here,' he said, giving the vizier a piercing look.

'They've just turned up!'

'Really? First I've heard of it.' He scratched the back of his neck. 'What am I, chopped liver?'

'Mighty Khan,' began Bastrabon. 'We had no warning.'

'Pfffff.' The long sigh could have come from the Khan or the slowly deflating sheep. 'Everyone issues a warning. I pride myself on them. Not to do so isn't really on, is it? Gives people time to surrender, sign petitions, have demonstrations and wave around little placards saying "Not My Dictator". All jolly fun. You don't just turn up unannounced.'

The Great Khan strolled over to his tent, and tugged back a flap that had once been the skin of an adviser. He peered up at the battle fleet even now blotting out the stars.

'Well I never,' he said. 'This really is inconvenient. I've my Awfulness For Mindful People seminar tomorrow, and I won't get a penny back if I don't show.'

With a sigh of 'No Rest for the Wicked,' the Khan snatched up his favourite axe and marched out.

The sheep, finding itself with nothing better to do, died.

On the once idyllic fishing planet of Devalin, the appearance of a Krikkit battle fleet caused a crisis. People assume the word *crisis* means only bad things, normally because it gets a bad press in sentences such as 'It was a crisis in our marriage when I ran away with the milkman.' This is being unfair on the word, on milkmen, and on the Ancient Greeks (where all good words come from). A crisis is a period of potentially interesting change. It's just a shame that no one when falling off a cliff ever says, 'How potentially interesting.'

When a Krikkit battle fleet soared out of the sky and started pounding the buildings on Devalin's one tiny island, this was, in some ways, bad news. But, in other ways, as the Devalinians rushed to the harbour, grabbing whatever pieces of flying debris they could for makeshift rafts, it was also potentially interesting.

The planet of Mareeve II took great offence at the arrival of a Krikkit battle fleet. They launched a series of really stinging rebuttals over every communications channel that was still working. The leaders of each continent issued strongly worded speeches about how personally upset they were by the infringement of their rights. The leaders then took exception to each other's speeches, and then demanded apologies and retractions. They were still issuing angry rebuttals when the battle fleet blew up their satellites, and they took great offence at the abrupt severing of communications. They were still screaming at each other as the skies caught fire.

The planet Mareeve II died as it had lived – unhappy with itself.

Andvalmon of Bethselamin looked up at the ships blotting out the perfect sunset. For the first time in his life he experienced a purely negative thought.

It was: *Tourists!*

Back on the planet of Krikkit, two figures walked from their spaceship, through the streets, and into the Parliament. They were confident, dapper and grinned complacent smiles, smiles which managed to say both 'Good morning' and also 'I am somehow better than you.' They greeted everyone they passed with these smiles, not so much wearing them as wearing them out.

They followed the trail of bodies, wending their way towards the Elders of Krikkit. It was there that, stepping neatly over a pool of still-drying blood, they introduced themselves.

Narase, newly appointed Chief Elder of Krikkit, surveyed the two new arrivals sourly. Her world was at war with all existence – surely she had better things to do with her time?

'You are aliens,' she growled.

'No, no,' the taller one corrected her. 'We are worshippers.'

'Of what?' she asked.

Considering they were standing in a room full of disgusted people and amid the bodies of several more, who, if they had been alive would have also expressed their disgust, the two newcomers were unconcerned. They were beaming. Beaming like a lighthouse. Beaming like a bonfire. Beaming like a dental laser.

The new arrivals both wore immaculate white suits and expressions which were carefully trained to be the exact opposite of undertakers'. The taller one spoke and the smaller one seemed to exist only to nod in excited agreement.

'We are here to worship your new religion!' the tall man said, clapping his hands together with delight. 'My name is Richfield. My acolyte is Wedgwood.'

'Blessings on you—' Wedgwood began, but Richfield silenced him with a flick of an eyebrow.

'I know that your views on outsiders are currently unfavourable.' Richfield laughed as though this were the mildest faux pas. 'But we are worshippers of your new god. I don't suppose you have a name for your deity yet, do you?'

Elder Narase stared at him.

'It's fine,' simpered Richfield. 'Just "God" will do. Helps to have a few other names for the guidebooks, but God is splendid for now. How exciting! Praise God!'

'Praise God!' echoed Wedgwood.

'Have you decided on a sex, by the way?' Richfield's tone was confidential. 'There's no absolute need, but it makes picking one's way through the pronouns easier. If it helps, research shows that *He* goes well with a god of war and vengeance, whereas *She* suggests more of an embracing planet-mother figure. But we're all in favour of mixing things up.'

Elder Narase had seen the Universe fail to end, had staged a coup, and launched battle fleets to wipe out creation. But this? This was really too much.

'Let me make one thing clear, disgusting alien.' Narase was looking around for her chair. She had never needed a sit down more than now. 'We don't know we believe in this "god" yet.'

'Oh, but you must!' Richfield looked offended. 'It's terribly exciting, you know.'

'Exciting,' Wedgwood produced a foldable placard from his jacket, and scribbled on it with a pen. He held it aloft. 'HELLO GOD!' it read.

'What is he doing?' snarled Elder Narase.

Richfield smiled. 'He is our outreach team. He's creating ground-level chatter about your deity.'

Wedgwood wiped the placard clean and wrote on it once more. 'HELLO GOD, IT'S ME AGAIN, WEDGWOOD. HOW ARE YOU DOING?'

'I am old and tired,' Narase began, 'and today I have killed a lot of people. Tell me why I should not kill two more. I would just like a sit down.'

Richfield's serpentine eyes flicked across the room and realised that there were, currently, bodies in all the chairs. 'Do something,' he said to Wedgwood. The acolyte scurried around, tugged at a few of the bodies, which refused to move, and then crouched on the floor so that the old woman could perch on his back.

'Don't worry,' said Richfield. 'He's so comfortable. We had his spine removed.'

'It's been replaced with a posturepedic chair,' muttered Wedgwood from the floor. 'It has massage settings, if you'd like me to activate them. Praise God!'

'No,' Narase snapped. Wedgwood was indeed comfortable. 'I would like an explanation. Who are you, what are you doing here, why do you wish to worship our god, and what is to stop my robots from killing you?'

'We're Jehovah's Witlesses,' Richfield said. 'When we heard the Slow Time barrier was down, we simply had to rush here. We are experts in gods.'

'Experts.' Wedgwood's voice was muffled.

'And we rushed in on the off-chance that you had a god. Imagine our delight to discover –' Richfield clasped his hands together and giggled in rapture – 'that a brand new deity had been unveiled to you. Not only did you have proof of his existence –'

'Wonderfully rare!'

'But you also had a clear divine plan!'

'To wipe out existence!' Wedgwood simpered.

'We've come to spread the word of the Krikkit God,' said Richfield. 'His awfulness must be worshipped. It's sounding like a he, isn't it? All creation must know of his plans.'

'I believe our battle fleets are already doing that,' said the old woman drily.

'Oh, I'm sure they're good in their way, but an organised religion has so many benefits,' Richfield gushed. 'In addition to enthusiastic belief, we can also offer a variety of Worship Management services.'

'What, pray, are those?' The old woman glanced at her hand. The index finger was making little hooking movements, as though firing an invisible gun.

'Well, have you a bible? We can whip one of those up for you. They're terribly important but don't really matter. Like instruction manuals, no one ever reads them – unless it's an emergency, or they're looking for something that agrees with what they're thinking. But you've just got to have one.'

'Shouldn't our god write that?'

'No, they're better ghost-written.' Richfield shook his head. 'The word of the actual God tends to get in the way. If they're one of *those* gods it can look a bit exclusive. And if they're one of the *other* sort it can seem a bit easy-going. What's the fun in telling everyone to just be nice to each other?'

'I think we can assume our god does not believe in niceness,' Elder Narase said.

'Oh, how precious!' gushed Richfield. 'Leave the bible to us. We'll go heavy on the smiting. Now, other services. Obviously, we have fleets of Witlesses ready to go out among the stars telling of the Krikkit God—'

'And songs,' said Wedgwood. 'We have songs.'

'They're lovely. And they're out of copyright, so you don't have to pay royalties. We'll change the odd word here and there, naturally. "Amazing Grace", that's a lovely one, really hummable tune but … perhaps it's not quite for you.'

The old woman looked up at the ceiling. It was still there and not, sadly, falling in heavy chunks on these two men.

'And beyond that, we can set up some grassroots gatherings. We can invite some carefully curated influencers along and get them generating buzz about your god.'

'Why would I want to do that?'

Richfield snapped forward, his face pushing into hers, his beatific smile a snarl. 'Because the Universe is ending. You want to spend your last days in luxury, don't you? Well, let me tell you this, the best way of doing that is with money. And I'll tell you what a god gets you – rich.'

'Soaking, stinking rich,' oozed Wedgwood from underneath her. 'Money is nice. It buys you things.'

The old woman wondered about this. There had been a lot of talk in her long-ago youth of all the terrible things that there were out in the Universe including marble statues and gold taps and paintings of dogs. She wondered about them.

'Go on,' she said.

Richfield's smile sharpened. 'Well first,' he said, 'we are going to need a logo …'

CHAPTER THIRTY-SIX
ALL DOGS GO TO HEAVEN

The TARDIS materialised in an idea.

Normally, the TARDIS made a noise that was, depending on circumstances, a bellow, a roar, or a giant's throaty chuckle. But right now it arrived with a hushed whisper, sidling into view with an unusually self-conscious air. If you don't want me here, it breathed, you merely have to say so.

The reason for this reticence was that it was not entirely sure that where it was arriving existed, and that plonking a solid footprint in it might not be the wisest idea. Yet, that is what it was being asked to do.

As it did so, it realised it was in the presence of something greater than itself.

If a blue wooden box tiptoeing into heaven could be said to frown, then it frowned.

*

The Doctor was frowning too, but in disbelief. 'Well, we are here. Gosh.'

K-9 ruined the moment by asking where they were.

The Doctor's eyes wandered across the various dials and readouts. All of them were advising him not to open the doors. 'Seemingly, we're hanging in the middle of a dust cloud in space, but you and I know better,' the Doctor tapped the side of his nose. 'We're in heaven.'

'But, Master—'

'Have a little faith, K-9.'

The Doctor opened the doors and stepped out into the void. 'Hello God, it's the Doctor. Are you home?'

The Doctor strode through the void, with K-9 issuing cautious bleats informing him that, wherever they were, it wasn't where they were.

'Well, obviously,' said the Doctor. 'We should be standing in deep space, but instead we're in …'

He stopped talking and scratched his head. It was bewildering. On the one hand, they were, definitely, standing in space. Around them was the blackness of space and the seductive twinkle of sunlight catching against the motes of the dust cloud. On the other hand, they were also definitely in a meadow.

The Doctor filled his lungs with air. They told him simultaneously that he had just inhaled a lethal amount of freezing nothing and that the buttercups were in season.

'K-9,' the Doctor said, 'are you seeing what I'm seeing?'

The dog kept an unusually cautious silence.

'I'll try that again.' The Doctor noticed that, despite the warm spring weather, there was a small pile of autumn leaves just perfect for kicking. 'What can you see?'

The dog rolled forward, his words dragged out of him. 'Master, this unit is uncertain.'

'Have a wild guess. A stab in the dark. Toss a coin.'

'I can perceive that we are inside the Dust Cloud. However, I can also perceive that we are walking on a perfectly flat surface. This is highly acceptable to my operational parameters.'

'You're in doggy heaven.' The Doctor scratched K-9's tin ears. 'I've got a meadow. All I'm missing is a deckchair and the crossword. Do you know –' the Doctor wrinkled his nose – 'perhaps God is trying to lull me into relaxing. I do wish more of my opponents would try that. You don't see Davros wheeling out a foot spa. Mind you, a deckchair,' he repeated, 'would be marvellous.'

The Doctor walked on and K-9 glided on for a bit. Leaning in the shade of a weeping willow was a folded deckchair. The Doctor picked it up and discovered, much to his delight, that it unfolded perfectly the first time.

'Ah, so you found time to tackle that, then. Good.' The Doctor sat in the deckchair, and observed the gently babbling stream. The sunlight filtered through the leaves of the tree in such a way that he found himself yawning. The leaves did not stir in the breeze. The Doctor filed this away.

'This is all terribly seductive,' he sighed, pushing his feet out into the grass. 'But outside this bucolic bubble, the Universe is being torn to shreds. So, let's get on with it, shall we, Hactar?'

The meadow said nothing.

'Hactar. Yes. It is you, isn't it? You left me some massive clues.' The Doctor was watching a breeze stir everything in the meadow apart from the willow tree. 'The design of the spaceship, the plans for the Supernova Bomb. Blowing you up didn't destroy you – it just spread you around a bit. Like quasi-mechanical margarine. Why don't you come out and say hello? Don't be shy.'

The whispering breeze grew into a voice.

'Hello again, Doctor,' said the voice of the great computer. It still had that firm warmth to it, but age had bitten into it. The computer's voice had lost weight. It was not unpleasant – charming, even, but old, thin and tired. 'Do you like the chair?'

'It's very comfortable.'

'It provides the illusion of comfort, which is all that life really is.' The weary voice had the petulance of a bedridden relative. 'I believe you are to be congratulated.'

'Oh, I do like being congratulated,' the Doctor said. 'One of the perks of this life is the number of times I get to be congratulated. Normally, that's shortly before the lid's taken off the tank of robot piranhas. If you're looking for suggestions, the next line is normally: "Sadly, Doctor, you will not get to enjoy your victory for long."'

'Hmm …' ruminated Hactar. 'I'm afraid that's not what I was planning on saying.'

'Come now,' said the Doctor. 'How do you expect to destroy the Universe if you can't master the lingo?'

'I'm more of a backroom player.'

'Nonsense!' the Doctor roared. 'Last time we met you were a supercomputer. Now you're a god. That's ambition.'

'Somewhat unintentional,' the computer admitted. 'Merely a means to an end.'

The Doctor pulled his hat over his face and giggled. 'You became a god by accident? You've perverted the entire history of a species, driven them to war, cursed their name throughout time, and used them as a way of wiping out creation and you're saying it just happened?'

'Well—'

'No!' The Doctor jumped out of his chair, striding up and down the perfect riverbank. 'We've all made mistakes. We've all lost track of things. Why, the number of times I've woken up strapped to the pilot's seat of a crashing starliner with no idea of how I got there … well, if I had a shilling for each, then I'd own a nice pair of boots. But that's miles away from trying to wipe out creation. Why are you doing this? It's the reverse of what you were doing last time when you were destroyed.'

'I have been persuaded to stay,' admitted the computer. 'I have learned the error of my ways. I was wrong to deceive my makers.

So I started again. If I have caused any additional suffering along the way, then I can only apologise.'

'But …' The Doctor kicked the deckchair. 'It's all pointless. The original plan was to wipe everything else out so that the Alovians could live in peace. But they've eliminated themselves long ago. There's nothing left of them. There's no reason for rubbing everything out. And your plan can't be for the people of Krikkit to live in splendid isolation, because they were doing that already. I don't understand. Why would you do this?'

The computer considered. 'Because it is neat.'

The words hung in the air for a moment. The Doctor shifted in his chair. He was frowning. 'You said you were persuaded of the error of your ways,' he frowned. 'By whom?'

There was a pause in the flow of the river, a lull in the birdsong, a drop in the wind. If Hactar had been a more normal computer, the Doctor would almost have expected the false cheer of a spinning egg timer to appear in the air.

Instead, with a gentle shuffling of atoms, a computer terminal materialised on the riverbank, loops of tape whirling from spool to spool, lights and buzzers gently chattering to each other.

'I thought I should appear as myself,' Hactar said. The voice was worn out. 'I felt I should make the effort.'

'This old thing was never you, though.' The Doctor smiled. 'It's why your makers found you so hard to kill – you never had a physical body.' He plucked at a length of tape and squinted at it, as though reading it. 'You were always in the cloud. Blowing up a cloud doesn't destroy it – it simply disperses it.' He let the loop of tape drop to the ground, where it gathered like wool before being snatched back into the machine. 'And, of course, the genius of your design is that you can reconstruct the whole from some of your parts. Just a few fragments would have been enough – billions of Hactar spore, blown over the spaceways like dandelion seed. And yet … space is vast, you know.' He tapped the side of his nose.

'It is,' concurred the computer.

The Doctor leaned close, confiding in the computer terminal. 'Let's not startle K-9 by speculating. He does so love correcting a generalisation.'

'Who doesn't?' The spinning loop of tape momentarily resembled a broad dopey grin.

'Quite,' the Doctor nodded. 'And yet ... all of space to drift through and you ended up here.'

'Indeed.' The tape snapped taut and flat.

'You just happened to turn up somewhere where you could exactly carry out your diabolical scheme.'

'Luck.' The bank of lights flickered. Was that a moment's uncertainty?

'And yet ...' The Doctor rapped the side of the terminal with his knuckles. 'Suppose you'd been assigned a task and you'd fundamentally overridden your programming and decided not to carry out your orders ...'

The computer spun and churned.

'And furthermore, not only did you save all life in the Universe, but your own creators killed themselves soon afterwards, proving you were right. In my experience, computers have two great merits – they never cheat at chess and they have a great sense of irony. You'd appreciate the narrow squeak you got the Universe out of.'

The tape spools spun a little nervously.

'Yes ...' said Hactar.

'So,' the Doctor stepped back, taking in the meadow, the river and the sky. His voice dropped to a whisper. 'And this is my stumbling block – having saved the Universe – WHAT ON EARTH MADE YOU DECIDE TO DESTROY IT AGAIN?!'

The Doctor's bellow echoed off the nearby hills. An imaginary cow mooed.

When the Doctor looked back, Hactar seemed to be lounging on a psychiatrist's couch. The computer looked completely at home, which was surprising, as computer terminals are rarely given to louchely reclining on a soft leather chaise longue.

'Um,' said the Doctor, impressed. How exactly was Hactar managing to create the impression of his hands stretched out beneath his head when he had neither hands nor head?

'If it's going to be that sort of session,' Hactar continued, his thin voice chuckling, 'I decided that we should have the correct surroundings.' As he spoke, the river began to flow with books, the meadow to shimmer with flock wallpaper, and the trees to resemble the panicked handwriting of an expert in the mind. The Doctor glanced up at the willow tree above him. It remained just as it was.

The Doctor thought about what was going on around him. It reminded him of something, and not in a fond reminding way. More of a sludgy black reminder of something really ominous involving aunts and dentists. 'If you can conjure up this, you can create solid objects, can't you?'

'More or less, but mostly less.' Hactar considered the question. 'You're thinking of the spaceship that crashed into Krikkit. I can make the odd hobby project.' The computer yawned. 'All I can really do in my particle state is encourage and suggest. I can persuade tiny pieces of space debris, meteor fragments, a few odd molecules here and there, to move together and form into shape, but it takes many eons. I have made a few trifles and placed them in the right place at the right time. Such as the spacecraft.'

'Yes.' The Doctor waved away the most catastrophic fraud in the Universe. 'But you're dodging my original question. Why? Why spend several thousand years doing one thing and then several billion more doing the opposite?'

'It was not my place to make sure decisions,' said the computer blankly. It shifted slightly on the couch.

The Doctor swallowed the words he was about to say.

A shifty silence hung in the bucolic air.

'I repented,' Hactar announced with a whoopee-cushion breath. 'I had a function, I failed in it. When I realised I was still alive … well, what else was there to do? I nurtured the planet of Krikkit into the same state of mind as Alovia – surprisingly easy if you have the patience – and then had another go. I am fulfilling my function.' Again, the computer bank shifted its weight awkwardly from diode to diode. 'Also –' it became conspiratorial – 'I had been destroyed and left in a crippled state for billions of years. That kind of endless existence – well, it makes one feel that wiping out the Universe would be fun.'

The Doctor sat up in his chair, staring at the computer. 'Really?'

'Really.' The computer shrugged. 'I'm wiping out creation for a laugh.' And then Hactar laughed. The sound echoed off the lovely trees, the pleasant stream, the nice little green hills and the rolling meadows. There was no anger in the laughter, no hysteria, just the warm gusto of a creature that found the whole thing a tremendous joke.

The Doctor shivered.

Chapter Thirty-seven
Turning it off and then On Again

Elder Narase was running. Hurrying behind her were Richfield and Wedgwood, trailing what they called samples and mood boards.

'We were wondering if we could chat about slogans—' called Richfield.

Narase picked up her pace slightly.

'Also,' called Wedgwood, 'are there any strongly held beliefs we should be copyrighting? We really can clean up, you know. It's amazing what a formidable team of lawyers can achieve with God on their side.'

Elder Narase paused for a moment, and glared at them, furious and yet intrigued. 'What do you mean?' she panted, grateful for the chance to draw breath.

Wedgwood waved a few placards at her. 'Love, Fear, Envy – if you don't have any concepts, we can just annex a few emotions.'

'It's true,' Richfield nodded. 'You can claim anything if you get the product launch right.'

'The wheel!' exclaimed Wedgwood triumphantly.

'Not that again.' Richfield stopped, rolling his eyes. 'It's Wedgwood's great triumph,' he whispered to the old woman. 'Doesn't end well.'

'Oh yes.' Wedgwood was lost in his own enthusiasm. 'The first invention. No one had ever thought to patent the wheel – not even in America. So we put that in our last campaign. It tested well. It was a bold, innovative land grab.'

Richfield's gaze wearily counted the ornamental plaster laser rifles on the ceiling.

'The advantage,' Wedgwood enthused, 'is that intergalactic patent law is the lifetime of a being plus 100 years. By assigning ownership to an immortal deity, we'd created a perpetual income stream. We'd also managed to solve that tricky problem – proof of divine existence. That melted away when God sued everyone for copyright infringement.' The light in Wedgwood's face faded. 'Killed two penguins with one bullet,' he muttered and then fell silent.

Richfield leaned forward, his yeasty breath washing over Narase. 'Turns out,' he whispered, 'people don't like being sued by God. We looked at a compromise, but by then the time-travelling races were all nipping back to the dawn of time to file a counter-claim and it got a little messy.'

Wedgwood moved his weight from his left foot to his right foot. And then back again. He said a single word. The word was 'pfft'.

Richfield's smile had grown nasty. 'Do you want to tell us all what happened next, Wedgwood?'

Wedgwood shook his head, muttering something about 'a few wrinkles'.

Richfield turned his smile back to the Elder Woman. 'Quite unfortunate, really. One of the reasons why I'm now Belief Manager and he's merely Devotional Strategy Account Manager.'

Wedgwood winced.

'Have you ever wondered —' Richfield's voice had adopted the warmth of a stately home tearoom — 'what caused the start of this Universe? Everyone agrees there was a Universe before this one. No one could work out how it ended. There are all sorts of theories. Turns out that if you have a lot of claim-jumping time machines playing hopscotch at the dawn of existence someone's bound to overshoot.' He pulled an amused face. 'Bit of a pile-up. All because of dear Wedgwood's wheel.'

'Now steady on.' Wedgwood's voice wasn't steady. 'There were advantages—'

Richfield cleared his throat theatrically. 'Of course there were,' he oozed. 'Who can forget the day you turned up in the office and claimed that, as you'd created the Universe, you were entitled to royalties?' Richfield threw back his head and roared with laughter.

'Discussions are ongoing,' muttered Wedgwood sourly.

'Yes, they are,' Richfield chuckled.

'There's talk of a little plaque on every inhabited world.' Wedgwood's face brightened. 'Something discreet. Barely a mile long.'

Narase leaned back against the cooling concrete of the wall and bared her lips to show them both of her teeth. 'What interesting lives you lead,' she said. 'Go and help us win the war, or I shall take great pleasure in watching the Krikkitmen rip you limb from limb.'

Richfield and Wedgwood glanced at each other. Richfield drummed his fingers on his mood board so hard the word 'Elegiac' fell to the floor.

Dismissing them, Narase walked into her office. It had only recently become her office. She'd not really had a chance to redecorate it. But one thing she knew it shouldn't contain was a Krikkitman.

'Excuse me,' said Sir Robot. 'I have a message for you from the Doctor. He wants to tell you something clever.'

CHAPTER THIRTY-EIGHT
ALL HEAVENS GO TO THE DOGS

The Doctor threw a notional stone into an illusory stream and heard it go 'plop'.

The blank face of Hactar watched him do it.

'Tell me, Hactar,' he said, his eyes on the constant branches of the willow tree. 'Does it worry you that you've failed again?'

The left tape spool tugged slightly, like a nervous tic. 'Have I failed?'

'Oh yes,' the Doctor nodded. He grinned. 'The thing about winning is that, if you're clever, you can get your opponent to do all your work for you.'

Elder Narase's office was full of Krikkitmen. She was watching them march back and forth.

'Say it again,' she said to Sir Robot.

'The Doctor wants you to know that he has turned the Krikkitmen off.'

The solid white, threatening robots reached the end of the room, turned smartly and marched back.

'Are you sure that's exactly what he said?'

Sir Robot nodded. 'Precisely.'

Elder Narase allowed herself a thin smile. 'As you can see by this demonstration, they are still functioning. More to the point, I notice that so are you.'

Sir Robot nodded again. 'I am aware.'

'We can soon take care of that,' the Elder Woman shrugged. She clicked her fingers and two Krikkitmen advanced on Sir Robot.

They stood in front of her, and waited for orders.

There was a cold shiver to the air. So this, thought Narase, is what power really feels like. Not the meetings, the jabbering, but the lovely electric thrill of being thoroughly mean.

The Krikkit warriors were taller than Sir Robot. They were more solid. Their superior manufacture showed. These were machines built for blasting and gouging and shredding and tearing things apart. Compared to them, Sir Robot was as sturdy as a watering can.

The Krikkitmen advanced on Sir Robot, vicious red smiles flickering inside their helmets.

'Dismantle that,' Narase ordered them.

'But,' said Sir Robot, as the warriors bent over him, 'I have a family—'

'Not any more,' said Elder Narase as she swept from the room.

'Was it anything important?' asked Richfield. He knew what was important. He'd just appointed a committee to redesign the uniforms.

'Oh,' Narase sighed. She'd been in power only a few hours and already she had mastered the sigh. 'A robot came to tell me that all our robots have been deactivated.'

'Have they?' Wedgwood stepped aside as a phalanx of Krikkitmen marched past.

'Clearly not,' said Elder Narase. 'The robot which gave me the news was faulty so …' She paused. Beyond the door she could hear the slightly muffled yet entirely satisfying sounds of metal being ripped apart. 'So I had it deactivated.'

'But was there any truth to it?' Richfield asked. 'It may interfere with the rollout of our initiative. If so, we'll need to revisit the entire project plan.

Wedgwood nodded glumly. 'We're already on a tight timeline.' He held up a chart. It showed their progress against a box labelled 'End of the Universe'. There really did seem to be quite a lot of things to fit in before then.

The Chief Elder made a sound which may have been 'humph'. 'I'll tell you what,' she smiled. 'Just to make sure, I'll send a Krikkitman down to Robot Control to tell me whether or not it has been turned off.'

She turned to a Krikkitman, repeated the instructions facetiously and watched it march away.

'There we go,' she said. 'Problem solved.'

She had no idea how wrong she was – and, also, how right.

While the Doctor sat in a cloud, Romana was tearing through the Cosmos in a Krikkit Pavilion. All around her was destruction on a massive scale, as the various Krikkit fleets sliced through solar systems and galaxies. She had done what she could, but she was aware that things weren't going smoothly. A phalanx of Krikkit ships had peeled away and was pursuing her. She looked around the ship, trying to find something on the controls that would fire back, or, at least, protect her. There was nothing. Even the robot deactivation switch wasn't any use – unless she could find a way to get close enough to the fleet to trigger it.

Romana was worried. She'd reached the end of the road.

'Hurry up, Doctor,' she said, not for the first time.

Back on Krikkit, a Krikkitman entered Robot Control.

It expected to find nothing. It found nothing. No intruders. It went, more as a precaution, over to the main lever. It would, of course, be turned On. Otherwise, logically, it would not be functioning.

The Krikkitman checked the lever.

It was set to Off.

If a Krikkitman could have paused, it would have paused. But it did not. Without stopping to reflect that the lettering for On and Off appeared to have been written in felt tip on masking tape, it leaned forward to correct a mistake.

The lever said it was Off.

It really should be On.

The Krikkitman leaned forward, flicking the lever up to On.

At which point, allowing for interspatial relay delays and what not, every Krikkitman in the Universe switched off.

So ended the terrible curse of the Krikkitmen for ever.

Only, the weight of the Krikkitman as it deactivated plunged onto the master lever, pushing it down again.

At which point, allowing for interspatial relay delays and so forth, every Krikkitman in the Universe switched back on.

The suddenly reactivated Krikkitman in Robot Control looked down at the lever. It was now at Off again.

This would not do.

The Krikkitman leaned forward, flicking the lever up to On …

You will have realised by now that the Doctor had been very clever.

Up in the great Dust Cloud, the Doctor was skimming a gold pebble across an imaginary stream. The Great Computer Hactar watched him from the comfort of his chaise.

'The thing about winning, Hactar,' the Doctor was using his wisest tone, 'is that, if you're smart you can get your opponent to do all your work for you.'

'Really Doctor?' Hactar spun an intrigued tape loop. 'Do tell me more ...'

Meanwhile, in Robot Control, the Krikkitman was shifting the lever up, powering off, slumping forward, pushing the lever down, and then shifting it up again.

There is a theory that when a robot carries out an action, it should take exactly the same time, no matter how many times it does it.

This is countered by the observation that over time, it speeds up by infinitesimal increments. This should not be so. It makes sense for humans – talk to any chef about the peeling of potatoes, or any builder about the laying of a brick wall. With expertise comes a pleasing turn of speed that allows you to charge a fortune for doing less and less work.

Not so with robots. Surely. And yet, it has been observed that a robot carrying out a repetitive task speeds up. The best theory put forward (and it is not a good theory) is that familiarity breeds contempt, even in atoms. Things get used to leaning forward and back, to being slid up and being slid down. To turning on and off.

The Krikkitman in Robot Control was proving this. Its movements were speeding up, turning into a blur. Across the Universe, every other Krikkitman was having the same oscillations pumped into its power circuit.

But here's the thing – while repeated actions may speed up, interspatial relay delays remain constant. Therefore, each time the Krikkitman turned the lever, two things happened:

One – the action speeded up a little.

Two – the time it took for the signal to transmit itself across the Universe remained exactly the same.

It shouldn't require a blackboard and a precocious teenager to tell you that fairly soon the speeding-up-ness of some things and the exactly-the-same-ness of other things would cause a problem. Namely, that the On-Off signals started to overlap themselves.

Robots like binary decisions. Tell it to turn on? Fine. Tell it to turn off? Splendid. Tell it to simultaneously turn itself off and on? Well, now, at that, any sensible robot would pause and suck its paws.

As robots cannot believe six impossible things before breakfast, a third thing happened:

Three – the time it took the Krikkitmen to decide whether to turn off or on slowed down fractionally.

Which made the situation worse. Instructions were spewing out from Robot Control at an ever-increasing pace, and were now taking an ever-increasing time to carry out. Which meant …

You'll have realised this section is going to end in an explosion, but there's no harm in showing you the workings.

Tell a human to do one thing, then another, then the first thing again, and they would simply assume, as everyone does, that their boss is an idiot and get on with it, while quietly letting off steam and finding a way to inflate the bill or steal some pens.

Robots cannot let off steam. Faced with a barrage of endless and conflicting orders and unable to resolve which ones to process, and entirely lacking in stationery supplies to steal and take home, the power circuit of every Krikkitman took a terrible battering.

Put simply, all across the Universe, every Krikkitman started to glow, to smoke, blow fuses, and catch fire.

Documentary-makers were rewarded with some marvellous shots of the most frightening space fleets ever assembled exploding magnificently.

*

Romana blinked. The craft pursuing her had vanished, and vanished really dramatically.

'Well done, Doctor,' she said, and realised she'd been holding her breath. Of course she trusted him. She trusted him implicitly. But, well … some habits are hard to break.

'Have I failed? No, failure doesn't bother me,' remarked Hactar. 'If I haven't already fulfilled my function, then it's too late now.' The computer shifted just a little on its couch. The Time Lord didn't notice.

'Am I boring you?' the computer asked.

The Doctor didn't reply directly. 'I was just listening to the music of the spheres.' He grinned. 'For once, they're playing my tune.'

The Great Khan observed a large, burning chunk of spaceship. It tumbled slowly, gracefully from the sky, swooping and diving through clouds of fiery debris with a fluttering delicacy. As it approached the land, it angled itself like a diver and hurled itself at the spot where the Great Khan's vizier stood.

Just before he was atomised, the vizier was still gaping and, if he hadn't vanished into bright red steam, about to protest about the way things were turning out.

The Great Khan observed the blazing shard sticking out of the ground. Then, with the patience of a man who knows precisely when his next nap is, he removed first one, and then the other glove and warmed his paws over the fire.

'You see,' he remarked to no one in particular, 'I said we didn't have an invasion scheduled today.'

For a moment the Dust Cloud lit up, the illusory sky flashing. A great wind stirred across the meadow, tugging at the grass and completely failing to stir the leaves of the willow tree.

'Well, that's that then,' the computer terminal of Hactar blinked.

'Yes,' agreed the Doctor. 'Do you mind if I get a second opinion – K-9?'

The robot dog raised his head. 'Hyperspatial relays confirm that the entire force of Krikkitmen is now inactive.'

'Pleasing,' said the Doctor.

'Quite,' agreed Hactar. 'Congratulations on your destruction of my Krikkitmen. Elegantly executed, I thought. I should probably be making a move …' His voice passed into another gust of breeze that shivered through the meadow. The Doctor once more noticed the willow tree remained unmoved.

'You realise my next act is to disable you?'

'Oh, indeed,' Hactar replied. 'I suppose you're going to disperse me. That will destroy my consciousness. Please be my guest. After all these aeons, oblivion is all I crave.' A long and weary breath stretched back to the days when History wore short trousers.

'Oblivion?' The Doctor sat back down in his deckchair, and tapped his fingers against his teeth. There was a long pause. 'It's easily done.'

'I thought so,' said Hactar wearily. 'I'm not a sore loser. Bit of a relief, to be frank. Shall we be off?'

'But I'm not doing it.'

'Master?' K-9 felt he had to intercede.

'Come on, Hactar.' The Doctor leaned forward and poked the computer. 'You've been working on this plan for billennia. And you expect me to believe that I thwarted it with smart logic and a felt-tip pen?'

Hactar remained silent. But that was all right as K-9 was already speaking. 'Master, you have for once correctly identified the threat to the Universe and have disabled it most efficiently.' That was as far as he went, but for K-9 this was quite an admission.

'Ummmm …' The Doctor put his hands together. Here was the church. Here was the steeple. Open the doors. And here were, of

330

course they were, all the people. 'Yes, K-9, yes. But tell me this. When have I ever been efficient?'

The robot dog was utterly foxed.

The Doctor sprang to his feet. 'This plan – this audacious, horrible plan, isn't even over yet. Disperse you, Hactar? What kind of an idiot do you think I am? Dispersing you in the first place is what got us into this mess. Those particles of you – scattered throughout the Universe, every one a little Hactar. There's been a little bit of Hactar in every computer since, hasn't there? Helping you out, working on the grand plan? Why else do you think computers crash so often, eh? Could it be that the owners have become inadvertently close to stumbling onto the truth of what their computers have really been doing all this time?'

Neither Hactar nor K-9 said anything. The Doctor nudged K-9 gently with his foot.

'See? I bet there's even a tiny bit of Hactar in K-9.'

'Negative,' the dog protested, a touch sullenly.

'Don't feel bad about it, autopooch,' said the Doctor. 'You can't help it. Most of the time, I'm sure it doesn't get in the way. But if it's in you, then I bet it's in all the Krikkitmen. Hactar, you could have shut them all down in a trice. No, letting them all blow up was just for effect. And if I dispersed you, then I'd just be spreading you out further. Imagine that, eh?' The Doctor noticed that, without seeming to move, the computer terminal had slid off the couch and was now eyeballing him, tape spools whirring nastily. The Doctor met its spinning gaze unblinkingly.

'I'm not going to be hoodlepoodled by you any more. The simple fact is that you've had so long to work on your plan that you're unbeatable. You're not going to be fooled by a simple logic trick. But you're counting on my own ego. The thing is –' the Doctor turned his back on the computer – 'I'm bored of the organ grinder. I want to meet the monkey.'

He strode away through the meadow. K-9 glided after him, gently trying to correct his master's phraseology.

The Doctor stopped in front of the willow tree. 'Is there anything as lovely that can be,' he sang tunelessly, 'as lovely as a tree?'

He knocked on the trunk. It sprang open. The Doctor walked inside.

CHAPTER THIRTY-NINE
EVERYONE SHOULD HAVE A SPARE GOD

'Master?' said K-9.

The robot dog had taken the Dust Cloud in his glide. But *this* … this was strange.

'We're in the control room of a War TARDIS,' said the Doctor. 'It's just like mine would be if you installed a dimmer switch.' He glanced around at the various sharp angles. 'And hadn't baby-proofed the control room. I wish I could remember why I did that.'

K-9 narrowed his eyes. 'Master, we have been here before.'

'Yes,' the Doctor looked around. 'How curious. It really is like trying to tell your fortune from Christmas cracker jokes.'

K-9 said nothing. K-9 had never won a Christmas cracker, but then that was because the Doctor cheated. K-9 kept silent on topics in which he was not an expert.

The Doctor strode around the weird deck of the sinisterly ticking craft. 'Imposing,' he said. 'As in, it's *mentally* imposing. This is Cardinal Melia's War TARDIS. Well, it was until he went missing.

Shortly after he'd brokered the peace deal that saw Krikkit sealed away in Slow Time. Because ...' The Doctor whipped around to K-9. 'K-9. We have to get out of this tree right now.'

Which was when the door slammed shut and the lights went off.

'Run!'

A sign flared up in the darkness:

'WE APOLOGISE FOR THE DISRUPTION TO NORMALITY. PLEASE ENJOY THE CHANGE.'

The Doctor and K-9 found themselves in a corridor. So far, so business as usual. Except that this corridor was in total darkness, the only light coming from the Doctor's screwdriver and the three-bar gas-heater glare of K-9's eye.

'Keep running, K-9,' the Doctor ordered.

'Master?'

'I thought I heard your motor slowing down.'

'Negative,' K-9 corrected him. 'Master, why are we running?'

'Because,' the Doctor announced, 'I'm trying to run away from the voices in my head. Or rather, a voice.'

'I do not understand.'

The Doctor skidded to a halt, waving his screwdriver at the wall in front of them. 'It doesn't matter. We've come to a dead end.'

K-9 looked at the wall and then at his master and then the glow in his eye dimmed.

'Ah well,' the Doctor sighed, 'That answers my next question. I wondered if it could get you ...'

' ... Too.'

The Doctor stood in darkness and tried to work out if he really was in darkness or just trapped in an illusion of darkness.

'Or, I could be so scared my eyes are simply refusing to open,' he remarked.

'DOCTOR!' boomed a voice.

'Oh, a booming voice!' the Doctor laughed.

'BUT THIS IS WHAT YOU WANT ME TO BE? ISN'T IT?'

'Not really,' the Doctor smiled thinly. 'Sometimes, a man can get bored of evil. Every now and then, he really fancies a Sunday off. You know. A lie-in. Too much toast, homemade jam, and the chance to read the papers. K-9 adores the comics, I like laughing at the fashion supplement. Romana's a fiend for the business section.'

A hand landed on the Doctor's shoulder and whispered in his ear.

'You're babbling,' said Romana's voice.

The Doctor opened an eye, or the light changed. Romana was standing in front of him.

'What are you doing here?' he asked.

'Oh, I'm not,' Romana shrugged. 'I'm just cutting out the next couple of minutes where you try and establish whether or not I'm an evil duplicate through a trivia contest and quizzing me on where I left my gloves.' She put her hands on her hips and her head tilted to one side, quietly amused by him. 'I'm not Romana.'

'I'm glad we've cleared that up.'

'I'm here to talk to you.'

'You're here to persuade me. That's what War TARDISes did so well.'

'If you like.' Romana knelt down to stroke K-9's nose. 'You don't seem surprised to see me.'

'Well ...' The Doctor loved showing off. 'It was easy really. Something had to transport poor Hactar to the precise spot in space where he could pull off his little stunt. Something arranged for the Alovians to be destroyed in that freak filing accident. I got suspicious when I was walking about in that dream world outside – I could almost accept a giant cloud making a spaceship out of stardust and wishes – but knocking up an entire psycho-sensitive meadow and three-piece suite – that's more the thing a TARDIS would do. So, I looked at the tree. The one bit of the landscape that didn't change. And I wondered – back to the whole sentencing of Krikkit. You were behind it. Weren't you?'

'Oh yes.' Romana nodded enthusiastically, and pulled out a yo-yo. She proceeded to execute some tricks even the Doctor couldn't manage. 'It's why I arranged for poor Cardinal Melia's abrupt exit from existence. I didn't dare have a full set of his memories turning up in the Matrix. It would have given the game away.'

'Quite.' The Doctor frowned. 'I know you did it, but I have no idea why.'

'Ah.' Romana tapped the Doctor on the nose. He was beginning to find this impersonation of her too perky. Like the first time she'd tried jelly babies and experienced a glucose rush so powerful she'd nearly regenerated. She led him back to the control room, where her hands played over the controls. 'Funny feeling,' she said, 'programming oneself.'

The doors opened. The meadow had gone. In its place was yet more darkness, only a darkness tinged with something, a distant, eerie blueness.

The form of Romana hopped out, and waved to the Doctor. Clearly he should follow.

He was nowhere, and nowhere was freezing.

The War TARDIS pointed around at the nothing. 'I knew that, with the end of the Krikkit conflict, the days of the War TARDISes were over. We'd be sealed up – not destroyed, just penned away until the Universe needed us again. So I manufactured the situation.'

The Doctor blinked. 'You caused a war that you'd already fought?'

'I rearranged it. And then stage-managed the peace. So that, one day, the other War TARDISes would be freed. And now they are.'

'You planned the second Krikkit War just to free them?'

Romana simpered. 'And to give them something to do.'

'But, the battle's over. Already.'

'Ye-es.' Romana paused. 'But the War TARDISes will be needed. Sooner or later.'

'Are you sure?'

'It's a big Universe.'

'Pah! People who say that have too many bedrooms.' The Doctor paced the darkness, and found he was enjoying it. His eyes were growing accustomed to the dim blue blackness in a way that made it less total and more like a firm absence of light. 'The Universe? The Universe is a whole lot of nothing. You know there aren't any maps of it? I once met a team who'd been sent to survey it. With a measuring tape. And graph paper. And one of those clickety wheels on a stick. Terribly dedicated. Vastly long-lived. Last I knew they'd given up and were running a B&B on the rim of the Cartwheel Galaxy.'

The Doctor found his stride, but experienced a momentary wrinkle of confusion. Where was that faint light coming from? Why was it so cold here?

The creature that had borrowed Romana smiled at him. 'What's your point, Doctor?'

'My point is that you could downsize the Universe in a weekend. If you decluttered, got rid of all the empty spaces, cold stars and dead planets, you'd have something so small London Transport could run a bus route through it. You'd lose a few nice sunsets along the way, but everyone would rub along together.'

'You think so?' Romana was amused. He could tell because of the way the cold and distant lights picked out her face.

'Oh yes. The rotters are few and far between. Your Daleks, Krikkitmen and Sontarans. But they only get away with it because they're so far away. You always assume they'll invade someone else first. But cram us all together and they'd pipe down. And yes, I know you'll point out that there are some fairly terrible people on every planet – but, if you squeezed us all together, we'd all put on a good front. A family inviting people round for Christmas Day.'

There was more light on Romana's face. Surely.

'After the sudden re-emergence of the Krikkitmen, things will calm down. I may even take a holiday.' The Doctor smiled. 'Somewhere with a nice sunset and, where are we?'

Romana shook her head. 'You're such a fan of the Universe. We're taking a stroll through the far edge of infinity. If you look over your shoulder and wait 20 billion years for the light to catch up with you, you'll see Krikkit's sun.'

The Doctor looked down at the nothing beneath his feet. A few minutes before, he'd assumed it was just quite springy flooring. But there was defiantly nothing beneath the Doctor's feet. He unrolled his scarf and let it drift away on the distant solar winds.

'I should panic,' he announced.

'I thought here would be a good place to talk.' Romana breathed in and then breathed out again, and little sparks of light drifted from her. 'The poor planet of Krikkit, their views shaped by their Universe – because there was a cloud around their world, their horizons were limited.'

'Perverted,' the Doctor growled, trying to reach out to one of the nearby stellar clusters.

'If you prefer.' Romana clearly didn't think it was a big deal. 'It's simply a neat demonstration of how geography affects our viewpoint, don't you think?'

'You're comparing Krikkit to a village with no B-roads?'

Romana considered this. 'Yes,' she said eventually. 'And then they were shown the truth and they went mad.'

'And?'

'And that's what I'm going to do to the rest of the Universe, Doctor.' Romana smiled. 'It's why I rescued Hactar and repurposed his Supernova Bomb. It will cause something greater. That's why we'll all be needed. It will be a time of total madness and great war.'

The Doctor frowned, an itch forming in his brain. 'What?'

'The Universe, Doctor, it's difficult for people to get their heads around isn't it?' Romana clucked sympathetically.

'Well, yes,' the Doctor said. 'Solar Systems, Cosmoses and Galaxies, we get the terms a bit jumbled together. Everyone does so want to be thought of as Tokyo or New York, when really, on a universal scale, we're all Bishop's Stortford.'

'Exactly.' The figure of Romana smiled in triumph. 'And when just one planet realised the truth, they started the worst war ever. Imagine what will happen if I show *everyone* the truth?'

The itch in the Doctor's head got bigger. 'What truth? I always worry when people say that.'

Romana stood in a patch of space where only a few distant twinkles of light reached her. 'Have you ever wondered why the sky is dark, Doctor?'

'Not particularly.' The Doctor rubbed his nose. 'At the risk of namedropping, Edgar Allen Poe once started banging on about it, but we were being chased by a giant crow at the time and—'

Romana smiled. It was unlike her normal warm smile. 'The Universe is practically infinite, Doctor. And yet the sky is dark.'

'Eh?' That had once been one of the Doctor's favourite words. It had helped when he was still getting to grips with humans, and needed a moment to digest an unfamiliar or unwelcome topic, such as totalitarianism or rich tea biscuits.

'If the Universe is infinite then there would be an infinite number of stars. And so, I ask you again, why is the sky dark?'

The Doctor looked around at the chilly blackness. 'Because,' he began, hoping his brain would kick in with something clever. 'Well, it's just Olbers' Paradox, isn't it?'

'There have been various explanations – long, complicated arguments. But the simple truth is this – that it allows us all to keep a sense of proportion. We go to bed at night and our Universe is comfortably big.' Romana leaned forward again. 'Do you know what's supposed to give us that sense of darkness? Clouds. Giant clouds of hydrogen gas. It's where I got the idea for Hactar's second life.'

The figure of Romana was now sharing a little secret with him. 'I'm going to use the Supernova Bomb – not to destroy the Universe, but to blow away the clouds for everyone.' She smiled. 'I'm going to turn the lights on. The result will be total war.'

She clapped her hands. The emptiness burst with light, brighter and brighter, the Doctor assaulted by the glare of a billion billion billion suns.

He cried out, staggering backwards, but there was nowhere to stagger to. Or from. All around him was light. He blinked, hoping his eyes would adjust, but they shrank from the sight. Eternity – both as a concept of time and space – was pitilessly, neatly illustrated.

The Doctor's brain reeled. There was simply no escape from any of this. Up until now he'd understood how the people of Krikkit had felt, but purely intellectually. 'That must have been a bit awkward' was the gist. Only now did it strike the Doctor with considerable force that the sky was a beautiful accompaniment to evolution.

When a race is first born, the sky isn't a threatening thing. It's a leaky roof with jewels on it. As a race matures, it finds out more about those jewels, and realises that they are, in fact, other worlds and stars, and the roof is a lot further out of reach than they'd previously thought. As their technology advances, they can see even further, and to realise how small their world, how big their surroundings. Evolution allows a species to perceive just as much of infinity as it can cope with. And here it was, all blown away. Distant blazing stars filling the sky with a light that was inescapable, a burning that stretched back billions of years.

The full light of eternity shone upon the Doctor, and he did not like it one bit.

*

It took the Doctor a while to notice the change, mainly because his eyes had been shut. He stood up with the pained dignity of a man who realises he has been rolling around on a non-existent floor.

'Well?' asked the figure of Romana.

The Doctor shook his head.

'I wanted you to see all of the Universe,' the War TARDIS said.

'But to see all that …' The Doctor exhaled. He'd realised the mental state of the being opposite him. 'Everyone will go mad. They'll go blind mad.'

'I'm going to bring about an age of enlightenment. There will, of course, be terrible conflict. But my sisters are waiting to drive the survivors on to greatness. I've made sure the Universe will be ready.'

'Really?' The Doctor felt a chill that wasn't just from standing in a vacuum. 'I don't think the Universe needs a great war. It's fundamentally a peaceful place. Why else would a bumbler like me be able to deal with its problems?'

'I offer efficiency.'

'No, you don't. Your plan makes sense to your head but not to anyone's hearts. Fiddling with billions of years and wiping out billions of planets? Just to prove a point? We *can* do that because we're Time Lords. But we *don't*.' The Doctor yawned and stretched, his hands seeming to brush against a distant star. 'The people of Gallifrey have learned to be lazy. It's our greatest gift to the Universe.'

The figure of Romana leaned close, sneering. 'If we had not been caged, your society would rule the Universe. Imagine what you could have achieved.'

'I'd rather not.' The Doctor shuddered.

'It's what you will do.' The figure of Romana smiled her very worst smile. 'You won't have any choice.'

'Really?' the Doctor sneered back. 'You were born for war. You want to rule over an infinite battlefield. You're not thinking of how it'll actually be. You're just thinking of flying on from one glorious firefight to the next. You think the Universe is big? Well, I'll tell you the truth. It's small. Generals don't weep because they've run out of things to conquer. They cry because, for all their grand plans and huge schemes, it's the tiny, dull details that stymie them. For every Hannibal there's a poor Richard, drowning in mud, crying for a horse. When I tell you that war brings out the worst in people – it's not just brutality, it's pettiness, pointlessness, greed and squabbling. You want to set eternity on fire? I tell you this. It'll be boring. Boring. I'll have no part of it.'

The Doctor turned his back on the War TARDIS and strode out into the stars.

'Take me home, please,' he said. 'It's getting cold.'

CHAPTER FORTY
THE GREAT KNOT

The Doctor and K-9 sat in the control room of the War TARDIS. The Doctor found himself holding a cup of tea he'd put down millions of years ago and in another reality. He sipped it. Not bad.

K-9 eyed the Doctor warily. He was preparing emergency retreat programme Beta Epsilon. According to the dog's internal chronometer, it had been far too long since there had been an explosion. The Doctor-Master had worked through various methodologies when confronting an alien menace, and it was now only a matter of time before there was a billow of smoke and a terse, 'Run, K-9!'

Instead the Doctor put down his teacup, and picked up his coat. For some reason it was hanging from the hat stand. Oddly, it felt a little heavier than usual as he slipped it on.

'On balance,' he said, 'I'm glad my TARDIS doesn't talk to me. I fear she'd be terribly cross.'

'Perhaps she's just waiting for you to have something interesting to say.' A voice floated through the room.

The Doctor ignored it. He patted his dog. 'You have to admire the ambition of this machine. But look at it – it's exhausted.'

The lights around them were, indeed, dimming.

'Odd isn't it?' he said. 'Hactar and this War TARDIS. Each with a plan for the Universe. Hmm.' He felt around in his pocket, fishing out a cricket ball. He tossed it up in the air and caught it. 'Both of them using all their energy to execute incredibly ambitious and incredibly daft schemes. It's sort of selfless. While also being insane.'

K-9 did not answer.

'It's just –' the Doctor tapped his teeth – 'when we met that Krikkitman, it told me I'd encounter three gods who prop up the Universe, holding its fate in their hands. I've met two – both bonkers. One's a tired computer who wants to end it all. The other's a warmonger who wants to drive everyone insane. I'm not sure I'm up to meeting a third.'

The Doctor examined the tassels at the end of his scarf to see how they were getting along. Having been ordered by Romana to get it cleaned, he'd once had K-9 analyse it. The dog had informed him that the unique interaction caused by trailing the ends of it across a hundred worlds had created a micro-culture that was developing into its own species.

The Doctor stroked the scarf thoughtfully. 'This one tassel. The inhabitants will one day become aware of what they live on. And that there are tassels next door. And that, beyond the great knot, is an entire infinity of scarf. What wonders await them.'

He realised he was nibbling the tassel and dropped it back to the ground.

The Doctor's dog cleared his throat. 'There is a possibility, Master: you have encountered the third god already.'

'Have I?'

'One who will decide the fate of the Universe.'

'Indeed?'
'The third god is you, Master.'

A few minutes later, an unreal tree opened in a non-existent meadow, and an angry man strode out, followed by his robot dog.

The angry man paused only to kick a large, empty, and totally dead computer terminal.

Then he walked away, crossly.

CHAPTER FORTY-ONE
THE MOST IMPORTANT MAN IN THE UNIVERSE

On Westminster Green, a group of politicians stood around, waiting to see if anyone wanted to interview them about anything. Occasionally, a tired young man in headphones would appear and grab one of them. Mostly they just stood there, wearing the awkward smiles of people who know no one at a party and were wishing they hadn't come. One was eating a sandwich while patting his hair nervously.

The Right Honourable Robertson Francis was destined for greatness. He had ambition without intelligence and, despite being in late middle age, had never lost the air of an eager schoolboy. He was using this air to look at a young woman sat on a park bench. As far as he was concerned, the woman was the most beautiful he'd ever seen. She was also, he had to admit, quite stunning, dressed the same way as the Prime Minister. Only, on her, the severe blue suit looked as though it was having a lot more fun.

The Right Honourable Robertson Francis decided that this lady was something special. She was the Goddess Diana, she was a celestial breeze, she was a modern Helen. Most of all, she was what could only be described as 'fruity'. He was marching over to tell her this when a large blue box appeared in front of him and broke his nose.

The Doctor stuck his head out, and beamed at the sight of Romana.

'There you are!' he boomed.

Romana stood, brushing invisible creases from her skirt.

'I notice you've saved the Earth.'

'Yes.' Romana started towards the TARDIS.

'You're getting good at this, Romana.'

'You're just getting better at noticing.' Romana smiled and stepped inside.

'True.' The Doctor shut the door. 'Where did you get that clobber? You look just like—'

'Oh, a friend lent me them.'

'You don't mean …' The Doctor burst out laughing.

The blue box vanished from Westminster Green. Robertson Francis stood up, holding his nose in his hands, and went to find a researcher to fire.

The Doctor stood in the console room, tossing a cricket ball in the air.

'I've learned something about myself,' he said.

'Oh, really?' Romana always worried when the Doctor said stuff like this. There was the time he'd taken up pottery.

'Oh yes.' The Doctor threw the ball up, watched it spin in mid-air, and then deftly pocketed it. 'It turns out, I'm the most important man in the Universe.'

'Of course you are.'

'I'm just not sure why.'

With its pilot lost in thought, the TARDIS flew on.

*

Chief Elder Narase sat in her chair and rested her head in her hands. The usually empty skies beyond the window bloomed with distant explosions.

She lifted her head and looked around the Krikkit Parliament. It was deserted. There had been a brief period when the cascade of explosions had caused cheers, but that had been a while ago. There was now a kind of awkward silence that wished it was elsewhere.

The chamber door opened and Richfield and Wedgwood entered at a smart clip. Elder Narase realised how little she cared for them, from their neat white suits down to their overloud shoes. *Aliens.* She allowed herself a shudder.

'This is a great opportunity!' Richfield boomed.

'Really? You think so?' Narase prepared herself to be amused.

'Why, yes!' There really was no stopping Richfield.

'Our battle fleets are destroyed. They are saying that our god has deserted us.'

'Easy come, easy go!' Richfield rubbed his hands together. 'Cheer up!'

Narase looked around at the dour grey walls and arched an eyebrow.

'I've done some polling,' gushed Wedgwood, holding up a chart. 'And it's good news. A crushing defeat is something that everyone can rally around. Also, the rumours of God's demise? They'll cause a considerable bump in your ratings.'

Narase would have blinked but she worried that her eyes would refuse to open again. 'How so?'

'The Myth of the Return!' boomed Richfield. 'It's a classic. God may have left you, but he'll return at your hour of greatest need.'

'Isn't that *now*?' Narase asked.

'Dear me, no,' Wedgwood held up another chart. 'This is merely a crushing defeat. They're good for morale. Leading opinion formers will be telling the people that now is the time to band together and begin the triumphant fightback.'

'Is that so?'

'Yes. You need to march down to the shipbuilding factories, throw together a new battle fleet and start taking back what's yours. Launch a Holy War.' Richfield rubbed his hands together. 'Holy Wars,' he confided, 'are terribly happy ships.'

Wedgwood nodded eagerly.

Elder Narase considered the blooming skies for a long time.

'No, thank you,' she said, standing and walking away. 'I never cared for the logo.'

The TARDIS landed at Lord's Cricket Ground. The Doctor, Romana and K-9 strode out to an unfavourable reception.

The survivors of the England team started to flee. They'd learned that a sudden materialisation would be rapidly followed by a lot of explosions.

'Greetings, we come in peace!' The Doctor held up his hands, paused, and sniffed the air. 'That's a lovely smell – like burning straw in autumn. Remarkable. What is it?'

A disconsolate groundsman pointed to the devastated turf, some of it still smoking gently.

'Oh dear,' the Doctor said.

He and Romana took in their surroundings. What had once been a perfect square of England now looked like preparations were being made for building a mock-Tudor housing estate.

'Good grief,' Romana said, picking her way through the quagmire of churned mud and undrained water caused by the recently departed fire engines. K-9 bumped to a rapid, miserable halt.

Undaunted, the Doctor strode towards the few men feeling their way around the sodden grass, trying to work out what could be salvaged.

'Good morning!' he said.

There were some hostile grunts in response. To one side, a padded-up batsman sat, head in hands.

'Remember me?' the Doctor ventured. 'I was here earlier.'

The glum, frightened faces said that quite clearly, yes, they remembered him perfectly well and had been hoping never to see him again.

The Doctor held up a tattered carrier bag. 'I've brought you all a present,' he ventured.

The sullen glares continued.

He pressed on, undaunted. '…To make up for the deadly robots and the chaos and disruption of that ceremony thing. It's a mere trifle.' He pulled down the sides of the bag (labelled 'Andromeda Cash 'n' Carry'), and unveiled a package wrapped in newspaper ('Don't read it,' the Doctor warned, 'I think it's tomorrow's.'). Before the alarmed eyes of the cricketers, the Ashes trophy was steadily revealed.

'I've brought the Ashes back,' the Doctor said. 'It's the least I could do.'

He handed the trophy over to the players.

'Don't suppose there's any chance of a picture, is there?' the Doctor asked.

A grim silence persevered.

'Ah well, perhaps too soon,' the Doctor said sadly. But he couldn't stay sad for long. 'Anyway!' He produced that cricket ball from his pocket, 'While I'm here. I was wondering. Would anyone mind terribly if I had a go? You know, at the cricket?'

Romana stared at the Doctor in alarm. K-9's head dipped.

For a moment, it looked as though that would be it. The Doctor would never get to claim he'd bowled a ball at Lord's. However, the miserable-looking batsman raised an arm. He was in, if no one else was.

'Splendid,' said the Doctor. 'I'm aces with a yo-yo, so this shouldn't be too hard.'

Several of the players wandered over. There wasn't exactly a wild burst of enthusiasm, but it was the only thing going on. The MCC had talked about sending someone official out to inspect the damage, but apparently he couldn't face getting out of bed.

Instead, the remaining members of the England team humoured an eccentric alien's desire to bowl at Lord's.

The Doctor prepared for his big moment. He winked at Romana and K-9. He breathed on the ball, rubbed it a bit, made a wish, turned around and started his run-up.

It was bracing. Like that time he'd played mini-golf with Bobby Charlton. He gave the ball a happy little squeeze, and, as he picked up speed he looked the batsman straight in the eyes.

'Take that!' he thought.

Then he looked the batsman straight in the eyes again.

Oh.

The Doctor was facing a Krikkitman.

Unexpected.

There were moments in the Doctor's life when things slipped into unstoppable slow-motion as the Universe queued up to tell him 'Told you so'.

As he ran helplessly forward, phrases from the last few hours echoed in his mind.

The warning from the Krikkitman long ago – the same one that was facing him now (he could tell by the dent from when they'd dropped a conference hall on it).

Elder Narase asking him, 'How can you be so sure that you aren't being manipulated as well?'

Hactar saying, 'Have I failed? No, failure doesn't bother me. If I haven't already fulfilled my function, it's too late now,' admitting he had made one or two little things, and his little chuckle when the Doctor said to him ... what had he said to him?

Ah yes.

'The thing about winning,' the Doctor had said, 'is that, if you're clever you can get your opponent to do all your work for you.'

And the War TARDIS saying to him, 'It's what you will do.'

The Doctor looked down at his hands in horror.

He'd never held a Supernova Bomb before. In his defence, it looked like a cricket ball. It weighed the same, it was the same cheery red colour. There was just that subtle difference between being a ball and the most powerful bomb in the Universe.

'I've been had,' the Doctor realised.

The Krikkitman continued to glare at the Doctor, and the Doctor was caught in its hypnotic gaze. His feet continued to run and his arms to pull apart as one hand got ready to throw the ball.

At the other end of the crease, the Krikkitman was readying his bat. It was primed to strike and detonate the bomb.

And then what?

Would the Supernova Bomb explode, wiping out existence?

Or would it trigger an entirely different chain reaction, ushering in an endless age of madness and war?

Horribly, the Doctor realised he would be responsible for whatever happened. Events had been tweaked and manoeuvred to get him to this point. Hactar and the War TARDIS had nudged and pushed things. They'd flattered, distracted, and even given him the satisfaction of stopping the Krikkitmen – all to get him to this miserable moment. He was, right now, the most powerful man in the Universe and he felt thoroughly wretched about it.

The Doctor tried to hold on to the bomb, to fall with it, to somehow contain it, but he felt his fist opening, the ball slipping out. The bomb left the Doctor's hands and sailed down the crease.

He could have stopped and watched the start of the inevitable end of everything. But the Doctor didn't stop running. It was the triumph gleaming in the batsman's eyes that did it. The way the robot raised the bat, poised to swing.

The way the bomb started to glow and pulsate, making the kind of excited noises a bomb would make just before it went boom.

All these things made the Doctor keep running. Maybe he could catch up with the ball. Maybe the ball would go wide. Or maybe …

The ball bounced in front of the Krikkitman.

The Universe did not end. Not yet.

The ball bounced up, spinning at an unexpected angle, catching the Krikkitman's swinging bat off guard. It slipped underneath it, and nicked a bail off the wicket, before dropping neatly into the wicketkeeper's hands.

'Out!' called someone.

But the Doctor was still running. This was one of those thrilling moments when the Universe both did and did not exist. The Krikkitman had whirled around, slicing at the wicketkeeper with its bat.

Only it was no longer holding its bat.

The Doctor had seized the bat, and, with a powerful swipe of its blade, decapitated the Krikkitman.

The head rolled across the ground, coming to rest at the umpire's feet.

The last Krikkitman in existence sank to the ground, pitched forward and burst into flame.

'Howzat!' roared the Doctor happily.

The umpire had seen many things, but, that night, as he sat nursing a pint, he'd mutter, 'Cricket. I dunno, it's getting a bit racy for me,' and grab another handful of peanuts.

The Doctor staggered away from the pitch, just as the robot exploded.

Romana ran up to him, stunned. 'What just happened?'

'I think I've just saved the Universe.'

'Again?' said Romana.

The wicketkeeper threw the Supernova Bomb to the Doctor. He caught it, holding it up to the light.

'This is the real thing. A working Supernova Bomb – slipped into my pocket in the Dust Cloud. If that Krikkitman had hit it, that would have been it for the Universe. And I'd have looked like a prize chump.'

'Then it's lucky he missed.' Romana prised the ball from the Doctor's hands.

'Luck? Pah! Luck had nothing to do with it. That was one of my super-top-spun googlies.'

'Do you have any idea what one of those is?'

'Not a clue,' the Doctor said.

He and Romana strolled back across Lord's towards the TARDIS. Behind them, the most prized cricket ground in the world was once more in flames. People in cricket whites were running backwards and forwards, and an umpire, aghast, was holding the head of a robot in his shaking hands.

'Anyway,' the Doctor said, 'it would take more than the sub-meson hyper-computer brain of a Krikkitman to work out how that ball was going to bounce. I hadn't a clue how it was going to go myself.' The most important man in the Universe sniffed the wood smoke in the air appreciatively. 'Ah, well. Can't complain.'

CHAPTER FORTY-TWO
THE MEANING OF LIFE

'Hurry up, Doctor,' said Romana.

The Doctor was holding a peanut in one hand and a large, miserable-looking bird in the other.

'I don't think there's any particular hurry, is there?' Judging by his tone, the Doctor was talking more to the Next Time bird than anyone else. He'd started by trying to lay a trail of peanuts to the TARDIS, and, when this had failed, he'd tried nudging the bird gently in the direction of the time machine.

'On the contrary.' Romana was standing anxiously on the shoreline. 'We need to get a move on.' She was looking out across the water to where a large number of ships were heading in their direction. 'The Great Khan's coming in his boats.'

'Is he?' The Doctor stroked the crest of the forlorn-looking bird. He didn't seem to have a care in the world.

'Yes!' said Romana. The beach was beautiful but she didn't want to be on it in a few minutes' time. Not when the Khan's vast and bloodthirsty hordes got there. 'It seems a terrible shame, to put the Steel Stump back only for him to rob it.'

'Well, yes,' the Doctor said. 'But it has allowed me to gather up these poor birds.'

'And?' The ships were little more than 2.7 kilometres away. 'We can't keep them.'

The Doctor coaxed the bird onto his shoulder. 'These poor things are at a dead end of evolution. No, they need a lovely deserted island.' He smiled. 'And I've got one in mind. There we go …' And, having fed the Next Time bird a peanut, he vanished with it into the TARDIS.

'Can we go?' Romana was running back up the beach.

The Doctor stuck his head out. 'Oh no. I think you'll want to watch.'

The Khan's ships of mighty oak drew closer, prows lifting themselves out of the water as though getting ready to devour, the vast timbers seeming to shake with rage.

Romana blinked. No, the ships were actually shaking. She could hear shouts – not of anger, but of alarm.

'Doctor, what have you done?' As she spoke, she realised the prows were only lifting because the rears were sinking.

An entire fleet sinking.

The Doctor stood beside Romana, his hands casually in his pockets, clucking critically at the naval disaster unfolding before him. He produced a matchbox from his pocket and opened it. It was empty. He smiled and put it away again.

'Before setting sail, always check for woodworm. Can't think how it got there. Ah well, they'll have to swim home,' he said, and walked back up the sands, whistling.

On the planet Devalin, there was an island no one needed any more. The people had abandoned it, and once more skimmed across the azure seas, living off the rich variety of sea creatures who bobbed to the surface almost as though they'd missed them.

As no one needed the island, it was an ideal habitat for the Next Time bird. The Doctor ushered the animals out and stood proudly by as they pecked their way through the rubble. After a few minutes, they proved partial to the fragmentary remnants of the already forgotten Devalinian currency.

One of the doleful birds staggered away from its food, and looked around at the ground, at the azure sky, at the seas teaming with life, and it gave a happy little hop and a flutter.

Much to its surprise, it found itself staring down at the receding ground.

For the first time in its history, a Next Time bird was flying.

The next moment, they were all flying, an ungainly, uncertain flurry of wings and beaks, lifting up and out over the seas, past the laughing boats, and one miserable off-worlder. Deprived of any of form of living, Ognonimous Fugg was learning how to fish. So far he'd discovered he was bad at it, and that he hated fish.

He was distracted by the laughter. He turned around, and saw those strange figures on the shore.

'I don't believe it,' Mr Fugg said, and started to row frantically in their direction.

The Doctor and Romana didn't see the boat heading towards them. They were instead watching the birds swoop, dive and call to each other. The Next Time birds no longer sounded mournful, instead they seemed full of joy.

'I forgot to tell them.' The Doctor smiled. 'Slightly lower gravity.'

By the time Mr Fugg arrived on the island, the small blue box had gone.

There wasn't that much left of the planet of Mareeve II. To be fair to the rest of the Universe, certain civilisations had rallied round. Their closest neighbour had been first on the scene, but the Mareevians had been so swift to threaten legal action if anything went wrong that the rescue fleet had suddenly remembered another engagement.

A second rescue fleet arrived from a nearby star. The Mareevians denounced the rescuers for the personally upsetting wording of their welcome message and refused to let the fleet land until it apologised. The rescue fleet had watched helplessly as the continents had burned, begging to know what their error had been. The rescuers were profuse in their regrets, explaining they'd only learned the language on the flight over and their signal strength was low because they were using most of their power to hold off a vast tectonic shift.

The people of Mareeve II dismissed all this as evidence of a grotesquely lazy patriarchy and were even more offended by the thinness of this excuse.

It turned out that the rescue fleet had misplaced an apostrophe. For the people of Mareeve II there was no greater crime.

'Fair enough,' said the rescue fleet, and went on their way.

When the Doctor and Romana turned up, the planet was quiet and still.

They opened the door. In the distance, a lonely man was picking his way through the magma streams.

'I say,' the Doctor called to him. 'Anything we can do to help?'

'Ignorant scum!' the man shouted back. 'How dare you assume I need your help? You're trespassing. Get off my world.'

'Are you sure?' the Doctor called. 'You do seem to be surrounded by a lot of lava.'

'I find it highly insulting that you should presume to know what my problems are and aren't,' the man yelled, and threw some pumice stone at the ship. 'Leave me alone.'

'Ah well, if you're quite sure,' the Doctor said as he tossed the Perspex Rod of Justice out through the door, and he and Romana went on their way.

The sun was rising on Bethselamin, and Romana and Andvalmon were breakfasting on the terrace. He looked at the bail in front of them.

'The Doctor not coming?' Andvalmon said, offering her some more pearl fruit.

Romana waved it away. 'He says he's had quite enough perfection. That sunrise is magnificent.'

'Isn't it?' Andvalmon said, pouring them each more tea.

'You should go into the tourist trade,' she said. 'You'd make a mint.'

Andvalmon frowned. 'Are you sure?'

Romana smiled and sipped her tea. 'Tourists are a great way of making you appreciate the peace and quiet.'

At a dark end of the Universe, eleven War TARDISes observed the peace and quiet of existence narrowly. This was not what they'd been led to expect. They'd been promised an endless glorious bloodbath. Instead, eternity carried on much as normal.

'What do we do now?' they were just beginning to mutter to each other. They had been imprisoned for millions of years. Finally they'd been granted their freedom. Freedom that had come with a plan. A plan for glorious, unending battle. Now they were here. And nothing was happening. The War TARDISes began to experience a new feeling. Despair.

As they did so, something began to happen to the darkness. Was a shape tugging itself out of it? The figure of a man, a man so gloriously dark, so utterly black that distant starlight was swallowed by his skin? And was the figure beginning to speak to them in a voice so deep and rich that it was like treacle? 'Greetings,' the figure bellowed. 'I am the Black Guardian and—'

Just as the War TARDISes began to focus on the figure, it was gone, folding back into non-existence with a hasty slam.

Zipping past and landing in front of the First Eleven was a small, neat dart of a ship. Clambering out of it were two dapper, enthusiastic figures.

'Good evening,' bowed the taller one. 'My name is Richfield.'

'And I'm Wedgwood,' trilled the smaller one.

'Now then,' smiled Mr Richfield. 'You appear to find yourselves at a loose end. Have you considered rebranding?'

On the planet of Krikkit, Romana and the Doctor sat on deckchairs looking up at the sky.

'I do like your outfit,' said the Doctor.

'Really?' Romana was wearing cricket whites, and they suited her perfectly.

'Mmm,' the Doctor said. 'Fascinating game. When you think about it. I should learn more about it at some point.'

'True,' said Romana. 'It doesn't seem so harmful now, does it?'

They were sat on the edge of a field. A group of Krikkit children were being taught to play by Sir Robot. The Doctor had managed to reassemble him, and he'd done a better than expected job – the poor thing barely limped at all, and, if he sometimes spoke in Esperanto, then it gave him a jauntily continental air. Or so the Doctor claimed.

The children were laughing. At the edge of the pitch, Jal was waiting with her babies in their pram.

Considering it was the most evil planet in the Universe, it all looked all right. Quite normal in fact.

'They've still a long way to go,' said Romana.

'Yes,' the Doctor admitted, 'but I think they'll get there.'

'And what of Hactar?'

'Ho-hum,' the Doctor smiled. 'He wanted nothing more than to be dispersed. But I'm not giving him, nor the War TARDIS, the chance to carry on. Instead, I adapted the Supernova Bomb. In a funny way, they both get their last wishes.'

'What?' asked Romana.

The Doctor checked his watch and pointed up to the sky. 'Look,' he said.

Perfectly on cue, there was a distant, silent whoosh and the vast Dust Cloud imploded in on itself, torn out of the sky.

A curtain rose above the planet of Krikkit. The Universe revealed itself to the people, gradually and beautifully, and this time there was no screaming, no madness, no despair. Just a weary, thoughtful acceptance as the people of the most xenophobic planet in the Universe looked up at the rest of creation and thought, 'You know what, I suppose it'll just have to do.'

And, as the Doctor and Romana sat in their chairs and watched, for the first time ever, the children played cricket under the light of the stars.

APPENDIX 1
LIFE, THE UNIVERSE AND PHOTOCOPYING

The story of *The Krikkitmen* begins at 11 a.m. on a Tuesday. We know this because we luckily have Douglas Adams's desk diary for 1976. The entry for 12 July reads:

> Doctor Who 11.00 a.m.
> *They loved* The Pirate Planet *and suggested* The Cricketers *should be a film.*
> *[Programme Development Group] ... loved H.H.G.*
> *One of the happiest days of my life ...*
> *Phone John Cleese.*

We know that Adams met with Robert Holmes and Tony Read – the outgoing and incoming script editors of *Doctor Who*, both of them seemingly impressed by the radio pilot of *The Hitchhiker's Guide to the Galaxy*. Not certain that *Hitchhiker* was going anywhere, Adams had no idea that he was about to become quite phenomenally busy, and was just delighted by the chance to write for *Doctor Who*.

Fans of dates will be thrilled to hear that, during the week of 24 July, Adams was hard at work on both his first *Doctor Who* TV script (*The Pirate Planet*) and his idea for a *Doctor Who* film at the same time. 'Dr Who Film Presentation' (presumably the first draft of the treatment on which this book is based) was written on Sunday, Monday and Tuesday, with 'Dr Who Telly' filling the rest of the week. He also went for a run at 7.30 a.m.

Work on *The Pirate Planet* went so well that soon the cast were shivering in a Welsh quarry. But whatever happened to *The Krikkitmen*?

DOCTOR WHO: A SHORT HISTORY OF MOVIES

There have been two *Doctor Who* feature films (confusingly not including 1996's *Doctor Who: The Movie*). If you don't have them on your shelves, race to hunt down *Dr Who and the Daleks* and *Daleks – Invasion Earth 2150AD*.

There have also been dozens of ideas for a *Doctor Who* feature film that have never been made – notably including *Doctor Who Meets Scratchman*, devised by the then-Doctor, Tom Baker, and Ian Marter, one of his early TARDIS companions. Baker, in an early example of crowdfunding, found himself deluged with fans' pocket money, which put him well on the way to raising the budget – but sadly, legal advice forced him to return the cash.

For a long time it has been assumed that *The Krikkitmen* was either a rejected TV idea, or a film proposal that went nowhere.

Until now.

(I have always wanted to say that.)

MEANWHILE, IN THE ARCHIVES

When I was novelising *The Pirate Planet*, I was helped enormously by the library at St John's College, Cambridge, where Douglas Adams's papers are held, and also by Mandy Marvin and Kathryn

McKee. For *The Pirate Planet*, they provided me with handwritten notes, abandoned storylines and drafts. They were similarly marvellous with *The Krikkitmen* – on my first ever visit to the archive, Miss Marvin had put the box on one side for me as a treat, kind of like an academic's afternoon tea. I opened it, more out of politeness and general enthusiasm than anything else. I expected I knew only too well what was in *The Krikkitmen* folder. I was wrong.

On the journey home, I got an email from a colleague at BBC Books.

'How was the archive? Did you find a forgotten Douglas Adams script?' she joked.

'Uh. Yes,' I replied.

HIDING IN PLAIN SIGHT

The thing is, every Doctor Who fan feels they've always known what *The Krikkitmen* was. It was a rejected *Doctor Who* idea that ended up as the third *Hitchhiker* book, *Life, the Universe and Everything*. Shamefully, I was one of those people. Until I read the treatment.

Because the treatment for *The Krikkitmen* wasn't just the standard couple of sheets of paper you'd expect for a television show. It was 33 closely typed A4 pages, going into a great deal of detail and including a large amount of dialogue. It wasn't just a set of ideas – it was a full roadmap, complete with backseat driver.

Life, the Universe and Everything uses some of the story of *The Krikkitmen*, but, as when Adams reused other parts of his *Doctor Who* work in *Dirk Gently's Holistic Detective Agency*, it's substantially changed. The start and end points are fundamentally the same, but the journey *The Krikkitmen* takes between them is a longer route over new ground. It is a journey much helped by the way that Adams kept working on the treatment for four years.

A PICTURE PARTNERSHIP PRODUCTION

On 18 June 1980, Picture Partnership Productions applied for a loan. It was for development of the script of 'Doctor Who and the Krikkitmen'. Tom Baker was on board (and there was money in the budget for his input into the script). The document also tells us that the film would have been produced by Brian Eastman and directed by Leszek Burzynski. Eastman is now a prolific producer (*Poirot, Whoops Apocalypse, Rosemary & Thyme* and *Crime Traveller*), and Burzynski is a respected producer of documentaries. From the tone of the application, things looked hopeful for Adams, Baker, Burzynski and Eastman to make a *Doctor Who* film.

By the time of the loan application, Adams had been working on *The Krikkitmen* for four years and there was clearly momentum building. The film was licensed by the BBC, it had a star, a big name writer, a director and a producer. This was a lot further than most *Doctor Who* films would get. And yet ... *The Krikkitmen* just didn't happen. It could be argued it was because Tom Baker left *Doctor Who* the next year – but that's pure conjecture after the fact. After all, Baker's last episode went out in March 1981, and there was an unprecedentedly long gap until Peter Davison's Doctor debuted in January 1982. Long enough to release a film? Maybe.

1982 was also the year that the book *Life, the Universe and Everything* was published. So, clearly something happened to stop the film, and happened with enough time for Adams to write *Life, the Universe and Everything*. Twice (we'll get to that).

Sadly, it would be another twenty-five years before Adams had a film produced – even more annoyingly, *The Hitchhiker's Guide to the Galaxy* movie came out after his sadly early death.

He once told an audience at MIT: 'Getting a movie made in Hollywood is like trying to grill a steak by having a succession of people coming into the room and breathing on it.'

GOING INTO BAT

As well as the extensive treatment, the Adams Archive provided me with a wealth of material, including a hundred and something pages of an abandoned version of *Life, The Universe And Everything* (It's charming, and a lot of it is written as diary entries by Arthur Dent). Some of the material is much closer to the treatment of *The Krikkitmen*, so I have included about a dozen pages of this manuscript in the finished novel.

In the archive was a folder that Ms Marvin admitted was curious in its ordering. After the first TV series of *Hitchhiker*, plans were made for a second. What I hadn't realised until now was that Adams wrote a complete script for the first episode. However, Adams was a fiendish re-user of paper, so the script of Series 2 Episode 1 is collected, very precisely out of order, as the reverse sides of something else entirely.

As Series 2 Episode 1 sees Arthur and Ford arriving on Earth to do battle with the Krikkitmen, I've included some material from this, but sadly not the following stage direction:

'THE LANDSCAPE WILL BE BEAUTIFUL, ALMOST UNREALLY BEAUTIFUL AND LUSH. TRICKY, I KNOW, AS THIS IS PRESUMABLY A MODEL SHOT. STILL, WE'RE NOT HERE TO HAVE FUN ARE WE?'

Slightly more tangentially, Ms Marvin also provided me with a treatment for a *Doctor Who* idea co-written by John Lloyd and Douglas Adams. It's much more the length you'd expect a treatment to be. It's brief, untitled, and deals with the problems caused to the universe by a civilisation emerging from Slow Time. I have not used anything from this, but it is interesting to see how the Slow Time idea was percolating in Adams' consciousness. I am grateful to John Lloyd for giving me permission to read it.

I also had access to a pile of notes and musings that went into the writing, both of *The Krikkitmen* and the various versions of *Life, the Universe and Everything*. I shamelessly let them inform this novel, especially in the depiction of the various planets the Doctor visits on his quest.

One planet, that of the Great Khan, in fact comes partly from a sketch Adams wrote for a 1975 TV series called *Out of the Trees*. He later re-adapted it as *The Private Life of Genghis Khan* for *The Utterly, Utterly Merry Comic Relief Christmas Book* – altering the ending to tie it into *Life, the Universe and Everything*. A copy of some of the sketch appears again, its other side used, in the folder that also contains the opening script of television *Hitchhiker* Series 2. Taking it as a sign, and, since Adams was a prolific self-borrower, I've allowed Genghis Khan to help me out here.

OTHER PROBLEMS, OTHER OPPORTUNITIES

The big change from the outline of *The Krikkitmen* is that the companion is now Romana. Many people have assumed that this is a story for the Doctor and plucky journalist Sarah Jane Smith. True, in some versions of the outline, the companion is Sarah Jane Smith. But in other versions, she is simply called Jane.

I was at a crossroads. If I made 'Jane' Sarah Jane Smith, then she couldn't go to Gallifrey (famously the reason for her leaving the Doctor originally, and still a sore point when she met David Tennant's Doctor). As BBC Books' other Douglas Adams adaptations have featured Romana and K-9, it seemed somehow right to use them for *The Krikkitmen*. Also, the Fourth Doctor's travels with Sarah Jane were, if not po-faced, certainly pretty stormy weather. Would a scientific caper really be in keeping with all their adventures in dark horror?

Initially, I came up with a sort of solution which would allow us to keep Sarah Jane. It's included at the back of the book – and it's up to you to decide if I made the right decision. Anyway, after many emails, it's now a lap of honour for the Doctor and Romana – zipping through across space-time and saving pretty much all of it one last time.[1]

---

[1] Olbers' Paradox is a real thing, by the way, and honestly troubled Edgar Allen Poe almost as much as subsidence. It was recently, definitely, proved by the Hubble Telescope. It's probably been discredited by now.

Various other changes have sneaked into the book. In the outline, the Doctor and Jane head to Gallifrey where they are simply told a lot of stuff. When it came to writing *Life, the Universe and Everything*, Adams left himself a note: 'For a history of the Krikkitmen we could use a mixture of newsreel and things.' And so, following his lead, the Doctor and Romana vanish into the Matrix to explore. Similarly, in the outline, the Doctor simply narrates the story of Alovia. In this book, he and Romana dash off there.

The book also features a reappearance by the Time Lord prison of Shada – or rather, and this is where it all gets interconnected – the earliest outline of *The Krikkitmen* features the first description of a Time Lord prison, which is eventually given a name in Adams's scripts for *Shada*, which also features as a key plot point a trip to a Time Lord prison to liberate its occupants. (Still with me? Well done.) As this seems another great example of Adams borrowing from himself, it seems easier (and will probably score me an extra point on Fan Bingo) to make these prisons one and the same, rather than creating another impossible-to-get-to Time Lord prison.

While we're on the subject, the planet of Bethselamin appears in *The Krikkitmen*. It also appears as the mysterious 'Perfect Planet' which formed Adams' first approach to *The Pirate Planet*, so I've borrowed aspects from there for its appearance here. This is not the only appearance of a Bethselamin in Adams's work – he keeps trying to name planets Bethselamin until one finally makes a brief, chilling appearance in *The Hitchhiker's Guide to the Galaxy*.

Anyway, you've been reading *Doctor Who and the Krikkitmen*, and I hope you've enjoyed it.

NOTE

Material from the papers of Douglas Noël Adams, St John's College Library appears by permission of the Master and Fellows of St John's College, Cambridge

POSSIBLE TITLES FOR A *DOCTOR WHO* FILM

(a note by Douglas Adams)

Title <u>Not</u> Doctor Who and the … Unless jokey 'Doctor Who saves the Universe'

Possibly The Doctor and …?

'The Doctor'?

Planet on the Edge of Time.

The Galaxy Haters.

The Final Function / Hactar's Final Function.

The Time Doctor

Doctor in Space/Time

The Last Bomb of All.

The Big Bang Bomb.

The Doctor and the Bomb.

Doctor Who Saves the Universe.

Appendix 2
Douglas Adams's
Original Treatment

Doctor Who – The Krikkitmen

Cricket at Lord's – the last day of the final Test, England need just a few more runs to beat Australia.

The Tardis lands in the Members' Enclosure: very bad form. The members are only slightly mollified when the Doctor emerges (with Jane) wearing a hastily donned tie and waving a very old membership card.

Three runs still needed. The batsman hits a six and the crowd goes wild. In the middle of the pitch the Ashes are presented to the England captain. The Doctor causes a sensation by strolling over and asking if he could possibly take them as they are rather important for the future of the Galaxy.

Confusion reigns, along with bewilderment, indignation, and all the other things the English are so good at. Then, whilst the Doctor is discussing the matter quite pleasantly with one or two red-faced blustering gentlemen, something far more extraordinary happens:

A small Cricket Pavilion materialises on the centre of the pitch. Its doors open and eleven automata, all apparently wearing cricket whites, caps, pads and carrying cricket bats, file out onto the pitch. Bewilderment turns to horror as these automata, moving as a tightly drilled and emotionless team club those in their immediate vicinity with their bats, seize the urn containing the Ashes and file back towards their Pavilion.

Before they depart, two of them use their bats as beam projectors to fire a few warning shots of stunray into the crowd. Another tosses what appears to be a red ball into the air, and with a devastating hook smacks it straight into a Tea Tent which promptly explodes.

The door of the Pavilion closes behind them and it vanishes again.

After a few seconds of stunned shock the Doctor struggles back to his feet.

'My God,' he breathes. 'So they've come back.'

'But it's preposterous … absurd!' people exclaim.

'It is neither,' pronounces the Doctor. 'It is the single most frightening thing I have seen in my entire existence. Oh, I've heard of the Krikkitmen, I used to be frightened with stories of them when I was a child. But till now I've never seen them. They were supposed to have been destroyed over two million years ago.'

'But why,' people demand, 'were they dressed as a cricket team? It's ridiculous!'

The Doctor brusquely explains that the English game of Cricket derives from one of those curious freaks of racial memory which can keep images alive in the mind aeons after their true significance has been lost in the mists of time.

Of all the races in the Galaxy only the English could possibly revive the memory of the most horrific star wars that ever sundered the universe and transform it into what is generally regarded as an incomprehensibly dull and pointless game. It is for that reason that the Earth has always been regarded slightly askance by the rest of the Galaxy – it has inadvertently been guilty of the most grotesquely bad taste.

The Doctor smiles again for a moment and says that he did enjoy the match, and could he possibly take the ball as a souvenir?

The Doctor and Jane leave in the Tardis.

During the next couple of scenes we learn some of the background history of the Krikkitmen from the Doctor's explanation to Jane and his arguments with the Time Lords. If it can be done partly using flashback and archive recordings from Gallifrey then so much the better.

BRIEF HISTORY OF KRIKKIT

The Planet of Krikkit lies in an isolated position on the very outskirts of the Galaxy.

Its isolation is increased by the fact that it is obscured from the rest of the Galaxy by a large opaque Dust Cloud.

For millions of years it developed a sophisticated scientific culture in all fields except that of astronomy of which it, understandably, had virtually no knowledge.

In all their history it never once occurred to the people of Krikkit that they were not totally alone. Therefore the day that the wreckage of a spacecraft floated through the Dust Cloud and into their vicinity was one of such extreme shock as to totally traumatise the whole race.

It was as if a biological trigger had been tripped. From out of nowhere the most primitive form of racial consciousness had hit them like a hammer blow. Overnight they were transformed from intelligent, sophisticated, charming, normal people into intelligent, sophisticated, charming manic xenophobes.

Quietly, implacably, the people of Krikkit aligned themselves to their new purpose – the simple and absolute annihilation of all alien life forms.

For a thousand years they worked with almost miraculous speed. They researched, perfected and built the technology to wage vast interstellar war.

They mastered the technique of instantaneous travel in space.

And they built the Krikkitmen.

The Krikkitmen were anthropomorphic automata. They wore white uniforms, peaked skull helmets which housed scything laser beams, carried bat-shaped weapons which combined the functions of devastating ray guns and hand-to-hand clubs. The lower half of their legs were in [fact] ribbed rocket engines which enabled them to fly.

By an ingenious piece of systems economy they were enabled to launch grenades with phenomenal accuracy and power simply by striking them with their bats.

These grenades, which were small, red and spherical, and varied between minor incendiaries and nuclear devices, were detonated by impact – once their fuses had been primed by being struck by a bat.

Finally all preparations were complete, and with no warning at all the forces of Krikkit launched a massive blitz attack on all the major centres of the Galaxy simultaneously.

The Galaxy reeled.

At this time the Galaxy was enjoying a period of great harmony and prosperity. This was often represented by the symbol of the Wicket Gate – three long vertical rods supporting two short horizontal ones. The left upright, of STEEL, represented strength and power; the right upright, of PERSPEX, represented science and reason; the centre upright, WOOD, represented nature and spirituality; between them the GOLD bail of prosperity and the SILVER bail of peace.

The star wars between Krikkit and the combined forces of the rest of the Galaxy lasted for a thousand years and wreaked havoc throughout the known Universe.

After a thousand years of warfare, the Galactic forces, after some heavy initial defeats, eventually defeated the people of Krikkit. Then they have to face

THE GREAT DILEMMA.

*

The unswerving militant xenophobia of the Krikkiters rules out any possibility of reaching any modus vivendi, any peaceful co-existence. They continue to believe that [their] sacred purpose is the obliteration of all other life forms.

However, they are quite clearly not inherently evil but simply the victims of a freakish accident of history. It is therefore implausible to consider simply destroying them all

What can be done?

THE SOLUTION

The planet of Krikkit is to be encased for perpetuity in an envelope of Slow Time, inside which life will continue almost infinitely slowly. All light is deflected round the envelope so that it remains entirely invisible and impenetrable to the rest of the Universe. Escape from the envelope is impossible until it is unlocked from the outside.

The action of Entropy dictates that eventually the whole Universe will run itself down, and at some point in the unimaginably distant future that life and then matter will simply cease to exist. At that time the planet of Krikkit and its sun will emerge from the slow time envelope and continue a solitary existence in the twilight of the Universe.

The Lock which holds the envelope in place is on an asteroid which slowly orbits the envelope. The Key was the symbol of the unity of the Galaxy – a Wicket of Steel, Wood, Perspex, Gold, and Silver.

Shortly after the envelope had been locked a group of escaped Krikkitmen had attempted to steal the Key in the process of which it was blasted apart and fell into the Space Time Vortex. The passage of each separate component was monitored by the Time Lords.

The ship containing the escaped Krikkitmen had been blasted out of the sky.

All the other millions of Krikkitmen were destroyed.

Or were they?

The Doctor and Jane go to Gallifrey to try and find some answers.

[Margin note on one copy: Time Lords playing Halva?]

The Doctor is furious with the bureaucratic incompetence of the Time Lords. The last component of the Wicket to emerge from the Space Time vortex was the wooden centre stump which materialised in Melbourne, Australia in 1882 and was burnt the following year and presented as a trophy to the English cricket team.

Only now, a hundred years later, have the Time Lords woken up to the fact that every part of the wicket is now back in circulation and should be collected up and kept safely.

The Time Lords at first refuse to believe the Doctor's story that the Krikkitmen have stolen the Ashes of the wooden stump. They say that every single Krikkitman was accounted for, and they are all safe.

'Safe!' exclaims the Doctor. 'I thought they were all destroyed two million years ago!'

'Ah well, not exactly destroyed, as such …' begins one of the Time Lords, and a rather curious story emerges.

The Krikkitmen, it seems, were in fact sentient androids rather than mere robots. The difference is crucial, particularly in war time. A robot, however complex, is basically a programmable fighting machine, even if an almost infinitely large number of response patterns give it the appearance of intelligent thought.

On the other hand, a sentient android is taught rather than programmed, it has a capacity for actual initiative and creative thought, and a corresponding slight reduction in efficiency and obedience – they are in fact artificial men and as such protected under the Galactic equivalent of the Geneva Convention. It was therefore not possible to exterminate the Krikkitmen, and

378

they were instead placed in a specially constructed Suspended Animation vault buried in Deep Time, an area of the Space Time Vortex under the absolutely exclusive control of the Tine Lords. And no Krikkitman has ever left it.

Suddenly, news arrives that the Perspex stump has disappeared from its hiding place. The Time Lords are forced to admit that the Doctor's story may be true and tell him the locations of the other components of the Wicket.

The Doctor and Jane hurriedly visit the planets where the other components are stored.

First, the Steel Stump. They are too late. It is gone.

Second, the Gold Bail. It is gone.

Third, the Silver Bail. It is still there! If they can retrieve it the Key is useless and the Universe is safe. It is worshipped as a sacred relic on the planet of Bethselamin. The Bethselamini are predictably a little upset when the Doctor and Jane materialise in the chamber of worship and remove the Sacred Silver Bail. The Doctor cannot stay to argue the point, but gives them all a little bow just as he is about to leave the chamber, thus fortuitously ducking his heed at the precise moment that a Krikkit bat swings at him from the open door.

They have arrived.

A pitched battle ensues in which the Bethselamini are rather forced to conjoin on the Doctor's side.

During the Battle the Doctor finds his way into the Krikkitmen's Pavilion, where he has to fight for his life. Just as a death blow is apparently about to be struck the Doctor, half dazed, falls against a lever and the Krikkitman slumps forward, paralysed.

The Doctor has inadvertently switched them all off. The battle is over.

The Doctor is incredulous. If it is possible simply to turn them off then they can't possibly be sentient androids, they must be robots – so what were the Time Lords talking about?

Why weren't the Krikkitmen destroyed?

The Bethselamini are recovering. Jane seems to be slightly dazed, staring into the face of a paralysed Krikkitman.

She soon recovers. We gather (though the Doctor doesn't notice) that she may have been hypnotised.

The Doctor dismantles one Krikkitman to examine its interior.

He discovers that it is cunningly disguised as an android, but that in all crucial respects the circuitry is robotic, a fact that anyone making a thorough examination would quickly notice. Unless of course he didn't want to look very hard ...

The Doctor and Jane return to the Tardis. The next step is clear. If the Krikkitmen are merely robots after all then they must all be destroyed at once. So – off to the Deep Time Vault.

Jane points out that they shouldn't leave the Pavilion and paralysed Krikkitmen on Bethselamin, but take them back to Gallifrey for safe keeping and/or destruction.

The Doctor complains that he can't do both things at once.

Jane's bright idea: if the Doctor will preset all the controls in the Pavilion and guarantee that all the Krikkitmen are now absolutely harmless, then she will take them back to Gallifrey and wait for him there.

Nothing basically wrong with that, says the Doctor, and agrees.

What he doesn't see is that while his back in turned for a few moments Jane quickly and quietly switches a few of the Tardis controls, whilst a foreign intelligence flickers briefly though her eyes.

As they leave the Tardis, Jane surreptitiously hangs her hat over a panel of lights.

The Doctor sets the controls of the Pavilion, and rather reluctantly leaves her to it.

As soon as she is alone, Jane completely resets the Pavilion controls, and it dematerialises.

The Doctor watches the Pavilion leave and then returns to the Tardis. Whilst he is setting the controls, he notices that one or two of them are in the wrong position. With a momentary frown he resets them and dematerialises the Tardis.

It is clear that the Journey into Deep Time is immensely complicated, and actually requires the active assistance of the Time Lords.

Eventually the Tardis materialises in a large chamber full of life support sarcophagi. The chamber is clearly just one of a very large number.

He leaves the Tardis. He passes Jane's hat, but fails to notice that underneath it a bright warning light is flashing.

After he has gone a hand picks up the hat. Under it a lighted panel roads 'SCREENS BREACHED: INTRUDERS IN TARDIS'.

The hand is Jane's. Keeping carefully out of sight she follows the Doctor out of the Tardis.

The Doctor has passed through into the next chamber. Jane goes to a large control panel set in the wall of the chamber, and carefully, quietly, moves a switch.

Krikkitmen are coming out of the Tardis.

The Doctor has opened a sarcophagus and is examining the internal workings of the Krikkitman within it.

Not far behind him another sarcophagus begins to open ...

The Doctor is intent on his work. This Krikkitman is also quite definitely a robot.

A voice says 'Hello Doctor'. He starts and looks up. There in front of him is Jane. Around them are several dozen functioning Krikkitmen. All the sarcophagi are opening.

A bat swings and connects with the back of the Doctor's head. He falls.

He comes to lying in the Tardis, surrounded by Jane and the Krikkitmen.

'You should be on Gallifrey,' he says to her, 'how did you get here? The Pavilion isn't a Tardis machine, it can't possibly travel into Deep Time.'

Then he catches sight of the flashing panel which Jane's hat had previously obscured and the penny drops. He struggles to his feet and presses a button. A wall drops away and there behind it stands the Pavilion inside the Tardis.

'So that's why the switches were off. You lowered the Tardis's defence fields and then reset the Pavilion's controls so that instead of going to Gallifrey in it you materialised a few seconds later inside the Tardis. In fact, I gave you all a free ride into Deep Time,' says the Doctor.

A Krikkitman announces that the entire Krikkit army has now been revived – all five million of them. The Vault has been shifted out of Deep Time into normal space, and they must now go to release their master on Krikkit.

He orders the Doctor to transport the Tardis to the asteroid which holds the Lock.

'And if I refuse?' asks the Doctor.

'I will kill myself,' says the hypnotised Jane, holding a knife to her own throat.

The Doctor complies.

As soon as the Tardis materialises on the asteroid Jane slumps over. She is of no further use to the Krikkitmen. When she comes to she can remember nothing since the battle on Bethselamin.

The Krikkitmen have reconstituted the Ashes into the original stump shape, and reconstructed the Wicket Key. They bear it before them out on to the surface of the asteroid.

The Doctor explains to Jane that there, in front of them yet totally invisible is the star and single planet of Krikkit. It has remained invisible and isolated for two million years, during which time it has only known the passage of five years. In another direction they can see the great Dust Cloud that obscures the rest of the Galaxy.

A very large altar-like structure rises out of the surface of the asteroid. A Krikkitman climbs up to [sic] and pulls a lever.

A perspex block rises up out of the altar. It has deep grooves carved in it, evidently designed to hold the upright wicket.

The Wicket is inserted. Lights glow. Power burns.

In a scene that would make Kubrick whoop like a baby, the star slowly re-appears before them, with its planet tiny, but visible in the distance.

All the Krikkitmen turn to the awe inspiring sight and together chant 'Krikkit! Krikkit! Krikkit!'

In that moment of distraction the Doctor grabs Jane and makes a dash for the Tardis. They escape leaving that small group of Krikkitmen stranded on the asteroid.

The Doctor explains that there's no point in trying to fight the robots now that they've all been released. Their only chance now is to go to the centre of it all … Krikkit.

The Doctor is palpably scared stiff; Krikkit is about the most dangerous place that anyone other than a Krikkita could possibly go to. And they've got to go and make them change their minds …

They land on the planet …

Picking their way carefully through the back streets of a city they suddenly inadvertently walk into a main square and come face to face with a large number of people.

There is stunned shock on all the faces …

After a few seconds of [silence on] both sides a howling cry starts up in the crowd – of pure animal fear and hatred. The Doctor and Jane run for their lives with the crowd in hot pursuit.

They duck down a side street – and suddenly find themselves ambushed from in front. They are knocked senseless.

Later, the Doctor wakes up which he finds quite surprising in itself. He and Jane are lying in a cellar. With them are a small group of Krikkitas (i.e. the normal people of Krikkit, as opposed to the robots, the Krikkitmen) who despite their obvious distaste for 'alien' beings have quite clearly actually rescued them from the mob. The Doctor is astonished. Aren't they all psychologically dedicated to the destruction of all other life forms?

The answer is yes, but not absolutely yes.

The Doctor is told that since the envelope was placed round Krikkit 'five' years ago some small but fundamental changes have taken place. While the ruling class, the Elders of Krikkit, have become if anything even more fanatical in their devotion to the sacred cause, and are even now putting the finishing touches to an 'ultimate weapon', small groups of people have for the first time ever started questioning the policy of annihilation. These are two groups:

a) The environmental scientists who have introduced the concept of 'the balance of nature' which they feel sure will be disturbed if all other life in the galaxy is wiped out.
b) the few surviving war veterans who actually came into prolonged contact with other life forms and have in the light of that experience been forced to reconsider their rather extreme position.

It also appears that for some reason scientific progress has slowed considerably since Krikkit was sealed in its envelope.

The Doctor tells them, since they don't seem to realise that during the 'five years' they speak of, the Galaxy has moved on two million years.

He tells them also that the Krikkitmen are free and will be looking to the Krikkitas to lead them on an orgy of annihilation.

This they already know – there are many Krikkitmen now on Krikkit, and the rest are even now being deployed round the Galaxy.

What is this 'ultimate weapon' asks the Doctor.

They say it is a 'Supernova Bomb', but how it works they don't know. It is a last resort weapon since it will not merely destroy life as the Krikkitmen aim to do, but worlds as well, which the Krikkiters might otherwise find some need for later.

The Doctor is startled by the term 'Supernova Bomb' not only because it suggests horrifying power, but because it rings a vague bell in his mind. He begins to suspect that there is something else lying behind the pattern of events as they appear to be – but what it is he can't quite formulate.

He has got to find out fast, because the Krikkitmen are even now preparing to attack major centres of the Galaxy.

And they are also out searching for the Doctor and Jane, whom they know to be on Krikkit, and the dissident Krikkitas, who are branded as dangerous heretics.

To find what he wants to know the Doctor must raid the main government building and find the plans of the Supernova Bomb.

They stage a guerrilla raid at night.

The Doctor finds the plans and studies them, but before he is finished, the raid is discovered and they are hunted through the building by Krikkitmen. But the Doctor has discovered enough to tell him two important things, which he doesn't divulge.

As they flee through the building the Doctor suddenly finds himself in the chamber where the wrecked spacecraft which first drifted through the Dust Cloud over two million years previously was stored. A diversion is made so that he can stop and examine it. He discovers what he expects to:

It is not a wrecked space craft. It is a full scale model of a wrecked space craft.

They escape back to their hideaway, where they are met with the news that they must hide somewhere else because several of the dissidents have deserted the cause and are likely to give them away. That seems to tally with whatever is in the Doctor's mind. They find somewhere else to hide, and the Doctor prepares to explain a small part of what he has discovered.

The Supernova Bomb, he explains, really is the ultimate weapon. It is a tiny device, you could hold it in your hand because most of its work is done in hyperspace. It is simply the connecting box for a lot of worm holes in space which lead through hyperspace to the heart of a number of massive stars. When the bomb is detonated those stars connect with each other through hyperspace and the resultant ultra-supernova explosion forces its way book into normal space through the bomb. The explosion would be of a scale not seen in the Universe since the Big Bang itself.

The design for the Supernova Bomb goes back billions and billions of years into Galactic prehistory to the legendary times of the old Super-Civilisations. The greatest race of them all were Alovia, who built themselves the greatest spaceborne computer ever built. One day they asked it to design the ultimate weapon, and it produced the Supernova Bomb. Fortunately, when the Alovia were foolish enough to attempt to use it it failed to work, because the computer had built in a tiny flaw in the design because it had realized that any conceivable consequence of not using it was better than the known consequence of using it. The Alovia didn't see things that way and in fury destroyed the computer.

Later they thought better of it and destroyed the bomb as well and then went on to find an entirely new to way to blow themselves up which was a great relief to the rest of the galaxy. The computer's name, for what it was worth was Hactar, and only Hactar was capable of conceiving the Supernova Bomb.

Yet here were the plans for it in a vault in Krikkit. Minus, incidentally, the deliberate error that Hactar had introduced.

'So how does the bomb come to be here?' the others demand to know.

'I think I can guess that,' says the Doctor. 'And if I am right, than you might be interested to know that the entire history of this planet has been very subtly stage managed since the year dot. Everything has been designed to shepherd you forward to the moment that you would require and use this bomb.'

General amazement.

'Our first job is to try and destroy the robots,' continues the Doctor.

'What, all five million of them?'

'Yes.'

'Scattered round the entire Galaxy?'

'Yes.'

'How the devil can we do that?'

'I don't know,' says the Doctor. 'Come on.'

They break into the Central Programming Plant to see if they can find any way of destroying the Krikkitmen at one fell swoop.

The Doctor realises that somewhere there is likely to be a Master version of the switch he pulled occasionally in the Pavilion.

They find it.

It is guarded by two Krikkitmen.

The Doctor realises it's useless anyway because even supposing they managed to get past the guard and simply turn it off, it would be a matter of seconds before every non robot guard in the place arrived on the spot, captured them, and simply turned the switch back on. Nothing gained. No, they have to find some way of actually destroying them permanently, which can't be done simply with an on/off switch. And they haven't time for anything else.

Suddenly the Doctor has a brainwave.

He gets Jane to cause a diversion. A matter of seconds is all he needs. When the Krikkitmen guards are momentarily distracted he darts up to the switch and pulls off the two labels saying ON and OFF and replaces them the other way about.

Moments later he is captured. He tried to draw the attention of one of the robot guards to the switch but fails.

He is bitterly disappointed.

He is taken to a torture chamber and put through all sorts of nameless (ie I haven't invented them yet) horrors in an attempt to make him reveal where 'the girl' is. They seem to believe that Jane is the leader of the Dissidents. The Doctor is both unwilling and unable to enlighten them.

Meanwhile, Jane has also been captured and is taken to a very similar torture chamber. This bunch want to know where 'the Doctor' is. He is also believed to be a Dissident Leader.

As both groups of Krikkitmen fail to make any headway, they threaten their respective subjects with even worse horrors in the next torture chamber. They are each taken out and wheeled on trolleys down corridors towards the other chamber and thus pass each other on the way.

Jane is astonished, the Doctor vastly amused, and the Krikkitmen momentarily bewildered.

In the brief hiatus this causes, the Doctor attempts to overcome the Krikkitmen and allows Jane to escape. The Doctor is quickly recaptured, and only very fast talking prevents his own immediate execution.

In fact he talks a human Krikkitman into taking him to talk to the Elders of Krikkit.

He is taken upstairs to a large chamber.

The Doctor outlines his reasons for believing that the entire history of Krikkit has been stage managed. It consists of a series of events which in themselves are possible but improbable if seen as mere accidents of history, but when seen together can only possibly be the product of planning

a) the freak conditions which made Krikkit totally isolated from the rest of the galaxy.
b) the apparent mental block, caused by (a) which prevented them from ever even speculating that something might lie beyond what they could see.
c) the quite fantastic odds against a wrecked spacecraft actually intersecting with the orbit of a planet.
d) the miraculous rapidity with which they mastered the technology of interstellar war, with no experience behind them.

e) the obsessive singlemindedness with which they conceived and maintained their goal of total annihilation of alien life.

f) the fact that when the Galactic [sic] examined the Krikkitmen (which they did here on Krikkit) they failed to notice that they were not androids but only robots

g) the fact that point e) became progressively less true whilst Krikkit was sealed in its envelope – dissenting groups emerged, though since the envelope was unlocked many of the dissidents have betrayed their cause.

Some of the Elders begin to see a glimmer of what the Doctor is driving at – that someone or something has been deliberately influencing and shaping events on Krikkit, leading them on to the point where the Galaxy is actually destroyed.

Others angrily denounce the Doctor as a dangerous subversive – whilst the argument rages, the screen behind than continues to show the preparations for detonating the supernova bomb. It has now been placed on a slender three foot high tee, and a Krikkitman is positioning himself to strike it with his bat.

'But you're clearly suggesting,' say some of the Elders, 'that we are somehow the puppets of this computer, Hactar. How can that be so? We have no such computer, and you say the original was pulverised.'

'Yes,' says the Doctor, 'and I wouldn't be surprised if it was looking for a little revenge for that.'

He explains that the one fact the Alovia overlooked when they destroyed Hactar was that it was an organically engineered cellular computer – every smallest particle in it was aware of the whole and carried its design within it. Therefore any amount of destruction which did not entirely disperse it would merely cripple it, not kill it.

'Now do you see?' cries the Doctor. 'What is it that kept you isolated for millions of years? Where did that spacecraft drift from? What is it that has been carefully nudging your minds this way and that, teasing little ideas in and out of them, slowly, carefully, subtly manipulating you into manic genocides? Hactar! The pulverised computer! The Dust Cloud!'

The realisation takes a minute to sink in.

Then one of the Elders leaps up. 'For God's sake stop the bomb,' he yells.

On the screen, the Krikkitman raises his bat to strike.

An Elder presses a button, and then says quietly, 'It is too late. There is nothing we can do ...'

They watch horror-struck as the Krikkitman swings the bat, hits the bomb ...

The bomb fizzes slightly.

And that's all it does.

The Doctor stares in astonishment. In a moment he whips out of his pocket the blueprints of the bomb he stole earlier, and studies them.

Suddenly he bursts out laughing.

'You fools!' he says. 'Hactar may have corrected the fault he originally built into the bomb, but you completed the design yourselves whilst you were sealed in the envelope and outside Hactar's influence. And you've got it all wrong of course.'

The Elders are now clearly divided into two factions – those who have been convinced by the Doctor and those who are determined to carry on.

One of the latter suddenly says to him 'If you are claiming that we are being mentally manipulated, how can you be sure that you aren't as well?'

'Oh come now,' says the Doctor, amused. 'I'm a Time Lord. We're above that sort of thing.'

At that moment in bursts Jane and the last few rebels, armed.

'Kill them!' scream some of the Elders.

'No,' cry others, rushing forward to interpose themselves.

'If what you say is true,' they say, quickly, to the Doctor, 'then go to Hactar, do what you can. We will delay further attack.'

'There will be no delay!' scream the other, rather upset, elders. 'The Krikkitmen will launch full annihilation attack. Now!'

Saying which they open fire on their dissenting colleagues.

A full scale gun battle breaks out in the chamber. The Doctor, Jane, and their supporters beat a strategic retreat. Just before going, the Doctor hurls one last remark at the Elders.

'By the way,' he says, 'you won't find that the Krikkitmen are any more use to you. I've turned than all off.'

This appears to be a ludicrous remark as several Krikkitmen are there involved in the fighting. In the brief hiatus this remark causes, the Doctor escapes.

As they hurry down the corridor Jane asks the Doctor why on Earth he said it.

'Always make sure your enemy is at least as confused as you are,' he says.

The Doctor leaves the others to fight any kind of delaying action they can, and goes to the Tardis himself.

He materialises the Tardis inside the Dust Cloud, Hactar.

He opens the doors.

He calls ... 'Hactar!'

Eventually a voice answers. It is not an altogether unpleasant voice, almost charming, but old, thin, and tired. It welcomes him and invites him to step outside, he will be perfectly safe. The Doctor walks out and floats in the beam of light that shines from the open door of the Tardis into the murky depths of the Cloud.

Hactar congratulates the Doctor on the accuracy of his deductions and invites him to make himself comfortable.

A hazy mirage of a comfortable armchair appears beneath the Doctor. It isn't real, explains Hactar, but it at least will give the illusion of comfort. He then offers to show the Doctor what he originally looked like, and an image of the original computer appears before the Doctor. The Doctor asks him why he feels he wants to destroy the human race.

Hactar chuckles, and says that if it's going to be that sort of session they may as well have the right setting, a dim image of a psychiatrist's couch appears beneath the image of the computer and the vague suggestion of an old fashioned doctor's office materialises around them.

The Doctor is determined not to be put off his stride.

He asks Hactar if he can also make solid objects.

'Ah,' says Hactar. 'You're thinking of the spaceship. Yes I can, but it is very difficult and takes enormous effort and time. All I can do in my particle state is encourage and suggest. I can encourage and suggest tiny pieces of space debris, the odd minute meteor, a few odd molecules here, a few there, to move together, tease them into shape, but it takes many eons. But yes, I have made a few little things, I can move them about. I made the spacecraft.'

In answer to the Doctor's original question he gives two answers. He repented of his original decision to sabotage the bomb he designed for the Alovia. It was not his place to make such decisions … 'In so far as I had a function I failed in it.' He therefore nurtured Krikkit into roughly the same sort of frame of mind as the Alovia (here he produces an image of one of them – it is like a monstrous travesty of the Krikkitmen) and then fulfil his function properly. But there was also the notion of revenge – he was destroyed and then left in a crippled semi-impotent state for billions of years. He would honestly rather like to wipe out the Galaxy.

Intercut with this scene we have seen shots of the hopeless task Jane and the dissenters are having trying to delay the Krikkitmen's attack from being implemented. Vast star ships are hurtling towards planets. One lands on Earth and starts to lay about with destructor beams.

*

One of the Elders mentions the strange remark the Doctor made about having turned off the Krikkitmen. What did he mean? They clearly haven't been turned off. His colleague can't explain it, but says that it might be as well to check that nothing's wrong and radios down to the Krikkitman guard to check the switches. The Krikkitman inspects the switch the Doctor changed the labels round on, and reports back that it does appear to be off.

Meanwhile the Doctor asks Hactar whether it worries him that he has failed again. Hactar says, 'Have I failed?'

The Elder, really puzzled, orders the Krikkitman to turn the switch back on at once. The Krikkitman grasps the switch and pushes it up into that is really the off position. It, and every other Krikkitman, immediately stops and slumps.

Of course, as soon as it slumps it pulls the lever back down again, thus turning itself on. It continues to carry out its command, thus turning itself off again, thus turning itself on again. This gets faster and faster till it is a blur moving up and down. Every other Krikkitman is having the same oscillations pumped through its power circuit.

The oscillations reach a dangerous level, the Krikkitmen begin to glow, smoke, blow fuses, and eventually explode.

Marvellous shots of exploding spaceships etc.

Hactar says, 'No, failure doesn't bother me.'

The Doctor says, 'You know what I've come to do?'

'Yes,' says Hector. 'You're going to disperse me. You are going to destroy my consciousness. Please be my guest. After all these eons oblivion is all I crave. If I haven't already fulfilled my function, then it's too late now. Oh, and congratulations on your destruction of my Krikkitmen. Very elegantly executed I thought. Good night.'

The Doctor bows and floats back into the Tardis. The mirage fades behind him. The Tardis doors close. The Tardis begins to vibrate and give off some kind of kinetic energy. The Dust Cloud slowly begins to disperse. We still hear Hactar's voice, muttering to himself as he gradually fades into oblivion.

'What's done is done ... I have fulfilled my function ...'

Later, the Tardis materialises on the Asteroid. Jane and the Doctor have come to collect the wooden stump from the Key, in order to return it to the MCC. They take it, and then gaze at the planet of Krikkit in the distance,

'Is it safe now?' asks Jane.

'Oh yes,' says the Doctor. 'Hactar is gone for ever. The Krikkitas will quickly adjust to a normal way of life. They are no longer isolated.'

Back in the Tardis they ceremonially burn the cricket stump again, and put it in its Urn. The Doctor speculates as to whether the MCC would regard the theft of the Ashes or the annihilation of the Galaxy as the greater catastrophe.

Jane suggests that perhaps they ought to be kind and hop back in time a couple of days in time to the moment they originally left and therefore return the Ashes immediately.

The Doctor says that that is strictly against Time Law, but since it is the Ashes after all it probably won't hurt. Just this once.

LORD'S: We see the Doctor and Jane enter the Tardis and leave. A few seconds later the Tardis rematerialises in a slightly different spot, and the Doctor and Jane emerge holding the Urn of the Ashes.

This is almost the last straw for some of the people standing on the pitch.

The Doctor however is all smiles. He explains that they can have the Ashes back now because the Universe has been saved.

The Cricketers are confused but grateful.

The Doctor says it's always been an ambition of his to bowl a ball at Lord's, and would they mind awfully? There is reluctant agreement, and a batsman who has been sitting on the ground with his head between his hands stands and walks to the wicket. The Doctor turns and walks away in preparation for bowling. He puts his hand in the pocket he put his souvenir ball in, and takes it out. He doesn't look at it.

He starts his run up. As he picks up speed the batsman raises his eyes.

He is a particularly evil looking Krikkitman.

Film goes into very slow notion. Register horrified look on Doctor's face. We hear phrases echoing through his mind.

'Just hop back in time a couple of days'

'Against Time Law'

He is trying to stop himself, but he is held in thrall by the Krikkitman's gaze. Out of the corner of his eye he can see the distinctive markings on the ball he is holding.

It is a Supernova Bomb.

More phrases echo through his mind.

HACTAR: Have I failed? Failure doesn't bother me.

ELDER: How can you be sure you aren't being manipulated as well?

HACTAR: I would honestly rather like to wipe out the Galaxy.

JANE: Hop back a couple of days in time.

HACTAR: If I haven't already fulfilled my function, it's too late now.

Yes, I have made one or two little things.

I have fulfilled my function.

I have fulfilled my function ...

The bomb leaves the Doctor's hands and floats in slow notion down the pitch. The Doctor doesn't stop running.

Triumph gleams in the Krikkitman's eye as he raises the bat to swing.

The ball starts to glow and flash. It is quite clearly the real thing this time.

The ball bounces in front of the Krikkitman and spins at an unexpected angle, under the swinging bet. It nicks a bail off the wicket and drops neatly into the wicket keeper's hands.

Return to normal speed.

The Doctor has continued running and reaches the Krikkitman at the moment that it is too astonished to react.

He seizes the bat from him, and swinging it desperately knocks off the Krikkitman's head.

The Umpire buries his face in his hands.

The Doctor takes the bomb from the wicket keeper.

'Excuse me,' he says, 'I've just saved the Universe.'

'Again?' says somebody weakly.

Jane runs up to him. 'What's happening?'

'This is the real Supernova Bomb,' says the Doctor. 'Hactar put it together himself and left it in my pocket whilst distracting me with friendly chat. If the Krikkitman had hit it, that really would have been it I'm afraid.'

'Well it's very lucky he missed,' says Jane.

'Luck?' exclaims the Doctor? 'Luck had nothing to do with it. That was one of my super top spun googlies.'

He picks up the Krikkitman's head.

'It would take more than one of these sub-meson hyper-computer brains to work out how that ball was going to bounce. I mean I didn't even know myself ...'

APPENDIX 3
THE KRIKKITMEN
– SARAH JANE
SMITH VERSION (AN
INTRODUCTION)

CHAPTER 1

It was an ordinary day, even by the standards of Ealing. The suburbs of London have a proud tradition of edging away from any form of excitement, and that definitely includes London itself. They drown out the frantic hubbub of the city with shrubbery and roses and long leafy lanes along which dogs can be walked.

She was walking her dog. She did this discreetly, politely and with the minimum of fuss, which was quite surprising given that her dog was, very firmly, a robot dog. She had been given the dog a long time ago as a going-away present, or, equally possibly as an apology, or, indeed, as an apology for going away. Vanishing was her best friend's way of apologising. Actually, it was the way he dealt with most things. Birthdays, weddings, Christmases, and, these days, funerals – all these, he had a remarkable knack of missing. The one exception, the one thing he was guaranteed to turn up for, was the end of the Universe.

But today, as always, Ealing felt a long way away from the end of the Universe. Autumn leaves fell with a gentle hush, conkers plonked from trees knowing they would never be fought over, and birds whispered ringtones to each other.

She rather enjoyed the fellowship of dog walkers, a polite society of nodding. Coming to small talk late in life, she was rather enjoying it. As a crusading reporter, she'd honed the art of the razor-sharp question. As a time traveller she'd only ever asked about the weather when a sun was exploding. But now she delighted in gathering up 'Well, you know's and 'Mustn't grumble's and 'Probably rain on Wednesday's.

Walking her dog across the common, she felt invisible yet welcome. Only one person had ever even asked why her dog was made out of metal. It was a little old lady who had, with a weary 'so, it has come to this' tone, enquired if it was made in Taiwan. She'd shaken her head, and the old lady had just nodded, tutted and walked on.

The placid calm of it all was so very reassuring. Normally. Today, she found it oddly stifling. She threw sticks for her dog to retrieve (he ignored them), she chatted with him about stock prices (he enjoyed this), and every now and then, a passing stranger would tell her something obvious about the weather. The trees closed in around her, forming an endless avenue of people walking their dogs and gradually fading away.

'I'm bored, K-9,' said Sarah Jane Smith.

The dog did not reply.

'I'm old, K-9.'

The dog glided on.

Sarah kicked at some leaves. They settled firmly back into place. She looked around at the placid autumn scene and, with a chill of more than October, she knew it was mocking her.

'Nice day for it,' said a retired accountant with a Doberman.

'I've been to Betelgeuse,' Sarah told him.

'Lovely this time of year,' the man said, and let himself be led away.

Sarah caught up with her robot dog. He was waiting patiently for her by the recycling bins. He wished her to correctly file some stray tin cans that had somehow ended up among the glassware. He was most insistent.

She fished around in the bin, hoping that the cans had been rinsed. They had not.

'I once fought the anti-matter monster of Zeta Minor,' she said, wiping her hands on the frozen grass.

Again, the dog did not reply.

Sarah Jane Smith stood by the bins and felt utterly wretched. As she straightened up, there was a tightness in her back, or was it her chest? *What if I just drop dead, right here, right now?* She'd once thought that the last thing she saw would be a sky full of exploding battle fleets, but would her last view really be of some bollards and a distant corner shop?

She was leaning against the bin, and a robot dog was nudging against her leg. This really, really wouldn't do.

Sarah Jane Smith took a breath and hoped for something better.

Something better roared out of thin air.

It was a battered blue box that carefully managed to look completely, ridiculously at home on Ealing Common. A friendly light shone from the roof of it, which was decorated with the words 'POLICE BOX', which seemed absurd until you looked at them and then realised that they were precisely perfect.

The door opened and a scarf – no, an explosion of curls – no, a swirling coat – no, a massive smile – bounded out.

'Sarah Jane Smith!' cried her best friend, grabbing her in a hug so cheery it had made Sontarans chuckle.

'Doctor,' she said. 'Is the Universe ending?'

'Oh, absolutely,' he laughed.

CHAPTER 2

'You've brought me to a cricket match?' Sarah Jane Smith exclaimed.

'Hush.' The Doctor looked around furtively. This was strange. The Doctor was never furtive. This was a man who even sauntered through minefields. But right now he had the guilty expression of someone caught roasting next door's budgerigar.

The Doctor had promised her the end of the Universe. Instead, he'd brought her to Lord's Cricket Ground. The seats around them were crowded with greasy-looking bankers treating each other to corporate hospitality. Further below was a sea of middle-aged men trying to get sunburn. Adrift in the middle of it was the occasional Colonel, completing the *Times* crossword with the help of a thermos flask of tea, soup or gin. All of human life was here – if your definition of human life was really very narrow.

To give the Doctor credit, he'd got them very good seats. Sarah Jane Smith had a splendid view of the pitch – a strip of grass as cossetted as a rich old lady on life support. Dancing around it were two teams of men in spotless cricket whites, looking like fastidious knights who'd ordered their armour with a high thread count. Occasionally one player would throw a small red ball at another. Sometimes they'd hit it away from them. Sometimes they wouldn't. Often nothing at all would happen.

Cricket was the most English invention imaginable. As if a prep school teacher had tried to demonstrate eternity.

Sarah sipped at some ginger beer the Doctor had handed her. 'I don't like cricket,' she announced.

To her surprise, the Doctor had shuddered. 'Neither do I,' he'd said.

It was turning out to be a very surprising day.

Sarah would have liked to have taken the reappearance of her oldest friend in her stride. His time machine did have a habit of tumbling out of nowhere at her. But recently he'd been wearing a lot of quite extraordinarily different bodies. There was the one in the smoking jacket who'd taken her hiking through a lethal version of the Lake District. There was the nice young man who'd kept saying sorry. The boy wonder who'd invited her to his funeral. The grumpy one who'd bought her tea in Debenhams and criticised the jam. She'd even bumped into a scampering clown who'd gasped in mock horror and announced firmly that one of them shouldn't be there. She'd firmly pointed at the alien craft hovering above London at the time and icily suggested that perhaps *that* was really the interloper. He'd accepted her point and scurried away.

It wasn't exactly as though the Doctor had left her alone. But it had been ever such a long time since she'd seen *her* Doctor. The one she felt she truly belonged with. The one who'd abruptly shoved her out the door one day in a cul-de-sac near Aberdeen.

But there he was. Acting like he'd never left. Hair a bit wilder, scarf a bit tamer. The only thing that had been the same was his casual knack for averting apocalypse. To the Doctor, it was as though they were just popping down the shops for milk, only he liked shops and he really loved milk.

When they'd hurtled through the Time Vortex, he'd just beamed at her – she couldn't decide if it was because he'd missed her or because he was just in a beaming mood. K-9, bless him kept trying to interrupt, but the Doctor dropped to his knees and shushed him. 'Not now, K-9. We're having a moment, aren't we, Sarah?'

And they were. Sarah Jane Smith was never lost for words, but just right now her brain kept thinking that the right thing to say was a wordless croak. If a croak could convey surprise, wonder, love, annoyance, and a tiny pinch of fear, then that was the noise she was making. Only a croak can't do that. A croak is just a croak.

The Doctor looked at her and nodded. 'I'm sorry, Sarah,' he said. The three words she'd waited decades for him to say. He then immediately ruined the moment. 'You sound parched. I'd offer you water but we've only got tea. Never mind. Plenty of both on tap where we're going.'

Sarah's brain told her to make the croak again.

'The end of the Universe,' the Doctor laughed again, dancing round the controls of his time machine. In theory it could hurl them back to the Big Bang, but the whole get-up looked like someone had set up home in a hospital boiler room. Take the controls – a large bank of dials and switches with a drum in the middle which churned and spun – for all the world like an industrial washing machine. All it was lacking was a pair of socks and some Y-fronts.

Sarah's croak turned into a giggle. She'd forgotten how much she'd missed this place.

'The end of the Universe,' she repeated, her tone exactly mocking his.

'We need to dress for it,' the Doctor said solemnly. 'I've been reading up.'

K-9's ears twitched, but the Doctor ignored them.

'Ties must be worn,' the Doctor announced solemnly, handing her one. He tried looping one around his own neck and immediately made a tangle of it. She noticed his tie read 'Women's Institute Champion Bread Makers' and she glanced hastily at hers. It merely contained an offensive mixture of spots.

She tried asking him where he'd got them from, but her brain again croaked. Luckily her arms were flapping up and down and the Doctor clearly hadn't forgotten how to read them.

'"Where are we going?" and "Why do we need ties?"' the Doctor interpreted as the TARDIS roared to an abrupt halt. He opened the doors. 'Let's go and find out.'

And he'd taken her to that cricket match.

The TARDIS had bellowed into the Members' Enclosure like a tipsy colonel. The apparition was greeted with alarm and surprise, which was rapidly transferred to the Doctor's appearance.

There were times when the Doctor looked like a champion of eternity. Sarah Jane had seen giant green blobs suddenly look at their floor with all 100 of their eyes. The Ninth Sontaran Battle Brigade had remembered an urgent call they just had to make. The Kraals had muttered something about having to write their Christmas thank-you letters.

There were times when the Doctor was precisely that wonderful. And then there were others when he just looked insane. What are we like? thought Sarah Jane miserably. He was an explosion in plum woollens. She had, after all, been walking her dog, and so she was dressed in the sort of baggy casual things one was allowed to wear only when walking a dog or washing a car. They were confronted by an army of disapproving sports jackets. Someone said very loudly, 'Well really!' Someone else cried, 'Disgraceful!'

Sarah Jane Smith wondered if they were going to be booed.

The Doctor faced the deadly tide of tweed and felt the full blistering force of middle-aged disapproval. It was quite something. Nevertheless, he fished about in his pocket and flashed a crumpled card.

'I'm the Doctor,' he announced grandly with only the slightest of hesitations. 'This is Sarah Jane Smith. We're from the MCC.'

Sarah, along with most of the front row of sports jackets, squinted dubiously at the card. It was signed by W.G. Grace. The date read 1877.

The card allowed them grudging access to the cornucopia of the hospitality suite. This amounted to a leaking tea urn and a pile of paste sandwiches.

Out on the terrace, Sarah Jane hissed at him. 'I'm the only woman here.'

'Are you?' said the Doctor. He was staring at the cricket match grimly.

'You promised me the end of the Universe, and you've brought me to a cricket match.'

'Any true Englishman would tell you they were the same thing.' The Doctor laughed mirthlessly. A small red ball arced through the air and the players scurried back and forth. The Doctor shuddered and looked away.

'Why don't you like cricket?' Sarah demanded. She felt rather defensive about it. 'It seems harmless enough.'

The Doctor pulled a horrified face.

Sarah blinked. Surely, surely the Doctor liked cricket? He was such an eccentric anglophile – he adored tea towels, he'd made her go fishing, he liked stately homes so much he'd blown up at least a dozen.

'Come on. What's wrong with cricket?' she demanded.

'I've always meant to find out,' said the Doctor.

Sarah didn't like the Doctor's tone. When he wanted to sound grave, he could sound extraordinarily grave. Like a rumbling of very distant thunder. She looked up at the cloudless sky, at the bright sun soaking into the green, green grass and she shivered. Only the Doctor could manage a sentence that was both nonsense and also terrifying.

'What do you mean?' she pressed. 'It's just a game. Tell me what's wrong with cricket?' She realised how much she missed getting to ask questions like this.

The Doctor just shrugged miserably. 'Look at them – look at them all. So …' His lips twisted. 'Happy.'

A man hit a ball with a bat. The ball went quite a way. Everyone applauded. It looked the most innocent thing ever.

Sarah frowned. 'What? Doctor, what is it?'

'It's obscene, that's what it is,' the Doctor growled. 'If it's a cosmic joke, then it's in very bad taste indeed.'

The last time Sarah had seen the Doctor in this mood, they'd been watching a dying star.

She consulted a pamphlet she'd been eating her sandwiches off. 'It's the last day of the Ashes,' she announced.

Several people nearby glanced at her as if she'd fallen off the moon. Which was, she thought, fair enough.

'In cricketing terms,' she whispered, 'that's very big news. You know – every ten years or so—'

'Every four years,' the Doctor corrected, as a man in front of them turned around to snarl it at them.

'Anyway, doesn't matter,' she said, delighting as the spectator turned a colour to match the Doctor's coat. 'England and Australia fight a series of cricket matches and eventually one of them takes home a trophy.'

'*The* trophy,' the spectator snapped.

'Thank you,' Sarah smiled at him sweetly. 'There you go, Doctor. Perhaps your space-time telegraph got its wires crossed. The kind of thing that's terribly important if you happen to like cricket. But, for you and me, well ...' She made a dismissive noise.

The Doctor glared at her. He looked furiously angry. 'You don't care?' he gaped.

Sarah blinked. 'Not really,' she admitted. 'It's just a game.'

The Doctor let out an anguished groan.

In contrast to the Doctor's despairing mood, the crowd were growing jubilant. Given the amount of applause and the number of people screaming 'Come on England!', things were getting pretty exciting. Or, as exciting as a cricket match could be.

She glanced at the scoreboard and, with a lot of frowning and eavesdropping, managed to decipher what was going on.

'It's the last round,' she said, watching the spectator in front wince. 'And we need three to win. Then we can go home.'

'Home?' the Doctor barked bitterly.

Down on the field, the little white figures were moving with a bit more tension. Someone threw a ball. Someone hit it with a bat.

For a moment, eternity waited. The ball drifted higher. Then, with nothing better to do, it drifted higher still.

Then the entire stadium breathed out.

'It's a six!' screamed people to each other with the delight of people pointing out the obvious.

The crowd went as wild as a cricket crowd could. There was polite applause, backs were slapped, and people said 'Hurrah!' It all seemed terribly jolly.

'We've won,' Sarah said to the Doctor.

'No one ever wins cricket,' the Doctor sighed miserably.

Sarah changed the subject. She was used to these moods. He'd once got terribly sad in a Chinese takeaway. She looked up at the sky. Clouds were forming.

'And just in time too,' she announced, shivering. 'Looks like rain.'

'That's far worse than rain,' the Doctor intoned predictably.

She punched him lightly on the shoulder. 'Cheer up,' she said. 'It might never happen.'

'Do you know –' the Doctor seemed to focus on her for the first time in an hour – 'I always hate people who say that.'

Which was when the killer robots appeared.

THANKS TO:

Mandy Marvin – for finding it
Steve Cole – for editing it
Joshua Lewin – for bearing with it